BLAISE

DAUGHTER OF LITTLE MERMAID

J A ARMITAGE

AUDREY RICH

Please contact the publisher Info@enchantedquillpress.com for translation and audio rights

www.enchantedquillpress.com

Edited By Rose Lipscomb

Cover by Enchanted Quill Press

Proof Reader: Tina Merritt

❀ Created with Vellum

KINGDOM OF FAIRYTALES

You all know the fairytales, the stories that always have the happy ending. But what happens after all those storybook characters get what they wanted? Is it really a happily ever after?

In this prequel, you will find out what happens next, be transported back to those lands you fell in love with and be prepared to meet some new characters along the way.

Kingdom of Fairytales is a new way of reading with one chapter a day and one book a week throughout the year beginning January 1st

Lighting-fast reads you won't be able to put down

Read in real time as each chapter follows a day in the life of a character throughout the entire year, with each bite-sized episode representing a week in the life of our hero.

Each character's story wrapped up at the end of every season with a brand new character and story featured in each season.

Fantasy has never been so epic!

READING ORDER

Kingdom of Fairytales is a 52 book series split into thirteen seasons. Each season has a four book story arc of a fairytale character with the last season seeing them all coming together. You can read any series first with the exception of thirteen, however it is recommended that you read in the order below...

PREQUEL

SLEEPING BEAUTY
1. Queen of Dragons
2. Heiress of Embers
3. Throne of Fury
4. Goddess of Flames

LITTLE MERMAID
5. Queen of Mermaids
6. Heiress of the Sea
7. Throne of Change
8. Goddess of Water

QUEEN OF MERMAIDS

29TH JANUARY

"*B*laise, where are you going in such a hurry with that humongous bag?"

Damn! So much for going incognito. My first trip outside the palace alone and I'd already been caught, despite hiding my conspicuous strawberry blonde hair under a hat and concealing my unusual golden-ringed eyes behind a pair of oversized sunglasses.

On reflection, wearing sunglasses on a dreary winter's day was bound to draw suspicion.

I turned to find my best friend, Hannah Fallon, eyeing me suspiciously. I'd hoped to get to the mail carriers as soon as possible, but there was no way Hannah would let me by without finding out what I was up to.

She placed her hands on her hips and blew a stray lock of dark hair from her face while she waited for me to answer. I could understand her surprise. As the Princess of Atlantice, carrying bags was not a usual occurrence. There was no need when I had palace guards to fetch and carry for me; a perk of being the daughter of King Ermias and Queen Antonella. Being let out of the palace alone was another thing altogether. It was not usually allowed without a guard to accompany me. Not a perk of being a princess! Still, I was out today, and apart from the anxiety of getting to the shop to pick up the invitations on time, I was enjoying my little piece of freedom.

For a second, I debated ignoring her, although it would be pointless. Tenacious was Hannah's middle name, and I knew that she'd not let me go without finding out what I was up to and why I was walking through the town square alone.

"Hey, Hannah, everything good?" I asked in an attempt at a distraction. "Your parents? Your fiancé? Please tell me about his latest romantic gesture."

"Let's forget the pleasantries or your poor attempt at distraction," she said, rolling her eyes and giving me a grin. "Are you going to answer?" She stuck her head out like a turtle, fixing her narrowed eyes on me. "Or evade?"

I snickered. "If that's an option, I'll gladly take it."

She shook her head and waggled a finger at me. "Nope. You know that dodging your best friend is prohibited." Her eyes traveled from mine down to the bag again. "Wait, isn't that the bag you love so much that it's usually on display by your decorative swords?" She eyed me suspiciously, and I knew that I'd never get past her without telling all. Miss Tenacity strikes again.

"Why are you using it, and why are you practically running? You never run."

She knew me too well. I patted the bag, which I did love because it perfectly matched the outer rings around my eyes. The gold was not a bright yellow like a sunflower but deeper as in the Colorita Ariane flowers brought in from the Kingdom of Floris. Almost the same color as my hair, too, a reddish-gold that was neither blonde nor deep red like my mother's, but settling somewhere in between.

"I'm dropping off the Valentine Day announcement to The Conch and picking up the invitations that our mail carriers will deliver; hence, the bag." I shrugged. "I felt like using it today. And I wasn't running."

She tilted head and raised her eyebrows. "Okay then, so why were you speedwalking?"

I wasn't going to get anywhere at this rate!

I sighed. "I want the ball and the prep work over with, plus I need to get there before the print shop closes."

The Valentine's Ball my parents had decided to throw this year was quickly shaping up to be the event of the year and a huge thorn in my side to boot. Carrying mail around like a commoner was one thing, but the fact that they expected me to go to the Conch offices to have them print an announcement defied belief. I still didn't know why they needed to announce it in the national newspaper. Just how many people did they expect to come?

Normally, I would have been allowed to ignore the whole thing. But this year, my mother expected me to help, and as she had all the palace staff sorting out the arrangements for it, I was dragged in.

"Are you freaking out?" Hannah asked

"A bit," I admitted. "There's so much to do, but at least the invitations are ready, and if I actually get everything done today we should be on track."

I thought about the magnitude of the task ahead and tried not to panic.

My mom had all the bases covered: The Conch would distribute the news throughout Atlantice, and our guards would deliver the invitations to our closest friends... if I ever managed to pick them up. The mail dolphins would distribute the invitations throughout the ports of our kingdom and the mainland.

"I don't have a doubt that our queen has everything ready," Hannah asked, reading my mind. "That's not why I was asking. Any important male guests I should know about?"

Her face showed a picture of mischievous delight at the mere thought of it.

I tapped my fingers on my thigh. "They invited a couple so you might have your chance," I replied, my voice heavy with sarcasm. Hannah had men drooling over her wherever she went. With her beautiful face with wide blue eyes and full sensuous lips, she never had to worry about going without male company. Besides, she was engaged to the commander of the fleet. She wasn't asking about eligible bachelors for herself. No, this was all about me.

She pointed to the large clock on the bell tower standing majestically above every other town building. "What about you? It's about time you snagged yourself a man. There aren't that many good ones around, and you're running out of time."

"Don't I know how fast it ticks," I sighed. It was okay for her. Men fell at her feet. As the daughter of the king, men acted weird around me. It wasn't that I wasn't beautiful. I would say that I rivaled Hannah in the beauty department, although we couldn't look more different. But men were either scared of me because of my position, or they sucked up to me to get in good graces of my father. Not one of them had actually seen me for me and not for the princess I was. "I just don't want to have to choose my husband at a ball."

"Would you rather have a decrepit king for a husband?"

I'd rather travel and meet different people with interesting cultures before settling down to the mundane life a married royal princess must lead.

"Don't remind me of my limited choices." I crossed my arms and narrowed my eyes. "But still, *everyone* needs to lay off the find-Blaise-a-prince bandwagon."

"Seriously, it's only because we care for you." Her voice rose higher than usual, and she touched her heart with her palms crossed. "We're all waiting for you to fall for the right one."

"Trust me, I know how much you want me betrothed," I scoffed. Everyone did, it seemed. Barely a week went by without The Conch printing a *why isn't she married yet* story.

"I'm still hoping for a double wedding," she sighed, staring out into space, no doubt imagining her wedding dress.

"I'd rather enjoy my freedom a bit longer." I kicked a small pebble into a dolphin-shaped bush by the baker's shop. "People should adopt a hobby and not worry about my lack of a prince to marry."

"They're just securing the succession since you don't have any siblings." She waved at one of the palace guards heading the opposite way. "I have to talk to Marianne about the meeting tomorrow. You'll be there, right?"

I jumped at the change of subject, glad to be off the future-husband topic.

"When have I ever missed a meeting?"

The members of the AML, Anti-Mermaid League, made it their mission to spread how evil the merpeople were. And if the AML obtained its primary goal, the merpeople would abandon their underwater kingdom and relocate far away from Atlantice. I couldn't wait for that day!

Atlantice was plagued with the foul creatures, being an island and having the waterways it did. With half the kingdom on land, another murkier kingdom lived below the depths, and it teemed with rotten half-fish people.

"Good," she replied enthusiastically, "We'll be discussing how we plan to execute... I mean, relocate them to other waters. See you tomorrow night!" Hannah's long legs maintained a steady march as she pulled out a small, blue notebook from her bag and ran after the guard. "Marianne, wait up for me."

Execute? Hmm, I better clarify the AML's mission. She never mentioned killing the merpeople in any of the meetings I attended. Rallying everyone in Antla to kick them off our shores was one thing, but I stopped at murdering them. Not that they didn't deserve it, but I was a princess, and princesses didn't go in for murder as a rule.

The aroma of fresh-baked bread drifted by, and Farina Martinez, the owner of Antla's Bakery, waved at me through the window. The rush of getting to the print shop momentarily forgotten by the heavenly scent, I headed inside. By the time I exited her bakery, I had filled my stomach with an empanada and a huge chocolate chip cookie that even the Badalah's bazaar merchants would envy.

Next door, the sign on the print shop still read *Open.* I pushed through the door, and somewhere a little bell tinkled to announce my arrival.

"Ah, princess," Mr. Worthpaper said, dropping into a shallow bow, "I have everything ready for you."

Five minutes later, Mr. Worthpaper handed me a package with the embossed invitations inside it. He carefully placed the heart-shaped container inside my bag.

"Thank you so much for preparing these with such short notice." I picked up the heavy bag and slung the handles over my shoulder. "My parents will send the shells over before you close."

"I'm not worried about the money." He bowed again. "And you're welcome. We're always here to serve the royal family," he said, opening the door for me to walk through.

Exiting the shop, I ambled through the cobblestoned streets of Antla back toward the palace gardens. On arrival at the palace entrance, I lifted my hat, and the guards uncrossed the royal glaives. I acknowledged their bows and headed toward the gardens.

The royal palace was situated on the shoreline, enjoying its own private inlet that boasted a beautiful white sandy beach and a small pier.

Large oak trees and tall urns filled with Queen's miniature decorative trees lined the path from the gardens to the sea. I ambled down the pathway while I thought about my parents. They'd been behaving as weirdly as the weather for a couple of weeks now.

My father had been getting more and more worried about the turbulent seas, complaining that the water looked darker than usual, a fact that the Conch had picked up on, and my mother was not her usual ebullient self.

It wasn't like her, especially when planning a party. She loved organizing them and always seemed to have an extra bounce in her step as she prepared for them.

Why is she depressed? Is she sick? I'd seen reports in the Draconis Sentinel about the Queen of Draconis being ill, and even though my mother had shown no signs of being cursed like Sleeping Beauty, the thought nagged at me, settling in my stomach like a lead baguette.

I shook my head to push back the nightmarish thoughts. Instead,

I concentrated on the waves lapping against the shore. So much for turbulent seas. The day was as perfect as any winter's day could be, and despite a bitter chill in the air, totally normal for January, the sky dotted with white fluffy clouds and the sea almost flat. I was pretty sure my father was worrying over nothing as usual.

The large red pavers switched to a stone path, and glass globes filled with seaweed replaced the urns. My bag seemed to be acquiring more weight with each footstep. Maybe I should have asked one of the guards to help me, after all.

I inhaled the briny air and sighed at the beauty of it and how lucky I was to live with such a view.

Whoosh. I squinted.

In the distance, two winged beings flew behind the clouds, and I blinked.

Dragons?

If they were dragons, why would they fly so close to Atlantice?

Goosebumps traveled up my arms as I stepped onto the sandy shore. There were more important things than focusing on dragons flying close to our kingdom: Namely, finding out what had prompted my mom's gloomy attitude.

So many questions ran through my head, bringing my mood down, and I wondered if the darkness of the sea was just a front for troubles in my parent's marriage.

My parents seemed happy, and although they did occasionally argue, I imagined it was not any more than other married couples. In front of the world, they always presented a unified, happy marriage without any problems.

But then the royal couple needed to maintain a harmonious front for the stability of the kingdom. They did a wonderful job because no one would know from looking at them that there were troubles. Maybe I was wrong about the whole thing. The only time my father stood his ground was when he needed to sail to the mainland, and my mom wanted to join him.

Atlantice was an island off the mainland of the other kingdoms. There were many ways to travel there. Boats were the easiest option, or the people could use one of two massive bridges that spanned the sea. One to the kingdom of Enchantia and the other to the kingdom of Floris. Where Floris was attached to the mainland, Enchantia, like us, was an island, so there was another bridge at the other side of Enchantia that connected it to Draconis.

My father always won those arguments, so my mom chose to fly on the large birds from Skyla to the mainland with half the guards flanking her rather than spend days crossing the bridges.

Not sure why my father held such a strong conviction about sailing alone, but he did.

These disagreements left a sour note in my mouth for marriage, which was another reason I was in no rush to marry.

Why they wanted me to find a spouse at eighteen boggled my mind.

Why couldn't I be free to choose when to meet my own Prince Charming? Not that my parents were pushing me as such, but the hints from my mother as to when I would find myself a man were growing stronger with each passing day. The upcoming ball was not helping the matter at all.

Maybe they were taking a leaf out of the king and queen of Draconis's book. Not that trying to marry off their daughter had done them much good. A competition to find her a husband had ended with her fighting for her own hand in marriage. Still, the Draconians were a weird bunch of people at the best of times.

I allowed myself a daydream of a handsome prince from a faraway kingdom, who would ride up on his white horse and fall madly in love with me one day.

Probably wouldn't happen, the way my luck with men was, but at least a girl could dream.

I continued toward the pier, my mood lifting as I watched a pair of pink dolphins flipping and twisting high in the air. With a large grin, I stepped on the wooden ramp and waved with both hands to get their attention.

As they raced toward me, clicking and performing their greeting dance, I shouted, "Hello, my lovely friends." I pulled off my hat and stuffed it back inside the bag's pocket.

The dolphins squeaked and trilled, approaching the pier with each leap. The heel of my boots smacked the wooden pier as I sprinted to meet our mail carriers, not minding if they splashed me when their slick bodies slammed into the water.

Lowering my bag slowly to the pier floor, I kneeled on the cold wood before I scooped out the invitations. The first dolphin swam alongside the pier, and I opened its waterproof mail pouch.

"Thank you, my dear friends, for delivering these. They must arrive to each of the ports as soon as possible."

They both bobbed their heads in agreement.

"You both are the best!" And they were. Dolphins never dallied when they delivered our mail, and they were a joy to watch too. To my knowledge, we were the only kingdom that used dolphins to deliver mail. As we were an island, it made sense.They were fast, dependable, and could get mail to the other kingdoms in half the time it would take to send the mail by the Urbis Mail Airship.

I finished packing the invitations in the dolphin's waterproof bag and fastened the straps to ensure they'd be safe. "All done. Be careful."

The dolphins whistled while bobbing their heads before their bodies disappeared into the water, leaving white foam bubbles in their wake.

Dipping both hands in the warm water, I caught the bubbles. The tiny spheres popped as the water slipped between my fingers. Blowing the rest of the bubbles out of my hand, I smirked, thinking that if a prince rode in on a white horse, I'd probably knock him down for abusing the horse.

In the distance, a red tail lifted out of the water and, for a second, floated perpendicular to the horizon. My legs trembled as I took in the sight. A red tail meant only one thing... blood. A shiver ran through me as I considered what would injure a defenseless dolphin.

I strained to catch a glimpse of the injured dolphin, but it didn't resurface.

My mind turned to the only creatures in the sea disgusting enough to hurt a dolphin. The merfolk! I hated them with a passion, and what else in the sea was big enough to go up against a dolphin? It had to be the merfolk.

Maybe I was wrong before. Killing them would be justifiable if they intended to hurt the sweet dolphins.

Splash.

The tail breached the surface again, closer this time. Now that I could see it a little better, I could see that I'd been wrong. It was not an injured dolphin tail at all. This one was iridescent, sparkling in the low light. It flipped and once again fell beneath the surface. I continued to search, but the sea creature didn't resurface.

Nothing.

Absolutely nothing out of the ordinary. I turned around to head back to the palace when a slight ripple disturbed the water. I turned to see what was causing the disturbance to find myself looking into the most gorgeous pair of green eyes I'd ever seen.

My breath caught in my throat as he bobbed in the water. His long brown hair skirted out behind him, floating on the surface, and I found myself wondering what it would be like to run my fingers through it.

"Can I help you?" I offered breathily, my voice cracking. I wanted to warn him about the sea creature I'd seen further out, but my cheeks were already flaming with embarrassment.

I quickly became aware that I was ogling him like I would an ice cream sundae with chocolate fudge on a hot day.

To keep from staring at him, I closed my eyelids but not completely. I couldn't help peeking from beneath my lashes, watching him lazily float on the water's surface.

In the back of my mind, I knew I should be outraged that someone was swimming on this particular stretch of coastline. It belonged to the palace and, therefore, was out of bounds to the public, but his overwhelming beauty had rendered me speechless, and I found I didn't care.

"Can I help you?" I tried again, clearing my throat.

He smiled, and two dimples appeared on his cheeks.

My heart flipped a bunch of times. If he were a snack, I would have gladly handed over half of the Atlantice Kingdom for just a tiny bite.

Oh gods, what was wrong with me. My first encounter with a hot man, and I was barely coherent. Not that he was doing any better. He had yet to answer my question.

I searched over my shoulder for his boat, but as my gaze landed back on him, he reclined, and the tip of his red tail exposed its ugly form.

My heart constricted as I struggled to take in the sight. He was a merman. Half a second ago, I was dreaming about running my hands over his perfectly chiseled chest, and he was nothing more than a filthy half-fish. A vile creature of the sea. It was him I'd seen swimming out there. Bile rose in my throat as I realized I'd been practically drooling over the disgusting creature. My stomach prepared to eject both the empanada and cookie, and I had to take in a deep breath to coordinate my senses.

The creature winked before he dove under and reappeared closer to the pier... closer to me.

He's revolting. His entire species are killers. So ugly!

I repeated the mantra to myself, thinking of all my friends at the AML, glad they couldn't see me now.

While he flapped his fin in the air, I repeated the lie that he wasn't gorgeous until I could almost hate him as much as the rest of his species and not look at him as a man.

Almost.

He waved at me before he nosedived under the water.

I needed to go back to the palace, to be away from the fish-beast, but something had me rooted to the spot.

He popped up and nosedived again, this time splattering water everywhere on the pier and on me. Suddenly, the spell was broken, and I could see him for what he actually was. He was my enemy, a man of the sea. He was practically a sardine, damnit!

"Ugh! My dress is wet, you jerk!" I shouted, taking a step forward and slipping onto the sandy pier. "Great! Now I have sand on my dress as well. Inconsiderate imbecile."

He popped up within touching distance, and I jumped as his deep voice spoke, "I'm sorry. I didn't mean to get you wet."

He had the audacity to give me a wide grin causing a small hurricane inside my body. I regarded him, trying to keep my emotions in check. His amazing green eyes, similar to the color of the seaweed that washed up on the shore, took my breath away.

Gorgeous eyes... in a face to die for... in a man-fish!

My heart pumped against my rib cage as if it wanted to fly out, and I hated myself for feeling it. Despite my attraction, the years-long loathing for merpeople fumed, twirling in my mind toxically until I could take it no more. Years of pent-up hatred exploded from my mouth. "How dare you talk to me?"

My tone could've made a shark hide behind an orca, but this guy didn't even flinch.

He twisted his head and scanned the shoreline until his eyes rested on mine again. His lips formed a smile.

"There isn't a sign prohibiting me from talking. Or do you carry one with you and decided to hide it behind your back so I'd have to guess?"

I wanted to rip his eyes out, but instead, I scoffed. "Ha, ha. Very funny." I crossed my arms. "You're a merman, so you're not allowed to even look my way, much less, talk to me. Do you even know who I am?"

Oh crap. Did I just say that?

He perused the area, this time with a scrunched forehead. "Forgive me, but I see no notice anywhere, and I do not know who you are." He beamed, showing off his perfect, white teeth. "No warning sign means I can talk to you all I want. Besides, why would someone prohibit me from talking to a beautiful young lady such as yourself?"

Despite my embarrassment of uttering the line *do you know who I am*, I continued along the same theme, unsure of what else to say. "You should know that you aren't supposed to speak to royalty."

"Ah, so you're part of the royal family?" He quirked an eyebrow and rubbed his chin. "You do not dress like any royalty I've seen. Usually, they have more jewelry than their bodies can carry and long ridiculous robes to trip on." His arm stretched out to one side, and with a slow movement, he brought it to the other side. "And they're surrounded with guards. Why isn't there a single guard to protect you? Are they so incompetent that they allow you to be here alone?"

He was trying to irritate me now, which actually made things a little easier. If it was easy to hate him for his rudeness, then I could look past the gorgeous eyes and dimpled cheeks and hot body and...

"It's none of your business," I snapped, crossing my arms. "But what should be your business is not talking to royalty."

I needed to leave, but once again, my body refused to move because of his audacity. Everyone knew that merfolk weren't allowed near the palace shore. No one was, but especially merfolk, and he should have known better.

"You're claiming that you're part of the royal family, but you don't have any of the tell-tale attributes, so how am I supposed to act?" His grin widened. The bastard was enjoying this. "I think you're lying so that I will bring you lobsters, oysters, and maybe even enough pearls for a necklace that would fit perfectly around that pretty neck of yours."

"You are too much." I huffed, pushing myself up from the pier and dusting the sand from my dress. "Don't ever speak to me again. Do you understand?"

"Ah, but that would be a huge mistake."

"Why?" I asked.

"Because I've enjoyed talking to you, and I can tell you've enjoyed talking to me."

"You're nuts, do you know that?" I grabbed my bag, pulled out the hat, and placed it on my head. "A smart man would leave the moment I asked him to leave."

"Ah, and a smart lady would have left already if she really didn't want to speak to me."

Crap!

"You're impossible." I pivoted and marched away along the pier, but the compulsion to peek at him one last time caused me to glance over my shoulder.

He hadn't moved, as though he knew I'd turn. His grin widened, which urged me to abandon the idea of the inherent evil in merpeople and kiss him.

Fish, he's a fish!

"Don't worry, princess, this isn't the last time you will see me." He chuckled. "We'll definitely meet again… soon. I promise you."

My heart quickened, and my feet moved faster than they ever had.

Back at the palace, I checked in to tell my parents I'd sent the mail and then headed up to my room. Throwing my bag on the dresser, I yanked the cord to summon Emma, my personal maid, and plopped on my bed face up.

With my eyes closed, a picture of him appeared in my mind, stained to the inside of my eyelids. I couldn't let it go. There was no point denying that I'd been attracted to him. Before I knew he was a fish, I was half-planning to jump in the water with him, and I was terrified of the sea. But he was a fish. A lower life form. I felt sick at myself for even thinking of him in that way. It was almost as bad as being attracted to a can of tuna because he was barely any different.

I needed to tell someone so I could talk it through, but who?

Hannah wouldn't understand my attraction. She would order the AML to hunt him down at the mere mention of him. But despite his boldness, rudeness, and being a merman, my heart tugged at the thought that the AML could hurt him. His beauty saved him from any revenge I could have unleashed on him.

"Princess Blaise, is everything okay?" My maid, Emma, asked

with her usual sweet smile as she curtsied without moving her blue cap.

I sat up and rested against the mahogany headboard trimmed with twenty-four karat gold. "Yes," I lied, "I'm fine." The whole interaction with fish-boy had left a sour taste in my throat and an ache in my heart.

"I brought in hot chocolate and your favorite banana nut muffin and chicken soup." Her strong, yet feminine, hands carried a tray with the steaming cup and two glass-covered plates. "Your parents said you'd rushed out of the dining room so quickly, you'd not even sat down to eat."

"Oh, that's because Farina Martinez fed me." Not to mention, a certain merman had captivated my every thought.

With the softest steps, she strode to the night table and gently set the tray down on the marble top. "Should I draw you a bath with the frankincense oil?"

"No." I fixated my eyes on the intricate golden fleur-de-lis patterned ceiling. My parents had chosen the motif because it symbolized life, light, and perfection, which they said reminded them of me. I didn't feel particularly perfect at that point. Disgusted with myself, maybe.

"Are you okay?" she asked again. "Do you want me to call your parents?"

"No, thank you, Emma."

She lifted the cover, and the deliciousness of chicken soup hit my nose.

"How about soup?"

"Nope." Food wouldn't help either. My brain was fixated on what had happened outside, and no amount of soup was going to purge the thoughts of him. At least it wasn't fish soup.

"Have you ever met someone you wanted to kill?" I murmured, looking up at her.

Emma's eyes widened. "No, never." She touched my forearm and whispered, "Did someone hurt you?"

"Yes... no, I mean, not physically." I formed a fist. "I met someone today. He was in the palace grounds... well, actually he was in the sea. He was the rudest, most killable person I have ever had the misfortune to meet."

She marched toward the door. "Should I call the guards?"

I waved the suggestion away. "The guards can't do anything about it now."

"Then I must call your parents. If he said something he shouldn't..."

"He didn't... he was just so infuriating." I picked up two pillows and threw them against the door.

Emma glanced at the pillows and placed both her hands against her heart. "But he was trespassing, right? Someone should know. What if he comes to the palace?"

I stifled a laugh. He could no more walk to the palace on his tail than I could sprout wings and fly. I took a deep breath and looked Emma in the eye.

"He's a merman, an infuriating one with absolutely no manners." I jumped out of bed and paced. "Where he found the nerve to even speak to me, I'll never know."

"Oh."

"They're the most disgusting, vile creatures of the sea, and they definitely shouldn't speak to us, like, ever, but this guy did. He should be held accountable, right?"

Emma slightly lowered her head.

Not the reaction I expected.

"It should be a capital crime for him to even look at me." I continued to pace, hoping she would verbally agree, but she didn't. "He has some nerve talking to me when he shouldn't."

The verbal tirade lasted another five minutes until my throat hurt. I picked up the lukewarm chocolate drink and sipped it. "Please take the food away because I just can't eat it. Not a single bite."

"Yes, princess. Maybe a bath will help, after all?"

"No! My skin is crawling just from thinking about him! Getting into water is the last thing I need."

Her hands picked up the tray, and she gave me a polite nod. "Will that be all?"

"Yes, and thank you for listening to me." The automatic thank you was ingrained in me. "Sorry..."

"Anytime, Princess Blaise." She opened the door and stepped out. "I'm always here if you need to talk."

She closed the door, leaving me alone with my thoughts. I'd hoped she would share my disgust of the merman, but she'd barely batted an eyelid at his mention. It was almost as though she didn't think they were beneath us.

Maybe I should invite her to the next AML meeting... or not. She needed an education, but some people weirdly thought that merfolk should have equal rights. Come to think of it, she had been quiet throughout my tirade. Urgh.

I lay back on the bed and closed my eyes. A picture of his perfect mouth grinning at me formed in my mind. "Urgh!" I screamed again, and my very last pillow flew through the air, joining the others on the floor.

2
30TH JANUARY

*L*oud clapping overflowed from the AML meeting hall as we spilled out into a quiet street of Antla. It felt like almost half the town had attended that afternoon, our largest turnout yet. I loved these meetings, and the one today was especially useful after my experience yesterday. I needed to purge any thought of the fish-man from my mind, and a meeting with like-minded mer-haters was the best way to go about it.

Several members left with Hannah and me, and while we strolled toward Hannah's home, she answered their questions with a grin that even a Cheshire cat would envy. She loved it when new members volunteered to help with the cause. We both did.

Saying goodbye to the others, Hannah and I headed toward her parents' home at the edge of the sea. Her father's position as admiral of our naval fleet entitled them to live in a manor by the water close to the palace, and it was here that my parents thought I spent the evenings I was actually at the meetings.

Hannah sighed and tucked her notebook into her bag. "We have so much to do. Hopefully, you'll be able to help us with the palace staff. I don't think I saw one of them on our roster. And most of your guards don't seem to be on board." She pursed her red lips. She never left her house without using lipstick.

For once, she didn't exaggerate. Apart from Marianne, the royal guard showed little interest in the purging of merfolk, but I was determined to remedy it. At least, I hoped to encourage Emma and the serving staff to attend the meetings and, eventually, the guards too.

"Don't worry, I'll speak to the staff and the guards. They'll, hopefully, join us when they hear how the merpeople are invading our waters. I swear there are more of them every month."

"Good," she said. "We must all do our part in recruiting more people. They're such a burden to Atlanticeans, and they've hurt us, killed our fisherman." She fiddled with a gold button on her custom-made navy jacket. "It's so unfair that no one has caught them and brought them to justice. I just wish we could eliminate them forever." Her lips twisted into a snarl.

I noticed she used the word "eliminate" too naturally. Had she always thought of killing them and not just banishing them from our waters? While I sought to rid them from our sea, killing them was too extreme. I thought back to fish-man.

My stomach turned over at the thought of a knife plunging into that perfect chest of his. I wanted him gone, not dead.

I regarded her closely, measuring her reaction. "Are you seriously thinking we should kill them, or just keep them away from the island?"

Her hand popped up within three inches of my face. "Ease up, Blaise. It's just an expression." She waved her hand as if waving the suggestion away.

"Glad to hear it. I won't be part of any genocide, even if they are merpeople."

Hannah wrinkled her forehead, causing it to form a weird pattern. "You're not becoming soft on me, are you?" She raised one eyebrow. "Because soft AML members are a weakness I can't afford right now."

"No way!" I shook my head. "I'm all in because they need to leave our waters."

She scoffed. "Good, because I'd have to remove your name from the AML list if you weren't on board with ousting those brutes."

"Trust me, I still want them gone, but..." An image of fish-man flashed in my brain. The way he'd looked at me with confident curiosity. He had been so close to me, he could have pulled me from the pier into the sea, but he hadn't. He hadn't touched me at all... *more's the pity.* "I just don't like killing anyone. It's too permanent."

"We're not planning to, but sometimes, I feel that it would be much easier than kicking them out of our waters. They're a bunch of disgusting, lazy creatures... And they reproduce like salmon since they have nothing better to do."

If they all looked like Fish, I could understand why the mermaids would want to have his merbabies. I shook my head at the thought of it. He was nothing more than a savage merman.

"Really, is that all they do?" I inquired, trying not to seem too interested in their mating habits.

Hannah nodded. "Our list continues to grow, and we spot more and more little ones in our waters every time my commander, almost captain, takes me to his battleship."

"Do you still call him by his title? Or is this just in front of me?" I raised an eyebrow. "Seriously, why can't you call him Geraldo?"

Geraldo was a rising star in the Atlantice Navy, totally gorgeous, and Hannah's fiancé.

"I could, but I love to hear his title, especially his future one." She smirked. "Can you imagine when I'm his wife, the wife of a captain?" She fanned her face with her left hand, and the diamond sparkled from the sun's rays. "I can't wait until that day. Everyone will have to bow down to me."

"Is that what you want? To have people bow down to you?" My skeptical tone should have silenced her, but it didn't.

She twirled her engagement ring. "Well, it is protocol when you're the commander's wife, so yes, I want them to bow down when I enter a room."

I rolled my eyes. While I did not like that royal protocol, which required everyone to curtsy or bow when I entered a room, I couldn't break tradition. But I asked my close friends and acquaintances not to bother in private. Her insistence on having everyone bow to her disturbed me. With a shrug, I said, "Glad I won't have to."

"We're friends, and all, but you'll have to bow down out of respect for my new position."

Deep heat, the kind that might push a person to say the cruelest words, spread from my heart to my face. I stopped at the fork between her home and the palace. "No, I won't, but if you don't adjust your attitude, I'll make sure you curtsy every single time we meet. And I mean every single time. Including when we're in private."

"And why would I do that?"

I crossed my arms and inhaled before I steadied my voice, "I outrank you, Commander Geraldo, and your admiral father. Remember?"

She waved her hand. "Of course, I know that."

"Based on your attitude, maybe you should sign up for a refresher course on royal protocol?"

"Don't let your princess title go to your head," she mumbled.

"I think it's the other way around. I've never asked you to curtsy because you're my friend. But I could. Maybe I should start right now before we part ways." I placed my hands on my hips. "What do you think about that? Do you want to curtsy?"

She sheepishly grinned. "I was just kidding."

My gut told me she was lying, but our friendship meant more to me than winning the argument. "Okay, but be careful when you kid around since the guards might haul you away for insubordination."

Hannah laughed, but her eyes scanned the area behind me. "I know you would never allow that. We're friends."

"No, I won't unless you overstep your bounds a little too far with your requirements."

"Whatever, my friend. My commander, uhm, Geraldo, is inside waiting for me. Night."

"Goodnight."

I shook my head and sauntered toward the garden. The conversation with Hannah disturbed me. While we had grown up together and bonded over our strong dislike for the merpeople, her recent statements concerned me. First, she'd implied that she wanted to kill them, and then, she stated that she would force everyone to bow down to her once she married Geraldo. Her position as leader of the AML and her upcoming wedding were going to her head, and although she was my best friend, I could feel a rift forming between us.

My feet led me to a small walkway by the sea. One I usually avoided because the narrow path lacked handrails, but it provided the most unobstructed view of the water.

I stopped at the edge and watched the undulating waves rolling toward the shore, calming me.

A seagull plucked a Goliath Grouper from the sea and soared straight for me. I quickly sidestepped a couple of inches to avoid being smacked in the head with the yard-long thrashing fish. As I did, my foot slipped on the wet wood, and I failed to remain on the pathway.

I lost my balance.

Splash!

Freezing water enveloped me in seconds.

A scream to alert the guards never made it out of my mouth as cold seawater rushed inside. I continued to descend into the deep waters until my feet touched the sandy bottom.

I can't swim!

Briny water burned my eyes as my lungs screamed in pain, desperate to inhale.

Not able to withstand the awful sensation, I shut my eyes, while my arms continued to flap like a baby turtle chasing its mom. My feet pushed off against the floor, and I pumped my arms faster, hoping that the salt in the water would help me to the top.

The effort failed. I probably rose three or four feet, which wasn't enough to reach the surface. If only I'd taken swimming lessons. If only I'd not been so afraid of the water, then I'd have been able to swim to the surface.

My body descended again, and with it, my chances of survival.

I was about to die if I didn't do something soon.

Without hesitating, I stripped off my jacket and kicked off my boots.

Crouching with my hands skimming the bottom, I shot my arms above my head, hoping that it would propel me all the way up. My arms swung faster.

My poor attempt propelled me about ten feet but still not enough for me to rise to the surface.

Why didn't my parents force me to learn how to swim? They could've bypassed my prejudices against the merpeople and made me take lessons.

Always those merpeople! They've always been the problem. And now, I'm about to die because of them.

Warm hands slid around my waist, pulling me quickly to the surface.

Once the cold air touched my face, I coughed, throwing up saltwater that burned my throat as it came up in great globfuls.

"Why don't you know how to swim?" a voice whispered in my ear, causing the hairs on my arm to rise.

I recognized the voice immediately. I'd thought about it enough over the past twenty-four hours. He held me tightly, and I was keenly aware that my body was held to his naked chest.

Without opening my eyes, I continued to cough. Loud, embarrassing coughs for several minutes. It didn't stop him from swimming with me away from land.

His warm chest provided a comfortable cocoon while my emotions drifted from happiness at being saved from drowning, to embarrassment, to fear, and, finally, anger.

Why did it have to be him?

The irony of him being my rescuer plagued me as I hacked my lungs out. He continued swimming, oblivious to my dilemma.

I opened my eyes and searched the coastline for the walkway I'd fallen from. I couldn't see it anywhere. In my addled mind, I wondered if he was taking me to a secluded cave and was planning to kill me? Did merpeople eat humans? Hannah had never mentioned it, but they were disgusting beings. I should have brought a knife for protection.

My eyes finally found the walkway, but it appeared to be a tiny dot in the distance. Controlling the adrenaline soaring in my body, I spat, "Where are you taking me? The walkway is back there. Return me immediately."

I was in no position to make demands, but that didn't stop me. He ignored me, continuing his path further out into rougher waters as if heading toward another kingdom. My heart raced, and my insides heated up. Fear and anger mixed. "Are you hearing me? Are you listening?" I raised my voice two octaves higher than usual and began to push myself away from him.

He gripped me tighter. "If you carry on doing that, I'll be forced to let you go, and as you can see, we are out in the middle of the ocean. I'm not going to hurt you. If I wanted to hurt you, I would've done it the last time we met. I'm trying to save you from drowning."

His tone and words seemed sincere. Non-threatening. I stopped pushing against his chest. He had a point. It was either go with him or drown.

"Where are you taking me?"

"I'm swimming to a place where you can rest, and we'll be able to talk. It's not too far from the palace but not close enough that the AML can use me for target practice." He chortled before he murmured, "We never know when their current strategy will change." Despite his words, his tone still held a hint of humor.

I shifted my head to confirm where we were. He hadn't lied. I could see the palace lights flickering in the distance.

"I'm not too sure about the intentions of the AML," he continued. "There are plenty of rumors that they want to exterminate us."

"You're relying on rumors?" I chided. "That's not always wise."

I gulped, wondering if he knew that I was a member of the AML.

"When there are too many rumors floating around, then it's always prudent to discover if there is truth to them. We now believe that those rumors are true," he answered, but not an ounce of humor remained in his tone.

I didn't know what surprised me more: that he knew about the AML or that rumors existed about the league seeking to exterminate merpeople.

Hannah had been snippy with me for weeks. At first, I thought it was because of her new engagement, but now I wondered if she and some of the executive members of the AML were keeping things from the rest of us. From me.

I wondered where he'd heard about the AML and if we had a spy in our midst. Atlanticeans who were sympathetic to merpeople coming to our meetings and passing information along.

It seemed unbelievable, but not at all implausible.

With the swaying movement of the water and the warmth generating from his body, my own relaxed, and my mental and physical exertion hit me all at once. Exhaustion caused my eyelids to flutter and finally shut out the world with all of its problems.

The peaceful state shattered when he whispered in my ear, "Princess, I'm sorry I have to interrupt your nap." His chest rose as he took a deep breath. "We're here."

I blinked a few times, getting my eyes used to the low light. My heart raced as I saw my fingers splayed on his chest, sending heat to my cheeks. I jerked my fingers away as though I had been physically scorched.

He frowned before scooping up an armful of seaweed lodged against the rocks and placed it on a rock. He gently lifted me above the rock before he set me on top of the pile.

Lowering my lashes, I evaded his eyes as he pulled away.

"Sorry, it's wet, but I'd rather you sit on wet seaweed and not on a hard surface." He shrugged. Now that he was not touching me, the cold began to seep in again.

"Uhm, it's fine."

His hand reached forward, and I jolted away from it.

But it didn't stop him.

I froze.

If he wanted to kill me, there wouldn't be any witnesses. Even though I could see the palace, it didn't mean anyone in the palace could see me. We were out here alone, just the two of us on a rocky outcrop. I was an easy target. A very easy target.

His palm grazed my cheek, and my stomach flipped over.

"What are you doing?" I snapped as his hand traveled up to my hair. My mind began to whirr as it filled with thoughts of him dragging me beneath the surface by my hair. I flinched away from him, my nerves in tatters.

He grinned and pulled away his hand. As he opened it, I could see it was covered with seaweed. "Don't think you want seaweed sticking out of your head. The Medusa look is out of style these days." His chest and shoulders moved as though holding in his laughter.

My fear melted away, but I forced myself to scoff. If he wasn't a merman, I would have laughed. But he was. Instead, I pursed my lips.

"How are your lungs?" he asked. "Better?"

I nodded, feeling foolish at the direction in which my thoughts had been taking me. "Still hurting, but at least, I'm not coughing."

He nodded thoughtfully. "Good. I've heard drowning is a painful way to die. Not that I'd know and all, what with me being who I am."

What he was... a merman. The AML protocol required me to continue a hostile stance, but I couldn't. His caring and jovial personality deserved, at least, respect. He'd saved my life. "Thanks for laying out the seaweed."

"All in a day's work." He chuckled. "I aim to please, princess."

The guilt gnawed at my heart until I decided to forget about rules and be a decent human being. "And thanks so much for saving me. I really thought my parents would have to prepare for my funeral."

"I don't understand how you can live in the Kingdom of Atlantice and not know how to swim. It's an island," he pointed out.

"I know that."

"So why did you never learn? Weren't your parents concerned about your lack of ability to swim?"

"Of course they were." I attempted not to stare, but his extraordinary aura beckoned me like a lighthouse beacon to lost sailors. He held my gaze for seconds before I lowered my head, focusing on his red tail. A fishtail. I couldn't ignore that he did not belong to the human race. He was a fish, a big part of the reason I'd never learned to swim.

"Then why not teach you how to swim?" He pointed at the palace. "It's not as though you live far away from the water."

"Uhm, I never wanted to learn," I admitted, hoping he didn't press me on the matter.

"Your parents should have forced you," he pointed out.

I lifted my head and took in a deep breath. "I refused every time they tried. After six years, they accepted my aversion to learning."

He jerked his head back. "Why refuse? All children want to play in the water and beg to learn how to swim and dive. Why not you?"

Why couldn't he let this go? I bit my lip while I plucked up the courage to tell him the truth.

"I didn't learn to swim because… swimming lessons in the sea meant that I might have to encounter a merperson, so I wasn't interested." I shrugged, not daring to look at him.

He was silent for a few moments while he took in my words. I hazarded a glance his way.

He stared at me with a tiny wrinkle in his forehead. "You would rather not learn to swim for your safety and possibly the safety of others because of my people?" He crossed his arms.

"Well, yes. Why would I put myself in waters with them?" I practically spat the last word out, hating myself more and more with each passing second.

"What did you think would happen?" The wrinkles turned to deep indentations creating horizontal paths across his forehead. He wasn't angry, but I could hear the hurt in his voice.

Self-loathing filled me, and yet now that I'd started, I found I couldn't stop. Years of AML meetings and hatred of merfolk poured out of me, and I was unable to make it cease.

"Everything bad and horrible. Merpeople are below us. Way below us. I've always heard that you merpeople cause all our problems." I folded my arms, using them as a barrier between us. My breathing came thick and fast at the way I'd just spoken to the man who had saved my life.

"Not sure who told you that, but we're peacefully living in our own kingdom. We may share and obtain our food from the same body of water, but we don't purposely cause trouble." He batted away a seagull that had swept close to my head.

"That's not what Hannah and the AML say." I stared at the retreating seagull. "She says that your people reduce both our fish and crustacean populations, and you hurt sea life for pleasure."

So now he knew. I was a member of the AML, the very same AML that he'd only ten minutes ago told me wanted to kill him. I'd always worn my membership with pride, but now it felt more like an admission of wrongdoing than a thing to be proud of. To give him credit, he didn't just swim away from me as I would have done in his position. I'd have left me to find my own way home over the slippery, seaweed-covered rocks. Instead, he spoke to me. His voice was calm like the gentle lapping of the ocean.

"I agree that we do eat fish and lobsters because they're our *only* food source," he explained. "We need to eat from the waters because we obviously can't walk on land." He lifted his tail. "But I have never hurt any sea creatures for the mere fun of it. Neither have my friends or family. We consider sea creatures our friends and not playthings. I can't say the same thing about humans who hunt for sport and not because they need to eat. Humans have a habit of destroying their environment instead of learning to live without harming it or using it for their entertainment."

"What? We don't do that." I raised my voice. I'd turned this into a shouting match. One I was ill-equipped to play because he was right. My own father enjoyed hunting.

"Think about how humans fish for sport, but once they catch the fish, they throw it back," Fish said. "And how about the hunters who kill and place the animal on their mantles as trophies? Do they kill those animals for food or for sport?" He pretended his hands formed a balancing scale. "Necessary nutrition or a sport? Which one is more destructive?"

I stared down at my fingers, wishing I'd kept my mouth shut. If I'd just thanked him and said no more, then I wouldn't have started this stupid argument.

His penetrating eyes prompted me to lean back, away from his heady scent of saltwater and something else I didn't recognize.

"The league says that you're savages, and they told us stories of how you sink ships and kill everyone on board."

Yet more AML hatred spewed from me in the same way salt-water had only ten minutes earlier. My heart and my mind fought with conflicting emotions. On the one hand, I believed every word I said. I'd grown up with it, and yet I had no reason not to believe him.

"They're lying to you because we're not savages," he whispered earnestly. "We live in our underwater kingdom in the same way humans live on land. Children attend schools, parents have jobs, our king rules the kingdom with a firm hand, everything that happens above land happens in a similar manner under the sea. We even fall in love and marry just as you do. Our lives are not that different from yours."

His tone sounded sincere enough, and his words natural, not contrived, and yet how could everything I'd ever known be wrong? My parents didn't even know I was a member of the AML, but I'd been with the group long enough for their doctrine to be ingrained.

"You can't judge all the merpeople because of the propaganda that the AML distributes," he continued. "Let's say that the rumor came from the bad actions of two or three merpeople; would you condemn the entire pod? Would you hang all of us for the crimes of a tiny minority?"

I shook my head. "No, of course not. That wouldn't be fair."

"Then we agree." He stared at the palace. "Are you ready to return?"

"Yes, I am," I said with a confidence I didn't feel inside. I didn't want to go back. I needed him to know that humans weren't all bad. I wasn't ready for him to leave me the way things were. I'd started an argument and didn't know how to fix it. After he'd saved my life, I'd actually sat back and told him how awful his people were. It was almost like I was trying to get him to believe it himself. *What was wrong with me?*

I'd thought he was going to leave me on the rocks for me to scramble home, but he pulled me back into the water and held me snug against his chest. He kicked off and began the short swim back to the shoreline in front of the palace. We reached shallow water, where he lowered me on the sand. "See you around, Princess."

"Not likely, Fish."

I turned away from him and waded through the shallow water to the beach, this time not looking back for fear he'd see the tears in my eyes. There was no point in being nice to him. We came from different worlds. Worlds that could not collide. Our argument might have been my fault, but it was valid. I couldn't be nice to him because I couldn't encourage him. And I couldn't encourage him because then, one of the AML would see him, and if the rumors were true, there was a chance they would kill him.

And I hated him. I hated everything he was and everything his people stood for... I just couldn't for the life of me remember why.

3
31ST JANUARY

"$\mathcal{M}$om, a bunch of the responses just arrived,"—I strode into my parents' bedroom, holding the cards in one hand and waving the fruity scented one in the other— "but the one from the Kingdom of Floris smells delicious. It's so good I'm almost tempted to eat it. How do they manage it?" I halted my stride four feet inside my parent's bedroom.

Sitting on her chaise with her chin resting on her hand, she gazed out the window, not even noticing I was in the room. Her long poofy skirt covered the entire lower half of the chaise.

"Mom, did you hear me?"

"What did you say, Blaise?" her toneless voice drifted over to me, but she carried on staring out of the window, not even looking my way.

Something was going on with her. This was not the mother I knew and loved at all.

I ignored the resentment boiling inside me because she did not confide in me and kept my tone steady when I answered, "The scent that is tempting me to eat this flower. How can they infuse it with this delicious smell?" I wandered toward the window, trying not to allow her distracted state to upset me further.

But I failed big time.

Her recent lack of *joie de vivre* pained me, tearing a gash in my heart.

I hated it.

Previously, my mom would have asked for the card and inhaled it, but now, she didn't even bother to take it from my hand.

Had running a kingdom filled with its protocols finally broken her?

Had she given up her joy and blended with the dullness of being queen after eighteen years?

"Mom, did you hear me?"

She finally brought her eyes to mine. Eyes that no longer sparkled.

"Ah, not sure, but they have wonderful gardens at the Floris palace. Perhaps the head gardener has developed a secret scent using their flowers?" she answered.

"He'll make millions if he patents it," I replied before bouncing on the bed and disturbing the pillows.

Three of them fell and landed with a plop, but my mom had already turned back to the window.

The fact that she didn't correct my unladylike behavior screamed major issues.

"I need the fresh air of the sea," my mom said as she swung her legs to the floor with a grimace and stood. "Will you accompany me, please?" My mom held the silk throw that had covered her feet by the two corners. She folded it and placed it on the chaise before she rearranged her long dress.

"Sure, Mom," I answered, picking up the pillows and placing them back on the bed.

"Please bring the notebook on my vanity table and the responses. We'll list everyone so we can finalize the seating arrangement. We must put the most desirable princes near you and their parents near the head of the table. The rest we can sit near the end of the table." She paused at the door. "Oh, and bring a couple of pillows." She ambled through the door while I gaped at her back.

Something about the way she walked caught me off guard. She usually strode with such confidence, but now, there was a slight limp to her gait, and she moved so slowly.

Grabbing the notebook, I hurried after her and stuffed the cards inside the pages. But there wasn't a need to hurry, as a sloth could have beaten my mom's measured pace.

"Mom, what's wrong? Are you in pain?" I whispered.

She hesitated before she answered, "It's nothing. Just have a lot on my mind right now." She continued to limp, not really answering my question. "Your father wants to leave for the mainland, and I want the Valentine's Day ball to be perfect. It is all too draining." She held her breath before she exhaled. "In a couple of weeks, everything will pass as it should."

Her cryptic answer drove me into hyper-worry mode.

"Why is Dad going to the mainland?"

My mom lowered her eyes before she spoke. "There are a couple of issues arising that he needs to have a face-to-face with the other leaders about. Nothing for you to worry about right now."

She winced through clenched teeth every time one of her feet touched the ground.

"Is everything alright with your feet?"

She nodded. "It's fine, Blaise, don't fuss so. I just broke in some new shoes, that's all. They were a little tight."

Her limp worsened as we continued down the path. There was no way it was caused by ill-fitting shoes.

She winced again and motioned behind us. I stepped aside as two guards positioned themselves on either side of her. They held out their arms and proceeded to help her walk.

Once again, my mind turned to Queen Briar Rose of Draconis. The papers said she was fine one minute and then in some kind of weird cursed coma the next. I knew this wasn't what was happening to my own mother, and I was overreacting, but something was going on. Something she wasn't telling me.

My heart plunged to my stomach at the awful thought of losing my mom. I wanted to beg her to tell me what caused her not to confide in me, to be honest with me, but a part of me was terrified that I wouldn't be able to handle the truth.

I trailed behind her and the guards with only the seagulls flying above us, their cawing breaking our silence.

When we arrived at the end of the path, she pointed. "Let's sit on those rocks over there close to the water. You don't mind, do you?"

I shrugged. "No, it's okay."

She half-smiled. "It brings back memories of when I first met your dad. Such wonderful times." She waved at the guards. "Please return to the path, we're safe here."

I held my breath at the thought that she'd brought me here for a reason. Maybe she was about to tell me what was going on.

Placing the two large pillows on the rocks, I held a hand out for her.

"Thank you, my sweet child," she whispered. "I've been so blessed to have you in my life."

"I'm not going anywhere, Mom."

"Yes, I know, but life has a way of disrupting our peace." She lowered her head. "It's been a wonderful eighteen years with you. I just don't want it to stop, but we'll be apart soon."

Then why are you pushing me to marry? If you don't want it and I certainly am not ready, why the rush? I refrained from screaming, but my eyebrows lifted.

"It'll be a while before I find my Prince Charming, and I'll still be close," I assured her. "Or I'll visit whenever I can." I leaned my head on her shoulder. "You'll just have to plan more balls so I can stay a month at a time." Despite my laughter, my heart ached to wail and relieve the pressure building inside.

"Your father would definitely enjoy more dances. And I'm sure there are enough reasons to hold at least a quarterly ball."

"Yes," I agreed, "and I can come up with plenty of reasons to have a ball on my end so you'll be able to visit me. It'll be like I never left."

"That would be good for your dad to visit his little girl often." She nodded.

It sounded as if she was writing herself out of our family.

Her hands gripped the edge of the pillows, and tears ran down her face. "Oh, this pain is unbearable." She slipped off her ballerina flats and placed her feet in the water. "I wish it would stop."

The calm water produced a wave larger than usual, soaking my mother's feet to the hem of her skirt.

"Can you please have a soothing tea made for me?" my mother cried urgently, pulling her dress down.

I stood, watching her hands lose their pinkness as they gripped the rocks. "Sure, Mom. I'll ask the guards."

"No, please, get it yourself," she urged, flapping me away. "You know how I like it. Make sure you find the fresh cinnamon from the garden."

"Okay," I replied, wondering why she suddenly wanted tea.

"Thanks, my darling child. Go quickly... quickly!"

With hurried steps, I reached the path, but a muted scream halted my next step. I turned to find my mother clutching her feet, her face screwed up in agony. As I watched, her feet changed from a light pink to blue. Seconds later, she hunched over. I glanced at the guards, but while they stood at attention, they did not move. Panic caught me and held me to the ground. I needed to bring a guard to help, but my mother needed me. I could hear her cries as she almost toppled into the water. Running back over the rocks. I caught her before she fell in.

"Go away," she cried, trying to push me away. "I need my tea now! Go!"

She shifted her soaked dress, and something in the water caught my eye.

As my eyes adjusted to the gloom, my breath caught in shock. There, where my mother's legs should be, was an iridescent blue tail.

I blinked a couple of times, trying to register how a tail could have replaced my mom's feet.

"Mom, what's going on?" I asked, panic filling my voice. "Why do you have a tail?"

"I didn't want you to witness this, Blaise. Please leave and forget what you just saw." Tears fell down her face, adding a little more salt to the seawater.

"No. Is this a trick? Is it your costume for the ball? What's happening?"

She lifted the tip of her blue-greenish tail. It sparkled. "No, I wish it was." She half-smiled, but she seemed about to cry. "But it's definitely not." She whispered, "I'm sorry, Blaise."

My breathing came thick and fast as I struggled to take in the sight before me.

"Did a witch cast a spell?" I asked, my voice shaking with each syllable. "Who can undo it?"

She shook her head, her long, flowing, red hair shimmering gently on her shoulders. "Sweetie, it's not a spell... at least not a new one."

"What do you mean?"

"Blaise, I didn't want you to ever find out about me. I thought I could hide it, but the pain has been getting so bad lately... Blaise, I'm a mermaid... Or at least, I was until I received my human legs." She smoothed out the fish scales on the spot where her calves used to be. "And now, it seems I'm reverting back."

I sank to the rocks, disbelief filling me. "What do you mean, you were a mermaid? You've always had legs."

"No, my dear," she said quietly, taking my hand in hers. "I was born a mermaid. After falling in love with your father, I asked for human legs."

I shook my head "How can that be? Humans can't change into mermaids, and mermaids can't change into humans. It's not possible."

Her hand shook as she spoke, her words coming out in a whisper. "They can when a Sea Witch uses her magic."

Tears streamed down my face. "It's not possible. It can't be. Why?"

She shook her head sadly. "I don't know why I've reverted back to my original form. I don't understand it myself."

I stood and gaped at her tail. "No, I won't accept this," I said, pulling my hand from hers and struggling to my feet. "I'll never accept that you were... are one of those detestable creatures. You're not my mom." Blood rushed to my head, and I screamed.

She raised her hands and yelled, "Stop. Stop! Sit down!"

I stepped away from her and glanced at the guards rushing toward us with their swords drawn.

My mother's voice rose up like the roar of a mountain lion when she saw them approaching. "She's upset and won't harm me, stay where you are. She is still Princess Blaise, my daughter. You are sworn to protect us both."

The guards stopped moving, but they did not sheath their swords. They shifted to their striking stances, waiting for her word.

Even though I was a princess they would protect with their lives, they would always protect her first. I turned back to look at her. Her tail was still visible. She'd made no attempt to hide it. The guards had not been taken aback when they saw it, which meant they already knew. That's why they had helped her walk down to the sea. They were helping her to change.

Taking a couple of deep breaths, I whispered, "Does Dad know?"

She nodded slowly. "Yes, he does. He's always known. I explained everything to him after we fell in love. I didn't want to hide it from him." Her lashes lowered. "There are no secrets between us."

I scanned the guards' faces, but not one of them seemed disgusted or surprised. "And these guards? Do all of them know? Who else knows?"

"Only these guards who are closest to your father and me, and they are sworn to secrecy." She let out a deep breath. "No one else knows. Not his family. Not our friends." She rubbed her arms. "We didn't want anyone to find out that I had once been a mermaid because people hold grudges against merpeople. Too many prejudices against us." Her hands reached out to me.

Moving back so she wouldn't touch me, I whispered, "How could you?" I glowered at her. "This is the ultimate betrayal," I said, allowing resentment to fill my tone.

She shook her head. "No, my sweetie. We did it to protect you. Protect your father, the kingdom. You were never supposed to know. It was in the past." Her fingertips touched her scaly thigh. "We thought it best to protect the family. There are too many Atlanticeans who hate the merpeople enough to hurt them. We couldn't chance it." She lowered her head, and tiny dots spotted the top of her dress.

Those tears meant nothing to me.

Nothing.

Not at that moment with my heart shredding into millions of pieces.

"You lied to me," I said through tears of my own. "Dad lied to me." I wiped the tears and retreated another foot. "Our lives have been a big, fat lie."

My mother raised her eyes. "Blaise, please don't go." She reached out a hand. "Please stay, and we can discuss this. How we did it for you."

"No," I shouted back at her. "There isn't anything you can say to change my mind. I'll never trust either of you again." I pivoted on my toes before sprinting back to the path.

Two guards crossed their glaives, blocking the path.

"Please, get out of my way," I snarled at them.

They didn't budge.

Not a single blink.

I pointed to their long polearms. "Uncross your swords. NOW!" I screamed.

They didn't even twitch.

From behind me, my mother shouted, "Please let her pass," using that commanding tone, she continued, "and escort her to her room."

Without glancing back, I marched up the long path, each footstep stomping against the wooden planks. *Is this what she'd been hiding? Or is it something else? This would be enough.*

The guards' heavy footsteps trailed behind me until I jerked open my door and slammed it in their faces.

For minutes, I paced my room, trying to figure out what to do.

I should pack my things and stay at Hannah's home. But I remembered the argument I'd had with her just the other day and decided against it.

I wanted to summon Emma, but I dreaded anyone seeing me so vulnerable. Instead, I plopped on my bed and closed my eyes.

Squeezing my favorite pillow in the middle, I rested my back against my headboard, tracing the gold trim with my finger.

I needed to talk to someone, or I'd explode. But telling Hannah was definitely out. If she found out, she'd have my parents thrown in jail for treason.

Emma? But could I trust her? She'd seemed so quiet the last time I'd talked about merfolk, but that didn't mean anything. It didn't mean she liked them. Maybe she was just doing her job.

My chest rose and fell as warm tears landed on the pillowcase and drenched my pillow.

Ignoring the several knocks on my door, I released the pillow and turned it over. From the other side of the door, I heard Emma's voice. "May I enter?"

I wiped my face with tissues pulled from my night table. My voice trembled when I responded, "Yes, and please lock the door behind you." My voice quivered. It reflected the same quivering inside my body.

"Yes, princess." Emma strolled into the room, and as she caught my gaze, her own hazel eyes widened. "Are you ok, Miss? Should I call the doctor?"

"No, nothing is physically wrong with me. Please lock the door," I asked her again.

She nodded and turned, locking the door.

"But something is wrong." She paused. "You've lost your color. Do you want me to prepare you some tea?" She spoke calmly, but her hands wrung together as though she was nervous.

"No, I wouldn't be able to drink it."

I lifted my arms and massaged the area below my neck with the tips of my fingers.

"Food, then? Chicken soup? Hot chocolate? Whatever you want, I'll make sure the cook makes it."

Emma reminded me of a sweet grandmother who thought food solved every problem, except she was about my age.

Holding back the tears, I responded, "Nothing will make this better. Nothing will help me. No one can. It's beyond anyone's help." I stifled my tears.

"There must be someone who can help you? Should I call Hannah? She's really good at solving problems."

"Definitely not her." I took a couple of deep breaths and locked eyes with her. "I'm sorry for being vague. I have a problem, and I don't know what to do. If I tell you, will you promise not to tell anyone? And I mean no one. Not your parents, not your siblings, not your friends. Can you promise me that you'll keep my secret?"

She hurried to the foot of the chaise and placed her hands over her heart. "Princess, you can trust me. I promise not to talk or judge."

I took a deep breath as I considered telling Emma such a secret. She had only been working at the palace for a few months, but she'd shown herself to be a trustworthy person.

"This afternoon, I watched my mother transform herself into a..."

I paused. Emma took my hands in hers.

"Into a what?"

"Into a... mermaid.'" I hiccupped, waiting for Emma to call me a liar or walk out the door. When she didn't, I continued. "She says that she was a mermaid before she married my father. Can you believe that? It was something to do with a sea witch. She's hidden that she is a mermaid for eighteen years because she didn't want anyone to know."

Emma's facial expression remained neutral, but she lowered her eyes. "Have you asked her why she didn't want people to know?"

"She said because people are prejudiced, and they hold grudges. I can't believe that she's a mermaid." All my fingers formed a fist. "It's disgusting."

With a hardened tone I'd not heard in her before, she said,

"Regardless of her turning into a mermaid, she's still your mother, and you love her. I know you do." I looked into her eyes to see not a look of disgust, but of one of understanding. She half-smiled. "No matter how upset you are right now, she will always be the woman you love because she is your mother."

I tilted my head, allowing my long hair to fall on my shoulder. "Aren't you upset that she's a mermaid?" I asked her. "That she has lied all these years?"

She'd not only lied to me, she'd lied to the people of Atlantice.

"Everyone has secrets, and no, I don't care if she's a mermaid. Queen Antonella has always been a fair queen who loves her people. She treats us all well." She strolled to my bed.

I picked up a strand of my hair and twirled it between my fingers. "I thought every Atlanticean hated mermaids."

"Not everyone hates them." Emma picked up the pillows from the floor and turned to me. "A couple of my friends are mermaids."

I was surprised by her admission. She'd never said anything about it before.

"Aren't you afraid of them?"

She laughed. "Not at all. They are my friends. One of them saved me from a shark when I swam too far from the shore once."

"They did?"

She nodded, arranging the pillows back on the bed. "Yes, and I'm not the only one they've saved. They do it all the time." She paused while she considered her next words. "I know you've never been fond of merfolk, but I don't think they are as bad as you think. They aren't monsters."

Why doesn't the AML mention this?

Fish's face danced in front of me, and I had to ask, "Do you know only mermaids, or do you know any mermen?"

"Mostly mermaids as the men don't come too close to the shore. But the ones I've seen are really cute." She giggled. "Super cute."

"The one I met the other day was cute," I admitted. I would never have mentioned it to anyone, but I trusted Emma.

"Really?"

"Gorgeous," I whispered, hardly daring to admit it. "My toes curl up every time I think about him."

"Do you know his name?"

"No." I bit my lip. I'd been calling him Fish, but it was such a derogatory term. I'd never paused to think to ask him his name. The admission to myself embarrassed me.

"What does he look like?" she asked, smoothing down my bed. For a second I worried that she would know him and he would tell her how horrible I was to him, but then I remembered she'd said that her mer-friends were female.

"He has long hair with a slight wave and the most brilliant green eyes I've ever seen." I touched my hair, where he had removed the seaweed. "And dimples. He has the cutest dimples when he smiles."

"Sounds like someone has a crush?"

"No!" I said, a little too quickly. I didn't have a crush. It was absurd. Like having a crush on a plate of fish and chips. He was a fish, damnit!

"Ok," she said, raising her eyebrows at me like she knew exactly what I was thinking.

"We are too different," I deflected.

"Hmm," she murmured, thoughtfully, pulling the covers on my bed taught.

"He's a merman. I can't like him. I should hate him. The merfolk are evil. Everyone knows it."

"Princess, I don't mean any disrespect, but the rumors about them are untrue. They're a peaceful people, who will only fight when they have to. They're not evil. Far from it. They've saved so many people, children, from the real predators of the sea."

"If that's true, why don't we hear about it?"

Emma shrugged. "Because most of the time, the merpeople don't show themselves to those they've saved. They leave the person on the shore, so the person doesn't know who saved them. Not everyone thinks the way you do. There are many people who are friends with the merfolk."

I thought back to when Fish rescued me. Was he just trying to be my friend?

Emma pulled a dust cloth from her pocket and began to dust. I sat on the chaise lounge and pondered my conversation with her. She had no fear or malice toward the merfolk, and yet, she seemed to not mind the fact that I hated them.

"You know I'm part of the AML, and my best friend runs it."

She nodded. "I know."

"Doesn't it bother you? I mean, if your friends are merfolk."

"I know who the AML are, and I know what they do. You profess to hate merfolk, and yet you've let one get right into your head. Maybe it's time to have a long think about your priorities."

I nodded. She was right, but the hatred of merfolk was so ingrained in me. It was easy for her to tell me to just change my mind, but not so easy for me to discard my lifelong beliefs. Besides, I didn't have many friends, and those I did have were all AML members.

I let her carry on cleaning my room as I watched on in silence. My own mother was not even human. I wondered what that meant for me. With a sinking realization, it hit me that I was half-mermaid. I was the object of my own hate. A half-mermaid that didn't even know how to swim.

A knock on my door, followed by my mother's voice, made me jump. Emma stopped what she was doing and looked at me, waiting to see what I would do.

"Blaise, darling. Are you in?"

Emma made to open the door, but I held my hand out to stop her. I brought my finger to my lips as my mother called out again. I couldn't speak to her. I wasn't ready to acknowledge any of it.

I could see the look of disapproval in Emma's eyes, but I ignored her as I was ignoring my mother. Eventually, my mother gave up, and when Emma left a half-hour later, she left without saying another word.

4
1ST FEBRUARY

*A*fter spending half the night tossing and turning, I finally managed a little sleep. The late morning sun's rays brightened my room. My eyelids fluttered open, and my gaze landed on the portrait of my parents and me. The corner of my lips automatically lifted at the sight of it. I remembered when it was painted. A gift for my seventh birthday. Pain came crashing down as I looked at my mother. In the picture, her legs were visible below her skirts, her ankles just peeking out atop her shoes. How could she have stood there smiling for the royal portrait, knowing what she knew? It didn't just impact her, it impacted me too. My whole life was a lie.

Blood rushed through my veins, warming every inch of my body, filling me with anger. It was one thing to be a mermaid and quite another to lie to me about it. My father too!

I pulled an old T-shirt over my head. Digging out a pair of riding pants from a corner of my closet, I shoved my legs inside them with a force that could have poked a hole. Luckily, the extra leather padding protected them from the brunt of my anger.

For a minute, I debated calling for Emma but thought against dragging her into my drama again. Not when I'd already divulged our largest family secret to her within an hour of finding out about it myself. If Emma found out that I wanted to avoid talking to my mother by leaving the palace grounds, she would only try to talk me out of it.

I could not put Emma in that position, but the anger still simmered inside me, and I craved alone time.

Grabbing a container of coconut water from my nightstand, I slipped on my favorite boots.

On the way to the path that would lead me to the beach, I swigged the coconut water, wishing I'd thought to bring some food with me. I'd need nourishment if I wanted to hide out by the beach all day long, and that was exactly what I planned to do.

Walking while drinking was another no-no with my mother. Royal protocol didn't allow it. What with the coconut water and avoiding my parents, I was really playing the rebel.

Rebelling felt good.

A little too good.

I generally didn't visit the beach much in the winter months, but it was the only place where I could guarantee I wouldn't be bothered. The strangest part was that while I feared the water, and disliked the merpeople, the beach was the one place that always calmed me. Even during the severest thunderstorms, it brought me a peace like no other place. Waves crashing against the shore never failed to push away the thoughts about the things that bothered me most.

I hurried down the rest of the path, desperate to be away from the palace and the threat of bumping into my mother, who, no doubt, would want to talk to me about the incident yesterday. I wasn't ready.

When I reached the beach, I tossed my boots underneath a sea grape bush and dug my toes in the cool sand. Draining the coconut water, I placed the empty bottle in the sand.

Finally, I'm free. At least, until Emma finds me gone and alerts my parents.

Despite the time crunch, I stomped my feet, leaving deep impressions in the sand as I paced along the shore. Deciding where to hide out for a few hours without my parents finding out and away from the guards' all-seeing eyes proved harder than I thought.

It was a long beach with not much in the way of places a princess could hide. My eyes drifted to the one break on the shoreline. The pier. Not that I could go to it. For a start, it was too low to hide under unless I wanted to wade into the sea, which I didn't, and secondly, there was the small matter of *him*.

If I walked out onto the pier, would he swim up to me as he had before, or would he be far away, not caring about seeing some rude princess? And I had been rude. Neither he nor my mother deserved it, but yet again, they were both merfolk. Lower-class citizens.

I turned to walk in the opposite direction to the pier, but the pull of it was too strong. The thought that he might come to me both thrilled me and appalled me in equal measure. My heart quickened as I made the decision to turn around and walk the short distance to the pier.

So what if he sees me? It's my pier. I can walk on it whenever I like.

I reasoned with myself all the way that I was only heading to the pier for the walk, but my accelerated pulse gave me away. I couldn't even lie to myself. I wanted to see him. I could blame it on curiosity, on any number of things, but the truth was, I wanted to see him again. Like the siren call of the ocean, he pulled me to him in a way I couldn't understand, nor was I prepared for.

The calm sea lapped against the pier struts, a contrast to the maelstrom whirling within me. With each step, I both wished to see the hint of a red tail and felt the desire not to. Two opposing forces pulling me apart. At the very end of the pier, I took a deep breath of fresh salty air. He was nowhere to be seen, which made me a little relieved and a whole lot disappointed. I had no reason to see him, and he had no reason to come back and yet... and yet, as I turned around to head back, the deep ache of disappointment increased, pulling my emotions down, weighing my heart and stomach.

A splash behind me had me pivoting back quickly, my heart leaping, but there was nothing there. Maybe a slightly larger wave hitting the endmost strut. Just as I had been uplifted with hope, I began the crash down, but then, I saw him.

He crested the water, his long dark hair fanning out behind him.

Could this guy be any more beautiful?

I swallowed thickly as he swam the short distance to me, sparkles on beads of water, giving him an appearance of otherworldliness.

"I didn't expect you to come back," he said.

I took a breath to tell him I was sorry again, to try to explain that my mind was conflicted, but he spoke first.

"I hoped..."

It was all the invitation I needed.

Lowering myself on the pier, my feet grazed over the water, and I whispered, "I don't know what I'm doing. My whole life has been a lie, and there is nowhere for me to hide from it. I was rude to you the other day. Very rude. I'm sorry."

I didn't mention that I might be half-mermaid. The thought still terrified me as much as the water did.

He grabbed the pier, his hand grazing my leg, sending goose-bumps up through my body. He was so close to me, his chest almost completely out of the water with just a hint of the tail visible beneath.

"No one will find you out here," he said, gesturing to the ocean with his free hand. Following his gaze to the horizon, the endless expanse of water sent a thrill of fear running through my body.

"I can't swim, remember?"

He locked eyes with mine causing me to inhale sharply. He smelled like the ocean, or perhaps the ocean smelled like him. I bit my lip, scared to speak anymore for fear of what might come out of my mouth. His gaze penetrated my skull, and I was keenly aware that his free hand had joined the first on the pier, although not quite in the same place. He had one at either side of my legs, both touching the leather of my britches, and as he pulled closer, my knees touched his naked chest. I couldn't breathe, could barely think. My eyes focused on his beautiful mouth, and when he spoke, it was barely above a whisper.

"No, but I can."

It was an invitation. An invitation to the sea. When I'd set out, looking for a place to hide, my brain had a half-assed idea to hide among the waves, but my fear was stronger than any ridiculous notion of jumping into something that could kill me as surely as any monster. Or at least it had been until now. Now, I had a shield from the cold, from the fear, although he was a big part of the fear too. Slowly I nodded my head.

His lips formed a mischievous grin. "Where do you want to go?"

I was barely aware I was breathing, but I heard myself speak, almost as though it was someone else.

"Anywhere my parents can't find me."

He held his arms wide open. "Jump."

I was already between them. All it would take was for me to quietly slip off the pier and be caught by him, but now that the magnitude of what I was about to do hit me, my fear caught up.

"No, I can't." I scanned the vast sea, wanting to abolish the feeling of drowning. "I really can't."

"Yes, you can. I'll catch you." Our eyes connected. "Trust me, I won't let you go."

With a dizzying clarity, I knew he would be true to his word. The desire to fall into his arms was almost as strong as the force pulling me back. Years of terror of the ocean was not something I could get over in a few minutes, but as he moved closer, wrapping his arms around my waist, the sea didn't feel so scary anymore. My body trembled, although I wasn't sure if it was the dread of the water or the intense physical attraction being held by him brought about. I eased my legs to the edge, allowing the water to hit my shins, soaking my pants. Holding on to the pier until my arms hurt, and taking a deep breath, I abandoned myself to him. I slid into the water without breaking eye contact. My T-shirt rose up, so I pulled it over my head and threw it onto the pier, leaving me with only my bra covering my top half.

"I will keep you safe," he whispered in my ear as the coldness of the water was swallowed up by the heat of his body against mine.

Snuggled against his chest, my mood transformed from fear to peacefulness, while my body reacted to his closeness.

I wondered if he could hear my pulse racing or my heart beating against my ribs as surely as I could feel it.

"You feeling okay? The water isn't too cold for you?"

"No, it's fine," I mumbled, the raw energy emanating from his body where our flesh touched more than warmed me. It surprised me just how warm he was in the cold ocean, although the heat between us was more than mere warmth.

"Okay. Once we reach the rocks, we can discuss our options."

The palace became smaller as he cut through the water, leaving tiny bubbles in our wake. The frisson of fear had not completely subsided, but because of the comforting way he held me and the strength of his arms, the thoughts of drowning were pushed to the back of my mind.

"How about when we reach the rocks, I teach you how to swim?"

"What if I drown?" I asked him, the apprehensive tone clear in my voice. I bit my lip, feeling ridiculous in this man's arms.

"In thirty minutes, you'll be swimming like a guppy," he assured me.

Leaning away from his chest a couple of inches, I replied. "No, I can't. It's too far from the shore and too deep. I'm definitely not about to risk my life."

He didn't understand the fear because drowning was not something he was capable of. He could swim and breathe underwater as easily as he could breathe above its surface.

His mouth twitched. "I won't let you drown, my little land-lover." He chuckled and continued swimming. "Trust me. Even if you were drowning, you know that I can save you."

I thought of all the things that could happen. Things I'd spent my life worrying about. I tried not to remind myself of the fact that the thing that worried me most was currently holding me in his arms.

"What about sharks?" I mumbled, feeling foolish. "They're crushing, munching killers of the sea."

He chortled. "Once a shark figures out that I'm a merman, it will stay away from me. It'll know that I'm not its prey and that I can kill it. Besides I think you'll learn how to swim fairly quickly."

"We're here," he continued. "You can sit on the rocks or stay in the water… with me."

He was giving me the choice, but it was a choice I'd been arguing both sides of in my mind since the very moment I first slipped into the water. His tail moved languidly under the surface, reminding me of its presence. He was a merman, and the feel of his scales against the skin of my feet was not about to let me forget it.

"I prefer to stay on the rock's surface," I said finally. "Not in the water."

He shrugged. "Your choice, but you'll be cold out there. My body heat is keeping you warm. I can't do that if you are up there and I am down here. I promise to hold onto you the whole time until you are confident enough to let me go."

"What if you let me go?" I asked.

He gazed into my eyes, holding my stare, and I swear, for a moment, I didn't care if he took me into the deepest depths of the ocean, for I would have gone willingly.

"I'll never let you go."

A thrill of excitement ran through me as I continued to hold his stare.

"Okay," I whispered.

He loosened his grip, and my body froze. He shifted my body so that it lay horizontal, his arm underneath my stomach. "You need to raise your arm and bring it forward like this."

For seconds my mind blanked. No thought but lots of tiny sensations in my stomach and the inability to breathe.

"Open your eyes and breathe," he encouraged me. "Come on, it's easy."

I blinked. "No, I can't do this."

"It'll be fine. I'm not letting you go. We're simply going over the arm movements first. I won't completely let go. I promise." He raised his arm again. "See how I lift my arm? Try it."

My fingertips pulsed from my strong grip on his upper arm. "No, this is too much." My heart raced, but I couldn't tell if it was a reaction to him or the memory of how the salty water rushed into my mouth the other day, choking me.

"Please," I cried, "I can't do this."

He scooped up an armful of seaweed and arranged it on the rocks before he set me on the pile.

"Okay, I won't force you." He tilted his head. "It's your choice to learn how to swim and when. But we can't stay here a long time." He held my gaze. "Unfortunately, you not being able to swim does limit our choices of where we can go."

"I don't want to learn how to swim, especially not here. The water is too deep. But I don't want to return to the palace... at least, not now." I bit my lower lip. Eventually, I would have to talk to my mother, but the anger inside me, much less than before, still simmered.

He lay back in the water for a moment, apparently in thought.

"How about the next town? There is a boat festival today, and you can blend in with the crowd. We'll hang by the pier. The bay has water shallow enough for you and deep enough for me." His dimples appeared. "And if you feel more comfortable, I can attempt to teach you how to swim there."

"Uhm, will everyone be there? People from Antla?"

"Of course, the fishermen of Antla were invited. They usually enter the races and the best-looking boat competitions. Some of their wives and children come along for the fun, so there may be people you know. There are walkways that you can walk through, and I can be beside you." He beamed. "It'll be a lot of fun."

If the public was there, it meant that the AML would be too. They were not ones to shy away from water events, preferring to go and cause problems for the merfolk that turned up. I couldn't remember the AML calendar, but there was every chance that a boat festival was on it. Someone would be tasked to attend and cause problems, and if they did, that meant problems for me too.

"I prefer that no one sees me."

"What do you mean?" he asked. "The royal guard won't be there, so you'll be safe."

"No, I mean that I don't want anyone to see us." I left out together, but he may have figured it out.

"Are you implying that you don't want to be seen with me?"

The heat rose to my cheeks. I didn't want to tell him how his presence might affect my relationship with the AML and Hannah, but I also didn't want to lie.

"It's just with the AML members and people talking and my parents…"

He held out his hand. "No need to go any further." He pursed his lips for a brief second. "How about the unused tunnels on this side of the island? I know where a couple of the entrances are. They have been closed off for years, but I know that they are still safe. I don't believe that the guards will look for you there. Most people don't remember them." He winked. "There is something I think you might like to see."

A quiver traveled from my stomach up my spine at the thought of it. It didn't matter that he had just explained that it was safe. "How close to the water are they?"

"They are waterways. Some are completely submerged, but the one I was thinking about is only half filled with water. Along the side there is a wooden walkway. While you walk, I can swim next to you. It's just like the path you were on the other day."

My voice croaked, "The one I fell from?"

"Yes, but that was because the seagull startled you."

"You saw that?" How embarrassing."

Heat exploded around my cheeks, turning them a shade of apple red.

"Yes, that is why I reached you sooner than anyone else. Your flailing arms would have alerted all merpeople that a human needed help, but it would have taken them a while to reach you." He grinned as if he held a secret he didn't want to share. "I just happened to be the closest one."

I nodded. He'd been watching me. I wasn't sure if I liked the idea or not.

"Look, we don't have to go if you don't want..." he said, as he watched my reaction to his words. "I mean, if you don't want to be seen with me..."

"No, that's not it. It's just..." The words tangled in my mind. "It's hard to explain."

"I get it. I'm a merman. You are a princess who enjoys a meeting or two with people who want to kill mermen."

If my cheeks got any redder, he was going to be able to use me as a lighthouse. And yet he didn't seem bothered or angry, more matter-of-fact.

"It's either that or being returned to the palace via the beach," he pointed out. He picked up a strand of my hair with the lightest touch that I wouldn't have noticed if I hadn't seen the seaweed he pulled from it.

"I know, but..."

"But what?" He waited a few seconds. "What are you so scared of?"

I picked at a prickly piece of seaweed that had penetrated my riding pants and threw it into the sea. How could I let him know that everything in my life had become a mess? That a maelstrom of fears wove through me, a patchwork quilt of neuroses. The water scared me. The upcoming conversation with my parents made me want to puke, and the thought of the AML members' reactions when they discovered my mother's secret made me want to hide in my room forever.

There were a million reasons that I shouldn't go with him, and yet, I found the one reason to stay with him was the strongest pull of all. I wanted to.

"Are you okay?" he asked, resting a hand on my leg, sending a shiver up my spine. "Maybe it's not a good idea to stay out today, and you should return to the palace?"

I shook my head, causing the water from my wet hair to land on his chest. "No, I'm fine. Take me to the tunnel, and I'll deal with it."

He cocked his head to the side, causing some of his hair to fall over his face. It took everything I had not to reach forward and tuck it behind his ear. "Only if you're sure."

I nodded. "Yes, I'm sure it'll be okay, but if you see any seagulls heading my way, please shoo them away."

He laughed. "No worries. I'll be your bodyguard as well as your transportation. Whatever you want, I'll be there for you."

I met his gorgeous green eyes. "Thanks, I really appreciate it."

"Any time." He held out his hand. "Now, make sure that you hold on tight, and we will be off." He cradled me against his chest and whispered, "Maybe we'll be lucky, and the guards haven't figured out that you're with me."

They would have realized I was not in the palace grounds by now. I doubted they would think to look for me in the sea, but they would definitely be searching for me.

I just replied, "Hopefully."

Ten minutes later, he swam us into a huge cave on the other side of the inlet with large signs posted both outside and inside the entrance. A narrow, wooden walkway lay adjacent to the water. Each sign had a large red cross and the words "Stay Out" and "Cave May Collapse" written on them.

My eyes widened, and I scanned the roof of the cave and the darkness beyond the entrance. "Are you sure we're safe here? The sign says it's dangerous. What if the cave collapses? It's so dark that no one will find us."

"Your parents placed those signs all over the entrance to keep people out of the cave and from using the walkways. Trust me, these caves are completely safe. There's a whole network of tunnels under the palace. I think they were built when your parents first started dating." He smiled. "And it's only dark for a minute or so. There'll be light on the exit side. Besides, I'm here to guide you, and my eyes adjust much quicker to the dark than yours do."

"Are you sure?"

"Nope, I'm not, but see the roof." He pointed to the large structure. "The cave is all one unit and not made of thousands of rocks. There isn't a single loose rock."

"Okay."

When we reached the entrance to the cave, he hoisted me up until I sat on the rickety wooden walkway sitting just inches above the water. My fingers trailed against a bannister fixed to the tunnel wall, and while a tiny layer of dust stuck to my fingertips, at least it didn't move when I pushed against it.

He must have noticed my testing it.

"Don't worry, it's secure." He quickly glanced at my dusty fingers. "I'm sorry it's not the cleanest, but I promise you that it is safe. What do you think? Can you walk on it? Or is it too narrow?"

"I think so."

He reached for my hand and squeezed my fingers. "You're safe with me. Trust me."

I pressed down my internal trembling at the dark, narrow path ahead of me. "It's all good." And with his reassurance that I'd be safe, the trembling and my anxieties subsided.

"Hold on to the railing, but you know that even if you slip and fall in, I'll be right here to catch you."

His words released the butterflies, and I stared into his eyes as he stayed by my side.

"How do you know about this place?" I asked, taking my first steps into the cave.

"I used to play here with my friends and cousins. But it was your mother who used these walkways to escape from her father and when she wanted to meet with King Ermias. Apparently, they used to meet down here. Maybe they even used them after they were married."

I stopped for a moment, surprised by his words. "Oh, so you know my parent's history?"

"Everyone knows about your mother and how she turned her back against her own people when she chose to stay a human and marry your father." He beamed. "Her father and sisters tried to stop her, but when love bulldozes its way into a heart, there is no halting it. Love can overcome everything, even between different species."

"Oh." He made it sound so simple, so normal, so... not disgusting.

My mother had turned her back on her family and way of life for love. Leaving everything she knew for love must have been the most difficult decision in her life, but she still had done it. She chose a totally different life for my father. I wondered how a love like that could work.

"All the merpeople were on lockdown for months after she left the underwater kingdom," Fish continued as I once again began the walk into the dark. "Nobody could go above water or talk to a human as they didn't want anyone else to leave, especially not to be obligated to The Sea Witch."

"Were you okay with it, or did you rebel?"

He chuckled. "How well do you know me? No, I didn't have to change my normal routine because I wasn't living here yet, plus I was very young when your parents married."

"So, you're not from my mother's world?"

"No, I come from the underwater kingdom near the Urbis Prison."

"Oh." I'd never heard of merfolk living anywhere else but in Atlantice, but it was a stupid assumption. Why wouldn't they live in other places? Just because Atlantice, with its city half in and half out of the water, was famous for them, that didn't mean there weren't other bodies of water for them to inhabit.

We walked in silence for a moment until Fish spoke again.

"You have such unusual but definitely beautiful eyes. The golden ring around your iris is stunning. I've never seen anything like it before."

His words lifted me, causing the flutter of butterflies. I'd always felt different because of my weird eyes, and here he was telling me I was beautiful, not despite them, but because of them. It was like he knew my worst thoughts about myself and could turn them around. I took a deep breath, glad we were in the dark, and he couldn't see the huge grin on my face. But then, I remembered he probably could. He'd said himself that merfolk could see better in the dark than humans. My smile dropped as I wondered what I was getting myself into.

I walked through the long cave that was more tunnel than anything else with one hand gripping the banister beside me and the other holding Fish's equally as hard. The sunlight behind us got dimmer with every step I took, but before it disappeared completely, another light source opened up in front of me.

"What is this place?" I asked in wonder as the tunnel widened to a set of stairs leading out of the water to a doorway. Small holes in the ceiling provided enough sunlight to be able to see again. I sat on one of the steps, and Fish joined me, pulling himself out of the water to sit beside me.

"Neat, huh? I've been told that your mother used to meet your father down here when they first started dating before the sea witch gave her legs. I believe that door leads to your palace, although it's been locked for as long as I can remember. You see that vase there?"

I looked to where he pointed. A small vase with the palace crest sat on the very top step near the door.

"Yes."

"Legend has it that your father put flowers in that vase as a code. If the flowers were pink, it meant that your mother should wait and that she was safe. If they were yellow, she should leave because the guards were on patrol. I don't know if it is true, but I always thought it was romantic. Of course, once she got legs, they didn't have to do that anymore."

I looked over at him, so beautiful in the low light. His tail splashed lightly in the water.

He was still a merman. A species the AML wanted to remove from Atlantice. No matter how much I liked him, no matter how safe and peaceful I felt around him, no matter how attentive, caring, funny, and wonderful he was, he was still a merperson.

I should not have developed any feelings for him in the first place.

And yet, despite everything, I had.

5

2ND FEBRUARY

*T*he Conch floated from my hands, and the pages scattered around my feet. I did not bother picking it up from the ballroom floor, where I was hiding from everyone.

After a perfect day spent with Fish yesterday, I'd forgotten my problems, and when he'd dropped me back at the palace, my mood had improved considerably. I'd even almost gotten used to the fact my mother was a mermaid. Or at least, I had until this morning's newspapers were delivered. *Queen Antonella is a Mermaid!* screamed the Conch's headline, followed by a quote from Hannah: "Queen Antonella has betrayed all Atlanticeans."

The words did not exactly state that she would also raise up the AML tribe against her, but my best friend would make it her mission to have my mother abdicate the throne.

She was my best friend… or, at least, she had been.

The Conch lay on the floor, spread out. My eyes focused on the second headline, halfway down the front page, reporting about the "Antla Town Riots." The pictures of riots on the outskirts of Antla as well as those in the town brought pangs to my already bleeding heart.

Another reporter announced that Atlanticeans from the other

side of the island might march to the capital and demand explanations from the monarchy.

The front-page news laid it out in black and white that nothing would be the same for me or my parents.

Not. One. Single. Thing. Ever again.

I inhaled, held it for ten seconds, and exhaled, hoping to stop an anxiety attack. I had never had one, but it seemed the likely response as my life crumbled.

Our lives crumbled.

Where was my father? Why wasn't he on damage control?

I'd asked Emma earlier to alert the head butler and the guards to bar all the doors to the palace and secure the windows, and she had not yet returned. With the curtains drawn, I ambled through the large room, wondering whether or not my parents would cancel the Valentine Day's Ball. A lot could happen in twelve days, but with my mother's transformation, the ball would surely have to be canceled. While she had set almost everything up, she would not be able to finish the last-minute details... or attend.

My fingers caressed the deep red velvet curtain the staff had hung up the day before specifically for the upcoming ball. The red tones were a shade of burgundy much deeper than the red-orange of Fish's tail.

I really need to stop thinking about him all the time. Focus on something else!

Across from the curtains, a pair of large glass urns filled with pretty fish were placed on either side of the twenty-foot tall double wooden doors, reminding me that my mother had always brought in pieces of her previous world into ours. She had decorated every part of the house with sea plants, sea creatures, even our paintings and statues contained bits of the sea.

I hadn't really noticed before now, but her underwater world had been brought into ours.

It seemed as if she hadn't just wanted the sea life to beautify the palace, but for the sea to be a part of our lives. It made sense, really.

Since yesterday, she'd been hiding away from the world in the palace's indoor pool with our guards protecting her.

A piece of me cried for her, and the guilty feeling from not responding to her invitation to chat an hour before invaded my peaceful state.

Why talk about her transformation and its effect on my life when we couldn't do a single thing about it?

Not one thing.

I headed toward the dais with the thirty mahogany chairs stacked up next to the three thrones. My mom had ordered the chair covers with colorful, embroidered crests and flowers from each of the kingdoms. The royal guests would know exactly where to sit without having to read their titles on the name cards in front of the table.

What a freaking waste!

The amount of Antlaicean's shells my parents spent on the order probably exceeded a day's salary for the entire staff, including the guards. She'd have to stop the orders before the seamstress finished making all the chair covers if she decided not to hold the ball.

I knew I should have gone to her when she sent one of the palace staff with a request to meet her, but despite the guilt burning in my chest, I wasn't ready to see her yet. The mermaid part I had just about wrapped my head around, but not the lies. I could understand why she had lied to the people. Merfolk were thought of as scum by a lot of the population, but she'd lied to me, her own daughter. I wasn't ready to forgive her just yet. I was a half-mermaid, a fact that the Conch was yet to make note of, but it wouldn't be long before they did, and I wasn't prepared. I should have been prepared. My mother should have told me.

The glint from one of the candelabras caught my eye, and I raised my head. Red bows had been tied to the bottom of each of the candle holders with streamers that fastened to the tops of the curtains.

She'd made it beautiful.

Knock, knock.

"Go away; I don't want to talk to anyone."

Knock, knock.

The desire to scream was immense. I wanted to be alone. How difficult was that to understand?

One of our butlers opened the door, stepped in with his jacket slightly skewed. A mere inch, not enough for anyone else to notice, but he pulled on the jacket as soon as my eyes landed it.

I raised my eyebrows. "Yes?" Unfortunately, my tone might have come across as rude or snotty. I half-smiled to compensate for my out-of-character tone. The last thing the family needed was an upset butler with the potential Antlaiceans up in arms.

He bowed. "I'm sorry to disturb you, Princess Blaise, but Miss Hannah Fallon has been most persistent in obtaining an audience with you. May I tell her you are accepting callers, or shall I have a guard escort her out?" His neutral tone could have won him the best butler award. "Or maybe ten to guarantee that she will not return?"

I gave him a sly smile at his words. At least the palace staff was on our side, a small mercy in the current climate.

My first reaction was to ask him to dismiss her, but my friend's determination and persistence might overrun even our best guards. They could beat hundreds of townspeople, but against a determined Hannah, they might just lose.

There was no way she would back down and return home. Not now that she knew there was a mermaid in the palace. It didn't matter to her that the mermaid in question was her queen. If I didn't allow her inside, then her intense hatred would push her to assemble a whole army to storm the palace, which would not help my mother.

"Let her in before she finds another way to enter." I half-smiled.

The servant bowed. "I will show her in…"

The door swung open, the force hard enough to knock it against the wall. The sound of wood against wood vibrated throughout the enormous room.

"That's right, you'll show me in. How dare you keep me from my friend!" Hannah barely missed hitting him with her bag as she marched past him.

His shoulders pulled back, and he glanced between the two of us. "Shall I leave you two alone, Princess Blaise, or would you prefer..." He trailed off with both eyebrows raised.

"It's fine, please close the door. Also, please order the guards to double up security at all the doors in the palace as well as the passages to the palace grounds." My eyes peeked at Hannah before returning to his. "We certainly don't want any other surprise guests today."

"Very well, Princess Blaise." He bowed again and closed the door.

Hannah stood in the middle of the room, underneath the chandelier with hundreds of candleholders throwing tiny beams of light against the walls. Her stiff back and her hands on her hips did not tremble.

"I'm going to ask you once and only once. I'm here as the head representative of the AML and not your friend, so I don't want any lies." She shook her long red hair. "Do you understand?"

The back of my neck and spine prickled as if a couple of bees had decided to have a stinging party. Without a word, I turned around and headed to the middle of the dais, stopping at the smallest of the three thrones.

I slowly turned to face her. She was right about something. We were no longer friends.

"Hannah Fallon, since you've barged in here without waiting for a formal invitation and you're on official AML business, I will accordingly act as a princess, a member of the royal monarchy, and not as your lifelong friend." Sitting at my throne, I motioned with my index finger where she should stand.

She didn't move a muscle, but her eyes opened wide.

"Step forward now before I have you escorted home with a note to your father... Or do you prefer a stint in the royal dungeon?" I asked in a cold, hard voice.

Her stance softened when she realized that couldn't win. All our lives, Hannah had bossed me around. She was above me in the

AML, a fact she liked to boast about as often as possible, but now, in our current circumstances, she knew that she couldn't win. This wasn't the AML office. She was in the royal palace, and I was the princess.

"Yes, I mean, no. I don't want to be escorted home. I just want to talk," she said in a friendlier tone and hurried to the spot I had originally pointed.

"Now, what is it that you want?" I asked.

She clasped her fingers before bowing her head for seconds. When she raised her eyes, it seemed as if all her anger had disappeared or she had stuffed it deep down into her soul. "Your royal princess, I must ask the question because I've seen no evidence, but the rumors have prompted a bunch of riots since last night." Her head turned toward the newspaper on the floor. "It is my duty as the head of the AML to ask if it is true that Queen Antonella is now a mermaid?"

I lowered my head and gaped at the newspaper. "You have no evidence, and yet you told the Conch that my mother had betrayed everyone."

She, at least, had the sense to look embarrassed.

"Yes, Hannah, it's true."

I raised my head as her light brown eyes widened.

She stiffened her back and pulled back her shoulders. "Did you see the tail with your own eyes?"

I nodded, and with a knot in my throat, I said, "Yes, I saw it. She turned in front of me after suffering from extreme pain."

Her face contorted into an expression of disgust. I imagined I looked the same way in front of my mother when I saw her tail.

"Blaise. She is not normal. You know that."

"She's the same woman she always was," I reminded her. "The same woman that invited you into our home and treated you almost as a member of our family. It's not the end of the world."

"Blaise, are you insane?" she spat out. "She's one of *them*!" She waved her index finger back and forth. "You need to see her as a mermaid. A disgusting water-dweller with scales." She flipped open her bag, pulled out the AML manual, and raised it up to chest level. "You've read this just as many times as I have. You know what it says. What horrible things merpeople have done. What they've done to sailors for centuries. How evil they are. You can't let your emotions blind you."

My mind raced to find the right words to counter her argument. She needed concrete facts, which, unfortunately, I didn't have at my fingertips.

"Hannah, what if those stories are false? What if well-meaning people attributed those stories to merpeople, and it was another sea creature?"

She shook her head vehemently. "No, it can't be. They're complete accounts from people who experienced them." She flipped the pages of the manual. "Look, on page one hundred fifty it says that a fishing boat off the Island of Skyla was completely destroyed and everyone on board was killed. Sharks can't destroy a boat. They don't have fingers. And they can't climb aboard and kill. It had to be the merpeople. No other explanation."

"But if nobody survived, you can't say it was them. Nobody saw them do it. What would be the motive of the merpeople? And how would they even manage to climb onto the boats? They don't have legs. They have tails that can't support their bodies like our legs can." I tilted my head. "What about pirates? Could it have been pirates? They would have more of a motive to kill the fisherman since they don't like witnesses."

She shook her head and placed her hands on her hips as though I was the one that had been brainwashed. "That's crazy. I think you're looking for excuses to protect your mother, and while I can under-stand that your love for her will influence your reasoning, you must also realize that it's wrong. Merpeople have always killed humans. This whole book has example after example. All the witnesses that you've seen talk at our meetings. You must believe it."

"Hannah, I can't blindly believe that manual anymore. And the witnesses never said they saw merpeople harming anyone. Just that they swam away from the scene."

She lifted her arms and waved them as though my change in heart was a magic spell that could be broken. "You're part of the AML, and you swore an oath to uphold everything in this book as the truth. And merpeople were involved, or are you calling your friends liars? Are you calling me a liar?"

I stood and joined her in the middle of the room. Reaching out to touch her arm, I lowered my voice, "No, not at all. I just think that you are wrong. Like I was wrong for all those years. I think we were both fed this stuff..."—I took the manual from her—"and we've both been led to believe it."

She brought down her hands. "No, you can't be saying that. You must believe that these stories are real," she said, grabbing the manual back from my hand.

"I'm sorry, but I can't." I exhaled, holding back the urge to raise my voice.

"That's ridiculous. Just because your mom is now a mermaid doesn't change hundreds of stories. You're not seeing clearly."

"But that's the thing," I said, measuring my words. "I *am* seeing clearly, and I think the conclusions in that manual are wrong. Pirates could have brought those boats down. Tempests at sea. Anything."

"You're wrong," she hissed through gritted teeth. "It wasn't pirates or storms. It's the merpeople. I know it is. They're evil and should be eliminated completely."

And there lay her biggest problem. She maintained the merpeople's culpability, despite the probability that there might be another explanation. My friend couldn't imagine that it wasn't the merpeople harming people.

Holding up my index finger, I attempted to hold my voice down because I didn't want her exploding any more than she already was and said, "What if it was the pirates who blamed the merpeople to avoid being targeted? Have you ever thought of that scenario? They may have even put together the manual and spurred the rumors."

She shifted her weight from one foot to another before she marched to the window facing the water. "No, that doesn't make any sense. Nobody would believe a pirate." She waved both hands. "No one will believe them because they're known for being liars."

"But weren't most of those accounts reported by the pirates themselves? It would make sense that the pirates themselves perpetuated the lies to save themselves." I tapped my finger against my chin as Fish had done. A small smile appeared as I remembered my time with Fish. "Perhaps the entire manual you carry with you is full of the pirates' lies."

Hannah dropped her bag on the floor and waved her hands. "Stop it, Blaise! Your mother has to be held accountable. She is a mermaid and must deal with the consequences of her species. She must be judged and sentenced."

"What are you talking about? She's guilty because of her species? My mom shouldn't be judged by the actions of her species but by her own actions, and right now, she's hiding. Guilty by association is totally unfair."

Hannah was not ready to back down. "Yes, guilty by association because the evil flows in their veins. They've killed people. Killed and injured."

I shook my head. "My mom has done nothing wrong. Nothing. And what do you even mean judged and sentenced? The last time I looked, it wasn't illegal to be a mermaid."

"Not yet, but it will be."

The way she glared at me made my stomach drop. What did she mean by "not yet?"

I shook my head. "No, it won't. We can't incarcerate people because of how they look. That is plain prejudice. And it's wrong."

She narrowed her eyes. "If it was someone else, you would be right there leading the pack."

I took a deep breath and lowered my eyes. My guilty conscience agreed with her. How many times had I jumped to the same conclusion of a mermaid's evilness because of my own prejudice? "You're right. Two days ago, I would have been feeling the same way as you. No hesitation at all." I drifted to the window overlooking the water and stared out at the waves hitting the shoreline. "But that was then, and now it's different. You know my mom. She is as normal as you or me."

"Bullshit!"

My hand flew up. "Please, don't interrupt. You need to hear me out." I glowered at her. "My mom is the same woman she was yesterday and the day before. She is no more a threat to society than I am, but you, on the other hand, maybe you are the threat."

Hannah, my best friend since forever, stood in front of me with clenched fists, a stiffened back, and a fighting stance as if she was prepared to fight me.

How had it come to this? I was as guilty as she was. She hated my mom for what she was, and I was beginning to hate Hannah for what she believed. The same thing I'd believed for a long time. I took a deep breath.

"My dearest friend, we're going around in circles." I stretched out my hands, hoping she understood my peaceful gesture. "Maybe we should leave this discussion for another day."

"Fine," she spat out. "But understand this, your mother is a mermaid and needs to abdicate as soon as possible. We can't have our queen be a mermaid."

I sighed. The rift between us had become too wide.

"My mother can't abdicate even if she wanted to. My father is the king. Only he can abdicate."

"He's as bad as she is. He married that foul creature. He should abdicate, then." She picked up her bag. "Make sure you tell them that I expect to see an announcement within one week, or I can't promise what the AML will do."

As she stormed out of the ballroom, my heart sank. Hannah was only one person, but the AML was a huge group. There was no telling what they would do.

I'd left it long enough. I'd been selfish in running away from my problems yesterday, but today I was going to do the right thing. I was going to see my mother, and I was going to tell her that I loved her, no matter what she was, for it was the truth.

I found her exactly where I expected to find her in the palace swimming pool. Even though I'd had enough time to get used to her with a tail, seeing her swimming in the palace pool still made me feel strange. She'd always been an elegant woman, carrying herself the way a queen should, but in the water, she was something else. The way she glided effortlessly in the water, making barely a ripple, was as mesmerizing as any ballet, as beautiful as any dance. I watched her for a while, not making my presence known. It was only when she caught sight of me that she finally stopped swimming and rested her arms on the side of the pool. She beckoned me over, and although her eyelashes already dripped with water from the pool, I could see the tears in them. I sat on the pool edge, my legs crossed.

"I'm so sorry, Blaise," my mom whispered.

I leaned forward and wrapped my arms around her, drenching my clothes in the process.

"It's me that should be sorry. I've spent my life looking at what people were, rather than who they were. I've been so wrong."

My mother pulled back, her eyes sparkling and a smile on her face.

"I guess I really should teach you how to swim now, huh?"

I laughed. My entire life, my biggest fear had been to swim near a merperson, and here I was, hugging one for the second time in a week. They'd gone from something I detested and feared to something I wanted to learn more about. I pulled my dress over my head and jumped into the shallow end of the pool in only my underwear. Fish wasn't the only one who thought I should learn to swim. So did I.

6

3RD FEBRUARY

*T*he sound of seagulls and waves beating against the shore woke me from a heavy sleep. The sun's rays filtered in through the slightly opened curtains, reminding me that, as a princess, I should drag myself out of bed.

For several minutes, I ignored all the unpleasant thoughts primed to filter through my consciousness and enjoyed the peacefulness of a brand new day.

I refused to allow any of Hannah's negativity to influence me until a man's loud voice interrupted my zen moment. He was shouting loudly enough that his voice projected through my closed door.

Father! I sat up in bed quickly.

Concern seeped in because my dad never raised his voice. Not in public. Ever.

I threw on a dress and slipped on a pair of gold sandals, but when I opened the door, the hall was completely empty.

My father had gone, but more disturbingly, the guard that usually patrolled the corridor was nowhere to be seen. Slipping out, I rushed along the corridor and ran straight into Emma. Once she'd gotten over being hurtled into by me, she curtsied and waved her hands. "Princess Blaise, you can't go downstairs yet. We need to return to your bedroom right away."

"Why?" I asked, my panic increasing. "What's going on? Why was my father screaming?"

Her eyes scanned the area as if she suspected a person would jump up in front of her. "He was instructing the guards to double up protection for Queen Antonella and the outside doors."

"Why more guards? What's going on?"

Emma remained calm despite my panic. She talked as she ushered me back to my room. "After he spoke to the crowd amassing at Antla's town center this morning, he wants to ensure that the palace is well protected. He even brought more guards from the mainland who aren't prejudiced against merpeople."

My stomach flopped as if the world was about to end. "They're still rioting?"

Emma twisted her fingers around. "Unfortunately, they continued throughout the night and haven't stopped. There are hundreds of people out there, and it doesn't look like anyone is stopping them."

I paced the length of my room, not stopping. "Are they near the palace?"

"No," Emma replied, "but although the riots aren't close to the palace, your dad is afraid they'll eventually march here and try to scale the outer wall or ram through the doors."

My arms flailed. "I don't get it. Why doesn't he try speaking with them again? He's always been a great communicator, and they love him. Surely, if he speaks to them again, they'll calm them down and return to their homes. One speech may not have been enough." I stopped pacing. I was babbling, and I knew it, but nothing like this had happened in Antla before.

She sighed, and her eyelids closed slowly over her brown eyes. When she opened them, they appeared discouraged.

My fingers gripped a piece of my dress, and I braced myself for more bad news.

"Oh, Princess Blaise, he's tried. He really has tried. Last night, he went to the town center. Only a few listened to him speak, and for a couple of hours they did stop rioting, but this morning they started rioting near the port. They had moved away from the center and waited for the boats to come in from the mainland. They assembled even more people with their hateful speeches about the merpeople. Not all of them joined the rioters, but a lot did."

A long silence filled the room. I could see the fear in her eyes. This had turned from a minor disturbance to something much worse. Hannah's words echoed through my mind. She'd told me that my father should abdicate or she'd get the AML involved. She had given me a week, but it seemed that the AML wasn't prepared to wait that long.

I looked at Emma, but she wouldn't look me in the eye.

"What else aren't you telling me?"

Emma's glistening eyes lifted, and her hands flew to her heart. "Your father doesn't know if he will be able to stop it."

I wanted to make everything disappear.

"There are rumors that some of the town's people are forming groups to hunt merpeople," she continued. "They want to capture and hurt them. Maybe even kill them." My thoughts immediately turned to Fish. He wouldn't know. I'd not been out to see him yesterday. I'd spent the afternoon with my mother, but I knew he would want to see me. I knew he'd be close to the shore, waiting for my return. I'd promised him as much, and because of that promise, he was in danger.

I needed to warn him.

"I need to get to the pier," I said to Emma. "Can you help me leave the palace?"

She didn't blink, didn't move, but stayed by the door, as stiff as a sentinel guarding a room full of the crown jewels.

"So sorry, but the palace is on lockdown. Nobody can leave or come in. Your father is so worried about anyone breaching the palace walls that he has everything locked."

Frustration gripped me. "I need to get out, Emma."

She stretched her arms out to the side and planted her feet

almost three feet apart, blocking the door. "I'm sorry, but King Ermias ordered me to keep you in your room for now. I can't disobey him."

"If you won't help me leave the palace, at least, let me out of my room so I can go and see my mother." I wiped a lone tear from the corner of my eye. "I can't let anything happen to her. I have to help her." My voice quivered, and another tear fell. "Please, help me. I must check up on her, even if it's for a minute or two."

She held her hand out, forcing me to back up, and her tone held a harder edge, "I'm so sorry. I can't. King's orders."

I'd never known her to disobey my own orders, but then I'd never known the king to even speak to Emma, and he outranked me. I could easily have shoved her to one side, but the poor girl was only doing her job.

"Did you ever imagine Antla would rise up against its royalty?" I whispered.

"Your father is doing everything he can to calm the people," she assured me. "He is planning to speak again later today. He will be heading to the port and pleading with the fisherman to be honest about their encounters with merpeople. It may help."

I laughed, but there was no mirth in it. "The AML has spread so many lies that the fishermen may be afraid to speak."

Emma stayed silent. She knew I was a member of the AML, and we both knew that I would be out there rioting if it wasn't my own family involved.

A couple of tears slithered down my cheeks to my jawline and wet my dress. I'd been a fool for so long. A bigoted, prejudiced fool, and now, we were all paying the price.

Emma walked over to my dresser and brought me a wad of tissues.

She hesitated before her hand reached toward me, pulled back for a brief second, and reached again until she placed a gentle hand on my shoulder. "I'm so sorry, Princess Blaise. I wish I could help more than I can. But the people of Antla will listen to the older fishermen when they return, and they will listen to reason. They'll listen to their king because he's always been kind to them. He will eventually calm them down. Queen Antonella has always been a good queen to all of us. They know that. Their hearts will be changed after your father speaks to them. And he'll do everything in his power to ensure that they don't breach the palace that so she's safe. So that we're all safe."

Despite her words, I read between the little hope she tried to provide. If they overran the guards and took my mom, none of us would be safe.

She dropped her hand. "Can I bring you anything to eat? You may feel better after you have a meal."

I meandered to the window facing the sea. "Maybe that might be better than trying to hash everything out on an empty stomach. A cup of peppermint tea, please. And a piece of wheat toast with butter."

"Good. I will prepare it myself and bring it up as soon as possible." She hesitated as if about to say something else but opened the door and walked through it. She curtsied and said, "Unfortunately, I need you to lock the door. Your father's direct orders. It looks like you now have guards outside to ensure that you're safe."

And that I don't leave.

For the first time, I obeyed a servant and locked the door. I leaned against the doorframe, listening to her retreating footsteps and the guards marching up and down the hallway. Their precise steps produced a musical rhythm, and I smiled. They would protect us with their lives. As long as they remained in their positions we would be safe.

Once the clicking of her shoes against the marble floor stopped, I plopped on my chair and thought of all the lies I'd foolishly believed. If anyone had told me just a few days ago that I'd no longer want to be a part of the AML, I wouldn't have believed it. In a world where I was supposed to be proper and act like a princess, the AML had been a relief of sorts, an escape from my princessly duties. My parents had never known about the meetings. I knew right from the start that they wouldn't have approved, and so for years, I'd kept it from them, telling them that I was just going to Hannah's house. At first, I was going to Hannah's house, and they sent me with a guard, but as I got older, I was allowed to make the short journey alone. It was at that point that Hannah had suggested I join her at an AML meeting. Before that, I'd not cared one way or another about the merfolk. They'd not really been a huge part of my life. I'd hidden myself under a hood, and sat at the very back at the first meeting, but soon I'd been accepted into the AML and become a part of something. They had become like family to me, and for the first time in my life, I felt as though I was doing something for me and not because I was supposed to. It took a while, but soon I began to believe the hate. Looking back, I realized I would have believed anything just to feel a part of a group where I was wanted for who I was rather than for my title.

Emma returned as promised, and I sipped the tea with a bit of honey, allowing the warmth to soothe my dry throat. Finishing my toast proved harder as it landed in my stomach like lead. After a couple of tiny bites, I abandoned the rest on the plate.

"I can't eat any more," I said, "but thank you so much for preparing it for me."

She smiled. "Any time, Princess Blaise. Do you feel better?"

I nodded. "I do feel a bit better, thank you."

She nodded and sat beside me on the bed, something she would never have done before. "There are a few fishermen waiting for your father to speak at the town center. He's asked that you accompany him."

"Why?"

"I think he hopes that if you are there, the people will be a bit more lenient. Your mother is a mermaid. He's going for the sympathy vote."

"Great!" I said sarcastically. Hadn't she mentioned before that they were rioting in the town center?

"Remember, he doesn't know you are in the AML. He's a good man, Blaise. He wouldn't take you if he didn't think you'd be safe. He's ordered half the guards from the navy fleet to surround the center, and they'll have a barrier set up so that it's only the fisherman in the square. He assured me that you would be safe. He also told me to tell you that it is your choice. He doesn't want to drag you into something you aren't sure of."

"No, I'll join him," I said, standing up. "I need to bathe and choose the right outfit for his speech."

"I'll find something," Emma said, rushing to my wardrobe. She reached for one of the purple day dresses that I usually wore to formal occasions. The dress screamed approachable royalty. Gold trim lined the hem and the bottom of the sleeve, and it had a sweetheart neckline and high waist.

"Emma, that's the one. You're amazing, as always."

She hung the dress on the hook inside the door. "I'll find you a matching coat while you bathe."

Once I was ready and dressed, I pulled on the purple coat Emma had found for me and went to find my father. A short carriage ride later and we were in the town center. A guard opened the carriage door, and, with my hand in my father's, we made our way to an erected podium. I kissed him on the cheek before I waved at the small crowd of fifty fishermen, dressed in their rubber overalls, holding their caps in their hands.

My heart ballooned in size as they nodded in unison when my dad asked for their help.

Behind the guards, a group followed a young woman with a blue bag. I strained my eyes until I recognized my best friend leading the pack.

As my father spoke, the crowd behind the barriers swelled, most holding placards.

I squinted to read the sign Hannah held.

DEATH TO ALL MERPEOPLE.

They were far enough away that my father could be heard over the noise they made, but Hannah's loud voice drifted over to me: "Justice for us. Justice for humans. Death to all merpeople."

Goosebumps covered my bare arms at her words. So the rumors were true. The AML was no longer interested in merely dividing the humans and the merfolk; they actively wanted to kill them. And now that my mother's secret was out in the open, they were no longer hiding the fact. Judging by the number of people chanting, it wasn't just the AML that hated the merfolk. Those who had secretly hated the merpeople were now crawling out of the woodwork to join their ranks.

"Traitor Blaise!" Someone I recognized from the AML meetings shouted out.

Anger swelled within me as their hatred spewed out. I was no longer a friend to these people. I was now a target.

4TH FEBRUARY

*W*ithout being able to leave the palace, my world had become so much smaller. The AML meetings, no matter how awful I now saw them to be, had become a beacon in the dullness of my royal life, and though I knew in my heart I could never go back, I missed the camaraderie, the laughs, the friends I had made. Friends that no longer were.

Picking up a blanket, I headed out to the palace deck that overlooked the shore. It was the closest thing I had to freedom, protected as it was by the palace guard. As I took a seat, a guard looked my way and nodded before turning his gaze back to the stormy ocean. Waves broke majestically on the beach, reminding me of the time of year and how lucky I'd been to catch a warm day the time I went out with Fish. Well, warmer than today, at least.

I'd not seen him in days. I wondered if he knew what was happening on land—if any of the merfolk knew just how reviled they were. The merfolk had only ever been tolerated by the humans and sometimes barely that, but now they were in danger, brought on by the uncovering of my mother's secret and the anger inspired by the AML.

I sipped the passion fruit tea Emma had prepared for me earlier, hoping that wherever Fish was, he was safe. I gave a small sigh. I didn't even know his name, and he didn't know mine. He was Fish, I was Princess, and neither of us had thought to correct the other. My term for him was much more derogatory than his for me. I wondered why he had tolerated it before I remembered that I'd never actually called him that to his face.

The wind lifted my long hair sending it flying out behind me and rustling the paper that someone had brought out. Picking it up, I glanced at the front page and immediately wished I hadn't.

The reporters had completely ignored that Queen Antonella had faithfully served her kingdom, generously giving her time and money, setting up foundations, and working with charities. Instead, they focused on the least important thing about her. The fact that she had a tail.

Not a single article throughout the paper portrayed an honest picture of her.

Apart from the one-sidedness, which was bad enough, what really pushed my blood to rush through my veins was the call to riot by none other than my best friend.

Hannah's face graced an article on the second page telling the people of Antla and the whole kingdom of Atlantice to turn against the royals. To turn against me.

My fingertips drummed a fast tempo on the arm of my seat. There was no rhythm, just my fingers moving quickly and pounding hard against the arm of the chair. My poor nails took the brunt of my frustration-releasing activity.

Luckily, no one witnessed their destruction as I figured out what possible options we had to stop more rioting and the AML's hurtful witch hunt.

If Dad reached the town's people today, then maybe they'll call off their riots.

But if that failed, we needed another plan to present to Hannah and her followers.

Proof that the merfolk had never hurt anyone.

She'd requested concrete evidence, but I'd had no idea where to get it. It was one thing to prove that something had been done, but it was another entirely to disprove it. And it wasn't just one thing. The AML handbook had hundreds of accounts. I sighed. I didn't even know for sure that the merfolk hadn't perpetrated those atrocities. But with what I knew now, with how gentle Fish had been with me and how wonderful my own mother was, it just didn't ring true anymore. The more I thought about it, the more I realized that most of the reports had come from Skyla, a kingdom notorious for pirates. Beyond the reports in the AML handbook, I'd not once heard of a merperson colony even existing in Skyla.

My fingers stalled, and I closed my eyes. The image of all the fishermen at the town center yesterday agreeing with my father came to mind.

Maybe if enough fishermen told their stories using their ship's logs as proof of the merpeople's goodness, or, at least, of the pirates' badness, she would stop the hunt.

Maybe.

My eyes flew open at the thunderous clacking of metal boots against the marble and stone steps.

Without counting, I guessed that between twenty to thirty guards were making their way in a fast trek down the stairs with drawn swords.

What is going on?

Another group followed them, but they halted until each step had two guards on it.

My heart raced as more heavy footsteps pounded against the marble floors. I peeked over my shoulder; four more guards halted a couple of feet behind me.

The captain of the palace guard, a tall reedy man with the bluest eyes, quickly bowed. He straightened before he said in the calmest voice, "Princess Blaise, we recommend that you head inside."

He said recommend, but this was no recommendation; it was an order.

"Why?"

Captain McDougall said, "We've had word that AML members

are marching toward the pier, and we want you safely inside in case they breach the barrier we're setting up to protect this side of the palace."

I scanned the empty beach. Nothing had changed, and no one had stepped foot on it... except for the many seagulls scooping their live prey from the water. "Either I'm blind, or they're wearing invisibility cloaks."

A couple of the guards snickered, and the captain's face turned as red as his hair. "Rest assured, they're heading this way."

He didn't have to tell me who led the pack.

I stood to face him, "I want to talk to them."

The captain shook his head. "I'm sorry, but it's too dangerous. The AML are becoming increasingly angry, and though they have not yet resorted to violence, they have threatened it on a number of occasions. I'm afraid I must insist..."

"I know the leader," I blurted out. My parents knew I was friends with Hannah, but they were yet to find out that she was a prominent member of the AML. It was hardly something I wanted to advertise, especially not now, but if it meant I could help solve this mess, then I'd happily admit to everything.

He stiffened his back. "The king will not approve of it, and therefore, we can't allow you to join them."

I sighed. My father would never let me speak to the AML, but then...

"Yes, but my dad doesn't need to know." I arched a brow. "There are always different ways to achieve what we want. Wouldn't you agree, Captain McDougall?"

"No, I wouldn't. It is my job to protect you." His voice was stern, and I knew then that I had lost. If I tried running toward the AML, there were half the palace guard nearby to stop me.

"Please," I whined. "I think I can help."

I could see the frustration in his face. He'd probably not expected to fall into an argument with a princess when he stepped outside. "I can't allow you to go, Your Highness. You could get hurt."

A scoff escaped my lips. "They won't dare touch a hair on my head. They know that their punishment would be swift and painful. Look at how many guards are out here." My anger at the situation spilled over, and I couldn't help running my mouth off without thinking of the consequences. "Besides, I've been a member of the AML for years. They're my friends, and I don't think that they'll hurt me. And Hannah will make sure that they've been instructed not to harm me."

His eyebrows raised at my confession as I realized what I'd said. I'd outed Hannah and myself, although Hannah was doing a pretty good job of it herself. The AML was no longer an undercover operation, but up until now, my involvement had been secret.

"Meaning no disrespect, I beg to differ, Princess Blaise," he began, not showing any surprise about my admission. "These people are no longer your friends. They are no more than an angry mob. Now please let me escort you inside before we put anyone else in danger."

The implication was clear. If any of the guards got hurt while the captain was arguing with me, I would be to blame.

I had no choice but to let him lead me inside. My first thought was that I should head to the palace swimming pool and tell my mother the truth about myself. The irony of it did not escape me. I'd been so mad at her for not telling me the truth, and I'd been hiding my involvement with the AML for years. I'd almost made it to the pool when I had an idea.

Captain McDougall was not going to let me run along the beach to speak to Hannah, but there were other ways out of the palace. Ways in which, now that most of the guards were out front, it would be easy for me to find a way out.

I rushed to my room and flung my wardrobe doors open. All my dresses, even the day ones, were too luxurious for the AML crowd. I spotted my daily outfits, which I had not worn to meetings, but I wore them around town. Hannah knew them all. I tapped the doorframe with my fingertips. No real tempo but it helped me think. Pulling out a black blouse and skirt, I quickly dressed. I completed my outfit with a widow's hat that had an attached veil to hide my face. I'd used it a number of times when walking to AML meetings so I wouldn't be seen by the public. As I pulled it from the hiding place at the back of the wardrobe, something else came with it, falling to the floor with a thump. I secured my long hair into a tight bun, placed the hat at a slightly skewed angle, and brought down the heavy veil.

The full-length mirror reflected a slim widow. I twirled around, loving how the skirt moved. Not one trace of Princess Blaise remained except for the long tendrils of red-blonde hair that escaped the veil when I twirled.

Pulling it back and securing it with pins, I let the veil fall over my face.

I spun myself around a couple of more times, and the hat stayed put. It wasn't the best disguise. Not many mourners ran through town in the middle of the day, but I'd used it many times before, it being more effective than a hood. This way, no one could see my eyes. My eyes fell to the thing that had fallen out of the wardrobe when I pulled my disguise out. It was the AML manual. The book of all the accounts of the merpeople's treachery.

I picked up the well-thumbed tome and sat on the bed. I'd read these stories so often that I could almost recite them by heart, and yet, I'd never really looked deeply into them. I opened the book to a random page. It could have been any of the stories, they were all the same. This one was from the captain of a ship in Skyla. His account ran along the lines that the merpeople had attacked the ship and stolen his riches after attacking the crew. It was so vague. No mention of how the merpeople got aboard, nor how they managed to get into the stow and grab the man's riches, all the while swash-buckling with the ship's crew.

All the stories were the same. Vague, no detail. Each one looked like it was written by the same hand, and yet it was doctrine to the AML. This book was the AML's proof that the merfolk were savages, and yet in the years I spent going to meetings, not once had anyone been brought in with a firsthand account. So many meetings I had spent jeering at the accounts of the members as they recounted throwing a bottle or some such at a filthy merperson. Now that I came to think back, they had all been the same and showed not the evilness of the merfolk, but the evil in us. Not once had an attack been provoked. Their crimes had been daring to breach the surface or look at one of the AML members in a way that the member hadn't liked. One member had thrown stones at a merperson for the color of her hair. I'd never been comfortable with these speeches, but I'd cheered along with everyone else for fear they would throw me out otherwise. I now knew my attachment to the AML was a result of loneliness in the palace. The palace was always full of people, and yet the only friend ever invited to my house was Hannah, and that was because her father was the admiral of my father's fleet.

I glanced down at the book again, deeply ashamed for my own actions. The lies in the book seemed all the more obvious to me now, and yet, we had perpetuated the lies. We'd all believed the stories the leaders told us came from the fishermen when it was painfully obvious they were the accounts of pirates, at the very least.

Thinking back on all the things I'd done, listening to the blatant lies and foul deeds of the AML, crushed me. I had never willfully hurt a merperson, nor gone out of my way to annoy one, and yet I was no innocent. I was as guilty as those that had committed the crimes because I had encouraged them. All because of a book and hearsay from the AML leaders. I threw the book across the room, where it bounced on the wall and came to rest on the floor.

I was not a nice person. I was a part of the problem. I knew that, but it was a problem I was going to rectify... or at least try. Captain McDougall might not want me leaving the palace, but I knew I'd never forgive myself if I didn't do anything. Maybe he was right, and I'd only get myself hurt, but it was no less than what I deserved.

Slipping my hands into black gloves, I took a back way out of the palace. An old corridor that was usually unguarded at the worst of times. As I suspected, it was empty, enabling me to slip out unnoticed to the back garden. Once outside, I avoided the scattered guards patrolling the garden by choosing my route carefully.

Picking the longest route to reach the terrace, I slid behind a group of trees to regroup my thoughts.

My acting needed to convince them that I could join the crowd.

I took a deep breath while I considered my options.

The guards watched both the stairs and the glass doors to the palace but not the outer wall. No doubt, guards would be positioned on the outside of the wall to stop people coming in, something I would have to be mindful of. The front gates would still be heavily armed even though most of the palace guards were out on the beach, but there was a back entrance that just might be without a guard. It was the entrance that the staff used when they were in a hurry. A small gate in the wall, it was mostly unknown to anyone who didn't live or work in the palace. I crept along the wall, keeping my eyes open for any guards, but when I skirted the corner, I saw a guard directly next to the gate. There had never been one there before, at least not on the inside, but there he was, and it didn't look like he was going anywhere in a hurry.

Stamping my foot in frustration, I pulled back so he wouldn't see me if he turned and tried to come up with another plan. The walls were much too high for me to climb, and the doors and gates were fully guarded. The beach would have been my first thought, but there were more guards there than anywhere else. I was just about to give up when a thought occurred to me. Hunching my body over slightly, I began to walk, along with a slight limp, to the beach. Just before I skirted the castle, I peeked around and saw Captain McDougall. He'd sent his men out to cover the beach. Only he remained by the beach entrance to the palace.

Hunching my shoulders, I hobbled forward, hoping my acting skills would pay off. As I approached him, I lowered my voice, making it huskier as if I had a bad cold. "Good afternoon, my dear guard. I must speak to the princess." I gestured with my hands, so unlike Princess Blaise.

The captain drew his sword immediately and stepped forward, his face guarded. His eyes scanned the area without moving his head, and in an authoritative voice, he barked, "Where did you come from? How did you get in here without the guards announcing you?"

Waiving one hand as if my appearance was inconsequential, I said with the sweetest voice, "The outside guards know who I am because I've been here before. But right now, can you please let the princess know that I'm here? It's urgent that I warn her about what I learned last night. She must help the queen leave the palace." I touched my heart with one hand. "You must let me speak with her. It's for the queen's safety."

My heart dropped as disbelief clouded his features.

"Who are you?" he barked, "and how do you know the princess?"

I needed to think on my feet if I was going to outsmart him. I looked like an old widow. Not exactly the type of person a young princess would associate with, but then I remembered I'd told the captain about my involvement with the AML less than an hour earlier.

"I'm with the AML. I know the princess from the meetings," I explained in a croaky voice. "They are coming here. They are on their way."

"I'm already aware of that. If you have no further information, I must ask that you leave. I'll show you out." He grabbed my arm in an attempt to usher me from the grounds. I was just about to pull back and snap at him with a rehearsed speech about how I must know the princess because I knew what her bedroom looked like, when I realized that being thrown from the palace was exactly what I wanted. My plan had been to send McDougall off on some wild goose chase, allowing me to run along the beach, all the while trying to dodge the guards positioned there. Yes, it was ridiculous, but it was all I had. The beach was an inlet of sorts and only accessible from the palace grounds. But it was easy enough to walk from the main public beach, over some rocks at low tide, which it currently was, and around the erected fence. The AML might have to get their feet wet to get around it, but I was sure it was a risk they were willing to take. In the distance, I could see them walking along the coast. They were almost at the fence already. I wasn't the only one to notice; the guards had begun to gather at this side of the fence, their swords drawn.

I didn't want any violence. I needed to get to Hannah before she got to the fence. I could no longer call her a friend, but she had been there for me in my darkest moments when loneliness had threatened to envelop me.

Pulling McDougall to the front gates, I practically sprinted through them the second he let me go. I ran down a public side street to the stretch of land on the coastline. The AML was nowhere in sight, which meant they were already over the cliff edge and on the rocks. Darting down the street, I peered over the edge. The whole group of them scrambled over the rocks as I rushed down a thin pathway to join them.

My heart leapt as I saw that I'd reached them in time. They still had a way to go to get to the fence. I could stop this before any blood was shed and hopefully talk some sense into them. Even at low tide, waves battered the outermost rocks, making this stretch of coastline treacherous. My feet slipped on the seaweed-covered rocks as I tried to catch up with them.

"Hannah!" I yelled out, but my voice was lost to the wind that had really begun to pick up. A stray gust caught the brim of my hat, sending it skywards.

Onwards I scrambled, racing to catch up with the group, each step slipperier than the last. Determination pulled me forward as sea spray, exacerbated by the wind, drenched me to my skin.

"Hannah!" I cried out again, this time a little more loudly. I looked up to find the group had converged around a spot at the water's edge about thirty feet from the palace fence. My first thought was that maybe they had seen me and decided to wait. Buoyed by the enthusiasm generated by this thought, I took another couple of hesitant steps on the damp rocks, but then something in the sea behind them sent my heart crashing to the ground.

"There he is. We've got this disgusting merman now. Capture the red-tailed monster," a man shouted.

With my heart pounding and my brain exploding, I inched my way to the waterline

Don't let it be Fish, please don't be Fish!

Blood rushed to my head, leaving my limbs cold and clammy as boats I'd not noticed before formed a semi-circle around something.

A flash of red confirmed my darkest thoughts.

"No!" I screamed.

This time some of the AML heard me. The members at the back turned. Some waved, either unaware who I was, or just happy to see me despite the fact they were here to overrun the palace.

Beyond them, the top of nets thrown from the boats bobbed above the water. As I watched, a couple of men jumped into the deep water from a boat, trapping Fish.

He was trapped, and as the crowd of AML members jeered, my panic increased.

The wind whipped up, almost sending me into the sea as I managed to get to the water's edge next to the group. The only hope I had of stopping this was to get to Hannah. I could just about see her over the heads of all the others, but she was surrounded. I could only grip onto the rocks for fear of falling in the water as the men in the sea closed in on Fish.

As I watched, he tried to dive below, but the water was too shallow, and the men had positioned their nets just so.

Time ticked slowly and quickly at the same time while I debated what to do.

I had to save him, but how?

Guards at the other side of the fence shouted for the crowd to dissipate, but they were ignored, and as the guards had been told to keep the people out of the palace grounds, none of them were rounding the fence to help. It wasn't their directive. I waved my hands so they'd see me. Without my hat, they'd know who I was, but all of them were watching the AML group intently, so none of them noticed my frantic attempts to grab their attention.

The members of the AML that had noticed me were now nudging each other, and my presence was no longer a secret. My hopes had been to talk sense into them, but now the ones at the back began to scramble toward me, and I saw the menace in their eyes. They didn't want to listen to sense. They were so riled up with hatred that capturing me would only be a boon to them. Hadn't overthrowing the monarchy been their primary objective? And here I was, giving it to them on a plate.

The only person that might stop this was Hannah, but her eyes were fixated on Fish. I wasn't trapped, I could outrun them—or, at least, out-scramble them on the rocks—but Fish had no way out. They were closing in on him quickly. Half the AML were still jeering and clapping, calling out vile names, while the other half had set their sights on me. I had two choices. One was to do what I always had and run away from my problems. The other was to face my worst fears.

Slipping off my boots and skirt, I did the unthinkable. My heart squeezed as I shouted Hannah's name as loudly as I could before holding my nose and leaping into the freezing ocean.

The cold gripped me, sending my body into shock. Without Fish warming me, I realized I'd underestimated just how cold the water could be. My feet found the sandy bed, allowing me to push. I needed to reach one of the boats.

My entire body shivered as I pulled maniacally at the nets. If I could loosen one from one of the boats, there was a chance Fish would be able to get through. I was distantly aware of shouting from the rocks. Men's voices. I ignored them all as I fought with the net. The man on the boat saw what I was doing and lunged for me, but it was too late. I'd freed the net and in doing so had let go of the boat and fallen below the surface.

I moved my arms the way Fish had tried teaching me, but the rough motion of the sea had me tumbling end over end into the abyss of the ocean.

Freezing water bit into me, causing pain like no other, but then warm arms enveloped me, spreading warmth through my body, soothing the pain.

We rushed through the water at a speed greater than I'd ever thought possible, getting deeper and deeper the further away we got from the rocky coast.

We swam under the water for what felt like forever until we breached the surface. I gulped back frigid air quickly, my whole body trembling.

He wrapped his arms around me more tightly as I fought to gain control of my own body. His warmth spread through me again, and my trembling began to subside.

"Thank you," he said, running his hand through my drenched hair, pulling it away from my face. "You saved my life back there." He nodded his head toward the mainland. From our position, I could just about make out the palace in the distance. We'd swum a good distance—enough to escape the AML.

"I should be the one thanking you," I whispered. "I'd been trapped in a way of thinking for so long, believing every lie fed to me, and you opened my eyes. You also saved me from drowning."

He leaned forward and kissed me so lightly, brushing my lips with his, only long enough to feel the warmth of them and taste the salt long after the kiss had ended. My heart raced, no longer cold, but sending tingles to the very ends of my nerves.

As he gazed into my eyes, he spoke. "Over raging tides, in the deepest areas of the sea, I will always protect you."

I stared into his beautiful green eyes, and the sincerity in his words caused a tingle from my stomach to my heart, touching my very soul.

My head spun with a gamut of emotion, but one thought I'd pushed to the back of my head now came crashing to the front.

We'd swum a long distance, taking a good ten minutes, at least. Not once had we come up for air.

I could breathe... I could breathe underwater.

HEIRESS OF THE SEA

1

5TH FEBRUARY

"*B*laise!"

My mother's screams cut through my brain, taking my thoughts away from the confession I was about to utter.

The pair of us were in the palace pool where my mother had been swimming around in the saltwater paradise my father had created while I'd sat on the edge, letting my feet and lower legs swish around in the water. Apart from my mother's complaining about the Anti-Mermaid League and the lies printed that very morning in the Conch, and the fact that I felt sick that I had been a very big part of her downfall, it had been a pleasant morning up until the smashing of one of the palace windows.

Moments later, I jumped up from where I'd been perched as a masked intruder ran through the hole he'd just broken in the full-length window. A shiver had run down my spine as the intruder turned his attention briefly to me. His face was covered, but I recognized his eyes. He was a friend of mine. A friend who now had a gun pointed at my mother.

"Who are you?" my mother had demanded, swimming to the edge of the pool.

"He's AML," I said softly. No point denying I knew him. I'd been on the verge of telling her my awful secret anyway.

Behind me, I heard the sound of the guards closing in, but I knew they wouldn't be able to do anything. Not while he had a gun leveled at the queen.

"Shut up, filth," the man screamed. "Anyone moves any closer, and you'll be fishing mer-brains from this pool for weeks."

I held my hands up, frozen into indecision. I'd not asked for this, but if my mother was to die at the hands of the AML, I might as well have pulled the trigger myself. This was all my fault. Years of recruiting for the AML and spouting their propaganda had led to this moment. I tried to remember the guy's name, but my mind fogged up with fear and let me down.

"You are everything that's wrong with Atlantice," he continued, walking closer to my mother, the broken glass crunching beneath his feet.

A winter wind whipped around the room, causing the temperature to drop several degrees.

"I'm the same person I always was," my mother said, showing no fear. I stood in awe of her as the gunman moved ever closer. Only moments before, she'd been complaining as though the AML talking about her was the end of the world, but now that danger was literally staring her in the face, she'd pulled herself together and fearlessly held her own.

"Let's talk about this," I said, trying to keep the situation calm. Escalating it with anger would not help.

"There's nothing to talk about. You are no better than she is," he replied, turning the gun on me.

It was at that point that my mother screamed my name. Now, I ducked as a bullet came whizzing over my head, missing me by inches.

As I ducked, I grabbed the brick that he'd used to smash the window and threw it at his head. It missed, but only because my mother had taken his lapse in concentration and grabbed his leg, pulling him over. As a stream of guards ran in behind me, the man fell into the pool, smashing his head on the side as he went. A stream of red blossomed, muddying the clear water. By the time the guards got to him, he was unconscious. Two of the guards grabbed an arm each and hauled him from the pool as I jumped in to hug my mother.

In all the years I'd lived at the palace, which happened to be all eighteen of them, it was only recently I'd found out that the pool was filled with saltwater rather than fresh. Since my mother's huge revelation, sand, ornaments, and sea plants had been added to the usually boring rectangular pool to turn it into a miniature ocean exclusively for my mother... and for me, if I desired.

Her beautiful tail moved up and down rhythmically as she swam toward me.

There, in the water, she took me in her arms and pulled me into an embrace. I still hadn't told her that I could breathe underwater, so she hauled me to the surface a moment later.

She must have thought me terribly brave to jump in to her, but the truth was, I wasn't brave. I was the exact opposite. I was a coward. I was just about to tell her everything when Captain McDougall rushed to the side of the pool.

"He's been taken care of, Your Highness. I'm awfully sorry this happened. Are you both okay?"

I nodded as my mother spoke.

"We are fine. The pool will need a thorough cleaning, though, and the window will need replacing."

"I'll see to all that. Would you like some assistance getting back to your room?"

"Yes, please. Could you have my maid fill me a bath with salt water?"

He beckoned a couple of his men forward to help her out. Seconds later, I found myself being pulled out despite not needing the help. I guess they didn't know that, though.

Back in my bedroom, after a quick shower, I gazed out of the window as I tried to puzzle out how I could breathe underwater. The simple answer was that I was half-mermaid. But before the intruder had interrupted us, I'd spent the last few hours sitting with my feet in the pool, and they'd remained exactly as they always had been. No tail, no scales, just two normal legs.

Plus, there was the fact that I couldn't swim. The mere thought of water turned my stomach to jelly. I'd jumped in this morning because of my mother, but diving in the heat of the moment was very different from wanting to swim for the mere fun of it. Just thinking about that scared me more than the gunman had.

What kind of mermaid was scared of water? None, I would wager. I'd have thought that being a half-mermaid, I'd feel it more. That I'd feel the call of the sea. I did, to an extent. I enjoyed the salty smell, the gentle lapping of waves. I even enjoyed watching the winter storms churning the sea... from the comfort of my own room through the window.

I didn't, however, have a deep urge to dive into the sea. Far from it.

Nothing made sense. Not when only five days prior, Fish had to save me from drowning.

I'd certainly not been able to breathe then. I'd ended up swallowing what, at the time, felt like half the ocean, but I'd certainly not breathed through it. So what had changed in the past week? If I was a half-mermaid now, I'd certainly been one before my mother's confession. Her telling me about it wouldn't have transformed me. I was either half-mermaid or I wasn't. There was no in-between.

My fingers drummed the window sill.

I understood that Fish and sea creatures breathed underwater because it was their natural habitat.

But a human breathing underwater?

Definitely mindboggling and unfathomable.

How did it happen?

I sighed. Sitting around in my room was going to drive me crazy. My mother was in her bath being looked after, and more guards had been brought in to keep us safe. That was all well and good, but it felt like I was in a prison. My father was out in town doing goodness knew what and guards still patrolled the beach, leaving me stuck here. There was no way my mother would let me go out now. I was going to be trapped at home whether I liked it or not, but there was another way. I'd seen it with my own eyes.

Rifling through my drawer, I found a dry bathing suit. Teaming it with a belt holding my knife—I needed to be able to protect myself—I pulled a robe over the top. A quick note later, saying I was heading out with my friend, and I was ready to go.

Stealing out of my room, I headed along the back corridors until I got to the servants' stairs. They were used more than the other stairs, but they were also the closest to where I wanted to go, and there was less chance a guard would spot me. As luck would have it, I encountered no one as I slipped down the stairs. Holding my breath, I sneaked past the large kitchen door and to the top of yet another set of steps. These led to the palace basement.

The basement was not somewhere I ventured often, but I had been down there a couple of times. It housed cold storage for the kitchens, a wine cellar, and a number of other rooms used for storage. It was also, if I wasn't much mistaken, where I'd find a door to a secret water-logged tunnel that would get me out of the palace without being spotted.

After finding a waterproof bag, I pulled a couple of bottles of water and some food from the cold storage and began to look for the door.

It took a while to find it, hidden as it was behind a unused dresser. A large bolt kept it locked from outside intruders. With a screech of wood on stone, I pulled the dresser away from the door, slid the bolt back, and ventured into the cold tunnel.

Freezing wind rattling down the tunnel took my breath away. I'd forgotten just how much Fish warmed me when I was in his arms. Without his protection, I would surely die of hyperthermia.

It was a risk I was willing to take to find out if he was all right. I'd worried about him all night, and the attack on my mother this morning had only compounded my worry. He'd promised me he'd avoid the coast, but I had a feeling he wouldn't be able to stay away.

Now that the AML had left the beach, he would be back, waiting for me.

At least, that was what I hoped as I stepped onto the rickety walkway that lined the tunnel.

I shivered from both cold and fear, walking through the darkness. Gripping the handrail, I edged along, heading towards the spot of light ahead of me, praying he would be close by. The tunnel would bring me out far enough away from the palace that I'd be difficult to spot by any guards patrolling the beach, but it would also take me to where the bitter cold winter wind roared, buffered by the jagged rocks. I would give myself just five minutes before heading back to the palace.

It had seemed like such a good idea when I'd thought about it back in my warm bedroom, but now that I was exposed to the elements, I began to rethink. Who went out in the middle of winter on a blustery day in only a bathing suit and robe? Well, me, but not many others. I shivered wildly as I scanned the horizon. The cold seeped into my bones, chilling me to my core.

I took a few steps out over the wet rocks, getting wetter every second from the sea spray whipped up by the wind. Wrapping the robe tighter around myself, I mentally chastised myself for being so stupid. But while I might not have a mermaid's call to the ocean, I was called to him. He had been my enemy for so long, and yet, I couldn't keep away from him.

"What are you doing?" he asked, breaching the surface. Spray pelted him as he bobbed violently on the water's surface, and he had to grab hold of a rock to stop from being carried away by the current.

"I c-c-came t-to see if you w-w-were a-alright," I said, my teeth chattering so hard I could barely get the words out.

"So jump in, and I'll warm you up," he shouted up at me.

I shook my head. If the water scared me when it was calm, that was nothing to the churning in my insides now. Even Fish was struggling to keep in one place. What chance did I have?

"Princess. You are practically blue. It might look scary from up there, but I assure you that under the turbulent surface, it's calm."

I shook my head again. There was no way the sea could be tranquil under the surface, not with the violence of the waves that hit the shore.

"Take my hand," he said, holding his free hand to me. "I promise you will be safe. Have I ever let you down?"

"You told me you wouldn't come b-b-back to sh-sh-shore," I reminded him.

"Yes, but I couldn't keep away, and neither can you, it seems. You're here now. You may as well join me. Unless you want to head back down the tunnel and go home?"

I thought about it. Turning back into the darkness was no more appealing than jumping into the ocean, but here, at least, I had Fish to catch me.

I took hold of his hand, and, all at once, warmth seeped through my body. By the time I pulled off my robe and eased myself into the ocean, my bag slung over my shoulder, I was toasty warm.

I barely had time to catch my breath before I was dragged under the water. Fish held me tightly as he pulled me through the ocean at high speed, returning to the surface every so often to allow me to take a breath.

"What are you doing?" I demanded when he finally came to a standstill in the water away from the coast. Wind whipped our hair around us, bobbing us fiercely in the petulant sea.

"AML," he said, pushing my hair from my eyes. I clung to him as one would cling to a life raft, fearful that if I let go, I'd be pulled to the bottom of the ocean.

"I'm sorry," he said. "I didn't mean to scare you, but I saw them clashing with your guards, and I thought we should get out of there before they saw you."

My life was crashing down around me. "Someone almost shot me today. He managed to get into the palace. He was there for my mom."

"Princess, are you all right?"

I nodded, but I wasn't. How could I be all right when people I'd counted as friends only a week ago wanted to kill me?

"Stay out here with me, at least for today. I can't keep you safe on land, but I can in the water."

"More guards have been brought in," I said. "The palace is probably the safest place for me now. This has given the guards a shock. I doubt they'll let it happen again."

"Princess." He took my face in his hands as my tears mingled with the sea spray. "I will keep you safe. I won't let anything happen to you while you are with me. Do you understand?"

I nodded again, hope filling my chest. I already felt safe around him. Even in the middle of the roaring ocean that had always been my most terrifying nightmare, I knew I was safe.

"Ready to go back under?"he asked. I hesitated, then nodded. I took my arms from around his neck and gripped his hand tightly as we slowly drifted under the turbulent surface.

He was right about it being calm under the water. The deeper we dove, the stiller the ocean seemed to be.

My arms and legs glided through the water as we dove deeper, and I found I no longer needed him holding onto me so tightly. My hand in his was enough. I breathed, air somehow filling my lungs. My fingertips skimmed the sandy bottom as we swam to a colorful coral reef containing plants that resembled flowers on land. Golden algae, orange finger sponges, and purple Kenya tree coral blended together in a dazzling display. The colors contrasted against the deep blue of the ocean beyond, akin to fireworks against the darkest of midnight skies, and my problems above the surface drifted away.

Fish lifted his index finger to his lips and pointed to a school of angelfish heading straight toward my legs. They whirled around me, a few touching my calves. Their scaly bodies tickled, but I withheld my laughter. Why disturb their journey?

A pair of tan sea horses hooked their tails as if holding hands. They hovered above a troupe of shrimp weaving in and out of a staghorn coral.

Fish's strong arms encircled my waist, and he pointed upward. I nodded my acceptance, and his strong tail thrust back and forth in rapid motion, propelling us to the surface.

My heart leapt almost as much as we did as we crested the water's surface, arcing over and then diving back in the way I'd seen dolphins do. When we breached the surface again, I couldn't contain my excitement.

"Amazing! I want to learn how to do that. Or is it only merpeople that can reach that high?" I treaded water, maintaining my body in one place, despite the strong waves pushing me side-to-side, although holding onto Fish helped.

"I'm not sure if you'll reach that height because my tail is stronger than your legs. Maybe learning how to pump your legs as hard as you can will help you jump out of the water." He scanned the area, his eyes focusing on the boats leaving the Antla bay. "Why don't we swim to the rocks so we can talk?"

We were close to a rocky outcrop in the next bay along from the palace. It looked to be only thirty or so meters away.

"I'm going to try swimming it by myself," I said with more confidence than I felt. If I couldn't swim to the rocks and ended up struggling in the rolling sea, I could slip beneath the waves and breathe while I waited for Fish to rescue me.

I wouldn't say that my fear of the sea had gone completely, but it had subsided now that I'd seen the beauty the ocean held.

Fish pulled a face that I hadn't expected.

"You tired?" I asked. "I think I'll be okay if you stay close. It's not that far."

For the first time since I had met him, he grimaced, his gaze darting this way and that on the water behind me. For a second, I thought that the AML had somehow followed us, but that sounded ridiculous, as we'd swum underwater, and there was no way the AML would be able to track us. Still, the fear in his eyes was real.

"What's wrong?" I asked, getting caught in his panic. I turned to see what had grabbed his attention, but apart from the whites of the waves, I saw nothing out of the ordinary.

Without warning, Fish's tail rose, and he slammed it down, splashing my face with droplets of water.

I met his eyes. "What was that for?"

"Sorry," he said, pulling me closer. "I didn't mean to splash you, but I wanted to warn a couple of sharks heading our way."

"Sharks?" I stammered, touching my knife that was still in its sheath. "You were warning them?"

"Yeah," he said, pulling me towards the rocks, clearly forgetting that I said I'd swim. "My tail splashing was a warning not to come too close. I think they've gone now, but you should sit on the rocks for a few minutes until I'm sure. I can fight and kill one, but while I'm busy brawling, the other would eat you whole."

My heart lurched at the mere thought of it. I scrambled out of the water while he swam around, his red tail appearing and disappearing in the water. The cold came back in a hurry, so I was glad when he swam back a couple of moments later.

"They're gone," he announced. "My warning did the trick."

He reached up to me, finding a loose strand of hair and tucking it behind my ear, creating a whirlwind of tingles that had nothing to do with the cold weather.

"I can't believe you scared off some sharks," I said as I once again eased myself into the water.

He shrugged. "Technically, my tail doesn't scare them away, but striking the water with it causes an echo, and they steer away from it."

"Wow," I exclaimed, genuinely in awe. "If only you could do that to scare off the AML, then we'd have no problem at all."

His hands gently touched my chin. "If you are worried about your mother, we can go back. I don't like the thought of you at the palace, but I'll understand if you need to get home."

My lips lifted to form a tiny smile. "My father wants to bring guards from the mainland because of these riots. He's not home at the moment, but McDougall—that's the head of the palace guard—has everything in hand. My mother is being very well looked after. I left a note that I was going out, so if they find me gone, they won't worry too much." A twist of guilt wrenched my gut as I thought of the vague note I'd left. There was nothing I could do about it now. "The leadership of the AML has lost its mind. Even when I hated merpeople, I never wanted them dead. I may have believed the AML's lies that merpeople were evil, but I pushed for their removal from our waters, not their death. Never their deaths." I looked into his eyes. "You believe me, right?" My beating heart raced, waiting for his answer. I wanted him to believe me. I needed him to believe me.

My toes curled up as the back of his hand caressed my cheek.

"I never thought otherwise," he said. "Do you want to see some more of the ocean bed? I know a spot that has the most beautiful coral."

I nodded. I'd go wherever he wanted to take me.

We swam together for hours, sometimes on the surface, sometimes underwater. A whole new world opened up to me, a world I'd never known existed. A world of beauty and silence deep beneath the noisy, chaotic world above us.

Hours later, we breached the surface for the umpteenth time, water dripping from us both. Now that I'd seen his world, I felt I understood him a little more. He was such a part of it, his beauty matching the world he inhabited. As he looked at me, I fought the desire to reach out and run my fingers through his hair, letting the water droplets fall through my fingers. I probably would have if he'd not spoken before I got the chance.

"How about we go somewhere else? There is an underwater cavern I want to show you. It will mean walking down one of those tunnels again."

"No sharks, though?" I teased, thinking back to how scared I'd been traveling through the tunnel the first time. This time, I could swim with him at my side and wouldn't have to walk along the rickety walkway, all the while worrying about falling in.

He chuckled and shook his head. "I assure you there are no sharks there nor any creatures with large teeth. Nothing for you to be scared of. Not with me."

I tilted my head. "Do you ever get scared?"

"What do you mean? In the sea?"

I twirled my hair. "In general. What would make your body break out in a sweat?"

"Interesting question. Obviously, I'm not scared of sea creatures humans should avoid because they normally stay far away." He stared at the boats in the distance near Antla's port. "Uncontrollable evil. Someone with hatred in their heart and the means to destroy everyone would scare me if I had to face them by myself."

"Yeah, that's frightening," I agreed, wondering if he was talking about the AML or someone else.

Behind him, a flash of color caught my attention.

"Can you see that?" I asked, pointing it out to him.

"Yeah, I've been watching it. It's one of your boats. I can see the royal insignia on the side."

"My boats?" I queried, suddenly worried.

"Not yours, your father's. It's a naval boat. Don't worry. It's not the AML."

His eyesight was amazing. I could only just make out the boat, although the strength of the wind was propelling it toward us at considerable speed.

"Want to dive under?" he asked.

I shook my head. "No." He wasn't afraid of the sea, and I refused to be afraid of my father's men. I'd left the palace without telling anyone where I was going. The note I'd left was vague, so it didn't surprise me at all that McDougall had sent out boats to look for me.

Ten minutes later, the small ship sailed to within about twenty feet from the rocks, and Sergeant Jimenez, one of my father's closest men, stood on the deck. He bowed before he asked, "Your Highness, are you stranded?" His eyes flicked over to Fish. I knew as well as he did that he didn't think I was stranded. He must have seen me through his binoculars and come to investigate.

"Nope, I'm perfectly capable of swimming back." I smiled sweetly, knowing full well this would get back to my father.

"I can escort you home now," he said, glancing Fish's way again.

"You'll have to swim over to the boat."

Crossing my arms, I responded, "I'm not ready to return right now. Maybe later this afternoon or tonight."

I could see the distrust in his eyes, singling him out as a mer-hater. A few days ago, this information would have thrilled me. Now, it only made me sad.

"Your Highness, I must insist. The situation in Antla is getting worse, and after the trouble this morning, your father has made the decision to leave the palace for a few days in the hopes that things will calm down. He ordered some of the guards to collect your mother and you. You can imagine your mother's shock when you were nowhere to be found."

"You mean he wants us to go into hiding?" I'd never thought I'd see the day when my father succumbed to the whims of rioters. Hearing of the gunman must have affected him greatly.

Jimenez nodded. "As I said, it's only for a few days. A vast number of people known to the guard as AML supporters have been seen entering Antla. Your father thought it prudent to take you and your mother away for a few days for your own safety. I expect they are searching the palace for you now; so if you'll come with me, I'll get you home."

I almost swam to him. I probably would have if he'd not uttered the next three words with such hatred.

"...Away from that."

"*That* happens to be a friend of mine and not the problem here. Quite the opposite, in fact. My friend is keeping me safe."

Jimenez shook his head. "I beg to differ. The merfolk are the cause of the problem. If they'd just leave, then half the people of Atlantice wouldn't have to abandon their homes to march against them."

I pulled my hands into a fist, anger burning within me. "You are aware that my mother, your queen, is a mermaid. Do you believe she is part of the problem here?"

He suddenly realized what he'd said and started to backtrack, but it was too late.

"Well, no, but… well."

"I'd appreciate it if you could send word to my parents that I'm safe. Tell them that I'm with a friend. I'll come back to the palace in a few days when they do. There is no need for them to worry. The rioters cannot get me out here."

"You're not seriously thinking of staying out in the ocean?" he blustered, his eyes narrowing.

"I assure you, I'm very serious. Now leave me be and let my parents know I'll be home in a couple of days. Tell them I'm perfectly safe and…"—I took a deep breath, hardly daring to say it— "I'm with a mer-friend. I think my mother will understand. I'm half-mermaid, after all."

There. That would stop him. He knew he couldn't disobey a direct order. My parents would be angry with me, knowing I'd sneaked out without their knowledge, but that was a price I was going to have to pay anyway. I knew my mother would get it. She'd lived on land but yearned for the ocean. She couldn't begrudge me finding out who I really was. Besides, I was an adult by law. I could make my own decisions.

Jimenez's mouth curled up in disgust at the term "half-mermaid."

"I don't think…"

"Sergeant, I'm well aware of what you think. I've given you an order, and I expect you to follow it. I'm eighteen now, and I can do as I please. Let my parents know I'm safe and pass on that I'm sorry for not telling them in the first place."

Sergeant Jimenez saluted. "Yes, Your Highness."

Not that he had any choice in the matter. He didn't have to like obeying my orders, but he did have to obey them. My parents were going to be pissed when they found out where I was, especially after this morning, but they would get over it. At least, they hadn't sent the whole fleet to look for me. Jimenez would have told me if they had. No, he'd just chanced to catch sight of me while I happened to be near his boat.

I thanked him and waited for him to turn around. Admitting to the world that I was friends with a merman was enough revelation for one day. I wasn't about to let anyone know I could breathe underwater too.

"You were magnificent," Fish said, throwing me up into the air once the boat was far enough away. I came down with a splash, and when I resurfaced, I did it with a grin on my face. I could tread water without Fish's help. I'd been doing it while talking to Jimenez and only just noticed. I'd be swimming before I knew it.

Swimming alone was one thing. Regulating my body temperature in the frigid water was another. I grabbed Fish's hand, and immediately, a bloom of warmth crawled up my body.

When Jimenez was far enough away, Fish took me once more to the depths, this time pulling me along at high speed. We slowed down as we came to the entrance to an underwater tunnel. He raised his free hand and pointed at the dark hole. All my fears came rushing back as I realized he wanted me to go in there with him, but as I was about to shake my head, I stopped. My biggest fear was the water, and I was already under it. I was with Fish. I nodded, and we entered the darkness.

A bright green glow emanated from the tunnel walls, allowing me to see where we were going. Phosphorescence, lighting the way. A whole network of paths branched off in all directions, but Fish seemed to know where he was going, so I accepted that I was safe and let him pull me where he wanted to go.

Eventually, we came to an underground room, half-filled with water and half with air. As we breached the surface, musty air filled my lungs, but it was breathable thanks to small holes in the roof of the cave.

"What is this place?" I asked, looking around. It was a little like the tunnel I'd walked through earlier, and, just like that one, there was a door with a small landing area lit by a solitary light.

"These tunnels are a little different from the tunnel you used to leave the palace, although that door also leads to it. Haven't you guessed what it is yet?"

I shrugged my shoulders. I had no idea.

"Let me give you a clue. Look at that."

He pointed to the door. Next to it, was a letterbox with a pull string.

"This is the mail network. The dolphins use a network of tunnels to deliver mail, and this is where they come when they want to deliver mail to your palace."

"But I always take the mail out to the pier and call for them," I exclaimed.

"You might." Fish shrugged. "But the palace staff doesn't. They drop the mail off here, and they pick it up from that box there. The network is connected to all the post offices in Atlantice, not to mention, the houses of Atlantice's richest inhabitants."

I'd never guessed that dolphins swam under Atlantice as well as around it. The whole kingdom held veins of waterways so frequent they were more common than roads. I'd just assumed the dolphins delivered the post that way.

"You brought me here to show me the mail?" I asked, turning to him.

"That's part of it, but there is another reason." He grinned at me. "Watch this." He swished his tail, and, as he did, the cave lit up with a shimmering glow. He pulled me into the water as the displaced phosphorescence glowed like a million twinkling lights in a dark, starry night.

We rose to the surface slowly, with me in his arms. As it had before, the urge to run my fingers through his hair was immense, but unlike before, I didn't stop myself. As I brushed the hair away from his face, the fleshy part of my palm grazed his temples. He lifted his hand up and gripped my wrist. I was about to apologize for being so forward when I realized his intention. He wasn't pulling me away. He was pulling me closer.

He was pulling me closer, and I let him. When our faces were mere inches apart, he stopped, allowing me, as he had always done, to make the decision for myself. It was an easy one. I leaned forward and touched my lips to his. Then and only then, he pulled my body closer, my bathing suit against his naked chest, and I abandoned myself to his kiss.

2
6TH FEBRUARY

ish's breath drew me out of a deep, peaceful slumber. I didn't want to wake and face the reality of what I'd done, but then I remembered the kiss. Almost subconsciously, I raised my fingers to my lips and grinned. I still harbored guilt over leaving my family when they needed me the most, but waking on a warm sandy bed with gentle waves lapping at my toes next to Fish made everything worth it. He'd taken me to a cave a little way down the coast where we'd held hands and watched the sunset until I'd fallen asleep in his arms.

"Morning, Princess. Sleep well?" He kissed my forehead.

I lowered my fingers and snuggled closer. My eyes fluttered open. "Definitely." I bit the inside of my cheek to stop my lips from spreading so wide that the corners hurt. "How about you?"

"Perfectly, with you in my arms." He planted a quick peck on my lips.

"You know, Princess isn't my name. I'm…"

As I spoke, another wave came in, higher this time, drenching the pair of us and cutting off my train of thought. The tide was coming in.

"What are the plans for today?" I asked, pulling myself closer to him, enjoying the warmth spreading through me. I couldn't go back to the palace, nor could I head anywhere on land, but I found I didn't want to. "Another beautiful coral reef? Or... we could stay here?" I said shyly. This was all new to me, but the feeling of lying next to someone, next to him, was not something I wanted to end in a hurry.

His laughter tickled my ears as his chest shook. I pulled back to meet the deliciousness of his green eyes.

His hair held a coating of sand, and it clung to the side of his face where he'd slept on it.

He spread his fingers and pushed back his long hair, allowing the waves to fan it against his neck. "This cave will be filled with water within an hour." He laughed. "I've been thinking about it, and I want you to see my home after we have breakfast."

My heart didn't know whether to stop beating or race or do both.

"You're taking me to the mer-village?"

The idea both prompted my nerves to pull tight and my heart to race from excitement. I'd seen the ocean with him yesterday. We'd explored reefs and swam with fishes, but I'd not seen another merperson all day. I knew they lived in their own version of towns and villages underwater, but until now, I'd not put much thought into it.

"The mer-village off the coast of Antla. It'll be safe there as long as we don't breach the surface, and you can see how we live." He cocked his head, and the back of his fingers caressed the top of my cheek before trailing to my jawline. "But only if you want to go. If not, there are a thousand other places I could take you." His dimples appeared. "So, do you want to see my home?"

Of course, I wanted to see it. I wanted to know everything about this new world. I found myself excited about the prospect of meeting Fish's friends and learning more about him.

"I'd love to see where you grew up."

A sadness flitted in his eyes before he smiled. "I'm not from Antla originally," he reminded me. "I'll take you to my birthplace one day if you want." He blew air out. "After everything has calmed down and we're not hunted. I wouldn't want to lead those rioters to my birth home."

Neither of us spoke. His thoughts probably headed in the same direction mine did, to when we could live peacefully together. Humans and merfolk.

"Let's find food and then explore other areas instead of brooding in this cave." He held out his hand, and I took it

We swam out in the ocean until we reached a new coral reef. In the middle of the reef, he signaled for me to remain quiet as he hunted a tuna.

Without his hand touching me, the cold began to seep in, but watching him weave through the water and masterfully blend in with the other wildlife took my mind from the biting cold.

He caught a fish and, after bringing me to the surface, filleted it on a rock using my knife to help.

"Normally, I'd just bite into this, but I know you land people are more sophisticated." He grinned, passing me a lump of the flesh.

Raw fish was not something I'd ever tried, but as my food supply was dwindling, I let it fall down my throat. It tasted better than I had expected, and I found myself wanting more. After a feast of fish swigged down with the water I'd brought from the palace, he led me to a passage in between large stands of seagrass. We stopped at a large coral reef with the grass growing at least ten feet tall around it.

"Let's go in."

He'd never spoken to me under the water before, always waiting until we were over the surface to talk. His voice sounded strange, almost like an echo reverberating through the water. I tried the same, expecting no sound to come out. I'd certainly never been able to talk underwater before, or at least, I'd never tried. I was surprised to find I could hear my own voice, albeit as distorted as Fish's was.

I squinted to where he pointed. "Where?"

He pulled the seagrass apart and pointed to a hole in the ground. "In here. The tunnel is about fifty yards long and will take us under the reef."

"Talk about hiding it really well." I wouldn't have seen it, shielded as it was.

"The entire village is concealed within the reef.."

My eyes took a while to adjust to the dark tunnel, but I found that the longer I spent underwater, the more quickly I adapted to my surroundings. Before long, I could make out the thousands of tiny fish that swam along with us. We dove deeper, then swam up toward a tiny light that expanded as we ascended. When we finally exited the tunnel, the underwater kingdom appeared. Its palace, almost the size of mine, rose above us with its splendor of towers and walls made from coral of every color.

"What do you think?" He grinned. "Stunning, isn't it?"

My gaze slid from one end to another, and my mouth hung open. "It's beautiful!" I murmured. And it was. Tall spires rose majestically atop the prettiest building I'd ever seen. The entire palace was a living organism with not a flat surface in sight. Fish swam in and out through the windows, making the whole place seem as though it was moving.

"I love coming in from the east corridor. Every time I see the palace arising from behind the village, it gives me goosebumps."

"I can see why." I couldn't stop gawking at the impressive structure.

He looked over at me. "I'm so glad you like it."

"Thank you for bringing me here," I whispered, reaching for his hand. "Is the mer-king as involved in the lives of the villagers as my dad is?"

"I'd say about the same. Since the palace is the center of our village, nothing occurs without the king's approval or knowledge. He's not listed as an official king of one of the kingdoms like your father is, as here underwater, we officially come under Atlantice's borders, but the merpeople have their own rules and laws that do not apply to the land folk. Twice a month, he holds court specifically to hear the villagers' troubles."

"Similar to my dad, except he does it once a week. Our villagers have many issues." I twisted my lips. "I guess that's a big understatement."

He placed his hand on my shoulder. "Don't worry about it, Princess. Everything will work out eventually. It may take a while, but it will work out. Your father seems to have the situation in hand."

"Thank you."

We continued along the path, similar to an unpaved street with a sandy floor in Antla. Intricate passages broke off from the main path, with more houses appearing on either side and at the end of them.

The village seemed devoid of any life. I scanned the area, but it seemed we were the only ones there.

He released my hand to point out the colorful plants on a window sill at the end of one of the paths. "They change the foliage every couple of weeks and during major holidays. You should come during Christmas. The plants brighten up that entire section."

"It's lovely now, and I can't imagine how spectacular it must be during Christmas." My eyes widened at the display of colorful plants along our path. "Do you think I could bring some back to the palace? I haven't ever seen these, and I think my mom would love them for her pool."

Fish shrugged. "Remind me when we pass the flower shop. I know the florist, and he can give us a good price."

It seemed weird to me that merfolk would shop as we did when they could hunt fish, but as they had houses and streets, it made sense that they would shop, too. If only Hannah could see how civilized it all was, how similar to our world on land.

The edge of the town appeared empty until we turned onto a wider street. A few merpeople swayed in front of the shops, talking amongst themselves. A few waved but most stared, narrowing their eyes, much the way Jimenez had at Fish.

There was no doubt in my mind they were staring at me.

Focusing my attention on the shops, I maintained my smile, ignoring the dirty looks as we passed. Up ahead, a couple of mermaids swam into the street, whispering to each other and pointing our way.

Fish halted. His eyes narrowed at the two mermaids, who caught his stare and turned around to laugh privately.

When I spotted the flower shop filled with all types of plants outside, I picked up my pace, dragging Fish with me. "I want to see the plants and buy a few," I said, pointing at the shop window.

He shook his head. "There's no time for shopping." The curtness in his tone startled me.

My mouth dropped open. "Why not? We don't have to be anywhere soon, do we?"

He raised his voice. "I've told you there is no time. Besides, you have no money."

Something had happened during our short swim. Only minutes before, he'd said that he'd get me a good price for the beautiful sea plants, and now there was no time? The coldness in his voice tugged at my chest, but his words sparked a fire in me.

"Listen to me, I'm the…"

He jerked me around until our bodies touched and whispered in my ear, "Don't you dare mention you're the princess. Here, in this village, you're just an ordinary girl with the ability to breathe underwater, do you understand?"

The pain in my chest magnified at the way he spoke to me. My eyes widened, and I restrained the tears welling behind them.

What was wrong with him? He'd never raised his voice to me. Not once. Not even when he was surrounded by the rioters. He had always maintained his cool.

"Understood, but when we reach our destination, you will tell me what in all of shellfish land is wrong with you," I whispered, gritting my teeth. "And I want answers. Do you hear that?"

He didn't acknowledge my words but released my arm.

Thousands of pins pricked my heart, but I pushed away the pain. It wasn't the right time for tears, but I was angry.

Whatever had happened just now had nothing to do with me. He was taking whatever it was out on the wrong person.

I pulled away from him to look at a statue of a young mermaid on a rock. I didn't want him to know he'd caused my tears. The statue was beautifully sculpted, though weathered by the sea and covered in places in green algae.

When I finally turned around, Fish hovered above me.

He crossed his arms. "We need to go."

Another prick punctured my heart, but anger replaced my hurt.

"You might need to go," I shouted, "but I can do what I want."

Embarrassed, I turned my head as a line of merpeople watched our little spat from outside their shops. I began to shiver with the cold, but I refused to hold his hand, even though without doing so, I didn't have the benefit of his heat.

"You are freezing," he exclaimed, taking my hand. I didn't attempt to stop him as he began to pull me through the water again. One day, I would have to learn how to regulate my body temperature in the icy seas, but I'd not quite managed that yet, and I needed Fish whether I liked it or not.

We swam past dozens of merpeople, each with their arms crossed, heads lowered, and tight lips on long, drawn faces. Their eyes followed us. Even the mer-children glared my way.

Why are they so upset? I wondered. These were not the merpeople that Fish described. He had said that they would help humans, protect them. But these merpeople looked at me as though I'd trailed dog dirt through their homes.

Fish glanced at me every so often, but I remained stoic. No need for him to see my anger.

Finally, he stopped in front of a large coral-made house. No fence or tall seagrass decorated the front, but it rested on top of a huge rock foundation, making it stand out from all the other houses we'd passed.

A huge merman with jagged short hair, hacked off no doubt by a knife or sharp rock, opened the door and bowed. "Good evening, sir," he said to Fish.

I followed Fish into his home, giving the merman a clipped smile.

"Evening, Alfred. As you can see, I've brought a guest. Can you make sure the guest room is ready?"

Alfred lowered his eyes slightly, then swam from the room, leaving me alone with Fish.

"What the hell was that back there?" I laid into him.

He sighed and placed both hands above his heart. "I'm sorry. No human has ever come down here before. I wasn't expecting the reaction we got, and it stressed me out. I didn't mean to make you feel bad."

I shook my head, my red-blond hair fanning until it landed over my shoulders and back. "Well, you did extremely well for someone who wasn't trying. You treated me like crap."

Alfred coughed, announcing his presence. "Sir, sorry to interrupt, but, some of the ladies of the town are here to see you."

"Ah, the welcome committee," Fish sighed.

Before Alfred could answer, five mermaids rushed in with their hands on their hips. They threw kill-her-now looks my way before a brunette yelled, "How could you bring her here?" She pointed at me. "Have you lost your mind?"

Some freaking welcoming committee!

He lifted his hands. "Please, ladies, calm down. Let's not shriek."

A voluptuous redhead waved her index finger at him, "She needs to know she isn't welcome here. We don't need any of those filthy humans in our village, especially her and her filthy…"

Fish pushed his palm in front of her face and shouted, "Stop. This is my friend. Don't insult her while she's in my home."

The blonde pointed at the door and yelled, "She needs to leave. Right. Now."

I wanted to grab her long hair and pull it until she begged for mercy and apologized, but I figured if Fish wanted to defend me against these witches, then I'd let him do it. He needed to make up for the way he'd talked to me earlier.

"Ladies, she's a guest in my home, so I'll be the one deciding if she stays or not. In fact, it's time for you to leave. Alfred, please escort them out."

They muttered obscenities but followed Alfred. Once they were gone, Alfred headed back to us. Fish whispered something in his ear, eliciting a nod from Alfred before he left.

"What is wrong with them?" I asked once the mermaids were out of earshot.

Fish stiffened his back.

"Why are they so hostile? Why don't they want me here?"

He glanced over his shoulder while he swam toward me. "Why don't we eat? You must be hungry."

"Don't try to redirect," I hissed, placing my hands on my hips. "I'm not a two-year-old."

He sighed before answering. "For the longest time, merfolk didn't much care one way or another about humans. We interacted with them on a daily basis. They stuck to land, we stuck to water, and on the rare occasion we met in the middle, everyone was pleasant."

"But?"

"A couple of months ago, the AML started getting more hostile. You should know about that. Merfolk stopped being welcome at the shops along the waterways. We found it harder to get the things we needed. It's caused a lot of resentment, as you can imagine."

"That's why they were whispering?"

"I didn't want you worrying, and I really hoped that they would accept you when they saw you breathing underwater."

It wasn't my fault that Fish was being an ass, but it was my fault those mermaids hated me the way they did.

"Maybe I should apologize for my part in that? Tell them how sorry I am that humans are hunting them and causing them problems."

His head dropped. "You saw them, they don't want to listen."

I lowered my eyes and stared at the sand. "Then maybe I should leave?"

He rushed over and held my hand. "It doesn't matter what they want. I want you here. I'll do whatever I need to do to keep you here. To keep you happy. I was a jerk earlier, and I'm sorry."

I went to the window. A group of mermaids swam by, pointing their fingers at me. They rolled their eyes and flipped their hair.

I wondered if it was just to do with resentment of me being a human. The way those girls looked at me felt personal. As they swam, one of them looked back. This time she wasn't looking at me. She winked at Fish, throwing him a small wave before sashaying away.

Then it hit me. It wasn't just because of who I was, but because of who I was with. They were jealous of me because of Fish, not that I could blame them.

They hated my legs, and they hated the fact that I was with Fish. Jealousy, pure and simple.

Double whammy!

I turned to Fish. Swimming toward him, I held out my hand for him to take.

He pulled me toward him, wrapping his hands around my waist. I only had eyes for him, but I hoped those witches could see me through the window.

"I really messed up back there. I mean it when I say I'm sorry. I brought you here, and while you are here, you are my responsibility."

"I'm no one's responsibility but my own," I pointed out.

He nodded. "You're right. I don't want to hurt you, though. The way I treated you was on me, and I royally messed it up."

I nodded. "You did." My lips curled up at the edges. It was hard to stay mad at him when he was so breathtakingly gorgeous.

He kissed my cheek and led me through his dwelling.

Fish's house astounded me in its size and beauty. The notion that all merfolk lived in gloomy caves was completely dispelled as he gave me a tour.

"This belonged to my parents, but they died a few years back," he explained as he escorted me through the winding passages. "It's all mine now. I inherited the house and Alfred, plus enough money to keep me going and pay Alfred's wages for a good few years."

"You have no siblings?"

He shook his head. "No, it's just Alfred and I. I've asked him to go to the surface and buy you some food. And bottles of water. I don't stock fresh water because I don't need it, but I've seen that your own bottles are nearly empty, and I didn't want to keep feeding you raw fish."

I was touched that he'd thought to do that.

"I thought the shops were refusing to sell to merfolk now?"

Fish nodded. "Most are, but I'm a good customer and pay well. Some are losing money because they are scared to sell to us. I'm telling you now, there can't be many shopkeepers in the AML. This is harming their businesses."

I thought back to all the AML members I knew. I couldn't think of a single shopkeeper within the ranks.

After a strange dinner of salty wet bread and cold, already cooked meat, which was all Alfred could source, Fish took me to one of the rooms in his house that he'd not shown me before. The entire room was filled with flowers of every kind clinging to the walls and ceiling. The only part of the room not covered in flowers was the floor, which held a raised area of sand.

"I asked Alfred to make this room up for you to sleep in. I wish I could stay in here with you," he said. "But if Alfred knew I slept with you, he'd talk. He's a great servant, but lousy at keeping secrets. If the townspeople found out..."

A shiver pulled at my heart when I realized he meant me to sleep here alone.

"We slept next to each other last night," I pointed out.

His smile disarmed me, and I wanted to grab hold of him and not let him go until morning.

"That was away from the townsfolk. There will be enough gossip with you just being here, and I don't want to make it harder on you. It doesn't mean I won't be thinking about you all night." He moved forward and cupped my face in his hands. When he kissed me, I kissed back, urgency in my lips, hoping it would make him change his mind, but eventually, he pulled back.

He smiled at me in a way that made my heart leap with joy and brought his fingers to his lips.

"Princess," he said, "with kisses like that, you're gonna kill me!"

He left the room through the long seagrass covering the door, and I fell back on the sandy bed, my heart jittering with happiness. Who cared if the people on land hated us, and the people below the sea hated us? We had each other, and I needed no one else.

3
7TH FEBRUARY

The sound of a commotion woke me from a deep sleep. Not exactly a peaceful one, but not a tossing-and-turning-all-night one, either. My body refused to leave the sandy floor to investigate the noise.

I rolled over onto my back and placed my hands underneath my head. The ceiling above me undulated in the warm current, a riot of hues that mesmerized me with their beauty.

The yelling became louder, forcing me to sit up. I could ignore it no longer. Fish's voice, the only male one as far as I could tell, sounded frustrated but in control. Not that I could hear his words. The women's voices shrilled, but no matter how much I strained to hear the context of their shrieks, I couldn't decipher any of their words.

I stood and ran my fingers through my hair. It was knotted from days of being underwater, but as I had not thought to bring a brush with me, I had to be content with using my fingers.

Their thundering voices died down for a minute before starting up again much more loudly. I rushed out of the flowered room and followed the sound.

A minute later, I halted in the middle of the front room, staring at the scene unfolding right outside the window.

The crowd, made up of eight mermaids, surrounded Fish with all their hands in the air, their wild gestures somehow in tune with their shouted words.

A cacophony of shrieks emanated from them as they all tried to speak over each other, resulting in a garbled mess of words. Maybe they were sirens who hadn't yet learned to lure their prey with sweet singing.

The mermaids pointed at the house, so I ducked back from the window. I heard one of them scream the word "princess" before going back to her incoherent babble. I gave it a minute, then peeked back out.

Fish was talking to them calmly now, and their focus was back on him.

Any other man might have lost his cool, but not him. He maintained his calm.

Alfred appeared beside me. "Is everything all right, miss? You look concerned."

I pointed outside. "A mob of mermaids seems to be accosting…" I didn't say his name, and it occurred to me I still didn't know it. After everything we'd gone through in the past couple of days, I'd not thought to ask him his name. "They appear ready to pull his arms apart and feed his body to barracudas."

Alfred chuckled. "Don't worry, they won't touch him. They're upset, and they'll scream and holler like starving banshees, but they won't touch him. They wouldn't dare."

I focused on the mermaids but peeked back at Alfred's face, wondering if he believed his own words. "Why won't they? They sound pretty upset. If they were piranhas, they'd have their teeth sharpened and ready to devour him until only his skeleton remained."

"They know he's protected by the king, and they wouldn't want to upset our king. Besides, they all like him too much to hurt him."

For some reason, I didn't like that any better.

"They like him too much?"

He grinned. "The master has never had to worry about being lonely. He has his fair share of admirers." When he saw my face, he added, "You are the first he's brought back here, though. Now, don't you worry about him. He can fend for himself. Is there anything I can get you? Some breakfast, perhaps?"

I was about to tell him that I couldn't face breakfast when Fish swam in, leaving the mermaids outside. He took one glance at my fingers and engulfed them with his hand. "I hope you weren't too worried about them. They're harmless." His dimples appeared. "I'm starving. Would you like to eat?"

I nodded. Now that Fish was back, my appetite returned with a vengeance.

"Alfred, I think the salmon should be available for pickup."

"Yes, sir." He bowed and left.

I stared out the window. More people passed by, waving their fists at me. "Are they all prejudiced against humans?"

"Not everyone," Fish said, wrapping his arms around me. I was no longer cold in his house, but his touch set my soul ablaze. "Unfortunately, because of the rioting, plenty are adamant about their dislike for humans at the moment."

I reeled away from the window. "What did that mermaid say about me?"

"What do you mean?"

"I heard one of them shouting 'princess.'"

"Let's leave it alone and wait for our food."

I circled around to face him. "Please don't hold things back from me. It's not fair to me. Why do they hate me such much?"

Fish cupped my face gently and placed a kiss on my forehead. "The last thing I want to do is hurt you." He hugged me, his muscular arms holding me tight without squeezing.

"Then don't. Tell me the truth and let me deal with it."

He pulled back, and his fingers stroked my cheek. "They know who you are. That's why they came back this morning. They found out that not only were you a part of the AML but that you spread AML propaganda. They want revenge for the AML hunting their men. Unfortunately, they didn't want to hear you weren't a part of the hunting rioters or that you never wanted to hurt anyone. They're out for their pound of flesh, and you're now their biggest target."

"How did they find out? You never mentioned my name."

He took a deep breath and exhaled. "Some of the mermaids recognized you." He looked away. "They know some of the merpeople you used to taunt. I tried to tell them that you've changed and feel remorse for what you did, but they wouldn't listen to me."

A slight pressure surrounded my heart as I admitted to myself that they had every right to be upset. I'd never personally taunted any merfolk, but I'd been right there with Hannah plenty of times while she had. I sighed. How would I make things right?

"I'm so sorry," he said. "I know that's not who you are. Not anymore."

"But it's only been since I've met you that my heart has changed. And Emma, my maid. Both of you pointed out that not all merpeople were guilty of the crimes the AML said they were." I placed my head against his chest. "I understand their reasoning because I'm guilty of what they accuse me of."

"No, you're not. Maybe you used to be, but all I see before me is a warm-hearted girl who wouldn't hurt anyone. I see the remorse for what you've done. But right now, they won't listen to reason. They've hardened their hearts despite my explanations. Even the merpeople who have friends above the water and know the truth can't talk sense into them."

"They may not be able to, not now. The reason for their hatred is too fresh in their minds," I said in a defeated tone, one I didn't like, but I couldn't control. "I can hardly blame them. They are no different from how I used to be not so long ago. It took a lot to make me understand how wrong I was. It took my mother turning into a mermaid."

"Turning back into a mermaid," he pointed out. "Again, I'm so sorry. Instead of protecting you from the rioters, I've led you into a den of hatred. It seems we are just as bad off down here. It never used to be this way. A couple of months ago, everything was fine, but then things changed. I'm not sure why. Our seas are much more choppy than usual, even for winter, and it's making everyone crabby."

I placed my hand on his chest, allowing my palm to feel his strong, beating heart. "It's not your fault. It's mine. If I hadn't joined the AML and been mean to all the merpeople I encountered, they wouldn't be upset with me now. My own actions have led to their hatred."

His hand caressed my hair, with slow, gentle strokes. "You were blinded by the words of the AML."

"Yes, but I could have investigated the AML's information, talked to fishermen, and come to my own conclusions. If I had actually used my brain, I could have discovered years ago that our information was derived from unsubstantiated pirate hearsay and not to be relied on. Maybe I could have even talked to merpeople and asked questions instead of blindly believing the propaganda. All those wasted years hating merpeople for nothing." I shook my head. "I've been so dumb."

He ran his hand down my head, tangling his fingers in my hair when he reached my nape. "No, you're not dumb. Misguided, maybe."

Guilt reigned deep in my soul. "My influence increased the AML's numbers."

"Please don't blame yourself." He rubbed my back.

The desire to sob until my tears ran out subsided. I needed to get a grip on my emotions and not fall apart.

I made a difficult decision, no matter how much my heart bled.

I leaned my head back to gaze into his eyes and take them in. "I need to leave."

Fish pulled back, lifted my chin, and met my eyes. "Where shall we go?"

"No," I replied, shaking my head. "You stay here. I'll return to the palace. My parents aren't there, but I should be. Not hiding here, away from all my problems. I'm only causing more for you.."

"They won't harm you here, no matter how much they yell and scream. You're safe in my home."

I smiled at his words. "I know you'll protect me, but I need to be at the palace. It was a mistake to come here."

"I don't think you'll be safe there," he said, furrowing his brow.

"The palace is full of guards. The captain of the guard won't let anyone in."

"The captain of the guard may well be with your parents," he pointed out.

I nodded. He was right. McDougall probably would be with my mother and father, but there were more than enough guards left to keep me safe.

I touched my hand to his face. "We have so many guards, and no one outside of the palace will even know I'm there. They'll think I'm with my parents or here in the sea with you."

"Are you absolutely sure?" He trailed his fingers down my cheek. "I don't want to lose you."

My heart skipped a beat. "I know that if I need anything, I just have to reach the water, and you'll magically appear."

He chortled loud enough that his chest trembled. "It's not magic, but I'll be close by."

I gazed into his gorgeous green eyes. "And how often will you search for me?"

"Every single minute of the day when I'm not with you." He dipped his head and kissed me.

My toes curled, my blood warmed, and tingles ran all over my body. The man sure could kiss.

The sound of coughing prompted us to end the kiss. Why did he have to come now?

"Sir, I have the salmon you requested."

"Oh, thank you, Alfred." He took the salmon and motioned for me to follow him

We brought the fish with us as we swam from the house. This time, instead of taking me through the mer-city streets, we swam around the edge and out into the open sea without anyone seeing us. Fish munched on chunks of salmon, but my stomach couldn't handle any more raw fish. A warm meal was the only thing I was looking forward to on getting home.

I kept the thought of having the cooks prepare a huge hot meal for me at the forefront of my mind. Anything to keep it away from the pain that was already forming.

I planned to come back to the sea often to see him, but in the current climate, I wasn't sure it would be possible. At least, we had the secret tunnel, so I wouldn't have to walk up to the palace across the beach.

An hour later, we arrived at the underground door through the extensive network of tunnels. Fish wrapped his arms around me. "Promise me that you'll stay in the palace and listen to your guards."

I raised my hand and touched my heart. "I promise to stay safe within the four walls of this palace and not venture outside it."

"Good. I don't want anything to happen to you, and I can't protect you out of the water." His tone sounded unsure. "I really wish I had legs."

I almost laughed. "Please don't worry about me. Between the guards and my trusty knife, I'll be fine."

He kissed me as his thumb trailed the curve of my ear and whispered, "Meet me tomorrow?"

"I'm planning on it."

He kissed me once more and then began to backstroke, not breaking eye contact. "Tomorrow."

I nodded my head.

He bent his body, flapped his tail in the air twice, and disappeared into the water.

The door was unlocked, exactly as I'd left it. I slipped through, bolted it from the inside, and pushed the dresser back in place. Apart from a tell-tale displacement of dust, it looked exactly as it had before.

This time, instead of sneaking into the kitchen, I announced my presence.

The cook, a sturdy woman in her early sixties who was kneading a ball of dough, glanced up and down at my bathing suit and matted hair and narrowed her eyes.

"We wondered when you'd be returning." She pulled out an assortment of food, which she assembled on gold plates. "Your parents have been worried sick."

Guilt twisted in my stomach. "Did Sergeant Jimenez tell them where I was?"

She returned to the dough she'd been kneading, bashing it roughly with her hands.

"I guess someone told them. I heard that you were out in the ocean."

"I was. How did they take the news?" I should have told them myself!

She stopped kneading and looked up at me. "Your father was annoyed and rightfully so, but your mother thought it was hilarious. I think she thought you'd be back within the hour, what with you being afraid of water. You should tell John you're back so he can get word to them."

John was the palace chief advisor and pretty much in charge when the royals were out.

I picked up a couple of finger sandwiches and nabbed a tall glass of coconut water before thanking the cook and heading to my bedroom. I would have killed for a hot meal, one that didn't involve fish, but I needed to take off the bathing suit I'd been wearing for days and wash all the salt out of my hair. A hot meal would have to wait.

I stood inside the doorway, smiling at how normal my room appeared. My sanctuary, which allowed me to ignore all the worries of the world and relax, smelled like the sea. It held all my favorite things. I removed the belt with my knife and flung it on the bed.

I meandered to the bathroom, washed the sand off my body, and thoroughly shampooed my hair. With a towel wrapped around me, I glanced at the lavender nightgown with gold trim and matching robe on my bed. Dependable Emma never failed. No matter what happened, she always made sure everything I required was at my fingertips.

Slipping on both the silky nightgown and robe, I sat on the bed and ate my sandwich. I slowly sipped my drink, leaned back, and closed my eyes.

Footsteps outside my door prompted me to open my eyes. My hand reached for my knife where I'd left it on the bed.

Emma entered the room with a basket full of my sandals and shoes, all shiny and almost new. Her mouth formed a slight O before her lips curved into a genuine smile. She bobbed and rushed in, setting the basket by the closet. "I didn't know you were back! I've cleaned your everyday footwear so that it all looks like new. This was my last basket." She said it all in one breath.

"Thank you, Emma. Do you know if my parents are all right?"

I still hadn't been to see John. It was on my list of things to do.

Emma nodded and sat beside me on the bed. I offered her a finger sandwich, which she took.

"They left yesterday. One of your father's naval men came to the door and told them he'd spoken to you out in the ocean. He said you were with a merman."

My cheeks colored at her words. I nodded my head, and she giggled.

"Your father was certainly surprised."

I cringed. I should have told them. "Was he mad?"

"More shocked than mad. Your mother told him in no uncertain terms that you were an adult now. She did ask that word be sent to her as soon as you got home, though. They were worried about you. I should go and speak to a messenger."

"Please, can you speak to the chief advisor? He will send word."

"Yes, ma'am."

"What's it like out there?" I asked her as she stood.

"The riots are still happening. It's like the whole of Antla is caught up in it, and both sides are arguing. It's like everyone has an opinion on the matter."

"Isn't it totally awful?"

She nodded, and I found myself wanting to tell her everything.

I took a deep breath, and all my guilt, my worries, the mermaids screaming at Fish—everything—spilled out like hot lava from a volcano. I kept nothing from her. Tears accumulated behind my eyes.

"Everyone hates me. Humans because my mom transformed into a mermaid, which I had no control of, and merpeople because of how mean I was to some of them. It was always Hannah that shouted the insults, but I never stopped her." I clutched my head. "They didn't want to hear my apology, my pleas for forgiveness. They only wanted to shout at me. It's why I came home. I was making things worse."

"Oh, Princess Blaise, that must've been awful. It is not fair for them to act that way."

"They had every right. The AML has been the cause of the troubles right from the start, and I was a big part of that." I sighed. "If you were me, what would you do?"

She sat back down and thought. "Princess Blaise, you are in a unique position. You are the only person who is an active member of the AML who has also been to the mer-city."

"Former member of the AML," I said, butting in.

She nodded. "I would speak to the people so they can come together." She wrung her hands. "They need to hear you talk honestly to them. Apologize if you have to. Even beg them to let go of their grudges because keeping them will only hurt them." She nodded. "You need to do whatever you can to get everyone to let go of these prejudices from both sides. There is no point in talking to only one side of this mess. If you can reach everyone involved, then it might work."

"If only it could be done. It would be amazing if both groups gathered and I could convince them that we should work together. But neither side will listen." I sighed. "There is nothing I can do. It's so hopeless."

She walked over to my jewelry box and picked up one of my tiaras.

"With both the king and queen in hiding, you're the only one the townspeople will listen to. You are the head of the kingdom."

"Me?" I almost laughed. "Oh, no. I'm not the head. I'm only eighteen. I'm barely old enough to do anything."

"Age doesn't matter. What matters is that you speak honestly and with confidence." She rubbed one of the jewels on the tiara with a satin rag pulled from her pocket. "You've been trained to rule. You need to make everyone listen to you."

I shook my head. "I'm not prepared. I know how to hold the right fork, to set up a royal ball, to wear the right clothes, but not to rule a kingdom. And definitely not to help these two groups of people heal their differences. I wish I could, but I'm not ready."

Emma continued rubbing each jewel on my tiara, with strong strokes. "You see this tiara?" She raised it to eye level, the jewels creating colored rainbows against the walls. "This is the one you were to wear for the ball. It proves that you are a princess. Not an ordinary Atlanticean, but its future ruler. It means that the people must listen to you."

My eyes widened as I gawked at the tiara my mom had selected for me to wear the night of the Valentine's Day Ball.

It seemed laughable now, and yet the ball was still set to go ahead, as far as I was aware. I took the tiara from Emma's hands and ran it through my fingers.

"Here," Emma said, taking the tiara back and placing it on my head.

I looked at myself in the mirror. I was no longer a little girl playing dress-up. I was the future queen of Atlantice, and I had a job to do.

I just wasn't sure I had it in me to do it.

Emma smiled at my reflection.

"I don't know," I said softly.

She pulled me into a hug. "One day, you will be. I just hope it's sooner rather than later."

We were no longer mistress and maid. Somewhere along the line, we'd become friends.

4
8TH FEBRUARY

*A*fter spending the evening debating Emma's words and having a very long talk with John, the chief advisor, who tried everything to get me to go to where my parents were, I was no closer to knowing what to do.

On the one hand, I knew Emma was right. On the other hand, I didn't feel as though I could accomplish what my own father had not. It was all well and good, Emma telling me I was in a unique position, but she wasn't the one who had to stand up in front of a group of people who would see me as a traitor. The more I thought about it, the more my anxiety kicked in.

After a fitful night's sleep, I decided to go and see Fish to talk it through with him... or to escape my responsibilities. One or the other.

After traversing the rickety walkway through the secret tunnel, my hand firmly on the banister, I came out along the shore. I sat on a rock and waited for him.

I slid the avocado and olive sandwich I'd brought into my mouth. The waves crashed against the rocks, splashing tiny droplets of cold water on my feet and shins.

The peaceful sound supplanted the turmoil both above and

below the sea as I concentrated on enjoying my scrumptious sandwich and not letting my mind wander to the job Emma had suggested I do.

In the distance, a red tail broke the shades of blue between the sky and sea.

True to his word, Fish appeared in less than ten minutes from me reaching the shore.

I finished my sandwich and quickly placed everything I'd brought with me on the rocks. I retied my bathing suit straps to avoid a wardrobe malfunction in the water and turned to face the sea.

Splash, splash.

Diving until my fingers skimmed the sandy bottom, I pumped my arms and legs faster in his direction. A few feet out from the pier, he hovered with arms wide open. I grinned and pushed my arms and legs even faster until he engulfed my body with his embrace.

The feeling of being protected and safe in his presence caused my heart to swell with emotion. He held me tight, his tail propelling us out to the open ocean and away from the guards that patrolled the beach. The water swooshed past us. Seconds later, we broke the ocean's surface. The world spun before we plunged back into the water.

Once we reached the depths, he kissed me. I surrendered to the kiss, and all my problems melted away. It was easy to get lost in him when there was no one around, no one to bother us.

"How are you, Princess?" he asked later after we swam up to the surface. "I was worried."

"Perfect now that I'm here in your arms, protected from the world. How about you?"

"Same." His dimples appeared, and his fingers smoothed my hair. "What do you want to do today? I'm all yours."

My toes curled in the water, and I took several deep breaths in a feeble attempt to control my heart.

I stared out into the vastness and spotted one of our navy ships a couple of hundred yards away. It wouldn't be long before they spotted us. We were probably the reason they were out here in the first place. "One of the caves? Secluded from everyone?"

"Sure thing."

Once we reached the bottom, we headed away from the pier. Away from the madness that had disrupted my world in just a matter of days.

The sunlight touched the tall seagrass as it swayed back and forth with the mild current. We bypassed the coral reefs I had already explored and the ones that led to the entrance to his kingdom. He rotated his body and pointed to a bluefin tuna swimming beyond a new reef, silently questioning.

I froze, ogling him as he used only his tail to propel himself forward. With one hand, he captured the seven-foot tuna and headed to a sharp rock. In one swoop, using the rock as a knife, he filleted the fish.

Seconds later, he motioned for me to follow him. We surfaced into a cave I'd not seen before. Gold and silver covered the cave floor almost up to the ceiling. The piles of treasure didn't leave any space to walk on.

I whispered, "Is this a pirate's cave?"

He sheepishly grinned. "Yes, but don't worry, it hasn't been used for years. We think they forgot how to get here or all the pirates on that ship died without leaving a map." He shrugged. "It's safe." He handed me a piece of the tuna.

"I'm surprised none of the merpeople have emptied it out." I bit into the tuna.

"We don't need these material things as humans do."

His simple answer reminded me of the problems in both kingdoms and the reason I wanted to talk to him.

"My maid... friend, Emma, wants me to give a speech in Antla. She thinks I can stop the riots, but I can't do it."

"Why not?" he questioned, moving a wooden chest to one side so I could sit down.

I shrugged. "My father has done nothing but give speeches, and they've not helped at all. If they wouldn't listen to the king, why would they listen to me? I just want to escape from all of it."

"Isn't this your escape?" He handed me another piece of the fish flesh.

"Yes, but it's so temporary. I want to leave everything behind forever."

I hated saying it, but that was the mood I was in.

"Wouldn't you miss your parents, your life in the palace? Your comforts? You'd no longer have a palace with guards patrolling the area, so you'd always have to look over your shoulder. It's not as easy as you think."

"You're right." I agreed with a sigh. "I would miss everyone, but I would gain freedom. Complete freedom from royal protocol, from friends turning on me, from people who hate me. I'd love to find a place with no other people and be free to make my own decisions."

With a neutral expression, he said, "The excitement would wear off in a few days. Being alone isn't all it's cracked up to be."

His eyes lowered, and he seemed to close himself off. I wondered if he was speaking from experience.

"I wasn't thinking about being alone. I was thinking of being with you."

His eyes lit up, and he nodded. "It sounds idyllic," he said, planting a kiss firmly on my lips and handing me more of the fish.

I rested my head on my hand with my elbow propped on a free space on the rocky floor. "No more, thanks. The rest is yours." I watched him devour the fish. "I know it would be a lot of work, but maybe that's what I need. I've spent my whole life doing what I was told and playing the part of the obedient princess. Maybe it's time to just be me."

He cocked his head. "You really think running away is the answer?"

"I don't know, but hiding in a cave of treasure isn't it, either. And although Emma means well, I think she exaggerates my abilities. My father is the king and ruler of Atlantice, and it's his job to stop the riots, not mine."

He gazed into my eyes. "If that's what you really want. I have nothing to stay here for."

I stood up, too eager to sit still. "You agree, then?" My voice croaked from excitement. I'd been half-joking, using him as a sounding board, but now that he wanted to come with me, I realized I'd never wanted anything more. I would come home at some point to let my parents know I was alright, but in the meantime, I'd carve out my own life away from the responsibilities of being a princess.

"Thank you," I whispered, bending slowly over to kiss him. In the shimmering light of the gold treasure, sparkles danced across his face, moving with the motion of the ocean that lapped the cave floor beneath us. His lips found mine, and I closed my eyes, kissing softly at first and then with dizzying intensity that sent the world spinning around us, locking the pair of us in our own little world and bringing me, quite literally, to my knees.

We should have spent the day planning our escape, but for a large part of it, our mouths were being put to better use than mere talking. Eventually, the tide pushed us further into the cave, and we had to either move or fall into the water. As I was already breathless from kissing him, I decided to move back. I created a path through the trinkets, on which Fish crawled awkwardly before settling himself on the sand next to me.

We did make plans then. I couldn't run away with only a bathing suit to wear. It was okay for Fish to be naked, all his people were, but I wasn't quite ready to abandon my modesty just yet. I'd spent years being lectured about the right way to dress, but no matter how much I wanted to throw caution to the wind, and truly be free, shyness dictated otherwise. I would have to go back to the palace at some point to pick up some things.

"I'll really miss my mother," I said, thinking about all the times she'd lectured me on proper attire. There was a sweet irony to it, really. "I wonder why my mother transformed into a mermaid now," I mused aloud. "All my life, she's had legs and all of a sudden, boom, she's a mermaid. She had no control over the sudden transformation."

He glanced at me. "Do you have any inkling what caused it? Did something happen beforehand?"

I shook my head. "I can't think of anything. When she and I talked, there didn't seem to be anything specific that triggered it. She'd been moody for a few weeks, which wasn't like her, but I'm attributing that to the pain. Her feet had begun to hurt. I remember wondering if she was unwell. I guess it had been going on for a month, maybe two, before she changed completely back to how she used to be."

"Was she in a large area of water when she changed?"

I shook my head. "No, she was on land the entire time beforehand. She placed her legs near the water when the transformation happened. I got the feeling that she'd been turning into a mermaid and back again for a few weeks, but by the time I discovered it, she couldn't change back."

"I wonder if it has something to do with her avoiding sea trips."

He knew a lot about my family!

"That was never her," I said. "She always wanted to ride in the ships to the mainland, but my dad insisted she fly. He never wanted her to be near water. That's why he installed our indoor pool. He managed to create a smaller version of the sea so she wouldn't miss it." I gave him a half-hearted smile. "But despite the pool, she still missed the sea."

"Hmm, so it's not as though seawater fell on her, and she transformed?"

I hesitated, remembering everything she said before I witnessed her transformation. Nothing solid came to mind, and I shook my head. "That last time, maybe, but I've seen her in the pool hundreds of times over the years, and I can assure you, I'd have noticed if she had a tail."

His long fingers rubbed his chin. "Rules out water triggering the change. But there must be a reason why it happened. Some trigger point."

"That's my thought exactly, but I don't know. I don't even know where she is to ask her. When I was at the palace, the guards told me that my parents were safe, but they refused to tell me where they were hiding." I thought for a few minutes about writing her a note and asking one of the guards to give it to her, but then something else popped into my mind. "My mom kept a diary. If we find her diary, then maybe it'll say if she suspected why she turned. It'll be much faster than writing and having to wait for a response."

He reached for my hand. "Maybe this isn't the right time to escape?" His thumb rubbed the back of my hand. "If something happened to change your mom, maybe we should find out what. There's been a lot of weird stuff happening over the last couple of months, and I wonder if it's somehow connected. The sea currents are changing. The sea is much more volatile than usual. All the merfolk have noticed."

"The land people have noticed too. It's been in the papers." I hesitated for a second. "Do you really think we should investigate why she transformed instead?"

"It may not be what you want, but it may be what you need… And," he cleared his throat, "it may provide clues that tell us if there's a chance for you to transform." His lips pulled tight.

My face might have blanched because his right hand reached out and landed on my forehead before it cupped my chin.

"Are you okay?" He lifted my hand and kissed the back of it. "I didn't mean to scare you, but…"

I gaped at him. I had never thought that if she transformed, then maybe I could. Although having half her genes made it a distinct possibility.

I squeezed his hand and tried not to let panic envelop me. I'd pretty much been living as a mermaid for the past few days. Maybe having a tail would make things easier all around. And yet, however much I'd learned to love the ocean, and despite the fact I could breathe underwater, I didn't feel like a mermaid. I couldn't keep warm in the frosty ocean without Fish, and he instinctively knew how to weave through the waves in a way I would never be able to match, mermaid or not.

I sighed at the weird way in which my life had changed in such a short period of time. The irony that I might grow a tail and turn into a mermaid after so many years being active in the AML wasn't lost on me.

The journey back to the waterlogged tunnel was quicker than I had expected. We didn't breach the surface the whole time for fear of being spotted, but I didn't need to go above water to know there was a storm coming. Another one. Fish was right. We'd had more storms than usual this winter. The sea was much darker than usual, too, which made swimming harder. Thankfully, I had Fish to propel me through; otherwise, I'd never get back. Some mermaid I'd be!

The tunnel was as dark as it always had been, but thanks to the thunder clouds outside, it was barely darker than the open ocean. Fish knew exactly how far to travel, and when he stopped, I found we were at the steps next to the blue door.

"I should be back in about thirty minutes or so," I said, jumping out of the water into the drafty tunnels. "Don't venture off too far if you decide to explore."

"I won't." He grinned.

I returned his grin and slipped through the door.

Once in my room, I showered the saltwater off and changed into a clean bathing suit. Wrapping a robe around myself to keep warm, I sneaked to my parents' room. Usually, there would be a guard on duty outside, but with my parents away, most of the guards were assigned to the beach area and outside.

My mother wasn't the type to keep a secret diary. At least, I didn't think she was. Her diaries were more like journals chronicling her life as the queen of Atlantice. I always thought that one day, she was planning to pull the best passages from them and have them published. I ran straight to her bookshelf, where leatherbound volumes told the story of her life since her early days in the palace.

Grabbing one of the books from the middle, I opened it to the first page and noted the date, January 1, from about ten years ago.

I flipped to the middle of the book, and memories crashed back as I recalled the scene she mentioned.

She had written about the time I'd learned how to jump rope. She'd captured my clothes, the way I was so uncoordinated that it took me hours to learn. I closed my eyes and our garden with the roses climbing up the trellis wavered in front of me.

Happy memories mingled with the present as I flicked through the book of my tenth year.

I thumbed to the back. The last entry was from December 31 of that same year.

I placed it in a bag I'd found in my room and pulled out the diary from this year. Without reading it, I placed it in the bag with the other one. I was about to leave it at that when I realized that my mother's transformation might have happened sooner.

The other books would help me figure out when this thing actually began. I pulled them all from the shelf and heaped them into the bag, then hoisted the lot over my shoulder. The walk down through the palace was much harder than the walk up had been, what with the weight of the bag. But if I wanted to find out what caused this mess, I needed to dig deep, and my mother's journals were all I had to go on.

"Having fun while I do all the work?" I laughed as Fish swam figure eights in the shallow water.

"I have to practice my moves to keep you interested." He chuckled and waggled his eyebrows. "Did you find the diary?" He spread his arms wide in a lazy stroke that pushed him toward the edge.

Sitting down and dipping my feet into the water, I set the bag down. "I found a whole heap of them." The low light was not bright enough to read, so I placed my bag in a waterproof mailbag the palace staff used to give the mail to the mail-dolphins and splashed down into the water beside Fish. His touch warmed me immediately, and, not for the first time, I was glad I had him by my side.

We swam through the tunnels and to the next cove where we would be sheltered from the view of the palace. As we swam around the corner, a flash of thunder lit the sky, and the first spatters of rain began to fall. I didn't mind getting wet—I was already soaked to the skin from swimming and had been for days—but the rain was somehow colder than the ocean, almost sleet, and we couldn't read anything if the books got drenched.

"There's a cave over there," Fish said, pointing out a gap in the rocks.

We'd just made it to the entrance when a crack of thunder pealed through the sky.

Inside the cave was cozy and warm compared to outside, and though the sky was rapidly darkening, it was slightly brighter here than in the tunnel beneath the palace.

I let out a yawn as we came to rest on a soft sandy bed.

"Maybe we should check the diaries tomorrow," Fish commented, taking the bag from me and laying it down beside him. I snuggled up to his naked chest for warmth as the storm battered the rocks, and the wind howled outside.

5
9TH FEBRUARY

a gentle breeze lifted a tendril of hair that tickled my face. I reached up to push it back, waking Fish from his peaceful slumber in the process.

His long, dark eyelashes fluttered. Turning my body onto my stomach, I watched him as he came to. His eyes opened a slit, and he threw a lazy grin my way, sending tingles down my spine. He really was a masterpiece of beauty, with his long hair spread out behind him. I kissed him lightly on the lips, eliciting another grin from him, and then skipped to the entrance of the cave to rinse the sand from me.

Silently, I scooped up water and rinsed my face, tasting the salt on my lips. Using my fingers, I braided my hair and used a hair tie I kept on my wrist to fasten the end.

The weather had cleared during the night, leaving a fresh morning and cloudless sky. I turned back to Fish to find him reading my mother's journal.

I stretched my arms and cleared my throat, he didn't respond.

He continued reading, oblivious to me.

"Morning?"

So much was his absorption in my mother's words that he didn't even look up.

I inched my way toward him, observing him as he read with his forehead creased from lifted eyebrows.

"Couldn't wait to dig into my mom's diary, huh?" I said, sitting next to him.

He jolted, and the book dropped onto the sand. "How did you sleep?"

"Like a baby." I winked. "Which one are you reading?"

"There are twenty books here," he exclaimed, holding one of them up. "Each book has three hundred and sixty-five entries, so I figured we'd better get started." He sheepishly grinned. "I'm learning so much about your life."

The corners of my mouth quirked up, but inside I trembled from not knowing what my mother wrote.

"I'm not sure about you reading my mom's diaries," I laughed. "Should I worry about you prying into my life with such intensity? My mom could have written anything about me. Even the embarrassing stuff. Actually, knowing her, she totally wrote embarrassing stuff." I reached for the book in his hand, but he pulled it out of my reach with a grin.

He gave me a side-glance. "I like reading her words, especially when they provide snippets of your young life. I can imagine you as a child getting into these scrapes."

I rolled my eyes, trying to keep the tone light, but my insides churned at how my whole life was laid out before him with every embarrassing detail written in black and white. If it had been anyone else, I would have insisted on reading the diaries myself, but there was something about him that made opening up to him exciting… and more than a little scary.

"After skimming a couple of the diaries from when you were young, I finally found the first one. The one where your mom explains how she fell in love and how she lost her tail to acquire her legs."

"It's all there?" A shiver ran down my spine at the thought of what I was about to discover. My mother had mentioned briefly that she'd fallen in love with my father after saving him from a ship-wreck, and that she'd asked a sea witch to swap her tail for legs, but she'd been hazy on the details and remained tight-lipped when I'd questioned her further.

I sat cross-legged beside him as he flicked back to the very beginning of the first book.

"This one starts before you were born," he said, pulling himself into a comfortable position. "Your mother started writing this when she first came to the palace, but she begins by writing a bit about her life under the sea and how she came to the palace in the first place."

A ripple of excitement came over me. I'd never heard the full story, and I'd certainly not heard about her life before she came to the palace.

"She starts off by saying that she first fell in love with your father as a child. A statue of him when he was a young prince was appar-ently erected near the coast at the other side of Antla to commemo-rate his sixteenth birthday."

"I know that statue!" I gasped. "He's looking out to sea in it because he wanted to be in the navy. He got his wish not long after the statue went up. He was a naval officer for years before his father died and he became king."

"Yeah. I know the statue too. I can't imagine anyone falling in love with it, but there you go."

I laughed as he pulled a face. Yeah, it was weird, but my mother might have led a life like mine, one of loneliness. Wasn't falling for a statue less weird than joining an anti-merfolk league? It was less destructive, anyway.

"She wrote that she made a flower garland and hung it around the neck of the statue." He raised his eyebrows at me.

"Just keep reading," I chided him. "What happens next?"

"Well, this went on for some time although she didn't say how long exactly. She does say that her six sisters made fun of her for doing it."

I sat up straight. "Six sisters? I have six aunts out there somewhere?"

Fish shrugged. "I guess so."

I had a whole family under the water that I'd never met. And my mother had never mentioned them to me, not once. "How could she leave her whole family and never talk about them?"

Just the thought of it broke my heart. I'd yearned for sisters when I was a child. I'd practically begged my mother for a little sister. Or even a brother, but my mother always told me I was perfect, and she would never be able to beat perfection. It was cute, but it had never consoled me. I was lonely. I didn't want perfection. I wanted someone to play with.

"I don't think she left on good terms," Fish said. "It seems like they teased her a lot as she was the youngest. I'm not surprised she never mentioned them."

"So she fell in love with my dad's statue. Then what?"

"You're going to love this," he said, shifting position and changing the book from one hand to the other. "As you said, your dad loved to sail. She wrote two whole pages about the first time she saw him in real life. It was the middle of summer... Hang on, I'll read this part out." He put a slight inflection in his voice, heightening the tone to sound like what he thought my mother sounded like. It would have been off-putting, but as I was so desperate to hear what he had to say, I let it go.

"It was a beautiful summer day," he read aloud. "My sisters had been royal jerks to me all morning, so I decided to head to the surface to see the sun. I'd always preferred the light to the dark. I hadn't expected to see him, the man that would become the love of my life. Had I known, I would have done something, although I do not know what. Mermaids have no access to the items land ladies take for granted. No makeup, no hairbrushes, and none of the beautiful clothes I'm now so grateful for. I only had my charms, and as a mere sixteen-year-old, they were pretty thin on the ground. I still remember that moment as though it was yesterday. His windswept hair was nothing like the perfect style on the statue, but I recognized him immediately. My heart was pounding so quickly that I almost forgot how to swim. He sailed past me in his boat, so intent on his destination that he didn't even notice me peeking out of the water. Not that it was a bad thing. My hair was messy and tangled with seaweed. I was torn between following him and risking him seeing me looking like the gauche adolescent I was or letting him go and hoping he'd come back when I was slightly less messy."

Fish flicked his own hair in an attempt to be my mother.

I laughed. "Stop it. Keep going with the story. Did she follow him?"

Fish nodded. "Apparently, she did. Not only that day, but many others. Once she knew his route, she waited patiently for him and followed him every day for a year."

"Did he see her?"

"She says not," Fish replied. "She was too nervous to ever speak to him. I guess that's because she was a mermaid, and he was a land dweller."

I couldn't imagine being so infatuated with someone that I'd follow him for a year without making my presence known. It must have been so hard on her, and all the while, my father had no clue.

"Be prepared," he continued, "because it gets better. One day, lightning struck your dad's boat, and it capsized, rendering your father unconscious in the process. Your mother saved him and brought him to land, but she was too scared to let him see her as a mermaid. She made sure he was breathing and left him on the shore to wake on his own."

I sighed at the thought of it. Knowing how it had ended made it all the more romantic.

"She'd heard of a sea witch with supernatural powers, so she swam for hours to a dangerous part of the sea, far away from the kingdom, and asked the witch to replace her tail with human legs."

I couldn't imagine how much she loved my father to do such a thing. "Why would she do that?"

Fish shrugged. "Why do we do what we do? She loved him so much that she wanted to be able to meet with him on land. Our desires can drive us to stupidity." He rested the book on his lap. "I never told you this, but your mother wasn't the only one. The day we first talked might have been the first time you saw me, but it wasn't the first time I saw you. It took me weeks to build up the courage to talk to you."

Without thinking, my fingers slipped under his hand, and I squeezed it. "I'm glad you did," I whispered. The urge to kiss him right there and then was immense.

He pulled the book up to carry on reading, but my heart was insistent and my lips ready for him.

Positioning myself between him and the journal, I leaned forward and pressed my lips to his, slowly this time. I wanted to remember every part of it, the feel of his lips upon mine, the salty taste of him, the way my heart beat like the pounding of the waves upon the shore. My fingers found his hair, gripped it, and pulled, bringing him closer still until our bodies touched, melting into each other. He rolled me over, and a slight thump told me the book had fallen into the sand.

His kiss took my breath away, and the weight of him on top of me brought about deep desires I'd never known, feelings of urgency, of closeness, and of never letting go.

I probably would have stayed like that forever, but a rogue wave engulfed us, taking the journal back with it as it finished its journey upwards and started back to the sea.

"The book!" I screamed.

Fish leapt up and caught the diary quickly before it was lost to the ocean. He shook it, letting water drip all over me.

"I think we should take a break while this dries out," he said, placing it on a dry rock in the sun. "I don't think the water has damaged it too much. The ink hasn't run. I'm starving. Do you want me to find us something for breakfast?"

I nodded, the taste of salt—of him—still on my lips.

"Oysters would be good," I replied with a nod.

He leaned in and placed a single peck on my forehead. "I'll be back with lots of oysters. Maybe while I'm out, you can put the books in chronological order so it's easier for us to select the time frame we're looking for."

Responding to his gentle kiss, the corners of my mouth quirked up, and I said, "Sure."

"I won't be long."

I'd been so caught up in my mother's history that I'd completely forgotten the reason I'd taken the journals in the first place. I would have to read through them to find out why the sea witch's spell had reversed, but I needed to hear the rest of my parents' story first.

Figuring out the order of the books was a much simpler task than I had anticipated. On the very first page of each journal, she'd written the year in big writing. I piled the journals up neatly and waited for Fish to return.

I didn't have to wait for very long. Within ten minutes, he came back with an armful of oysters. With his bare hands, he pried open four and handed them to me.

"What about your breakfast?" I asked as he placed the rest next to me.

He sheepishly grinned. "This is my dessert. I sorta had a bluefin tuna."

The morning sun caught the side of his face, making the droplets of water still clinging to his hair glisten. As I ate, he sat next to me, doing nothing but watching me. Small tingles ran through my veins as, once again, I felt exposed to him in a way I never had with anyone before.

"Why don't you go and see if that journal is still legible," I said when I could stand it no longer. If he'd been eating, too, it would have been fine, but to have him watch me as I tipped oyster after oyster down my throat left me feeling almost naked.

"Where did we get up to?" he asked, picking the book up from the rock and prying the damp pages apart.

We'd gotten to the part that had made him admit he'd been watching me for a while before speaking to me, which in turn had made me want to kiss him, but I skipped past that. "Find the bit about the sea witch," I said, throwing the empty oyster shells back into the ocean.

Fish nodded and found his place. "The Sea Witch provided her with the legs, but it caused her an excruciating amount of pain when she walked. She wrote that it felt like the points of a sword jabbed the soles of her feet every time she stepped on them."

I gasped. "My mom had that same pain before she turned back into a mermaid. The guards had to help her walk."

Fish nodded. "She wrote that the Sea Witch warned her, but that she'd rather have the pain than not be able to win your dad's love."

"I can't believe she'd do that."

"Ah, well, there was another young lady who liked your dad." He cleared his throat. "And this young lady was not only beautiful but a princess. When your mom witnessed them together, her heart almost broke, which is when she started asking around about transforming herself."

I shook my head. She'd never mentioned any of this. I knew the royal families of all the kingdoms. Many of them attended the balls that my mother put on every year at Valentine's Day. Could one of them have been a rival for my father's affection? I wondered which princess it was and if I'd met her.

"Yes, and she wrote, 'My love for Prince Ermias is a thousand times greater than any pain I may suffer. I'd rather die than not be with him.' And she told the Sea Witch as much when she begged her for the legs. She really loved him, huh?"

I nodded. "She still does. It sounds weird when you read it out like that, but their love has lasted all this time. It's sweet, really. She went through so much for him."

"The rest of the entry is how she met your father with her human legs and how she danced with him while being in pain."

"My mother loved him so much that she underwent all that suffering and left her family for him. What a sacrifice. Now it makes sense why my dad never wanted her in the water. It's the one disagreement they always had when they needed to travel to the mainland. My mom always lost."

"Love will make us do crazy things." He leaned his head back, his gorgeous wavy hair fanned out on the sand behind him.

"The Sea Witch did this to her. Maybe she knows how to help my mother. Does the journal say where the witch lives?"

"Unfortunately, there's nothing else about the process or how the Sea Witch did it. She may be dangerous."

"Not all witches are dangerous," I pointed out. "Look at Enchantia. It's full of them, and most are really nice people. Queen Snow is lovely!"

He stared at me for a minute, his face contorting as if he tasted bad seafood. "Are you absolutely sure?"

"The Sea Witch gave my mom legs when she asked for them," I pointed out.

"Yeah, but she also made them painful. Who knows how long the pain lasted? We've only just started on the first book. Maybe the pain went on for years. What if your mother's feet always hurt?"

"They didn't!" I said a little too quickly. The thought horrified me. "She only started complaining of pain before her tail came back. One or two days at the most. She was in a weird mood for a few weeks before that, but at Christmas, she danced with my father for hours with a smile on her face. She wasn't faking. She was so happy. I doubt she would have been able to do that if her feet were killing her."

Fish shrugged as though he wasn't convinced. "You want to go find her, don't you?"

I thought of our plan of running away together. Before I'd read my mother's journals, it had been my only wish, but my mother had sacrificed so much to be with my father. Even though she'd been through all that, she was back to where she started with a tail instead of legs—and she was being vilified for it.

"Yes," I said. "I do."

6

10TH FEBRUARY

*P*lanning to find a witch in the ocean, as big as it was, was not an easy feat. But with a bit of careful reading, plus Fish's extensive knowledge of the ocean, we pinpointed a section of the ocean where we thought she might be. My mother had mentioned a part of the sea near Atlantice's unofficial borders with Floris, and Fish had worked out the rest with his knowledge of that particular area, which was very little. It was a fool's errand, and we were unlikely to find her, but if I did, maybe I could make my mother human again, and the mess happening in Atlantice would go away.

Or at least, it would lessen for my parents. If my mom could walk again, she would be able to return to the palace, and my father would be able to run the kingdom instead of being forced into hiding.

By the time Fish had made his mind up yesterday about the best place to look, the sun had already been high in the sky. We didn't want to be caught so far out at sea after dark, so we'd decided to get a good night's sleep and set off in the early morning instead.

Which is why I'd come back to the palace, and I was once again sneaking around my own home. I needed to pack some things, and I didn't particularly want to tell anyone why. My mother's history was hers to share, not mine, and I didn't want to be put in a position where I'd have to lie about where I was going.

After packing a number of bathing suits into a bag and filling the rest with packaged food, I slipped my knife into the side pocket and headed back to meet Fish in the secret tunnel. As my parents were away, the staff presence in the palace was pretty thin, and I managed to gather everything I needed and get back without being caught. We'd left the books in the cave, knowing they'd be safe there as no one could get to it from the land. I'd put them right at the back, high up on a rock, and weighed them down with a heavy stone in case a storm blew in and pushed the tide higher than it usually went.

Fish smiled sheepishly as I slipped through the door. "I'm not a hundred percent sure exactly where we need to go," he admitted.

I furrowed my brow as I slid into the water beside him. "Yesterday, you said you thought you knew where my mother was talking about."

He rubbed the back of his neck as his other hand moved lazily along the water's surface. "Yeah, I thought I did, but I want to make sure. I don't want to drag us on a wild goose chase. It won't take long. We can head back to the mer-city, and I'll ask around, just to confirm."

Blinking a couple of times, my voice creaked as I asked, "You want me to go back to the mer-city? Great. Excellent. Seaweed hanging in trees, fantastic!"

"What?" Fish asked, confusion clouding his features.

I covered my mouth to avoid spitting at him as I chortled. "You haven't heard of that expression? And you, a merman. I thought it came from your people."

"I have no idea what you are talking about."

It took a couple of breaths to ease off from my mirth. "Take the first letter of each word and spell it out." I repeated the phrase but emphasized the first letter of each word, using my finger to spell out the words for him. "Seaweed. Hanging. In. Trees."

His eyes widened before he chuckled. "Shit, indeed. I promise it won't take long."

I pulled the bag over my shoulder and took his hand. Just before we submerged into the water, I heard him mumbling "seaweed in trees" and following it with a laugh.

A rush of emotions flooded me as I remembered how the mermaids had treated me. Amidst the array of colors, my own color faded as the blood drained from my face and limbs. I was hated as much under the sea as my mother was on land. A trip to the mer-city would only draw attention to us, and then everyone would know where we were going. I didn't want everyone to know. As we exited the tunnel and daylight hit my eyes, the fear of heading back to the mer-city became too much.

I hesitated, pulling back on Fish's arm.

When he glanced over his shoulder, I shook my head so emphatically that my hair drifted in front of my face. I pointed up and continued my ascent to the surface.

As he breached the surface next to me, his eyes adopted a look of concern. "What's wrong? Are you okay?"

Shaking my head and waving my hands side to side, I shouted, "I'm not going back there. The merfolk hate me."

He lifted my chin, and our gazes met. "They don't hate you, they are just wary. Why don't we head to the pirate's treasure cave? You can wait there, and I'll find out where the Sea Witch resides. I'll come back as soon as I'm done."

I closed my eyes. "How long?"

"I'll be as quick as I can. I've heard rumors of the witch before, so she is known to the people there."

He took me to the cave and left me to wait. Without him, my temperature plummeted rapidly. It was so strange how he kept me so warm. I pulled a sweater from the bag and pulled it over my head.

While he was gone, I took a granola bar from my bag and chowed down on it. I was getting pretty sick of eating fish, though I'd never tell Fish that. It was all he ate. After taking a couple of swigs of juice I'd brought with me, I wandered around the cave. So much treasure hidden away where no one could find it. It seemed an awful waste, and yet, I had no desire to steal any of it. It was beautiful, but no more so than the treasures the palace already held. I might have been tempted to take a necklace or ring, but anything I took would only weigh us down, and I had no use for trinkets.

Without my watch, I had no way of knowing how long Fish took, but it was long enough for me to worry that he might want to leave our trip for another day. I didn't want to wait anymore. This had gone on long enough.

Eventually, though, he came back. His expression was enough for me to know that he'd found out the information we needed. I pulled the sweater off and bundled it back into my bag along with the empty granola bar wrapper.

"Let's go," he said, holding his hand out to me. I took it without question.

Less than a week ago, doing much more than dipping my toes into the ocean would have put me into a cold sweat. Now, here I was, swimming out into the deepest part of the sea, and I was looking forward to the adventure.

The sun was out, and although it didn't make much difference to the temperature of the water, which was still icy cold, it gave the impression of summer. Sharing Fish's body heat helped cement the impression.

I still didn't know how that worked. He only had to touch me with the tips of his fingers to warm my entire body. I was glad of it. Our friendship, or whatever it was, was only possible because of the weird magic. On my own, my body would succumb to the cold, and I'd be dead in less than thirty minutes. It was a scary thought, and one I tried not to dwell on as the land behind us got smaller and smaller. Before the land was out of sight completely, Fish pulled me under, and we continued our journey below the surface.

We swam for hours, skimming the seabed—or, at least, Fish swam, and I let myself be pulled along by him. My swimming wasn't particularly strong yet, and I'd never have kept up with him if I was left to my own devices. With little to do, I watched the underwater world pass me by, marveling that there was a whole other world down here, one so different from my own.

Eventually, the beautiful reefs of coral of every color gave way to boring sand with the odd sea plant. The deeper we swam, the darker it got, and before long, the sun's rays barely penetrated the water, and I had to squint to see. My head filled with tension, making me feel dizzy until the pressure became unbearable. I yanked on Fish's hand and pointed upwards. We swam up slowly with him stopping every minute or so for a break. My desperation to breathe clean air made me struggle to get out of his grip, but he wouldn't let me go, and it seemed to take forever to reach the surface.

"What did you do that for?" I wheezed, pulling air into my lungs. Immediately, the headache subsided.

"I forgot for a second that you are human," he explained.

"What?"

"Merfolk can withstand immense pressure under the sea. Humans find it tough. You can go down quickly, but if we'd surfaced too quickly, it could kill you. As soon as I saw your expression, I knew I had to get you to the surface. Your head hurt, didn't it?"

"It did. It's better now."

He nodded. "Next time we go down, I want you to hold your nose and blow to equalize the pressure. It will stop the headaches. Okay?"

"Okay."

"And when we resurface, we'll take it slowly."

I held my thumbs up, feeling foolish. I'd never thought about the water pressure. This time, when we traveled down, I did what he said. It worked, not that I had thought it wouldn't.

"Do you think the Sea Witch will hurt us?" I asked, suddenly feeling nervous now that we were so deep I could barely see. I honestly didn't believe she would, but I wanted to hear his voice next to me to reassure me that he was still by my side. He was still holding my hand, but it didn't feel like enough somehow.

"The person I spoke with said he didn't think she was dangerous. And while I didn't ask about her being mean or malicious, I don't think she is. We need to be careful and not ask her for anything. Apparently, she only barters for things she really wants, and she never accepts money as payment."

I wondered what she'd taken in payment for giving my mother legs.

We continued through fathoms dark and deep, slowing down to minimize bumping into a dying coral reef. Bereft of bright hues, this one contained various shades of grey tones.

I pulled closer to Fish, afraid of the sea creatures that might lurk around the corner.

"Princess, we're getting close. There will be another coral reef completely draped with the bones of dead sea creatures." He slowed his pace and pointed to the coral reef a hundred yards away. "I'm sure that's it."

I shuddered. "What? Is everything dead there?"

"From what I hear, yes, almost everything will be dead. Stay next to me when we meet her."

Like I was going to go elsewhere. I gripped his hand more tightly as we neared the decaying reef.

With nearly no light reaching this depth, I was having a hard time seeing exactly where we were headed, but my eyesight had strengthened over the last week or so, allowing me to see enough. Enough to know, I wished I'd stayed at home, at least.

A dark shadow rose at our right, but when I looked, there was nothing there. We inched closer, and as we did, the water became noticeably colder. A cold that Fish's warmth couldn't penetrate. I was about to suggest we leave this for another day when a grey shape loomed over the coral in the distance.

Had I been on land, I'd have inhaled sharply, and it took everything I had not to open my mouth at the sight of her. Fish stopped and swam slightly in front of me.

"Greetings! We want to speak with the Sea Witch. We've been told she lives in these waters."

As she moved toward us out of the murk, her figure took shape. I was surprised to see that she wasn't a mermaid, but something else entirely. A creature I'd never heard about. While her top half was that of a beautiful woman with long flowing hair, her tail was more akin to that of a seahorse than a fish. Her striking purple tail curled around at the end into a swirl, and I was sure that it would be rather striking if there was more light.

"I'm known as the Sea Witch in these waters." She spoke with a clear and pleasant voice, which put me at ease. I'd been expecting something horrific, especially after passing through the dead reef, but as she came closer I saw a kindly face set in a smile. She lowered her head and inspected us. "How may I help you? Is there something you wish to barter? Something in the bag, perhaps?"

She swam to us and then whipped around me, fingering the bag. As I turned my head to look at her, she arched her brow.

"There's nothing in there beyond some old clothes and a bit of food," I said.

"We are here because we were hoping you'd be able to answer some questions for us," Fish said.

With a sly smile, she asked, "What are the questions you desire me to answer, handsome merman?"

Handsome merman?

"Do you remember a young mermaid you helped get legs about eighteen, nineteen years ago?" I replied for him, making sure I was between them. She could keep her mitts to herself if she thought Fish was on offer.

The Sea Witch glided around me, her tail curling and uncurling slowly while her fins beat faster than a hummingbird's wings. "Ah, the little mermaid from the kingdom far away. You know her?" She narrowed her eyes, light emerald dotted with black specks, beautiful with a hint of secrecy behind them.

"You remember her?" Fish asked with a hitch in his voice.

Her eyes fixated on his. "Of course, I remember everyone I help. As a witch I have a lot of power to help those without any." She grinned.

"You can't imagine how much pleasure it gives me to grant people their wishes, especially those who are good. And she was one of those people..." She looked to the sea behind us as though she was thinking back. "Maybe I can help you?" She pointed her long, thin fingers at Fish. "Whatever your heart desires, I can grant for a lifetime."

He bowed, lowering his eyes. "I will definitely keep that in mind, but right now, I want to know about her transformation and the forever part."

"Anything your heart desires," she repeated breathily, getting close to him. "What is it you desire?"

The way she gazed at him made me nervous, almost as though she was casting a spell on him. I desired for her to get out of his face, but I could hardly say that.

"Can you tell us what happened to the girl you helped?" Fish asked.

"Ah, yes," she said, swimming away a little. "Sometimes, my mind wanders. But that sweet child was so special, one of a kind. I could never forget her. She had so much love for that prince." She sighed. "She so desperately wanted human legs that she would do anything for them." Shaking her head, her cobalt blue and emerald hair fanned until it gently landed on her shoulders.

"Her tail is back," Fish said. "After all these years, the spell reversed. Did you have something to do with that?"

The witch ran her index finger across her lower lip. "That's odd. The spell should've lasted her entire life. It was one of my more powerful spells." She tapped her lips with the same finger. "You're sure she lost her legs and regained her tail?"

"I actually saw her transformation," I said. "One minute, she had human legs, and the next, she had a tail." I shrugged. "We can't figure it out. We thought you would know, as you were the one to give her the legs."

"You saw it happen? You know her? I heard she went on to become the queen of the land."

"She did become queen. She is my mother."

On hearing this, the witch's eyes widened briefly before going back to normal. She placed her hand on my shoulder.

"I'm sorry to hear your mother is having problems," she said, playing with my hair. "Such a nice girl to come this far to help her. I notice you haven't got a tail. Would you like one?"

I shook my head. "No, thanks."

A school of fish swam near us, heading in her direction, then quickly returned our way. I watched them move in one humongous circle.

"Hmm." She studied me up and down. "You are not a mermaid, and yet, you swim underwater. Interesting… and strange."

Fish swayed his tail impatiently. "Could your spell have worn off? It's been eighteen years."

She waved her hands. "Oh, no. Once they're transformed, they cannot return to their original state. It is permanent and irreversible. All my spells are."

"Maybe she wished for her tail back. I know she missed the sea."

"That could never happen," replied the witch. "My spells are so powerful that neither the power of a person's mind nor the passage of time can undo them. It's funny, but I never expected…"

I waited for her to finish the sentence, but when she didn't, I asked her. "Expected what?"

"Oh, nothing," she said gaily. "I'm just intrigued by you. A half-human and half-mermaid, and yet, you are neither of those things."

"What do you mean?"

"Oh, nothing. Pardon me. I don't get many visitors, and I forget myself sometimes. Is there anything else I can help you both with?"

Fish bowed. "Thank you so much for assisting us. We appreciate you answering our questions. You've been most gracious and generous with your time."

But she hadn't helped us. She didn't know why my mother transformed back any more than we did. According to her, it was impossible, and yet, I'd seen it with my own eyes. Maybe she wasn't as powerful as she made herself out to be.

She beamed. "Won't you stay and join me for a light supper, at least? You've come a long way. You must be hungry."

He shook his head. "No. Thank you for the generous offer, but we have to return."

She nodded, but her piercing eyes remained on mine. "It's been a pleasure, and please don't hesitate to return, my dear merman... and you with the beautiful golden-ringed eyes... Such stunning eyes."

Fish pulled me away slowly after we'd said our goodbyes. The witch had been perfectly nice to us, and yet, our meeting left a sour taste in my mouth—and I wasn't just talking about seawater. There was something odd about the way she looked at me. When we'd first shown up, she'd only had eyes for Fish, but the second I mentioned who I was, her attention fixated on me. And that thing she said. Neither mermaid nor human? Was she talking about me being half of both or something else entirely? When I'd called her out on it, she'd passed it off as her forgetting herself. What did that even mean?

Once I knew we were out of earshot, I spoke to Fish. "She's hiding something. I don't know what, but I think she is."

He turned to face me. "I think you're right, but there is nothing we can do about it."

As we swam toward the light and away from the Sea Witch, I began to feel better about things. We'd not learned anything that would help my mother, but I wondered if I had worried too much about the witch. Now, in the light of day, the whole thing seemed silly.

And yet, I couldn't shake off the feeling she knew more about me than I did.

7
11TH FEBRUARY

I awoke the next morning in the sea cave where we'd spent the previous night. A grey mist clung to the rocks, mirroring my own mood. I pulled myself up and headed over to my bag. Fish always kept me warm, but I craved the warm hug of my sweater. I'd been wearing bathing suits for days, and I was sick of it.

I pulled the sweater over my head, then grabbed another granola bar and bottle of water, and made my way back to where Fish was sleeping. He'd slept with his arm around my waist, but now that I'd moved away, it was splayed out on the sand. Stifling the urge to take it in mine, I ripped the packaging off the granola bar and swallowed it in two bites. Dinner last night had been raw fish again, and while Fish never seemed to get enough, I was thoroughly sick of it.

I didn't want to admit it, but I needed to go home. How could I have thought about running away only days before? It made me want to laugh. Out in the sea, I would have lived a life of bathing suits and cold fish for every meal. Meanwhile, I craved normalcy and a hot meal. I wanted a shower and to wear socks. All the things I'd taken for granted, I now wanted more than anything.

Most of all, I missed my parents. While they were hiding from threats of being killed, I was hiding away from everything. The kingdom was going to crap, and its leaders were nowhere to be seen.

It wasn't fair. It wasn't fair to the people, it wasn't fair to my parents, and it wasn't fair to me.

I looked over at Fish, and my heart did a double beat. If he wasn't so inordinately beautiful, this wouldn't be so hard. If he was ordinary or pedestrian in any way, or in any sense of the word, I wouldn't feel so conflicted, but he wasn't. He was special, and wonderful, and all the other words people used to describe the person they loved, none of which were quite enough.

And I did love him. I'd suspected it for some time, that my feelings were growing stronger, but it wasn't until the sea witch looked at him so intimately that I felt a sucker punch of jealousy to the chest. It wasn't as though she had even wanted him, per se. She had only wanted to barter, and yet the thought of her, or anyone, having him made me feel sick to my stomach.

I didn't belong with him in the sea, but I no longer belonged on land either. Like the Sea Witch had said, I was neither mermaid nor human, but somewhere in between. Someone that fit in nowhere.

I wanted to wake Fish to tell him I needed a break, but the thought scared me. I didn't want a break from him, merely the sea, but what if he didn't see it that way? If I could have taken him up on the land, I would have, but he wouldn't be able to go anywhere with his tail. Just like my mother and father had been, we were destined to be apart, and yet hadn't my mother broken her own destiny? She had until now, anyway.

Fish stirred, breaking me out of my thoughts. I swallowed, knowing what I was about to say would hurt him.

"Hey, you," he said lazily, turning in the sand, his eyes focusing on me.

"I need to go home. I'm sorry."

Tears welled in my eyes as I waited for the backlash. But there was none. He held his hand out to me. "I've been thinking the same thing," he said, pulling me into a hug.

As he wrapped his arms around me and the heat pounded through my body, I wished I could stay exactly where I was forever.

"You know where I am if you ever need me."

"I don't mean forever," I said in a rush.

He pulled me tighter. "I know you don't. You are a land dweller, and it's where you belong. I'd feel pretty weird being out of the sea for more than a few days."

"But doesn't that make you sad?" I asked. "You belong in the sea; I belong on land."

He turned me to face him. He was so close, I could feel his warm breath on my cheek, and when he looked at me, I could see forever.

"It doesn't mean we don't belong together," he said, stroking his hand through my hair. "It just means we can't be together all the time."

"But I want us to be together all the time." I sighed.

He sat up, pulling me with him. "I do, too, but I've seen your reaction every time I give you raw fish."

He pulled a face, making me laugh. "I look that bad, huh?"

"I can't cook underwater, and any food I can get from the shops will inevitably be waterlogged. I can't change that, but I can let you go home to eat every once in a while. I've got things to do anyway. I've neglected my own life."

"I'm sorry."

"Don't," he said, pulling me toward him. He kissed me lightly on the lips. I closed my eyes and inhaled his salty scent. "Don't apologize for giving me the best week of my life."

My heart warmed to his words. I knew that the last couple of weeks had been amazing for me, but it was nice to hear he felt the same way.

"If only the merfolk liked me. Things might be different."

My own prejudices against them had influenced how I treated them, which, in turn, led them to hate me.

A vicious cycle of my own doing.

I could have blamed it on Hannah, on her influence as my best friend, but at the end of the day, I was the one who had made the choice to mistreat them, to show them hate, not her. The AML may have influenced and misled me, but I hadn't stopped to meet merpeople and find out the truth.

"If only the land folk liked us," he countered.

"Ugh, you're right. I just don't know what to do to rectify things."

"Beats me how we can bring both groups back to a semblance of civility." He ran his fingers through his long tresses. "This whole situation seems to have been blown out of proportion, and it's asinine. Both worlds are as bad as each other. It's never been perfect, but in the last few months, things have become intolerable. I wish I knew what had changed so suddenly."

"My mother turning into a mermaid?" I offered.

"I think that's a symptom of the problem and not the cause of it."

"What do you mean?"

"Things have been different for a while. Way before your mother's transformation." He drew closer, leaning in real slow, and kissed me. "I'm so sorry that I can't figure this all out. I wish I could."

We gazed into each other's eyes, and I could see how much this bothered him. As much as it did me.

I sighed and began to stand, but he pulled me back down to the sand before lifting my chin and gazing into my eyes. "Don't allow what we're going through to destroy who you are. I know it's tough, but we'll get through this."

My fingers intertwined with his. "I hope you're right."

He shrugged. "We've been away a while. Maybe there's been a breakthrough that we don't know about. Your parents could be back in the palace waiting for you to come home." His dimples appeared as he smiled.

I loved his optimism, but I knew he was wrong. I could feel it in my heart.

"I want to swim to my own kingdom and see what is happening there," he continued. "It's not just the land dwellers with the problem. The merfolk have developed a major attitude, too. You do what you need to on land, and I'll work on the merfolk."

Having a plan made me feel a little better about the situation and made me more determined to face my problems.

I gathered the books up and slotted them back into my bag in preparation for going home.

I remained silent on the short journey around the cove and into the tunnel that would take me home. What else was there to say? It felt like something was ending as I left him at the secret door to the palace, but he assured me he'd be back as soon as I needed him. I gave him a quick goodbye kiss and slipped through the door.

My room looked exactly the same as when I'd left it. Nothing had been moved, no new clothes had been laid on my bed, and the basket of cleaned shoes Emma had brought to me the last time I was home was still on the floor where she'd left it.

Strange. Where's Emma?

After a quick shower, I slipped on a dress, loving the feel of the fabric after days of wearing a wet bathing suit. Pulling on a jacket over it, I headed toward the dining room.

My mouth dropped at the emptiness of the room. A fine layer of dust coated the dining table, and while the table was set, no one had eaten in the room in days.

Not one single item was out of place.

I rushed out of the room and sprinted toward the kitchen.

Empty.

The entire hallway was devoid of guards and staff.

Where did everyone go?

I pushed open the kitchen doors and stopped dead in my tracks. The room sparkled as if the staff had spent days cleaning it, but there was no one there.

I brought my hand up and rubbed the back of my neck.

I ambled to the main rooms on the first floor. But every room remained unoccupied. It was as if the entire palace was uninhabited.

What is going on?

Clink clank, clink clank. Silence. Clink clank, clink clank. Silence.

The loud noise sounded as if it came from the ballroom.

I pivoted on my toes and hurried to the source of the noise.

Emma hurried from the outside terrace doors, holding a step stool in one hand. She grinned at me. "You're back. Thank goodness you're back." She placed the stool on the floor and curtsied.

"Emma, where is everyone?"

Clink clank, clink clank. Silence.

"And what is that noise?"

"Someone forgot to properly lock the window in the ballroom. The lock doesn't automatically return to its place unless you force it to, so every time the wind blows, the metal hits both glass and metal. It's the one on the top, so I was looking for the step stool to fix it." She picked up the stool. "Care to help?"

"Sure." I followed her to the windows.

She stopped and gently set the stool next to the window. I held it for her as she stepped on the first rung

As she fixed the lock, I took a look around the ballroom. It was decorated for the ball with beautiful sashes of purple and pink and tables and chairs laid out, waiting for party guests. A huge tank stood at the far end filled with water

"Why is the room decorated and what's that tank for?"

Emma fixed the lock and stepped down. "Just in case your parents return, and we have the Valentine's Day ball." She smiled. "The queen sent word that they're still hoping to be home by then. The tank is for her for when she returns. Repairs are still being done to the pool room."

"You've heard from her? Is she all right? When did she say they were coming back?"

"She didn't specify a date." Emma sighed. "She just said she hoped this would all end soon. I think she wanted us to decorate the ballroom so she could remain hopeful about everything going back to normal. Her letter also had instructions to send all the palace staff home until further notice. A few of the guards are still here, although most are out in the towns dealing with the problems there. I elected to stay behind, as did a few others, but as you can see, the palace is mostly empty."

I'd never heard the palace so quiet. With the normal everyday hustle and bustle of staff, advisors, and guests gone, the place seemed desolate.

"I don't suppose she mentioned where they were staying, did she?"

Emma shrugged. "I didn't read the message. I'm only relaying what was told to all the staff by the head palace advisor. He's still here if you want to ask him."

I nodded my head. I needed to see my parents to make sure they were okay. The head advisor had already told me that he'd organize safe passage for me to wherever they were.

"If you'll forgive me, Your Highness, I don't think you should go to them."

"What do you mean?" I asked, furrowing my brow.

Emma tapped her feet on the floor and wrung her hands as she plucked up the courage to say what she had to say.

"You have the ability to stop the people from creating more havoc."

I held my hand out to stop her from speaking.

"I can't do it, Emma. If my father can't make a difference, why should I be able to? I'm only back to see my parents. I need to talk to them."

"You doubt your own abilities. One day you will be the queen of Atlantice, and you won't be able to wait for your father to make a difference. It will be all on you. Do you want to lead a divided kingdom when your time comes, or do you want to heal the divide now while the rift is still young?"

Emma picked up the stepstool and hurried out, but she halted at the door and glanced over her shoulder. "It's not always been this way, and you know it. Your father doesn't know the AML, but you do. Your father doesn't know the merfolk. You are the only one who knows both well enough to get them to listen. I guess you need to decide what kind of ruler you want to be."

She left the room, and once again, the silence deafened me.

Her words impacted me in a way I had never thought they

could. She was right. I'd spent so long figuring out how to run and hide when I should have been working on coming up with a solution.

I meandered around the room, touching the glass vases and silk chair coverings. I traced a couple of the names that had been embroidered with gold thread on the sashes tied to the chairs. Even the linen table runners had been ironed until there wasn't a single wrinkle.

Standing alone in the room, I felt a burning desire to rise above my insecurities brought about by the people of Antla, by the merpeople who decided not to extend grace, by Hannah who didn't respect my title.

I straightened my shoulders and marched out of the ballroom.

Those rioters were my people, people I loved, and who loved me. Maybe she was right, and they would listen if I showed up and pleaded with them to hear me out.

"Emma, where are you?" I raised my voice. "Emma? Emma?"

She sprinted back from the terrace and took a couple of deep breaths before she answered, "Yes, Your Highness?"

"I'm going to speak to the chief advisor. I'm going to do as you say. Please, can you make sure the west terrace is clear? I'm going to make a speech to the public."

Her eyes opened wide, and she nodded. "Of course." She gave me a little curtsey. "When do you want to speak to the people?"

"One hour from now. That should give us all enough time to collect everyone." I hesitated before I built up my voice. "I can do this!"

Emma bent her knees with a huge grin as if I had gifted her a million shells. "I'll have the others spread the word. We'll get everyone to gather by that balcony," she said before she ran out of the room.

My next visit was to the palace chief advisor. He was the highest-ranking person in the palace after the actual royal family.

"John?" I said after knocking on his office door. Almost immediately, the chief advisor opened the door. John was a tall, reedy man in his early fifties, always immaculately dressed with never a hair out of place.

"Your Highness." He greeted me as enthusiastically as only John could do, which wasn't a lot. "It's good to see you. I'm sure your parents will be happy that you have returned. Would you like me to send word to them?"

"Yes," I replied hurriedly. "But after that, I need you to get the staff back in as quickly as possible. I also need you to send word to the townsfolk to come to the palace. I'm giving a speech in just under an hour on the west balcony."

John's eyes widened. "A speech? What kind of speech?" He clearly didn't think I was up to the job.

Perhaps he was right, but I was determined to do it anyway.

"I was in the AML, and I've just spent the last few days underwater with a merman. I think I'm the only one in a position to see both sides."

His eyes almost popped out of his head at my admission, his mouth hanging open comically.

"John!" I shouted, to snap him out of it.

"Oh, yes, right. I'll get to it." He disappeared into his office before coming right back out again. "I wonder if it would be prudent to let me help you with the speech?" he said, reverting back to his normal efficient self.

"No, thank you, John, I've got it."

I gave him a wink, feeling more confident than I had any right to, and headed back to my room. If I was going to deliver a speech in front of goodness only knew how many people, then I was going to look my best while I did it.

After carefully applying my makeup and finding a better dress to wear, I began the walk to the west balcony, rehearsing what I was going to say in my head.

Emma found me halfway along the main corridor. She had to run to keep up with me.

"The messengers have gone out, and the west balcony is ready. I've instructed the few guards I found to help out and..."

"Thank you," I said, cutting her off mid-flow. My brain was scrambled enough without needing to know more. Either people would show up, or they wouldn't.

I had no doubt the Conch would send some reporters out at the first hint of the princess making a speech. I wondered if they already knew where I'd been for the past few days. Probably. I thought back to the way Jimenez had looked at Fish. It was the same look of disgust I'd used when I first saw him.

Still, I didn't have time for regrets. I was on my way to make things right. If Jimenez had told The Conch that I'd been in the ocean with a merman, then so be it. It would come out one way or another, and if the people didn't already know, they soon would.

We headed to the west end of the palace and climbed the tower to the balcony overlooking the town. The very same balcony where my mother and father had kissed on the day of their wedding and where I'd been introduced to the people. I rarely ventured to this part of the palace except for royal occasions that dictated I must parade myself in front of the public. Two guards stood in front of the doors and pushed them open at my nod. They sounded the trumpets, and I stepped onto the balcony.

Nothing prepared me for just how many people had turned up at such short notice. I'd purposely left as little time as possible so I wouldn't have to speak to so many, but the square at the other side of the palace wall was heaving with people. The noise was deafening.

Underneath my long dress, my legs trembled. The people shouted obscenities and raised their fists in my direction. A quick sweep of the crowd told me that there were many AML members in attendance. I couldn't see Hannah, but I knew she had to be there somewhere.

"People of Atlantice!" I began, my voice wavering.

Barely anyone stopped their own yelling to listen to me. I cleared my throat, pulled myself up to my full height, and tried again.

"People of Atlantice!" I shouted.

More people raised their eyes and lowered their arms, and then silence cut through.

"I come to you today to beg you to halt the rioting and to stop the fighting. We're better than this."

A few more lowered their arms, but only to cross them, their faces filled with acrimony as they stared at me.

"As Atlanticeans, we are better than this," I repeated, trying to remember everything I'd rehearsed on the short walk through the palace. "We have always known how to converse with each other so that we are all heard."

"You traitor!" someone shouted from the crowd.

I guessed my days with Fish hadn't gone unnoticed after all.

Emma drew closer and reached for my hand, keeping a step back so she wouldn't share the limelight.

Taking a deep breath, I allowed the multitude of boos to be subdued by my silence.

I raised my voice an octave higher, "We are from a small island, but we are mighty and strong. We are passionate about our beliefs, but we're also caring and can listen to the other side."

I met the glances of several, who nodded.

"I've been underwater and spent time with the merpeople."

The group that had originally booed shouted more obscenities again along with the AML crowd, but I waited, scanning the area and lingering to meet the eyes of those who seemed to be listening.

"Yes, I've actually met a few merpeople, and they're not the killers we've been led to believe. They are not evil. They're not killing our fisherman." I shook my head. "They're actually like us. They've been hurt like you have by the lies the AML told. You know that I was part of the AML and that I also believed their propaganda, but that is all it was."

I took a deep breath and looked around the crowd.

"Propaganda brought to you by hate-mongers. I'm ashamed to say I was one of them. For a long time, I listened to them and believed them, just as you have been listening to them, but I was wrong. I was very wrong."

The crowd paid attention with only a handful protesting now, their voices lower as other people waved at them to stop.

"And those lies that I, along with many of you, believed and spread hurt us all. They pitted us against the merfolk and them against us." I placed my free hand against my heart. "I'm truly sorry that I was deceived, and in turn, I passed on the lie to more members of the AML than I care to list."

The crowd buzzed, but they, at least, no longer shouted.

"I was saved by a merman just eleven days ago. He didn't have to save me, but he did. Does that ring true with what you've been told?"

I paused as a group of AML people jeered "liar" and "traitor." Finally, my eyes rested on Hannah, who had muscled her way to the front. She glared at me from her position on the street. I could tell this was hurting her.

Emma leaned back and pulled on my hand but didn't release it.

Ignoring Emma, I continued, "Can any of you honestly say that you know of a firsthand account where a merperson hurt you? Or did you wrong? I'm not talking about the garbage spewed by the AML, but something you've witnessed with your own eyes?"

The crowd was noticeably quieter now, so I carried on.

"I know the business owners are struggling. I know they are losing money because of all this hate. I can see some of you down there. Shop owners that had a roaring trade a few weeks ago, thanks to the money brought in by the merfolk. Now that you've allowed yourselves to be bullied into not selling to the merfolk, aren't you suffering as much as they are? I know a lot of you want to open your shops to everyone, and I know the AML has threatened you if you do."

More and more people nodded their head, and a dozen or so actually clapped. Hannah screamed, "All lies," and her people booed as she began to lead them out of the square. I watched her barging past the rest of the townsfolk, her AML cronies in her wake.

"Please help me to heal our town and establish good relationships with the merpeople so that we can live in peace. If we are able to work with the merpeople, then our fishermen will be safe from sharks and any other threats in the water."

The AML reached the edge of the crowd and shouted, "Death to the merpeople" and "We'll hunt them down until they're all extinguished," but I continued encouraging the people who stayed.

"We can get along with each other and work together to restore peace to our great island."

Surprisingly, only a dozen people stormed out with Hannah, and I smiled at the majority of the town who remained.

"Thank you so much for your willingness to listen. To help me stop the disruption these riots have caused our town." I blew a kiss out to the crowd. "I love you all, and again, thank you for listening to me. We can work together to return to our peaceful state."

The crowd clapped as I left the balcony.

Emma squeezed my hand. "Princess Blaise, you did amazing. I knew that you could do it!"

I could barely breathe from the anxiety that speaking to the people had produced. My stomach was in knots, but as I looked into Emma's beaming face, I knew I'd made a change.

How much of a change remained to be seen, but I'd gotten through to some of them. That was as much as I could hope for.

"Thank you for having faith in me." I beamed, bringing Emma into a hug.

The palace had come to life in the short time I was out on the balcony. The sounds of the staff coming back filled me with joy. At the bottom of the tower, John greeted me.

"You did very well, Your Highness. The king and queen would be proud of you."

It was high praise indeed from John, the man of few words. I thanked him and headed out to the beach. A couple of guards patrolled the perimeter, but nothing like the presence from the week before. They paid me no mind as I kicked off my shoes and ran out onto the sand.

Meandering to the pier, I scanned the vastness of the sea with a huge grin.

I wondered how Fish had done with the merfolk. After all, I wasn't the only one trying to win the people over. Fish had been trying to do the same.

I waited impatiently for him to surface, dipping my feet into the cold water. Without him holding me, it was much too cold to keep them in for too long, and yet I longed to jump right in. After all that time in the water, I was confident I could swim without Fish's help. What I wasn't confident of was not turning blue.

"Fish, where are you?" I shouted, pulling my feet back up onto the pier and wrapping my arms around my legs.

A thought occurred to me that he might be waiting for me in the tunnel, so I stood up and headed back into the palace. Inside, I was greeted by many members of staff as I rushed to get to my destination.

Pulling open the secret door behind the bookcase, I headed out into the underground tunnel. There, waiting for me, was Fish. Ripples on the surface gave him away. In the dim light, I could barely see a thing, but I could hear the splashes in the water. Sitting down on the steps, I began to pull my clothes off so I could join him. I laid my jacket neatly to my side before pulling my dress off.

"I think they listened to me," I jabbered excitedly as I folded the dress and placed it on the jacket. In only my bra and panties, I took a breath and leapt into the water to the spot where Fish was waiting for me.

As it always did when he touched me, warmth shot through my body, but this time, it was accompanied by a strange buzzing sensation. Something flashed in front of me, lighting up his face, but it wasn't him at all.

I was looking into the face of the Sea Witch.

THRONE OF CHANGE

12TH FEBRUARY

*T*he blackness receded, a nightmare that had run through my thoughts all night. My neck twinged from the awkwardness of the position I'd slept in. Pulling my arm back to massage my neck, I opened my eyes. And that's when I realized the nightmare hadn't been a product of my imagination at all, but very real.

Jumping up, I almost slid over on the slippery surface beneath me. I was in some kind of bubble, which explained the lack of purchase under my feet. I wasn't standing on a flat surface, but the inside of a sphere.

Outside the sphere, the darkness moved weirdly. It was only as I squinted my eyes and peered out that I saw that I was under the sea.

I had no recollection of the night before, beyond the yellowing eyes of the Sea Witch staring at me. I'd swam toward her thinking she was Fish and then the horrible reality of who she was came crashing down, right before she grabbed me. Just thinking back to the night before broke me out in a cold sweat, and my breath caught on the inside of the weird bubble I was trapped in. Once the Sea Witch's arms had enveloped me, everything became hazy. The very last thing I remembered as the world around me went black was the sound of her poisonous cackling, a sound that was still reverberating through my brain all these hours later. At least, I assumed hours had passed, although under the sea as I was, with little light, it was hard to tell. The air-filled globe encapsulating me was made not of glass but of something else. It was transparent enough to see out of, but it's edges undulated, not quite keeping their spherical shape. I found that if I pushed the edges, I could make it move slightly. It had the consistency of rubber, but it was not rubber that held me. The whole thing was magic. It had to be. I could breathe in it perfectly normally, despite being under the ocean. It wasn't like the way I breathed through the water, but how I breathed on land. I felt down to my clothes to find they were dry. I wondered if magic was involved in that, too, or if I'd been unconscious long enough for my underwear to dry. It was all I had on. I couldn't see anything tethering the bubble to the seabed, and yet, it hovered in one position, only swaying gently in the slight current.

Darkness surrounded the outside of my prison, and I squinted. Everything appeared devoid of life with only the dark greyed reefs nearby. Even the seaweed below the see-through enclosure contained only hints of a pale green color amidst the putrid tone.

Sitting down, I ignored the seagrass basket full of grey-colored seaweed and shucked oysters by my feet and picked up one of two glass containers filled with water. I swigged it back, desperate to rid myself of the salty taste in my mouth.

Delicious, fresh, water.

It allayed my fears that the witch wanted to kill me. At least, not yet.

I grabbed at the spot where I kept my knife, only to find that I'd lost it somewhere on route. Not that I knew what I was planning to do with it. I doubted a small knife could cut through magic and if it had, then what? If the bubble popped, I'd still be stuck at the bottom of the ocean far from land,...alone. It was like my worst nightmare had come true.

I took a deep breath to steady myself. Yeah, I could breathe underwater, but I'd freeze to death long before reaching land. I was in a no-win situation. At least, I was warm inside the bubble.

Something moved outside the bubble, prompting me to jump back up. The now-empty water bottle fell to the base of the bubble as I stood. As the moving shape solidified, I saw it was the Sea Witch gathering seaweed. Her tail created a tiny wave as it quickly flapped against the water.

A shiver ran up and down my back for a brief moment, and I had to take another breath to keep the panic at bay.

Just two days before, the Sea Witch had told Fish and I that she'd helped my mom, the Little Mermaid, over eighteen years ago to win my dad. The Sea Witch's spell transformed my mom from a mermaid to a human before I was born. And now she was a mermaid again. The witch had lied!

"Hey!" I yelled, banging my fists against the walls of the bubble. Not that it did any good. My fists sank into them soundlessly, and my yelling seemed to be having no effect either.

The Sea Witch continued to pick up enormous quantities of seaweed and dumped them in a large container. "Hey!"

She glanced back; her eyes narrowed, and they appeared slightly wild as if she wasn't quite sane. Her hair floated around her head, a messy halo of wild gray-green, almost the same color as the seaweed she held in her hands. When she saw that I was awake, she threw her head back and cackled--the same raucous crowing she'd done the night before. I pounded against the sides once again, even though I knew it to be pointless.

The Sea Witch turned back to her task, evidently tiring of laughing at me.

My hands smarted, but I continued to pummel to no avail.

The bubble remained an impenetrable beast of a barricade.

In the distance, I could just make out a school of Bluefin tuna headed toward me. They quickly turned around at the sight of the witch. The tuna reminded me of Fish. It also made me realize just how hungry I was, not that I was planning on eating the Sea Witch's oysters.

I watched her, wondering what use she would have for a container full of seaweed.

She suddenly perked up, lifted the container, and swam around the outside of the sphere, dumping the pile of seaweed on top of the globe. The seaweed drifted down the sides until it covered the entire perimeter.

Not only was I imprisoned in the bubble, but she had removed my ability to see outside it.

"Oh, I'm glad I found you." *Fish!* The sound of his voice filtered through the bubble, lifting my spirits. He sounded relieved, but not more than I was at hearing his deep voice close by.

"Well, hello, handsome merman." She purred like a cat receiving a bowl of milk. "What brings you to my abode?" She asked with a sweet voice.

Too sweet. My fingers formed a fist.

"My friend is missing." Fish said.

"The one you were with the other day? The underwater-breathing human with the incredible eyes."

I leaned forward, putting my ear to the bubble and held my breath, waiting for Fish's reply.

"Yes. Have you seen her?"

"Such beautiful eyes," The witch replied, ignoring Fish's question. "Have you ever seen eyes like that before? So unique."

"She is beautiful all over," Fish said, causing my heart to lift. My mouth curled up at the edges hearing how he thought of me.

"Has she been here? I've looked everywhere, but I'm at the end of my tether."

His voice maintained an even tone, but I could hear his frustration.

"Ah, yes. Forgive me. I've been busy with a... situation." Her voice hardened on the last word. "But, of course, I remember your little friend. I've not seen her. I'm sure I would have remembered."

I slammed my fist into the thin wall of magic separating me from Fish.

"I'm here," I screamed. "Fish!" I could hear him, so it stood to reason he'd hear me.

"I've looked everywhere," Fish repeated, sounding despondent. "She's not at home. At least, I don't think she is. I asked a guard on the beach in front of the palace, and he told me she wasn't."

I stopped pummeling to listen. He'd spoken to one of the palace guards?

"Maybe she is avoiding you. Have you considered that?"

I gritted my teeth at her manipulation and hoped Fish would see through it. I had no reason to avoid him. The last time I'd seen him, we'd arranged to meet up.

"I don't think so. It doesn't sound like her."

"Just how well do you know this girl?" she asked. I peered through the seaweed, trying to find a gap big enough for me to see out. "I'm assuming she is your girlfriend."

I held my breath, awaiting his answer. Yeah, it was stupid wanting to know if the guy I had a major crush on considered me his girlfriend or not when I was magically imprisoned under the ocean.

"We're close," he said.

"Oh, my handsome merman, have you thought that she might have run away? I got the sense from her that her responsibilities were troubling her. She is a princess, is she not? Life cannot be easy for one with such responsibilities."

The urge to take her apart with my bare hands grew exponentially. What did she know of my life in the palace? Precisely nothing, and yet, she'd hit the nail on the head. I had tried to run away from my responsibilities.

"She wouldn't do that," he replied with a hint of irritability. "She wouldn't run away from me. She's not the damsel in distress you are painting her to be. Only yesterday, she took her father's place and gave a speech to the people of Antla. Does that sound like someone evading their responsibilities?"

My heart fluttered as he defended me against her. He stood his ground and didn't believe her lies. I loved how he knew me.

I banged my fists against the barrier, only stopping when she spoke again.

"Well, maybe she wouldn't normally run away," the witch continued, "but her circumstances are bleak. Word has it that her speech didn't go over so well in some circles. The people that she was trying to reach the most left halfway through it...or so I'm told. Such a shameful outcome could upset a young impressionable girl. I mean, if even her town people, who have watched her grow up, who are supposed to love and respect her as a fellow Atlanticean, didn't stay to listen to her then who will? Certainly not the rest of the island people," her voice sounded sincere. Almost as if she cared. "She probably was so upset that she has left the palace and not told you or anyone else. You know girls at that age are not very stable. They live by their emotions, and they do not bother to really think through their actions."

"I don't think so," Fish said, maintaining a confidence and restraint in his tone. "She's strong and doesn't let her emotions get the better of her. Besides, I heard the opposite. The townspeople have been talking about her all morning, and most had nothing but good words to say."

A slight sharpness invaded his voice, but probably not enough for her to hear. I loved how he spoke with sureness but never arrogance.

She, on the other hand, needed a huge wakeup call: one that might have involved a couple of swift clouts to the head. And I would be the first one in line to administer them, as soon as I found a way out of this godforsaken bubble.

"Look, if you haven't seen her, I should be on my way."

I crouched and jumped as high as possible, hoping that bringing my feet down hard would find a weak spot. Beneath me, the bubble wobbled, causing me to fall over. I used it as an excuse to see if I'd perforated the bubble

Nothing.

Absolutely nothing.

Not a hairline crack.

Not a single scratch.

My heart plummeted with the realization that the bubble remained without a mar from all my efforts. I needed to break this damn bubble while Fish was nearby, or I'd never get away.

Opening my mouth, I let out a scream. "Help me, Fish. I'm right here. Help me!"

I waited for some sort of response from him, but it was the witch that spoke next. Frustration bubbled within me that I could hear them perfectly well, and yet, Fish couldn't hear my screams, shielded as I was by magic.

"Of course, I can ask around, but I seriously doubt anyone will know anything," she said, smarmily. "You need to accept that she might never return. If I were her, I would have come to you. Asked you for your help. But maybe she was too proud?"

"No, I will not accept that she just disappeared without telling anyone."

"Without telling anyone, or without telling you?" The witch asked.

I was ready to kill her, I really was.

"She would have told me if she planned to leave. She would want me with her."

The Sea Witch scoffed, but when she spoke, she changed her voice again. "You're very confident that she'll return."

"She will." He cleared his throat.

Hot tears surged from my inability to break free and from not being able to swim and embrace Fish. The whole thing made me want to tear the witch apart with my bare hands.

But all that anger was useless. It may have helped me to release my emotions, but it did nothing to help me escape. What I needed was more thinking and less acting like a two-year-old whose toy has been ripped from her hand.

I wiped away the tears and concentrated on finding another way to draw attention to the massive wall of seaweed she'd surrounded the bubble with.

Echolocation! If I could transfer my movements to the seafloor, he may feel it and suspect that the seaweed wall is hiding me. He'd shown me before that he could sense things in the water.

I turned over on my stomach and banged on the floor with my fists and the tips of my toes to no avail.

"Look. I've traveled a long way to get here," Fish huffed. "Have you seen her or not?"

"I'll give you this much young merman. You are tenacious. Why don't we take a swim around the area, so you can be satisfied that she isn't here?"

I listened, holding my breath, but the two of them drifted away, their voices getting quieter and more distant. I sat back in the bubble and admitted defeat. If Fish couldn't see or hear me, I was at the whims of the witch, though goodness only knew what she wanted with me. I was nothing to her. I lay back and waited for their return. I didn't hear anything for what felt like hours.

Thoughts of what she might do to him clouded my thoughts. She had me captive, why not take Fish too? Or perhaps a merman was too commonplace to hold her interest. She'd certainly shown more interest in me upon finding out who I was. And still, I couldn't see why she should care. So I was a princess, and yes, I could command a good ransom, but what use did she have for riches? She lived at the bottom of the ocean. I was also an abnormality, neither a human nor a mermaid. Maybe that was what interested her. Thoughts of her performing experiments on me made me feel sick to my stomach, so I picked up the other canister of water and concentrated on listening for her return instead. A while later, I heard her, her low voice growing louder as she approached.

"Now, you can see that she isn't here," she said. She was talking to Fish. He'd not left without me. Maybe I still had a chance.

She carried on talking, and I held my ear to the bubble. "Maybe you should try and search somewhere else. Have you tried the perimeter of the mainland? They may have seen her there. What about the fishermen? Did they see her run away?"

"She hasn't run away," Fish maintained, his voice hardening. "But if you haven't seen her, I'll be on my way."

"No!" I screamed, pummeling the interior edge of the bubble. He couldn't leave, not now. He didn't answer, and after screaming for a solid five minutes, I had to accept he'd gone, and with him, my chance to escape.

2

13TH FEBRUARY

I awoke from a dream so beautiful that I could happily have stayed asleep for a long time. Unfortunately, the truth has a habit of creeping in when it's not wanted. It jolted me from my sleepiness.

I peeked through a tiny gap that had appeared during the night between the fronds of seaweed. Granted, I had to lie on the floor to see out of it, but at least, I could glimpse the colorless coral reef and gloomy water that still surrounded me. No denying the same desolate scenario.

Sitting up, I strained to hear movement of any sort, but being so far under the water, all I could hear was the desolate silence that only a few days before I'd found a solace in from the noise of the above-water world. I'd do anything to hear the chaos again, the noise of people chattering, of horsehooves on cobbles. Of anything, but the relentless penetrating silence that was suffocating me.

My stomach grumbled, and I debated eating from the basket of food she had left. I grasped the box and picked up the seaweed, a vibrant green, the only thing of any color for miles around. At least, she'd tried with the food, not that it would make it any more palatable. I closed my eyes and tried not to picture the lumpy wet fronds of disgusting seaweed as I popped it into my mouth and began to munch. It was hardly a delicious salad, but it was edible, and that was as much as I could hope for. I swigged it down with another bottle of water I found in the bottom of the basket. It was the last one, but I figured if she wanted to keep me alive, she'd have to replace the water at some point. May as well make it sooner rather than later.

The water, however, reminded me that I had nowhere to answer the call of nature, and if the water was going in, it would have to come out. I'd had to go yesterday, a thought that had made me feel sick to my stomach at the time, but after I had gone, the liquid somehow managed to seep through the walls of the bubble, leaving it perfectly dry. So water could get out but not in, and nothing else it seemed could penetrate the strange walls. It was a strange but, I supposed, necessary form of magic.

A sliver of light streamed in through a tiny hole, and I jerked my head toward it. The Sea Witch swiped a few pieces of seaweed away from the bubble. My eyes widened, but I didn't say a word, not wanting to upset her. I watched her take away more seaweed, allowing more of the dim light into my enclosed darkness.

"Hello, my pretty, little girl." She stared from the top of the sphere for a minute before her lips curled up, and she asked, "How was breakfast? Good, right? Did you like the seaweed?"

I tried to keep my tone steady in the hopes that if I was nice, she might think about freeing me. "Yes, it was good. Thank you."

"Excellent. I had to venture way out of my sanctuary to find it for you. We wouldn't want you to complain about the food or starve," she said, using that sweet voice with an underlying tone I disliked.

I detested her whole fake sweet tone. Period.

"Why am I here?" No point beating about the bush and discussing the pleasantries of a seaweed diet.

For a brief second, she glanced behind her shoulder. "Can't you figure it out?" She cackled. "You're a real mystery, you know." She swam to the far side, where the seaweed completely blocked her.

I moved to the other side of the bubble where the top of her hair appeared between two more displaced fronds. "This is a lot of work. Maybe I shouldn't have added this much seaweed."

"What do you mean?" I tried to keep my dislike for her out of my voice, but it wasn't easy.

"Can't you see all the effort I'm making to give you a better view?" Her voice hardened. "I needed to hide you, but now that we've seen the back of that merfriend of yours, I think it's only fair that we be able to see each other as we chat, don't you?"

I bit the inside of my cheek but remained silent.

She scoffed. "Not answering me now?" Another piece of seaweed fell, and she peered through. Her beautiful emerald eyes were now yellow, just as I'd seen them when she'd captured me. Her emerald and cobalt hair had faded overnight to a dull green and blue-black. She'd been using some kind of glimmer when she'd spoken to us the other day. "Should I go away and leave you? Is that what you want?"

I stared at the gap, and she peered in as she tapped her chin with her sausage fingers.

My head moved from side to side as my fingers drummed slowly against my thigh. "No, not at all." Being trapped was one thing; not being able to see out of my prison was another.

"What were you saying about me?" I lifted my eyebrows. "That you consider me a mystery."

"Of course, I'm talking about the fact that you can breathe underwater but have no tail. Three weeks ago, you didn't know how to swim, did you?" Her piercing eyes met mine. "Doesn't it seem bizarre that one day you can't swim and the next day you're swimming as if you've been doing it since you were born? And breathing underwater? It's so strangely remarkable. Some would say it's unbelievable."

It was unbelievable. I'd asked myself the same question. "My mother is a mermaid, remember?"

The Sea Witch shrugged as though this didn't answer her question, then swam away. I tried to find another gap in the seaweed so I could see where she went.

She swam about ten feet or so and then changed her mind and turned, swimming back to me.

Another chunk of the seaweed drifted away, and she watched me with an evil grin. "Is that your take on how it happened? Your mother being a mermaid, somehow caused you to be able to breathe underwater? I'm not sure that's how things work. "

I shrugged. "What can I say? It just happened."

Her eyes narrowed. "Just happened? No child, it did not just happen. Things like this do not just happen. There are greater things at play here."

I shrugged. What could I tell her that she didn't already know? She was the peddler of magic, not me. Still, I got the feeling she was hiding something. She knew more about me than she let on. She'd let slip, just moments before that she knew I was afraid to swim a couple of weeks ago. I'd certainly not told her that. What else did she know about me that she wasn't letting on?

She drifted away from the newly exposed section. More chunks of seaweed drifted down to the floor. "Much better, now that I can see you." She winked. "This is a lovely way to protect someone, isn't it? Nobody can hear you or see you—just moi," she chortled. "You're safe away from the world."

My hands hid my face from her as I didn't want my expressions to give away my thoughts.

Lady, you have issues. Serious issues about how to keep someone safe.

I cleared my throat and bit my lip while trying not to show how upset her words made me. Once I thought my expression concealed my true feelings, I uncovered my face and said, "No, I have no idea how it happened. If I did, I would tell you. But why am I here? Who or what are you protecting me from? And why was I put inside here?"

She swam around the perimeter, and I shuffled, trying to make sure I faced her.

One of her hands landed on her heart, and she sighed. "That's for me to know at the moment. I'll make sure you have food and fresh water. Don't you worry."

Don't worry, huh? Easy for her to say.

"I need to check on a couple of matters right now, but I'll be back to chat some more. Don't leave."

I almost laughed. Don't leave. As if I could.

I plopped down on the floor and yawned. Not sure how I could have become tired from doing absolutely nothing, but I had.

My eyelashes drifted down, and I nodded off, just to become startled when my head dropped to the side. I lay on my side, shut my eyes, and allowed the slumber to take over.

An evil laughter interrupted my nap, but I didn't dare move. Maintaining my body in its position wasn't easy, but I didn't want her knowing that I had awoken.

Eavesdropping under the circumstances might prove to be useful.

"Good timing, dear child, for a nap as it's time to leave you some food and clean out your cage," she mumbled, but her closeness allowed me to hear her words clearly. "I really need to find some help if I going to keep her here." She laughed. She mumbled again, but I couldn't understand the short phrase or sentence she had said.

My eyelids opened a sliver, just enough that through my eyelashes, I witnessed the Sea Witch's hands penetrate the shield.

How?

She pulled out the near-empty basket and picked up a new one.

She touched the surface with her fingers, mumbling some weird word. "Vallume, unlock," she whispered. She shoved the box closer to my torso. "Good, now off to do my own work. This girl is keeping me much too busy. Maybe I should..." her voice trailed off as she swam away.

Her last statement worried me, and I decided that my safety required a quicker exit from my prison. Either she wanted to kill me or to find someone else to do so.

But I wasn't ready to find out.

Scanning the area to ensure that she wasn't anywhere watching me, I placed my fingertips on the cool surface. I quickly whispered, "Vallume, unlock." My finger went through the sphere as easy as a warm knife through butter.

My heart beat faster with excitement. There was a way out, and I'd found it. Now, I only had to figure a way to get past the witch and back to the coast without freezing to death on-route.

I brought my fingers back inside and sat pulling the basket toward me. While I ate the seaweed, I hatched an escape plan. The trip back to Atlantice would take hours, and during the middle of the night, my visibility would be hindered. I also had the problem of the coldness to deal with. Funnily enough, I was more willing to risk hypothermia than hang around waiting to see what the Sea Witch wanted. At least if I left, I might come upon another merperson to share their warmth. There was a chance I might survive.

I needed to take a risk or be stuck with the witch, and there was no telling what she had in store for me.

In the far distance, she screeched like a hungry hyena about to feed, and I wondered what had happened? Maybe Fish had returned? My heart pounded at the thought.

Dropping what was left of the seaweed, I knelt up and peered through the bubble walls.

A short time later, she swam toward me at record speed, her seahorse tail waggling out of control.

I plastered a smile on my face in an attempt to hide my nervousness. The thought that she'd seen me figure out her secret was too much to bear.

She approached the bubble and, with one look at me, narrowed her eyes.

I swear, my heart almost beat out of its ribcage, and yet, I breathed evenly and tried to keep my emotions in check

Her mouth opened and closed before a small smile appeared. "Everything ok? Is there anything else you want?"

Keeping my voice steady, I said, "I would love to have some more of the seaweed." I pointed to the pile outside.

It must have raised her suspicions because her tone shifted. "Why?"

"If I have to sleep here another night, the seaweed would make the bottom more comfortable, but I can help you if you want." I stood, to show I was willing, not that I thought that she'd let me out to pick seaweed, but I wanted to gauge her reaction. I also needed an excuse to get out.

"No need." She picked up a pile and dumped it into the container. "I'll bring you some later."

"Thank you."

She chuckled. "I will bring you back more food for tomorrow morning because I may not be able to return with your breakfast in the morning." She sneered and placed her hands on her hips. "I have things to attend to, things that cannot wait."

Her words sparked excitement within me. If she was going to be away, it would give me a chance to escape. I wondered if it had anything to do with her screech a moment ago.

I strived to keep my voice steady and as nonchalant as I could manage while my heart thumped against my ribs. "Is everything okay? Maybe I can help you."

She waved as if erasing my words. "Everything is fine, but it's late at night. And since you asked nicely, it's just a matter I have to take care of." She twirled around with her hands spread wide. "My sanctuary is heavenly because it's far away from everyone, but it also means that it takes me longer to reach all the other kingdoms."

She was heading to another kingdom. Great news! I would need to be careful so I wouldn't bump into her in the open ocean, but it was my perfect opportunity, and I was going to take it.

"Then I would appreciate the food." She gave me a strange look that turned my insides to jelly. I'd never been much of a liar, and the way she looked at me made me feel that she could read my mind. I kept still, trying not to smile too much, and it was only when she turned to leave that I let out a breath I hadn't realized I'd been holding.

She would be back later with another basket. It would give me enough time to come up with a plan. I pulled another oyster from the basket and downed it in one. The salty taste was becoming too much for me, and I was sick of it. I needed to escape before I was forced to eat another one.

Planning my escape didn't take much time. What was there to plan? Get out of the bubble when the witch wasn't looking and hotfoot it out of there, hopefully getting to a source of warmth before I died of exposure. I was still in my panties and bra, neither of which would protect me from the freezing temperature of the ocean.

I had to come up with something better, but I couldn't think any further than getting away from the witch. It took hours to swim here from the coast and with the sea as cold as it was, I wouldn't have hours.

I was still thinking about how I'd manage to beat the cold when she returned an hour later with another basket.

She mumbled, and a second later, she shuffled behind me and whispered to herself. Keeping my back straight, I continued to look ahead as though nothing was happening. When I did turn, the basket was in the bubble, and the original basket was in her hand

She asked, "Are you okay?"

I looked over my shoulders to meet her eyes. "Of course, why wouldn't I be?"

"Hmm, no reason."

She was obviously insane. Of course, I wasn't alright. The woman had me trapped in a bubble. And yet she kept asking if I was ok. Did she actually think I was enjoying being here? Maybe she did.

"I've been wondering why you would want me here?" I said, holding my breath. This was to be, hopefully, my final encounter with her, and I needed to know what her interest was in me.

"I thought it would be the best place for you." She touched her chin with her fingers, pulling at her chin hair. She really wasn't the glamorous woman I'd seen when I first met her. I guess now that I was a captive audience, she didn't have to make herself beautiful for me.

"You must be a powerful witch if you can grant wishes. I would imagine that giving my mother legs would have been difficult."

"Ah," she sighed, gazing off in remembrance. "It was my finest moment. One of my most difficult spells, but oh, what a masterpiece. I hear she's doing well at the palace."

I detected a frown beneath her calm exterior.

"She was until she turned back into a mermaid," I reminded her.

This elicited a grin from her which surprised me. Why would she be happy that her spell had ended? She'd said herself she had no idea how it had.

"All good things must come to an end," she said airily as though the loss of my mother's legs was an inconsequential thing.

"I have no tail," I said. She looked back at me. "And I'm happy. I don't want one. I don't want anything from you."

"Why child, I never thought you did."

"I was just wondering if that's why you brought me here. I thought that maybe you thought that I might want a tail."

She narrowed her eyes. "Why would I think that?"

"Well, you've seen me with the merman, and you saw that we had feelings for each other. I wondered if you'd come to the conclusion I wanted the same as my mother, albeit the opposite way around."

She shook her head and swam around the bubble, coming back to face me. "No, child. I didn't for one instant think you wanted something from me. In my experience, when someone wants something, they ask for it...sometimes they just take it. I'm of the second group."

"Like you took me," I whispered.

"Yes, exactly. Just like I took you. I wanted you, so I took you."

"Why did you take me?" I held my breath, waiting for her answer. She pulled closer to me, pushing her nose almost right up to the bubble wall. A shiver ran through my whole body as she spoke. "My dear child, you really have no idea what you are, do you?"

3

14TH FEBRUARY

$\mathcal{A}$ warm blanket wrapped around me, protecting me from the biting cold. Flurries of snow drifted down around us, landing on my eyelashes, which were already frozen in clumps from the moisture of the sea. Someone thrust a warm drink in my hand, which I sipped gratefully, all the while trying hard not to spill a precious drop of it with all the shivering. I was aware that someone was rubbing my feet, by the sharp stabbing pains shooting up my leg. The pain was not from turning into a mermaid, which I most definitely hadn't, but from the frostbite that was setting in.

It had been a ludicrous idea, but one I'd thought through thoroughly. It had probably saved me from death or worse, yet it had left me shivering with the very real chance of hyperthermia.

The person, a kindly fisherman, finished with rubbing my feet then pulled a pair of thick woolen socks onto them

"T-t-thank you," I muttered through chattering teeth. I thought about how I'd come to be out in the middle of the ocean during a winter storm. My journey had begun the night before when the witch had left to do whatever it was that evil old hags like to do in their spare time.

When I was sure she'd gone, I'd inched over to the edge of the bubble and stretched my arms to allow my fingertips to touch the barrier. I whispered, "Vallume, unlock."

My fingers had slipped into the water. and I'd managed to roll my entire body through the bubble walls.

Immediately, the sharp sting of the cold water hit me like a thousand needles. The shock almost had me wanting to return to the warmth and relative safety of the bubble, but sheer desperation had me swimming away.

My first instinct had me swimming along the ocean floor, but as orange colors rising from the east lit up the ocean, I'd swum upwards towards them, stopping every so often as Fish had taught me until I hit the surface. With no land in sight, I'd only had the sun to guide me. I'd barely been able to see it through the thick snow clouds that had gathered above, but it was enough to know which direction to swim. I'd struck out toward the coast with long, fast strokes periodically glancing over my shoulder to see if I was being followed.

Looking back, I would never have made it. If it wasn't for the fishermen who just happened to be heading back to shore, I would surely have succumbed to the cold.

"How in all the kingdoms did you manage to get out so far?" the kindly fisherman asked. I was way too cold to formulate an answer. He hadn't recognized me, which was a blessing. I could only imagine how the Conch would have a field day if they knew I'd been found in the middle of the ocean in only my underwear.

"I've alerted the coast guard," another fisherman said. The hospital in Antla is expecting you. It's a wonder you haven't died.

I tried shaking my head. I didn't want to go to the hospital. The fishermen might not have recognized me. I expected that they didn't come across many half-naked princesses during a normal day, but I couldn't hope no one would. I needed another escape plan. This time, not away from someone who wished me ill, but from these well-meaning fishermen, who were taking me back to one hell of an embarrassment even if they didn't know it.

I pulled the blanket more tightly around myself as my body

began to get feeling back. Snow hammered down around us. I would say that it was unusual to have snow this late in the winter, but nothing about the weather had been normal recently. Snow was just par for the course this season. I'd been ushered under cover, but still, the snow seemed to find me. I gazed out into the distance as the fishermen held a whispered conversation amongst themselves. I could see the coast now. Although it was a fair distance away, I'd be there before I knew it. I needed to get out of the situation I was heading toward. Once someone recognized me on land, it was all over. I'd done everything I could to get the people to listen to me and to understand that the merfolk weren't the monsters they were painted to be. If it got out that I was found in my underwear in the ocean, all that work would be rendered useless. Who would believe me, or want to listen to me after I was stupid enough to get myself in such a situation? I doubted anyone would believe my story of the Sea Witch

As the shore loomed, I knew I had no choice. It sounded madness to my own ears, but the alternative was worse. I jumped up from my seat, threw the blanket to the floor, and leapt from the boat back into the freezing water.

This time I was ready for the needles of pain. I opened my mouth and let out an underwater scream, shouting out Fish's name as loudly as I could. I recognized the area I was in. One of the more beautiful reefs I'd seen in the days previously. I also remembered the way to the mer village. If Fish wasn't around to save me, another merperson would. They might not like it, but I doubted even they would want the death of the land princess to muddy the already muddy waters. Swimming as fast as I could, I pulled broad strokes, heading to the gap in the seagrass. I'd almost got to the reef in question when heat flooded my body, and the pain fell away. Turning my head quickly, I saw Fish behind me.

"I never thought I'd see you again!" Fish's deep voice brought joy to my heart.

I twirled around, and seconds later, his arms encircled me.

He touched my chin, drawing me in before he dipped his head

and kissed me. Heat of a different kind enveloped me, warming my body so much better than the hot chocolate had.

He caressed my fingers as he pulled back. "Where have you been? I've been searching for days. I even went to see the Sea Witch, but she had no answers."

I scoffed. "She was the one who took me. She was holding me in a bubble." I shook my head. "I heard you talking to her, but her strong spell didn't allow you to hear my screams."

"You were there?" His voice became harsh. "I had a feeling she knew something. I didn't think she had you, though."

"I don't even want to think about her right now." I really didn't. I wanted to get back to normality as soon as possible. I'd talk about her later when I was ready. "What is happening back home?"

His eyes opened wide, too wide. He touched my cheek. "I hate that she took you. I hate that I wasn't there to stop her."

I caught hold of his hand. "It's ok. I escaped, but we both need to be careful in the future. She didn't tell me why she took me."

"Did she hurt you?" He ran his eyes down my body, looking, no doubt, for scratches or bruises.

I shook my head. "No, she kept me warm and fed, but I had a feeling that she wasn't planning to let me go. She said I didn't know who I was, but I don't think she was referring to me being a princess. I think she was interested in me because I'm half-mermaid."

Fish shook his head. "I doubt it. Half-merfolk are extremely rare, but not completely unheard of. One of the elders in the mer village is a half-merman. His mother was a mermaid, his father, a fisherman. There have been other instances."

I thought it through. I'd never heard of a half-merperson before, but then I'd not put much thought into the people living under the sea. I'd been too busy vilifying them. "He has a tail?"

"Yes. All the half-merfolk I've heard of have had tails."

I wiggled my toes. I was still wearing the fisherman's socks. "Maybe that's the issue. Something about the witch's spell on my mother made me a half-mermaid, but with legs, so I look totally human. Anyway, like I said, I don't want to even think about it." I pulled off the socks and tucked them into the side of my underwear. "What's been happening here?"

Fish took my hand and began to pull me slowly through the ocean as he talked. "I've been talking to Emma, and you really need to see her as soon as possible. I'll take you there now."

I let go of his hand and swam beside him. "But why?" A horrible thought crossed my mind; I reached out and squeezed his arm. "Are my parents okay? Is Antla okay? The people?"

He smiled. "Your parents are fine, and the town is holding up well, considering all the rioting and the AML still on the warpath. But she's been reading your mom's diaries, and apparently, she's learned information you need to know."

"She's been reading my mom's diaries? How do you even know?"

He stopped where he was and turned to me. "When I was looking for you, I want to the palace. One of the beach guards fetched Emma. She introduced herself as your maid. She was the one who told me that your speech had gone over well. She also told me that you hadn't been seen since. I left her then and came looking for you, but when I couldn't find you, I went back to the palace to see if you'd gone home."

"She told you she'd read my mom's diaries? Why would she do that?"

"Did you leave them on your bed?"

I thought back to when I'd last been home. I had just tossed them aside, thinking I'd come back to them later.

"Probably."

"She told me she found them and thought they were yours. She said she only read one because it might say where you had gone."

I guess that made sense. Emma wasn't the type of person to snoop. "So, what was it she found?"

My breath hitched as his fingertips outlined my face with slow, tiny circles until they reached my chin.

He shook his head. "I'm sorry, but when I asked her, she said she thought it would be better if she talked to you first."

"Was it to do with the Sea Witch?" I asked. Maybe my mother had written more about her. Something that would explain why she wanted me so badly.

"Not sure, but you should talk to her as soon as you can. She made it sounds as if it's important."

He leaned in and kissed me again. "You must be tired. Please, let me hold you, and I'll bring you back."

"Thank you." I lifted my arms, and every single muscle and tendon cried out in pain as he pulled me close.

I yawned.

"Tired?"

I nodded too exhausted to speak.

"Then sleep, and I'll take you back."

I closed my eyes and let him take me through the water.

Later a light kiss touched my temple, and my eyes fluttered open.

He smiled and pointed. "Just in time for the welcoming committee."

I looked over to where he was pointing. On the beach in front of the palace, a row of palace guards stood gazing out to sea. Sergeant Jimenez was among them.

"I think it's time for me to leave." He released me and ducked under the surface.

I waved at the guards, and it seemed as if I had waved a red flag to a dozen bulls. As they caught sight of me, they ran to the pier.

My voice hitched as the guards stood at attention, waiting for me. I bobbed under the surface to where Fish was hiding. "Can you wait until I find out why they need me?"

"Of course. I'll be underneath the pier." I gave him a quick kiss and rose to the surface.

As I headed toward the group of guards, Sergeant Jimenez bowed.

"Sergeant, it's good to see you."

"Your Highness, thank goodness you are home. The guests have already started to arrive. We've placed them in the west wing. We didn't know what was the best thing to do in the situation. They are all being cared for, and we haven't explained to them that you are missing. We hoped you'd just be out here." He scanned the sea behind me with a slight look of disgust on his face. He was obviously looking for Fish.

The blood drained from my face. "What?" I managed to squeak out. "Who has arrived?"

The sergeant scanned the area before he met my questioning eyes. "The guests that will attend the Valentine's Day Ball. Today is February 14th. The ball is tonight."

My head hurt as I thought of the ball. A few weeks ago, it was all I had thought about, but what with everything else going on, it had slipped my mind.

"Didn't we send out cancellation notices so they wouldn't come?"

Sergeant Jimenez shrugged. Of course, he wouldn't know. It wasn't his job to know about invitations and cancelations. He was only there to find me.

"Turn them away." I waved my hands. "Turn them all away. I don't care if they're the rulers of their kingdoms; we're not prepared to host them."

He grimaced. "We can't turn them all away, Your Highness. Some of these guests have traveled from the far side of Atlantice, and you know some of the foreign royals are coming. As I said, some have already arrived."

Seaweed hanging in trees. Double triple seaweed in quadruple trees! Damnit all. The idea of a party gave me a headache.

"As the only remaining royalty left, you are expected to host the ball." He reminded me. "For your people."

All the saliva in my mouth dried up, and my hand touched my throat. "I can't. I've just spent two days tra…" I decided not to tell them about my imprisonment. "I've been gone for two days, and nothing is prepared for a ball. We would need to order food, and there simply isn't enough time."

He half-smiled. "I'm under the impression that Queen Antonella ordered everything before she left the palace, she provided specific instructions with a schedule, and the cook has been cooking since yesterday morning. Trust me, everything is set. The rooms are prepared, the food will be ready, and the staff returned for the ball yesterday afternoon. There is nothing for you to worry about except for you to host it."

My fingers massaged my temple, trying to push back the negative thoughts. I took a deep breath. "Can you please ask Emma to come down here?"

"Emma, Your Highness?"

"Emma, my maid."

He nodded, although he didn't look like he wanted to leave me. He must have known that Fish was nearby. He probably thought that's where I'd spent the last couple of days, and he'd probably have preferred the truth to that. I wasn't sure his thoughts on Sea Witches, but he sure disliked mermen.

I waited until he was out of view before dropping back beneath the surface.

"What's the matter?" Fish asked when he saw my face. "Is your mother ok?"

"We have an annual Valentine's Day Ball at the palace."

Fish furrowed his brow. "So?"

"So, today is Valentine's Day."

"Ah." Comprehension dawned on his beautiful features. I'd managed to find myself in another pickle. At least, this one beat being trapped in a bubble under the ocean by a maniac...slightly.

I gave him a quick kiss. "I'm going to have to go. I'm needed."

Fish ran his tongue across his teeth. "Okay, but don't go in the water unless you know I'm in there. I'll hang around this area tonight. You know where I am."

Just knowing he was close by was enough to get me through the upcoming nightmare. "You know, I almost regret escaping from the Sea Witch now." I pulled a face, which made him laugh. It was the image of his happy face I took with me as I ascended to the surface and swam to the shore.

Emma ran down the pier, performed a quick curtsy before she plopped down on the edge of the pier. "I'm so glad you're safe and well, Your Highness. I was worried about you."

"Safe but not at all well," I managed to respond. I inhaled as deeply as I could. "Please cancel this ball. Tell the guests that we're no longer holding it. I'm in no shape to host it."

I expected her to be on my side, but I'd clearly forgotten how important the monarchy was to her. "Your Highness, with all due respect, it is your duty to host it. Antla needs you right now."

My voice croaked, and my head shook. "Duty? I've done enough. I'm in no shape to host a ball. I didn't sleep last night."

Emma smiled. "So nap first. Antla needs this ball, and so do you. You might need a hairbrush first."

I stuck my tongue out at her.

"I'm serious. Think about how much it'll help the people come together when The Conch prints it in their newspaper. The kingdom is in a dire mood. It needs some frivolity."

"But..."

"But nothing," she said, holding her hand out for me. "The Queen has sorted everything out. The food is being taken care of, the guests are already arriving. Literally, all you have to do is host it. I'll help in any way I can."

I stepped out of the water, and she threw a towel around me. "You do know that I'm your boss, right?"

She gave me a grin. "Of course, Your Highness, now get up to the palace and get in the shower. You have a ball to host."

Goodness, I loved that girl to my bones. I gave her a grin and began the walk up the beach. Before I'd taken too many steps, a thought occurred to me. "Is the tank still in the ballroom?"

Emma furrowed her brow. "Yes, but the staff is going to take it down to make more room on the dance floor."

"Don't. Tell them to fill it with seawater." She appeared surprised but didn't question me. "Can you go and tell them now? I would imagine it will take a while. I'll meet you in my room in ten minutes."

She nodded, narrowing her eyes at me. Before she could question me further, I ran back to the pier. Almost immediately, Fish appeared.

"Everything ok?" Fish whispered.

"I want you to attend the ball."

He pulled back and sounded unsure when he asked, "What? How?"

I cleared my throat. "I need them to see you, a merman. Besides, it's a Valentine's Ball. I'll need a date."

His lips pulled up at the side. "You want to take me on a date?"

"Sure," I said.

"I'm not sure this will go down well with the people. They are struggling to accept a princess whose mother is a mermaid. What do you think they'll do when they find out you are dating a merman?"

I leaned over and kissed him. "I don't even care. If they can't accept you, then I can't accept them."

"You know I can't dance, right?" He looked down into the water. "I don't even have two left feet."

I laughed. "Don't worry. I have a plan. Meet me in the tunnel early evening. I'll be the one in a dress."

I gave him one last kiss as he slipped beneath the surface.

Back in my room, Emma was nowhere to be seen, but she'd laid a dress out on my bed, and I found the bath drawn in my bathroom. After so long in cold seawater, it felt heavenly to drop into the hot bath. She'd filled it with a heavily scented bath oil, a delicious change from the smell of salt and seaweed. I stayed in the bath until it cooled to lukewarm, at which point, I got out.

The dress Emma had picked out for me was perfect, with tiny pearls forming a shell on the left side of it. Diamonds surrounded the outer shells, and another set of diamonds lined the sweetheart neckline.

Before pulling it on, I found a bikini in my drawer. It was the only one I owned and guaranteed to cause a stir. Seeing as what I was planning was going to cause a stir anyway, I figured it didn't matter. I pulled the bikini on and lay down on the bed. Within minutes, I was fast asleep.

By the time the clock bells struck four, I was standing in front of the mirror, twirling, with my arms wide open. The full skirt opened like a budding rose. When I stopped, the skirt returned to its place.

Emma knocked and entered with a huge grin. She dangled a pair of sandals in one hand and a box under her other arm but stopped short. "Your Highness, you look amazing. Wait until everyone sees you."

"Thanks," I said, taking the sandals from her hand. Slip-on shoes would be mandatory for what I had in mind. My mother would have wanted me to wear my hair up, but if the night shaped up as I planned, having thousands of pins in my hair would only hinder me. I ran a brush through it in front of the mirror and placed the tiara on my head. Make-up was something I would have to do without.

"You really are beautiful," Emma said.

I gave her a smile then looked down at her maid's uniform. "I'm giving you the night off."

The smile dropped from her face. "Why? What have I done?"

"You've been a great friend. I want you to take one of my dresses, get yourself made up, and come to the ball as a guest."

Her face brightened immediately. "You mean it?"

Staff was never invited to the balls. They only came to help, but Emma was no longer staff to me, she was my friend. Without her, I'd have stayed in the sea and hidden away from the ball. If anyone deserved to go, it was she.

"Of course, I mean it. Find a necklace to wear too. I'll see you in the ballroom in an hour. There are a few things I have to attend to before the ball starts."

She gave me a quick curtsey, and I left the room, smiling. My first port of call was with John. As the host, I needed to know exactly who was coming, and I had to remember their names.

He opened his office door on the first knock. "Ah, there you are. I have the lists and the times here," he said, thrusting a pile of paper into my hands. "The guests have been shown to their rooms and told to line up outside the ballroom at five precisely. I've organized a number of staff to coordinate them. You'll stand on the inside of the ballroom and receive each guest. You remember the protocol?"

I nodded. I'd been doing this my whole life. I knew who to curtsey to, who to call your majesty, your highness, your honor, and the myriad of other titles that had been burnished into my brain since I first learned to talk.

"I wanted to ask you about security," I began.

John held his hand up. "It's all in hand. Sergeant Jimenez is arranging everything. Extra guards have been brought in. We both thought it prudent in such times."

I nodded. He was right. We needed all the guards we could get.

"Thank you. Is there anything else I should know?"

John shook his head. "The orchestra is already here and warming up, the catering is being dealt with. Everything is ready for the five o'clock start. I must say, the only thing I've been worried about in this whole thing is you."

"Me?"

"You have been out in the ocean for a long time. There were rumors that you'd eloped with a merman and that you weren't coming back."

I laughed. "Since when do you listen to rumors?"

"I don't as a rule, but you were out a rather long time. I must admit to being relieved when I heard news of you being home."

"I assure you that if I do decide to elope, I'll tell you in advance," I said, throwing him a wink. He cleared his throat as if uncomfortable about the mere notion of it.

"I'm not sure my heart would stand it, Your Highness. Is there anything else I can do for you? I'll be beside you the whole evening if you need me."

"Actually, there is one thing."

He narrowed his eyes. "Do I even want to know?"

"You most definitely don't want to know. Just have a couple of guards head down to the basement. I'll meet them down there in five minutes."

An hour later, I strolled to the entrance of the ballroom and took John's hand. His eyes almost fell out of their sockets when he saw who else was there with us.

"Do you really think this is wise?" he whispered to me as we got into our places at the door.

The staff had added to the decorations, filling the entire room with heart-shaped balloons in pink and purple to match the rest.

"Just do your job and let me do mine," I whispered back as sweetly as possible. At the back of the room, near the head table where I'd be seated for dinner, was the tank my mother had ordered installed for her to attend. Except my mother was still in hiding. I glanced over, and Fish gave me a wave through the transparent side.

Despite the emotional rollercoaster, my body was experiencing from the potential chaos that could ensue when the guests walked in, my lips formed a grin.

John nodded to the orchestra, which began to play a soft tune. The doors opened, and the first guests walked in.

"His Royal Highness, Sultan Aladdin, and Sultana Jawahir, from Badalah." John read out loudly.

I shook Aladdin's hand, and he slipped me a wink as he always did when we met. Jawahir's beam reached from ear to ear. Dressed in a long red sari with bright red lipstick and perfectly white teeth, she was the epitome of beauty. I noticed her eyes widen slightly as they came to a rest on the tank, but she merely smiled even wider at me, a gleam in her eye. A couple of courtiers came over and escorted them to their seats.

"His Majesty King Bennet and Her Highness Queen Renée of The Vale."

King Bennet took my hand and shook it strongly. I watched his expression as he caught sight of the tank, but it barely changed. Queen Renee didn't even look at it.

"I'm sorry Eliana couldn't make it," she said with a grin. "She's getting close to her due date, and it's a long way to travel. I can't wait to be a grandmother." She clapped her hands together, and I couldn't help but smile. I'd have bet Fish could have grown wings and flown out of the tank in front of her, and she wouldn't have noticed.

As John introduced the other guests, a process that took an awfully long time, I watched their reactions. Most were surprised, but I saw very few who appeared angry. That was until the dignitaries of Atlantice started to file in. Hannah came, arm in arm with her beau, which surprised me. Her father would have been expected to come as the commander of the naval fleet, but I didn't expect Hannah would want to come.

"Hello, Hannah," I said. "I didn't think I'd see you tonight."

"Someone had to come and make sure this evening didn't descend into a mer-loving fiasco."

My stomach tied in knots as she slowly turned her head toward the room. I knew the exact second she saw Fish. Her skin reddened, and her lips turned downward in an expression of disgust.

"You brought one of them here?" she hissed under her breath.

"I did. He is my guest."

She didn't wait around long enough for me to explain, which was good, because I didn't plan to. She pulled on her fiancée's arm and practically dragged the man out of the room.

Part of me wondered if I should be upset, but a bigger part of me felt only relief. After Hannah left, I continued my greetings, now to the hard workers of Antla who were the last to come in. As the final name was called, I heaved a sigh of relief. I'd barely eaten all day and was ready for food. Just before the doors closed, a girl appeared. A girl so beautiful, she took my breath away.

Beside me, John rustled his papers and got as close to panic as John ever got.

"She's not on my list!" he exclaimed, turning the papers over in his hand as though her name would somehow appear.

"It's alright, John. I've got this." I took Emma's hand and found her a spare seat myself. "You are the belle of the ball!" I said to her.

She gave me a shy giggle as the prince next to her offered her his hand to shake.

The food was excellent, and although I didn't go to him throughout, I made sure Fish was taken care of. Out of the corner of my eye, I watched as he took his very first bite of steak. His expression was rapturous as he chewed on the juicy meat.

The meal gave me time to assess the situation. Nobody wanted to do too much talking as the food was too incredible. I noticed many people glancing Fish's way and heard the faint whisperings of gossip, but it seemed Fish was oblivious. When he'd finished a number of steaks, he swam around the tank and waited for the rest of us.

Once the last of the dessert was finished, we all retreated to the edges of the room to allow the staff to clear the tables and pull them back to make space for the dance floor. In the commotion of moving tables, I headed to the tank. The orchestra ramped up the tempo as I pulled the dress over my head. Leaving it next to the tank, with the tiara and shoes on top, I climbed a small set of ladders and cleared my throat.

"Your majesties, your highnesses, ladies, and gentlemen. Tonight marks the first time I've held a ball. I know some of you are disappointed that my mother and father are not here to attend, but I'm sure you are aware of the reasons why. Atlantice is currently divided. There is a rift between the land folk and the merfolk. As you can see, I hope to heal that rift, but this merman is not here to make a statement. He is not some political protest. He is here only as my date. Now, it is customary that the host has the first dance so if you'll excuse me."

I dived into the tank and swam into Fish's open arms.

Over the sound of the music, I heard applause, but I didn't care. All I could think of was Fish and how breathtakingly beautiful he was. He spun me around in time to the music as it almost faded to nothing behind the sound of applause.

"I thought you said you couldn't dance," I murmured as he twirled me around in the water.

"Not on land, maybe, but in here, I'm a master."

We swayed to the music, which sounded distorted under the water's surface. Out of the corner of my eye, I watched as some of the guests got over their shock and stepped onto the dance floor. A light flashed somewhere, and I knew without looking that it was a Conch photographer. I had no doubt that we would make the front page tomorrow. I truly hoped we would.

I only had eyes for Fish. The guests didn't need me. My mother had taken care of everything before she went into hiding, so those not dancing were served a constant supply of drinks.

The orchestra continued to play my mom's prescribed song selection until the end of the night.

As soon as the notes of a slow song played, Fish drew me into his arms. He leaned in and whispered, "You were amazing. Jumping in here, dancing with me. I believe you truly made a difference tonight." He winked. "If not for our people, definitely for me."

My heart raced, but I still managed to squeak out a few words. "Thank you. I really hope so."

The lights dimmed as the last note played, and Fish inched closer.

My heart pounded as his lips touched mine, and somewhere outside the tank, the light flashed again.

4
15TH FEBRUARY

The morning light, which seemed to shine brighter than ever, flooded my bedroom and invaded my eyelids.

My head pounded, and I pulled the covers up to cover my face, letting out a moan as I did.

As I'd spent the night in the tank and not drinking much. I could only attribute the pounding in my head and my aching muscles to dancing all night and getting very little sleep.

Someone knocked at my door, but I pretended to be asleep. The door opened, and I moaned at the loud footsteps.

"Get up sleepyhead. You've caused quite a stir."

I wondered if I stayed very still under the covers, Emma would leave me alone. As my covers were pulled back, and a cup of coffee was placed on my nightstand, I figured probably not.

"I've brought all the papers," Emma said, placing them down next to the cup. "You might want to drink the coffee before you read them," she warned.

"That bad, huh?" I asked, pulling myself into a sitting position and rubbing my eyes.

"See for yourself... Thanks for last night. I got to dance with a prince."

I grinned at her, despite wanting to crawl deeper into my bed. "I'm glad you had fun."

She gave me a quick nod and then left me to my own devices.

While I wanted to sleep in, I knew I'd needed to read what the newspapers had written. Picking up The Conch and the other newspapers, I dragged myself out of bed and plopped on my chair next to the window, facing the sea.

The Conch had printed a picture of Fish and I dancing in the tank with the words underneath the photo, "Her Highness Dances with a Merman at the Valentine Day's Ball in Antla" in bold, huge letters.

I peeked at the other newspapers, and they repeated the picture with similar verbiage.

Sensational headlines aside, most of them focused on my budding romance. Budding romance, a term that had been used liberally throughout the papers from the other kingdoms. I drank my coffee down as I read through all the articles. It could have been so much worse. I'd expected worse.

Later, Emma knocked on the door and peeped her head through, asking, "May I come in?"

"Seeing as you so rudely awakened me this morning, you might as well come in," I said gaily. "You'd better have porridge and fruit with you, though."

"I've got better than that," she grinned, passing me a hot breakfast on a tray.

"Did I ever tell you that I love you?" I murmured, inhaling the delicious scent.

"Not often," she said. "There is so much gossip buzzing around Antla that I figured you would want me to wake you up."

"I figured there would be," I said, between bites. "What are the people saying?"

She headed to my dresser and pulled out a pair of jeans and a sweater, which she rested on my bed. "Your Highness, everyone, and I mean everyone, is talking about him. They're on street corners, in front of shops, inside the shops; they're everywhere, chatting about it. I went to pick up the thank you notes that Queen Antonella ordered, and all I heard was gossip about you and your mysterious merman dancing at the ball. Everyone wants to know who he is."

I blew air out. "I bet they do."

She laughed, pulling a duster out from her apron and beginning to dust. "So far, the reaction has been positive, even for those under the sea."

My head turned quickly. "The merpeople? When were you out there?"

She turned around and waved her hands. "Not me. A couple of my mermaid friends said that everyone in the underwater kingdom is talking about it. Their world has been rocked, as well, by the news."

"Oh." I bit my lip. "I guess my action to unify everyone has turned into gossip sessions. Not so sure that's what I wanted."

She stopped dusting and walked toward me with a hesitant step and not her usual bounce. "Did your merman tell you about Queen Antonella's diary?"

I snapped my fingers. "Yes, I totally forgot about it. Thanks for reminding me. What did you read that's so private that you couldn't tell Fish?"

She reached inside her pocket and pulled out one of the diaries. "First, I want to apologize for reading it. I first thought it was yours. I wasn't going to read it, but when you were away for so long, I thought it might give me some clues as to your whereabouts."

I gave her a kind smile. "It's fine. What did it say?"

"It might be best if you read it yourself." She said, handing the book over to me. I noted the year embossed on the spine. It was the year I was born eighteen years ago.

My eyes widened, and my heart missed a beat as I accepted the book. I'd expected her to hand me a more recent one. "Thank you." I met her eyes. "Is it bad?" I asked, my voice quivering.

Her eyes lowered before she took a deep breath. "To be honest, I'm not sure how you'll feel, but it will definitely be a shock." She lifted her eyes. I'll leave you to it.

I waited until she had left before putting the tray with the empty plate to one side and opening the book at the bookmarked page. Very quickly, I realized that it was my mother's account of her wedding day to my father. Happy tears filled my eyes as I read pages and pages of how happy she was and how perfectly her life had fallen into place. Her only regret was that her own family couldn't attend the wedding and her father wasn't there to walk her down the aisle.

I skim-read the part about the wedding itself and moved on to the reception. My mother had described in great detail how she and my father had danced all night, including all the songs they had danced to. By the time I got to the end of the day, I was none the wiser as to why Emma would think it would shock me. Perhaps she didn't know that I'd already found out that I had a grandfather and aunts somewhere out in the ocean.

The next day's entry was much the same, many declarations of love and how happy my mother was. I remembered back to the royal wedding portrait in the palace hallway. She'd looked happy in it, with her long white dress.

I was almost about to put the book down, figuring that Emma had panicked over nothing when I noticed that my mother had written about her honeymoon being canceled.

She'd never mentioned it before, although thinking about it, she'd never mentioned her honeymoon at all before. It just wasn't something I'd ever asked her about.

Sitting back in my chair, I continued to read.

Our bags were packed, and we were to set off at first light the next day. My head was still in a whirlwind after the excitement of the wedding and my new position in the royal household. I'd gone from a simple mermaid to the queen of Atlantice overnight, and my thoughts were overwhelmed. If only I'd have known then what I know now just twenty-four hours later. Worrying if I'd make a good queen was nothing compared to worrying about what kind of mother I'd make.

Wait, what?

I stood up, my heart beating wildly. My mother hadn't been pregnant with me on her wedding day, surely?

No, in the official wedding portrait, she's appeared slim, her dress hugging her. There was no way she was hiding a baby bump under it. I flicked back to the start of the book and skimmed through it to almost the end when their wedding was. Not one mention had been made of any pregnancy. It was so odd. Why wouldn't she mention it? Even a few words to say she was pregnant? Nine months earlier she had been talking about getting herself ready for royal life.

It didn't make sense. I flicked to the next page to pick up reading but noticed a tear where a page had been ripped out.

I didn't want to read what came after, but morbid curiosity had my eyes wandering to the next page.

As I gazed down at this picture of beauty, I knew I was in love. I'd thought the biggest love I'd ever be able to feel, I'd already felt on my wedding day, but my love for Blaise eclipsed even that. Her father is besotted with her, and why wouldn't he be? As unexpected an addition as she was in our lives, and in the very short amount of time she has been with us, she has filled us with so much joy. Our beautiful Baby Blaise.

My throat tightened as I took in the implications of her words. I was adopted. Not two days after my parents' wedding, I'd been adopted. How could they not have told me?

"Seaweed hanging in trees," I shouted my childish swear over and over again as I marched around the room, banging my hands against the dresser.

I not only was adopted, I was unexpected! How could I possibly be unexpected? One doesn't simply walk into an adoption agency and then forget about it until the baby is plonked in your arms. Surely, they would have spent months filling out paperwork? And why so soon after their wedding? Didn't they have enough on their plate? None of it made any sense. I flung myself on my bed and cried myself dry.

A knock on my door interrupted my misery. "May I enter, Princess Blaise?"

"Don't call me princess," I said as Emma walked in. "I'm not a princess. I don't know who I am."

She hurried over and put her arms around me.

My shoulders shook as I cried on her shoulders.

"You're still their daughter. They raised you as their daughter, and they never had any other children. It's clear that they love you with everything in them. You're still a princess. In their eyes, in our eyes, you are still their daughter. Please, don't doubt that."

Her words soothed me enough that I stepped back and nodded. "What do I do now, knowing that I'm not their biological daughter?" I raced to the mirror on my vanity table and stared at my eyes. The golden rings around them were not like my parents or anyone I knew. "Emma, do you see my eyes? Have you ever noticed that they are not like everyone else's?" I'd always wondered about it. People remarked on them all the time. Even the Sea Witch had picked up on them.

Her words came back to haunt me. "Don't you know what you are?" she'd asked me. Apparently not, it seemed.

She peered into the mirror and smiled. "Yes, you have eyes that are unique" She lifted her shoulders slowly. "People assumed your eyes were from your maternal side as no one knew her family history. It makes sense."

My mother's eyes were bright green and nothing like mine. Certainly, they didn't have the golden rings around them.

"You knew that she was a mermaid before she transformed?"

She bobbed her head. "Yes, my mermaid friends told me last year. I wasn't sure whether to believe them. No one on land knew of it as far as I was aware. She kept her secrets very well."

"And still, you didn't try to persuade me to leave the AML?" I cocked my head. "You never spoke badly about them or even tried to talk me out of the organization."

She wrung her hands. "It wasn't my place to say anything. You were so fixated on helping them that I didn't want you to be upset with me."

My head lowered from all the negative thoughts. So many things had happened in such a short period of time that my poor brain was whizzing from it all.

"I think I need to see my parents, uhm, Queen Antonella and King Ermias."

Emma gave me a kindly smile and sat on the bed next to me. "Your highness, they're still you're parents. There is no doubt in anyone's mind that they love you as their daughter. And I think they would be deeply hurt if they heard you calling them by their royal names."

I turned away from her to watch the ships entering and leaving the bay before I turned to her. "Emma, do you think you could have the guards prepare the carriage without our insignia? I need to visit my parents, and I don't want anyone to know."

She stood looking grateful for something to do. "Of course. When do you want to set out?"

"Tomorrow, really early in the morning before anyone is up."

She strode to the door, bobbed, and said, "I'll speak to John to get your ride ready. Do you want me to bring you anything?"

"No, thank you. I have to see the staff and thank them all for their help last night at the party." I gave her a half-smile. Meeting any of the staff or guards was the last thing I wanted, but hiding in my room wouldn't help me any. Until my parents announced that I wasn't their biological daughter, I would act as a princess.

After thanking the staff and saying goodbye to the guests that had stayed in the palace overnight, I headed to the kitchen. The cook prepared a light brunch full of breads, cheese, and fruit and a tall glass of coconut water, which I took out on a plate to the beach-side terrace. The weather was better than it had been in weeks, with a weak hazy sun warming the sky. I sat my food on the table before I gazed at the sea, whose ebb and flow had me imagining a different kind of life. Fish didn't appear, but I was neither close to the water, nor had I called for him. I wanted to speak to him, to tell him how he was the talk of the town, but I knew if I did see him, I'd only end up crying.

A guard tapped his heels together a couple of times before I heard him. When I looked up, he bowed and said, "Your Highness, Hannah Fallon is here, insisting on seeing you."

"Oh, she is? Did she say why?"

Great!

He pursed his lips. "No. I asked her a couple of times, but she didn't respond and continued to ask to see you. I'm sorry, I couldn't dissuade her."

I waved my hand. The last thing I wanted to do was listen to Hannah's diatribe about Fish. No doubt, she'd seen the papers by now. And yet, I was only putting off the inevitable if I didn't see her. She was not a girl you could easily say no to.

"Let her in, and please can you ask one of the maids to bring in a selection of drinks, I think both hot and cold, just in case."

"Yes, Your highness. I'll let her in now."

"Thank you."

He bowed and strode to the door, leaving me feeling even more agitated than I already had been.

I took the last bite of my sandwich and drank the rest of the coconut water, hoping that she didn't cause my stomach to revolt from our conversation.

Hannah marched in with her shoulders back, gripping a newspaper. She opened and closed her other hand as if preparing for a fight.

"Hello, Hannah. How are you and your family? Your fiancée?" The formal greeting should have screamed for her to be careful, but Hannah usually ignored social cues unless they slapped her in the face.

She pursed her lips and slammed The Conch on the table. "Yeah, let's just skip the useless pleasantries as if we're still close friends. Because right now, we're definitely not."

I cleared my throat and swallowed. "I'm sorry to hear that you don't consider us friends. I know that our relationship is a bit strained, but I still consider you a friend."

She scoffed and placed both hands on her hips. "You know that we're not. Not anymore. So you can stop trying to pretend because it's not going to work."

"Fine," I sighed. "Have it your way. What do you want?"

She pointed at the newspaper with the picture of Fish and I dancing in the tank. The corner of my lips turned up as I remembered him leaning over and whispering how beautiful I looked just after the picture was taken.

"I guess you believed it was a good idea to jump into the tank and dance with a merman?"

"Of course, I did. Otherwise, I wouldn't have done it." I tapped my fingers against my jeans.

"Do you realize how bad this looks? How people will see this? You are almost naked for goodness sake." She paced in front of me, but I held my words, waiting for her to finish. "Blaise, you know how this will look. What people will say?"

She picked up the newspaper and turned to a page I hadn't read yet. The photo of Fish and I kissing filled up a quarter of the page. My body still tingled as I remembered the midnight kiss.

"Should we ever really be concerned about what people think?" I said lazily. Right then, I didn't care one jot what Hannah or any of her cronies thought of me.

"You're a princess! The daughter of the king of Atlantice, who will one day rule here. And you kissed a fish! You. Kissed. A. Fish!" She enunciated the last four words with loathing. "How could you? After all the AML training, I'm surprised that you could do that. It's disgusting. Simply disgusting..."

A knock interrupted her next words giving me time to formulate an answer that wouldn't be considered rude. It was harder than I thought it would be.

"Yes?" I asked, fully knowing that the staff would be bringing our drinks.

The door opened, and the maid came in carrying drinks.

While Hannah paced the terrace as if she were on fire, the maid put the drinks on the table next to me and gave me a quick curtsey.

"Anything else Your Highness?" she asked, appearing nervous, not that I could blame her. Hannah looked on the verge of exploding.

"Thank you, but I think we have everything we need."

"Hannah, please sit down and join me," I said as the maid hurried back into the palace. "They've brought every freshly squeezed fruit drink you usually enjoy." I picked up the container of freshly squeezed papaya juice. I poured out about a fifth into my glass and took a quick sip.

She halted her steps and marched over. "How can you act so nonchalant?"

"Why wouldn't I?" I pointed to the sea and the sky. "It's a beautiful day after a beautiful night, where the people of Atlantice were able to forget their daily life and enjoy themselves with plenty of food and dancing. You should have stayed."

She sneered. "Really? After what I read and saw in the newspaper, I'm really glad I decided to skip this sham of a ball. Your parents would've been ashamed of what happened here last night."

Maybe she was right. Maybe I didn't care about that either.

"The night was magical," I offered, which only seemed to anger her more.

"Yes, dark magic is what happened here. You kissed a fish. If I didn't know you aren't interested in getting married soon, I would say you were desperate. Didn't you learn anything from the AML? All those years of proof of what they do to our people? They kidnap and kill them for pleasure." She threw her hands in the air. "You, of all people, should know that."

I was sick of her whining. I'd heard this spiel so often coming from her lips I could recite it verbatim.

I stood and faced her. "You're wrong, Hannah. So wrong. He's the best man I know. His heart is genuine. He saved me from drowning. You, of all people, know how terrified I was of the water. How I refused to learn how to swim for years. How I wouldn't step in further than my shins into the sea and only when forced to because my friends, including you, begged me to join them. He risked his safety for me by allowing himself to be captured because he wanted to make sure I was safe. He has done more for me than anyone else, and that includes you."

"No, I won't believe your perception of these people. They're evil. They've killed. They're worse than savages."

"He's not like that. He's incredible, and you would see that if you spent some time with him."

She wrinkled her nose up. "I won't spend any time with those smelly fish. They're disgusting and dangerous. I'm surprised that he hasn't kidnapped or killed you yet. You need to wake up before he does."

I took in a deep breath, trying to keep my cool. "You are the one who needs to wake up, Hannah. You've spouted so many lies that you wouldn't know the truth if it slapped you in the face."

She strolled to the doors, while furiously shaking her head. She pivoted on her toes and barked her words. "I will not listen to you try to convince me that these people are anything but the disgusting creatures we've always believed they were. You have been hood-winked by him."

"Maybe I have, Hannah, but I'd rather be hoodwinked by him than knowingly be part of an organization that hurts others and spreads lies for their own gain. Not anymore."

She moved close to me, pushing her face into mine.

"You are disgusting," she spat.

My blood boiled, and I couldn't help myself. So much for staying calm. I pulled my hand into a fist. "Get out!" I ordered, my tone leaving little chance of misunderstanding.

"You won't hear the last of this!" She huffed. And as she stormed out, closing the gate behind her, I knew she was right. This was only the beginning.

5

16TH FEBRUARY

*E*mma entered my bedroom with a bounce in her step and humming a tune I didn't recognize.

The delicious smell of hot chocolate mixed with an unknown spice wafted by my nose.

"That smells heavenly," I said, offering up a smile. The day before had been one of the worst in my life, but a good night's sleep had put a few things in perspective.

"Good morning, Your Highness," She cried with false cheerfulness. She placed the tray with my morning drink on the table by the window before she bobbed. She glanced at the bag by my bed. "You're all set to visit your parents, I see."

I covered my mouth as I yawned. "I've been up since four, making sure that I have everything I need. I'm not sure how long I'll be staying with them."

Not seeing my parents for nine days had been difficult. Despite everything, I missed them.

I sat at the table and moaned as the hot chocolate warmed my mouth. "This tastes as good as it smells."

"If I'd known that you were awake, I would have brought you a cup up earlier. Do you need me to bring you breakfast and your clothes now?"

Running my fingers through my long hair to untangle the ends, I said, "No, thanks. I'll have breakfast downstairs. Do you know if the carriage is ready?"

"Yes, Your Highness, John organized everything last night. How are you feeling this morning?" she looked at me warily. No doubt me shouting at Hannah had got back to her. I'd completely unraveled, and Emma knew it.

"I've been better," I admitted.

She nodded. "You will be fine. Remember that they love you." She was back to talking about my parents.

I already knew that. I just wished they hadn't lied to me. There were too many secrets in this palace. First, the mermaid stuff, now about me being adopted. I didn't want to tell her I was afraid there was more.

"How many guards are accompanying the carriage?" I asked, instead. It seemed a safe topic of conversation.

"There will be two guards driving and two at the back, or so John told me. There will also be five guards ahead and five behind the carriage on horseback. All will be in the red uniform."

I glanced up at her. "I thought I was to go as inconspicuously as possible."

"That's what I said, but John told me his thinking, and it makes sense. Anyone seeing the guards will believe that a guest from the ball is leaving the palace, and they should not suspect that it's you inside."

I guess it made sense.

"If anyone does follow you, I believe there is a contingency plan. I'll go and alert the cook that you're nearly ready to eat; shall I?"

"Please."

Once she was gone, I pulled on my jeans and sweater. The weather had been mild yesterday, but it was volatile at the moment, and though it was still too dark to tell, I didn't hold up much hope that the weather would continue to be nice.

I headed downstairs, my head full of conflicting thoughts. I'd not seen Fish all day yesterday, and who knew when I'd see him again. Taking a detour around the breakfast room, I headed down to the tunnel beneath the palace.

Fish was already there, resting his head on one hand, his arm on the platform allowing his almost dried long hair to spread behind his back and shoulders. "Good morning, Princess. I thought you'd forgotten about me."

I knelt down to him, getting my knees soggy in the process and kissed him. I could really taste the salt on his lips now that I'd been away from the ocean for two days. "Never...although, I have to go away again. I need to see my parents."

"I understand. I hope there wasn't too much trouble for you after the other night. I spent the day in here hoping you'd come to me. I worried when you didn't."

I sighed. "I'm sorry." I told him everything; about my spat with Hannah, about finding out I was adopted, and about the missing page from the diary.

Wow, he exhaled sharply. "You didn't know?"

"My parents are quite adept at keeping secrets from me; it seems. That's partially why I'm going. To find out if there is anything else they are hiding from me."

"I wish there was something I could do."

I slipped my hand into his and felt his familiar warmth. "You've done more for me than you could know."

His smile almost broke my heart. "I don't think I'll be too long. I'll come straight down here when I get back." I let go of his hand and stood.

"I'll be here."

As I opened the door to the basement, I turned back to him. "I'm going to ask Emma to bring you the newspapers. You are quite famous up here after the other night."

"Famous?"

"They are calling you my mystery man."

"Beats what I used to get called at school."

I laughed, and after blowing him a kiss, I headed back into the palace.

A short time later, the carriage rolled out of the palace grounds and followed the road to my parents' hideaway house. No one had told me where it was, and I wasn't allowed to look through the carriage curtains lest someone see me, so I had to content myself with reading a book in the dim light the carriage afforded.

The jostling of the carriage calmed me, and at some point, my eyelids closed until the swaying completely lulled me to sleep.

Sometime later, I awoke, and as we were far from Antla, I was finally able to open the dark curtains. The journey took longer than I had anticipated and I whiled away the hours watching the world go by.

Eventually, we came to a stop, and Captain Jimenez's voice drifted down from the front of the carriage. "Your Highness, we're here."

I didn't wait for him to insert the keys into the lock; instead, I unlocked it myself from the inside, carefully swung the door open, and dropped to the ground without using the stairs.

The captain bowed and held the door. "Welcome to Coventry Cottage."

A thrill of delight filled me as I took in the thatched roof and the quaint cottage with a small garden out front. Behind the cottage, rolling hills filled the horizon, and out of the chimney atop the cottage, smoke rose lazily, drifting upwards to nothing. Behind me a path wound its way down to the sea.

My father, dressed in a peasant's Sunday best, stood outside the door with his arms wide open. He appeared tired as if he had not slept in days, but his grin brightened up his face.

I sprinted toward him, almost toppling him over. "Father, I've missed you so much. So, so much." I rested my head on his shoulder.

Parental love flowed from him as he tightened his arms around me. "I've missed you too, my little pumpkin." The name I'd hated since the time I hit twelve suddenly sounded beautiful. "How are you? Have the staff been taking care of you?" He stepped back. "You look well-rested."

"I slept the whole way here," I laughed. "Where's mom?"

He sighed. "She's at the cove," he said with a low voice. "It's been difficult."

"Oh." Of course, she was. She couldn't live in a cottage.

He led me inside the cottage filled with flowers in handmade vases. "She's not happy here."

A guard popped out of his seat by the front door and bowed as we headed in.

"Shall I fix us some tea?" My father asked. I almost laughed before I realized he was being serious. I'd never seen him make tea in his life.

"Actually, I'd like to go and see mom."

"Of course." He gestured to the door we'd just come from. I left my bag in the house and headed back outside.

Down by the cove, my mom waved excitedly as she saw us approach. Her smile brightened her face and reminded me of happier times, times when we'd talked for hours about silly difficulties at school that I thought meant so much, or when I'd fought with my friends and sworn my world was collapsing.

If only I could return to those simpler problems and not the ones we now faced.

I jumped into the water fully clothed, and once I reached the deeper water, I lunged. "Mom, I've so missed you." I hugged her, and just like it did with Fish, warmth spread through my body.

We bobbed like two buoys tied together during a storm. "Oh, sweetie. I've missed you more. Much more." Her tears mingled with my own. "It's good to hold you in my arms, my sweet, precious Blaise. My darling daughter."

The words aching to be spilled stayed unsaid as I smelled the salty water in her long hair.

Minutes later, my mom and I leaned against either side of a pale green rowboat with my father in the boat itself.

My dad smiled. "It does my heart good to see my two beautiful ladies safely next to me. We are so glad you are here and safe. We worried about you. We got word that you had disappeared. We also had word that you were out in the ocean with a merman. Is that true?"

The questions burned in my mind. I'd come here to ask them about their secrets, and here they were interrogating me.

I told them everything, about how I'd met Fish, about how we'd kissed at the ball. I only left out the part where I'd been taken by the witch. For some reason, I knew it would only scare them more.

"I don't know how you survived out there," my father said. "What did you do? How did you eat? How did you survive in those temperatures? I must say, I thought the whole thing was a joke."

"It isn't a joke, Father. I ate what Fish brought me. He kept me warm, transferring his heat to me."

My father's face was a picture of shock, and my cheeks reddened as I realized how it sounded. "It works with all merfolk. When I hugged mother, she transferred her heat to me too." As I said it, I realized the cold was beginning to creep in again. I swam around the boat to the other side where my mother held on.

"But how did you stay in the water so long?" she asked.

Neither seemed in the slightest bit upset I was dating a merman. Mind you, how could they be, given their own personal circumstances?

"I can breathe underwater."

She gave me an odd look. "You can?"

"Yes, because I'm a half..." I was about to tell her that I was a half-mermaid, but I wasn't. If I was adopted, I couldn't have been. So, it begged the question, what was I?

I shook my head, trying to get rid of the Sea Witch's face. She'd told me that I didn't know what I was, and she was right. Not only did I not know who I was or where I'd come from, I had literally no idea now how I could breathe under the water either.

I took a deep breath and spoke again, my body shaking slightly. "I found your diaries. I know I was adopted."

They glanced at each other, and beside me, my mother gasped. "I guess I have no right to be angry at you for going through my things. You were never meant to see those."

"Maybe not, but I did see them. I saw what you wrote the day after the wedding, but there was a page ripped out."

She closed her eyes, and pain radiated throughout her features. "I'm sorry. We should have told you."

"So tell me now," I demanded, anger coursing through me.

"We didn't adopt you," my father said quietly. "Not properly, anyway."

My heart jumped into my mouth. Not adopted me? "So, what did you do?"

Mt father looked down at my mother, and she nodded her head, so he continued. "The day after our wedding, we were planning for our honeymoon. I'd booked us a couple of weeks at one of Skyla's beach resorts. In the middle of the night, one of the maids woke us, telling us that there was someone to see the both of us who had said it was urgent. I was a new king. My parents had died only a couple of years prior, and I still did as people asked of me, and that included getting up at midnight to speak to strangers on my doorstep." He gave a cough and stopped speaking. Up on the clifftop, a guard watched us. We must have looked so funny to him, two of us in the water holding onto my father's boat. At least, he was too far away to hear what we were saying.

"Carry on," I said impatiently.

"It was an old woman."

"It was two women," my mother corrected him. "The older one came to the door, but the younger one stood behind her, covering her face with a hood."

"That's right." my father agreed. "The older one handed over a baby...you. She said that a spell had been broken, and the kingdom would shine again."

"Would shine again?" I asked.

"Before you were born, there were lots of troubles. A little like it is today. The woman said our troubles would be over as long as we took you, no questions asked. She wanted you to go to a good home."

My eyes widened. "What? You just took me from her?"

My mom gently patted my forearm. "I know it seems unbelievable, but it's what happened. When you opened your eyes and gazed at me, I asked to hold you and fell in love instantly." She slowly breathed in. "Your sweet smell. I will never forget it. And when I touched your cheeks, you grabbed my fingers and didn't let go. I loved you from the very first moment."

"I understand that you both fell in love with me." I glanced at both of them. "But did neither of you think to ask questions? Do you know who my real mom and dad are? Do you know anything about me at all?"

I glanced between the two of them incredulously. The king and queen of a kingdom and they did something so utterly reckless, so out of character.

"Of course, we asked questions," my father said. "The old woman refused to tell us anything except to say that you were very loved and not given up lightly."

"But surely taking in a baby without papers is illegal."

"Yes, but there was something about the woman. It was like we were compelled to take you. She was right too. After you joined us, the kingdom began to thrive."

"Why didn't you tell me?"

"We discussed it early on," my mother said, slipping her hand in mine. "We wanted to raise you as our own. We worried that if people knew you were not born to us, they wouldn't see you as a lawful princess. We told the world that I found out very late in my pregnancy that I was actually pregnant. We told them that I was very lucky that my bump didn't show and that I'd kept it well hidden. A lot of people thought it strange, but over time they forgot. You were such a sweet little thing that you wowed the public and press, and questions about your birth stopped coming. A little trickery and a bribe involving a local doctor helped. We didn't tell you because we told no one else. We were never blessed with biological children, but I never felt I needed them because I always had you. I have never regretted taking you in."

She pulled me into a hug. Once again, her warmth seeped into my body.

My whole life was a lie. I didn't know who I was or where I'd come from, and yet, the look on my mother's face was so earnest. I could make the decision to forgive her or to break her heart. In the end, I couldn't do it. I couldn't hurt her more than she already was hurting. My parents had given me the best life anyone could hope for. Did it really matter what had happened at the start of it?

"I saw the Sea Witch," I said. They'd told me their secret. Now it was my turn to tell them mine.

My mom's hand touched her chest, and her eyes widened. "When did you talk to her?" Her voice quivered on the last word.

"A couple of days after you went into hiding. I read a few of your diaries, and when the curiosity took hold, I went to see her."

They both gasped and instantaneously gawked at each other. Their reactions kept me from mentioning that she had trapped me in the bubble.

"You need to stay away from her!" my mother said quickly

My dad sneered. "She tried to kill your mother."

"What? When?"

"Before you were born, when we were still courting. I knew your mother was a mermaid, but no one else did. We met in secret. There's a tunnel under the palace."

"Yeah, I know," I said.

He raised his eyebrows but didn't question how I knew.

"Your mother had fallen in love with me from afar..." My mother held her hand up and rested it on my father's arm. "Why don't you let me tell this part?"

My father nodded.

"I had fallen in love with your father. His ship was wrecked, and I saved him. He knew right from the start that I was a mermaid, but no one else did. We hid away, meeting in secret until the day he asked me to marry him. I said I couldn't. How could I? I had a tail. It was then that I went to the Sea Witch. She promised me legs in exchange for my voice. I agreed, but once I had my legs, I got scared and swam away before she could take my voice. She followed me to the surface, but your father was waiting for me in his boat. He pulled me over the side, but not before the Sea Witch hit my new feet with her magic."

"She hit you?" I asked, amazed. "Did she hurt you?"

My mother's eyes clouded over as if remembering something awful. "Every day after that, walking was almost unbearable. I was introduced to your grandparents as your father's fiancé. They accepted me, but they must have thought I was strange, sitting down as often as I did. My feet felt like I was walking on knives. Your grandparents died before we got married, so they never knew me when I was not in pain. I must have seemed so odd to them. A few weeks before the wedding, my feet just stopped hurting."

"They just stopped?"

"Yes. One day I woke up and was able to walk properly. I danced all night at our wedding. It was wonderful. I'd not had any pain since...well, not until it returned at about Christmas time. The pain started coming back. It wasn't too bad at first. I could pass it off as bad footwear, but throughout January, it got considerably worse. You saw yourself what happened next. I'm back to the way I was before."

My heart bled for her. How awful it must have been to walk in agony for all that time. It just brought up more questions, though. Why did the pain suddenly stop all those years ago and why did it come back last month? The Sea Witch probably knew, but I wasn't planning to go back to find out.

6

17TH FEBRUARY

The morning sunlight chased my carriage as we headed back toward the palace at breakneck speed. It jostled from side-to-side as the horses' metal shoes pounded the road.

I had visited my parents because I missed them and wanted answers, but everything I discovered on my short trip had pushed my mind into overdrive. During the long return trip to the palace, my mind filled itself with uncertainty about my parents' confessions and excitement on reuniting with Fish. My heart pounded against my ribs, thinking about him.

I wasn't sure if the good night's rest without waking up before the roosters or the anticipation of returning to Fish's arms kept me awake during the ride. Not once did I nod off to the horses' rhythmic beats, but instead, I observed how the carriage whizzed by the countryside and cottages with large chimneys, their dark smoke filling the light-orange sky.

Every few miles, a person or two appeared next to the road, but more often than not, it was empty. Nobody waved, and certainly, no one ever imagined that part of the monarchy rode inside the nondescript carriage speeding toward the town of Antla.

Perhaps the reason my mind didn't surrender to the rhythmic

carriage ride was that, among all my other thoughts, the one that stood out was the one about my royal status.

Who was I? Who were my biological parents, and why had they given me up? More importantly, how could I find out the answers to my questions?

The familiar odors of the town drifted in from my open window. The smell of fish wafted by as we passed the dock, and I wrinkled my nose. I loved eating seafood, but the smell of so much fish wasn't pleasant.

Pinching my nose, I stared out the window at the busy loading dock filled with people. Nothing appeared unusual. Nobody rioted, nobody shouted.

Everyone appeared to be in excellent spirits, working their jobs without a need for intervention.

I wondered how the merpeople were doing.

As the carriage entered the town center, the smell of fish was replaced by the delicious aroma of baked breads flooding the inside of the carriage. I inhaled and yearned for a meal from the palace cook.

The carriage finally came to a stop inside the palace grounds. Captain McDougall opened the door and bowed his head before he said, "Welcome home, Your Highness."

"Thank you."

McDougall had come back with me on the orders of my mother and father. He was to return to them once I was safely home. After the talk in the sea, clinging to my father's boat, my mother had decided it would be better if we headed inside. A guard had been brought down to help carry her up. She'd stayed long enough to talk me through the specifics of me arriving at the palace as a baby, and then returned to sleep in the ocean.

I'd had time to think about not really being a princess and had come to terms with it. I was no longer angry at my parents; however, their explanation had left a lot to be desired. I knew that if someone had turned up at my doorstep in the middle of the night and handed me a baby, I'd have certainly asked questions. And yet, they hadn't. They'd accepted it. I think they believed that somehow I was good luck and that my mother had been able to live peacefully with no pain in her legs for the past eighteen years because of me. The notion was ridiculous. All of it was ridiculous, but the alternative could have been much worse. My birth parents obviously wanted more for me than they could give, and they'd brought me to the royal palace. I guessed they hoped I'd grow up to be a princess. I allowed myself a smile. They'd got their wish. And yet, a pang of sadness pulled at me. It wasn't the fact I was given up as an infant. It happens. Babies are adopted every day, but the not knowing where I was from almost crippled me. If I came from an orphanage, I'd have been able to ask to see their records. As things stood, unless my birth parents made themselves known to me, I would never find out. After eighteen years, it didn't look likely.

I ran through the palace and headed straight down to the tunnel beneath. As I'd hoped he would be, Fish was there and greeted me with a smile. This time, it was most definitely him.

"Welcome home, Princess." He winked, and his lips curled up. "I hope your trip was everything you wished for."

Resisting that gorgeous face became nearly impossible, I dropped my bag and sprinted toward him. Slipping out of my shoes before I sat on the edge of the platform, I leaned in to meet his kiss.

For some unknown reason, after our kiss, I lowered my head and bit my lip. A weird shyness overcame me.

He lifted my head with his fingers. "Is everything okay? Are your parents fine?"

I nodded and croaked out. "Yes, they were in great health. Everything is good. I have a lot to tell you, but later. How are you?"

"Better, now that you're here. Did your parents admit to you being adopted?"

I sighed, holding my hand out to him. "They did...but..."

He picked up my hand and intertwined our fingers, gently squeezing them. "I'm all ears."

The hinges of the huge door creaked before the person knocked. "Yes?"

The door opened about an inch, and in a low voice, Emma asked, "May I come in?"

"Yes, of course."

She pushed the door ajar, slid in, and curtsied. "Welcome back. How are Queen Antonella and King Ermias? How was your trip?"

I beckoned her to join me on the edge of the steps. Her eyes widened before she kicked off her shoes and dipped her toes in the water.

"They're as good as can be expected. I wanted them to travel home with me, but my mother is reluctant to. She is free to swim in the waters around where they are. Here, that would not be possible without a barrage of media people hanging out on the coast hoping to get a glimpse of her. I spoke to them about my adoption. Now that you are here, I might as well tell you both at the same time."

I breathed in and closed my eyes for a few seconds before I told them everything I'd learned.

Neither spoke as I told them about the night I was brought to the palace and the aftermath where my parents had concealed me and pretended my mother was pregnant.

"Incredible. Did they know these women?" Emma asked while she gaped at me.

I shrugged. "Nope. Not at all. My parents opened their door in the middle of the night. Someone handed them a baby, and it sounded like they just took it...me. I mean, who does that?"

Fish tilted his head. "That's so weird."

"Trust me, it's super weird. They didn't question the women, didn't ask them where they were from, who they were. Nothing. They took me in without knowing anything except that they fell in love with me the moment they saw me."

Beside me, Emma aahed as though this was some kind of romantic love story and not the nightmare of my life.

Fish winked, his grin lightening up his face. "Of course, they fell in love. Just look at you. Who wouldn't have fallen in love with you?" He squeezed my fingers, causing my breath to hitch and my cheeks to heat up. "But it's still strange that they would just hand over an infant like that. Who gives up a child to complete strangers?"

Emma lowered her voice. "What if they stole the child from someone else? They would've been in big trouble. Even the royal family must obey the rules. The authorities would force a trial or something."

It had crossed my mind. Stealing children wasn't completely unheard of and babies especially, but the way my parents told the story, no money exchanged hands, and no one had ever come forward to ask them for money.

"I really don't know what they were thinking. The whole thing is completely insane, but it is what it is."

"Do you think you'll search for your birth parents?" she asked.

I shook my head. "How can I? All I have to go on is that I was given up by two women, an older one, and a younger one. The younger one's face was hidden by a hood. I'm guessing my mother and grandmother, but who knows. There is no way I'll ever get to the bottom of who I am."

"So you're not going to at least try?" she asked incredulously.

"What can I do? Do you know how I could find them? My only real option is to put a call out via the Conch, but if people know my mother lied to them twice, I doubt they'd be so forgiving. We've had enough troubles lately. This would destroy the monarchy. I need to keep it a secret."

"I see your point," she said. "I just wish there was another way."

"I do too, but I can't think of it. That's not all I spoke to my parents about. Before their wedding, the Sea Witch tried to kill my mom."

"What?" Fish's jaw dropped before he shut his mouth. "The Sea Witch who held you captive?"

"Yes, the only Sea Witch around these parts."

Emma picked on the hem of her uniformed skirt. "Why?"

I told them both the part about my mother swimming away from her and the pain in my mother's legs until around the time they married.

Fish held out his hand, pointing his finger upward. "That's why she took you. Revenge! It had nothing to do with who you are or the fact that you can breathe underwater. She wanted you in exchange for your mother."

It made sense. Perhaps the witch planned to take my voice in exchange for my mother's tail. Maybe she was going to use me to lure my mother to her so she could take her voice. A shiver passed through me as I thought of what might have happened if I'd not escaped.

Fish squeezed my hand. "No wonder you're shell shocked. You've been through a lot."

"She might have killed me," I murmured.

Fish's thumb caressed the back of my hand. "Try not to think about it. Let's talk about something else."

Beside me, Emma nodded her head. It was as if the pair of them wanted to cheer me up. It was nice to feel so cared about.

"Tell me about the townsfolk. I noticed it was quiet when I pulled in this morning."

"Not one single riot since you gave your speech!" Emma grinned. "I told you, you could do it."

My speech felt like it had happened so long ago. So much had happened since, and the state of the kingdom had been pushed from my mind.

"What about the merfolk? How are they doing?"

Fish raised his eyebrows, and his mouth fell into a lazy grin. "I spoke to them. The news of the above world filtered through. I think they understand that you are on our side now. They are certainly happy that they can go to the land shops again."

"Merfolk use land shops?" Emma questioned. "How?"

Fish laughed. "They don't go inside. A lot of the land shops are situated along the many waterways. On one side they have doors to the street which the land folk use, and at the back, many of them have other doors...windows really just above the waterline. The merfolk knock at the window and give their orders. The shopkeepers bring it to them. We also have shops of our own under the water."

Emma gasped. "I wish I could go see."

She would never be able to swim to the mer-village. Unlike me, she couldn't breathe underwater.

"I'm not a half-mermaid," I said. When neither of them spoke, I carried on. "I shouldn't be able to breathe underwater."

Fish's eyes widened. "Then how can you?"

I shrugged. "I don't know."

The three of us lapsed into silence. I'd told them everything I knew. There was nothing left to say. Neither of them had any idea why I'd suddenly uncovered this new ability.

I stood up. I'd hoped that speaking to Fish and Emma would bring some clarity to my situation, but if anything, it had left me feeling more despondent.

"Now that I'm back, I should go and talk to John and see what's been happening in my absence."

"Wait, you've just got back."

I turned back to Fish. "I know. I'm sorry. I'll see you later." Emma jumped up and slipped her feet into her shoes. With a small wave, the two of us left the tunnel and headed back into the palace.

I found John exactly where I expected to find him. He opened his office door and ushered me inside.

"How has everything been"? I asked, once I was certain the door was closed behind me. I took a seat in one of his leather wingbacked chairs while he took the other.

"Things certainly seem to have died down a bit Your Highness. Word is that your speech had an impact. I suspect the AML haven't changed their views, but the other townsfolk have stopped blindly listening to them. You did a good job, Your Highness."

I gave him a small smile. Any praise was high praise coming from John.

"Thank you. Do you think that's it now? Are we over this?"

"Hmm." He lifted his fingers to his chin. "I wouldn't like to say. Yes, it seems that things have calmed down, but you never can tell what is going on under the surface...and I'm not talking about the water."

"So, what are you talking about?"

"Nothing really," he answered, sitting back in his chair. "But the AML is still active. One speech isn't going to sway them, and just because they have been quiet for a few days doesn't mean they aren't planning something."

The only way I could think of to find out what they were up to, if anything, was to go right to the source, but there was no way I'd be able to go to an AML meeting and remain inconspicuous. I'd managed it for years because the AML always met in a small building in a back alley, and no one would ever think to look out for a princess. Now, the second I headed out into the streets, I'd have all eyes on me. It occurred to me that I wasn't the only one that people would pay attention to. Until a few weeks ago, not many people had heard of the AML. Their rise to fame was swift, and now, everyone knew about them. It meant that the Conch would be keeping tabs on what they were up to.

"I'd like to go to the Conch head offices in town," I said, standing up.

John's mouth opened in surprise.

"Why ever would you want to do a thing like that?" he asked. "I've had them sending messengers here at all times of day to request a meeting with you. I've been almost fighting reporters off all day and night."

"In that case, they'll be happy to see me," I said, opening his office door. Before I was halfway through it, I heard his footsteps following me.

"I don't think it's a good idea for you to be heading into Antla," he said, striding in front of me and turning to stop me.

"I'm not suggesting I go alone. I was hoping you'd get a carriage ready for me. I'll take a couple of guards, and I'll be taking my maid."

"Your maid?" he furrowed his eyebrows. "What do you need your maid for?"

"I don't need my maid for anything," I replied, smiling sweetly. "I just want her to come. I'll go find her and pick up the carriage by the main door in ten minutes."

It didn't take long to find Emma. I'd only just left her a few minutes previously. She almost brimmed over with excitement when I asked her to come with me.

"Why the Conch?" she asked as we stepped into the carriage. I hated to get back into one so soon after getting out of one, but walking through the streets just wasn't an option.

"I needed to confirm if your perception of the state of Antla is accurate. I mean, you've seen it from the palace, and Fish has seen what's going on in the mer village, but neither of you has spent time in town."

"I've been through town. I live in the center," Emma pointed out.

"What I actually meant was you haven't been following the AML and seeing what they are up to."

"Oh!"

The journey to the newspaper offices was mercifully short.

A tiny bell jingled above the Conch's front door, and as we walked in, the smell of old newspaper invaded my nostrils.

I headed to the counter, and two young men bowed. The older of the two gawked at me without saying a word, but the younger one got over himself and managed to speak. "Good day, Your Highness. Welcome to the Conch. How can we help you?"

"Hi. I'd like to talk to Mr. Scribble."

Mr. Scribble was the owner of the Conch. He was also the chief reporter when he felt brave enough to leave his two sons in charge in the office. I'd met him on a good many occasions as he was the official royal reporter.

"Yes, he's in the back, and it'll take just a minute to get him." He sprinted through the back door, leaving his brother still gawking.

I picked up a newspaper left on the counter with the photo of Fish and me at the ball. We looked amazing on it. Such a wonderful night.

A couple of seconds later, Mr. Mark Scribble scurried in with a pencil behind an ear, and his fingers darkened by ink. His head must have touched his knees when he bowed. "Your Highness, it's a great pleasure to have you here. What can I do for you?"

"Hello, Mr. Scribble. Nice to see you again. Can we talk in the back?"

He bowed again, this time a little shallower and beckoned me through to his back office. Emma came with me, but the guard who had accompanied us stayed at the front door.

"I'm here about the AML, Mr. Scribble."

The second I mentioned those three letters, his face lit up. He pulled his pencil from behind his ear and grabbed a notebook from the desk.

"I'm not here to give an interview," I said, seeing what he was about to do. "Quite the opposite, in fact. I'm here to ask you for information. I trust that our talk will remain just between the three of us."

The poor man looked almost devastated that I was denying him his interview of a lifetime, but he put the notebook back down and put the pencil back behind his ear.

"Of course. My lips are sealed. What do you want to know about the AML?"

"I trust you've been following them?"

He steepled his fingers. "I've had a number of reporters on the case, yes."

"My main concern is that the current lull in the riots is a temporary thing, and the AML is planning something huge. My guards are working around the clock to keep the palace safe. Some of them are with my mother and father. They aren't taking time off because of the potential threat."

"I understand your concern, Your Highness. Far be it from me to tell you how to run the palace, but from what I've heard, the tide has changed considerably. Not long ago, a great many people were joining the ranks of the AML, but after your speech, the shopkeepers began thinking for themselves. People stopped being scared to speak out. A lot of the newer AML members left. I don't think it's a matter of what the AML is planning; I think it's more a matter of what they realistically can plan. At the moment, very little."

"So, everything is all right then?"

He sat forward. "I wouldn't say it's back to normal. There are a lot of issues in play. The bad storms affecting the area are still happening, your parents are still in hiding, and your mother is still a mermaid...isn't she?"

I ignored his question. I wasn't here to provide him with snippets of gossip for him to print in the next day's paper.

"What about the underwater people?" I asked. "Have you heard of any issues with them?"

He quickly shook his head. "They're quieter than us humans. I haven't heard of any problems or potential problems. I like the merfolk. No bother. Not much to write about, though."

"That is really all I needed to know. Thank you." I stood to leave. Beside me, Emma also stood. Mr. Scribble looked stricken that his favorite piece of tabloid fodder was just about to walk out of his office without so much as a smidgen of gossip.

"Anything else I can do for you, Your Highness?" He ran around the two of us to open the door.

"No, I appreciate your time, Mr. Scribble."

"Anytime."

I'd almost left when a thought occurred to me.

"Actually, Mr. Scribble, there is something you can do for me."

He gave me a toothy grin before running back to pick up his notebook again. "Name it!"

"Can you print an announcement for me?"

The poor man looked like I'd just asked him to kill his own mother. "I'm going to be holding a party down by the marina tomorrow night. I'm going to invite the public. There is a little fish restaurant there called El Mar. I'll have my guards in attendance."

He nodded as he wrote the information down.

"I'll have it out before four if you wish."

"I would like the merpeople to receive the announcement as well."

He nodded. "No problem. I'll have the dolphins deliver underwater notices."

"Thank you... Oh, and Mr. Scribble?"

"Yes?"

"I'd like you to cover it in the paper."

His face brightened considerably at the invite. It made up for the lack of gossip anyway.

Before heading back to the palace, I made a quick detour to the fish restaurant to let them know that they would be busy. The owners were ecstatic, especially when I let them know I'd get the palace to help with catering and food, and I would pay them a handsome amount of shells for their troubles.

"Why are we having a party?" Emma asked when we were finally on our way back to the palace.

"It's one thing to talk about coming together. Now, I want to practice what I preach. I want the Conch photographing me with the merfolk and the landfolk."

"Great idea! Aren't you worried that the AML will show up?"

I turned to her. "I'm actually hoping they do. They are the ones that need convincing the most."

7

18TH FEBRUARY

*B*efore the roosters crowed, I had met with the palace cook and with the El Mar owners to make sure the preparations were running smoothly. The palace cook had ogled at me as though I was insane when I'd announced I needed her help the evening before. I didn't like putting so much on the palace kitchens at such short notice, but the restaurant wasn't equipped to deal with the numbers I expected.

It meant I had to help source the fish, but I had someone ideal to help.

"The freshly caught fish has been delivered," Fish beamed up at me from the water in the tunnel. "Did the merfolk mind helping out?" I asked after first bending down for a kiss.

"They were happy to help. I think we can safely say that they have forgiven you."

I gave him a grin. "In fact, they asked if I'd bring you to meet them this morning so they could formally apologize."

"I wish I could, but it's not just the fish we have to deal with. The palace cook is having kittens over the whole thing, and I've had to send a message to Mrs. Farina's bakery to order as many deserts as she can make. It wasn't a very well thought out plan." I conceded.

"You are planning much more than a party. You are doing for the kingdom what needed to be done. I can't speak for the land folk, but the merfolk are greatly impressed."

When I didn't reply, he continued. "Are you worried about the party, or is something else bothering you?"

"It's not really the party." I bit my cheeks before I said, "The people listened to me, and it was great, but I wonder how they will be when faced with the merpeople."

"They will be fine. You've got to remember that this is a recent thing. Before the beginning of this year, the land folk and the merfolk got on reasonably well. The insurgence of the AML has caused all this."

"It's the AML I'm worried about. The editor for the Conch told me that they weren't up to anything, but he's not been inside their meetings. How much can he really tell by following them to and from the meeting rooms?"

Fish shrugged.

"They get off on violence, and that's what worries me."

Fish furrowed his eyebrows. "I've not known them to be violent. A bunch of asses maybe, but not violent."

"It's low-level stuff. We used to do this thing where we'd sit in a circle and tell stories about how we'd been awful to a merperson. Some people would throw stuff, some would call them names, or generally inconvenience them."

"You did that?"

I felt my cheeks redden at the admission. Just saying it aloud made me feel sick about the whole thing.

"It wasn't my finest moment. Anyway, the point I'm making is that some of the AML would hurt the merfolk. They often talked about doing much worse. You've heard yourself about the death threats."

"They are all talk," Fish scoffed.

I wasn't so sure. "They are angry. Having such a turn-around of the people won't make them happy. I know Hannah. She doesn't like to lose."

He swam closer and took my hand. "You have organized half the palace guard to be there. The merfolk are on your side now after your speech." When I didn't look convinced, he squeezed my hand. "If everything goes horribly wrong, just jump into the water, and I'll whisk you away."

He made it sound so easy.

"How about I whisk you away right now?" He pulled me closer, wrapping his arms around my waist. Saltwater dripped from his arms, seeping through my dress.

The temptation to just dive in and hide from my problems was immense, but that was the trouble. It always had been. Spending time with Fish was all too easy, but it didn't mean it was the right thing to do.

"I can't," I sighed. "I've made a lot of work for the palace, and I really should be there to help."

"Aren't you supposed to be in charge?" he asked, scooting my whole body closer to the edge of the water. "So delegate." He brought me into a kiss, and as I inhaled the salty smell, I knew I was powerless to resist him. Pulling my shoes off and throwing them to the stone floor, I pulled my clothes off, leaving me in only my bra and panties and slipped into the water. Fish reached out for me and pulled me back into the kiss that I'd just interrupted by taking my clothes off. His heat thrilled me, and as we sank below the surface and the dark water enveloped us, I knew I never wanted to let this go. Of course, we had to. A dark tunnel was no place for a make-out session. It might have been if it wasn't for the very distinct possibility that Emma would be asked to come look for me. After checking my bedroom, this is the very first place she would look. Fish's plan had been to take me to the cave in the next cove, but the choppy sea had ended that idea, so he took me to the treasure cave instead. Not that I cared. I probably should have. Another storm blowing in meant that my party would probably be a bust, but right in that moment, I didn't care. He lay me down in the sand and there, in amongst gold and jewels and treasures rivaling those of the palace, he kissed me again, his emerald eyes locked onto mine. I'd always kissed him with my eyes closed before, but watching the way he looked at me as our lips touched, brought about sensations I never knew existed. My pulse raced as he pressed his naked chest against me and soon, I couldn't keep my eyes open any longer. I fell into the kiss until that's all that there was, just the sound of the storm outside the cave, the taste of salt, and the heat of his lips upon mine.

He ran his hand down the skin on my side, sending fire through my veins, igniting feelings I'd never known. Goosebumps appeared on my arm, and suddenly I was more aware of my body than I'd ever been before. The feel of the damp sand on my back, the slight ripple of wind on my arms, and mostly, the feel of Fish against me.

Water lapped at my feet, not as turbulent as the sea outside the cave, but enough to drench my legs and up to my waist. Fish's tail was damp against my thighs, and for the first time, I paid attention to the feel of it. In my AML days, I'd always thought of a merperson's tail as being something gross, wet, and slippery, but his scales were soft, almost like velvet against my skin. I reached down and touched the scales where his thigh would be if he had legs. Beneath the skin, I felt hard muscle, powerful from constant swimming. He kissed me again, and this time, I let go. I let go of his tail, of everything, and abandoned myself to the moment. A rogue wave caught us, drenching us from head to toe. Beside me, some of the lighter treasure moved with a clanking sound as it hit other pieces.

"I should probably get you back," Fish said, pulling back. My heart tugged at the thought of returning to the palace, spending the day without him, but there was always tonight. He'd be at the party, and there was nothing stopping me from spending the night out in the ocean with him.

The ocean tossed us from side to side as we swam back to the tunnel. "I might have to call the party off if the weather continues like this," I sighed as we saw to the basement door.

"This is just a squall. It will clear up."

I gave him one last kiss as I climbed up onto the steps and pulled my clothes on over my wet underwear.

In my bedroom, Emma had laid out my clothes for the party. A smart pantsuit that looked more business than princess, but I trusted her judgment. After a quick shower, I ran some red lipstick over my lips, a nice contrast to the navy blue jacket, and headed out to help with the preparations. Despite her bluster, the head cook had everything under control, and when I peeped in the kitchen, she had her army of staff were busy making food. As I watched, a number of staff members came in and picked up the items that were ready to go and took them out to be loaded into carriages to be taken to the restaurant.

Not wanting to take up the cook's time, I went to see John instead. Expecting to find him in a similar panic, although much less obvious, I was surprised to see him, not only out of his office, but outside, organizing the food into the carriages. He held an umbrella over his head as the staff walked past him, filling each carriage with food from the kitchen

"It's not like you to be outside," I remarked, stepping up next to him. The rain pelted down, making a pitter-patter sound on the umbrella above us.

"It's not often I get to be involved in this side of palace life, and I must say, I'm rather enjoying it."

My mouth curled up at the corners. At least, someone was having fun. As each box of food was placed in a carriage, John checked it off his list.

"Actually, I have some good news for you," he said, waving his hand to send the full carriage on its way.

"Hmm?" I could do with some good news. Everything had been doom and gloom lately. "I hope it's a weather forecast saying that the sun is going to come out this afternoon."

He gave a very un-John-like smirk. "It's just a little rain. Half the people invited will be in the water anyway, and the rest will have to lump it. No, it's not about the weather. I got word from Captain McDougall this morning. He sent word that your parents are heading home."

My heart leaped at the news. Maybe everything was going back to normal after all.

"I've assigned someone to the tank in the ballroom," he continued. "The queen would not like a tank with just water, so I've had some of the staff bring in the plants and rocks from the palace pool. It's not ideal, but it's only temporary while the pool room is fixed up."

It was breaking royal protocol, and it would probably give him a heart attack, but right at that moment, I didn't care. I turned to him and hugged him. He stiffened up as I put my arms around him, but he didn't murmur a word. When I pulled back, I noticed the tips of his ears were cherry red.

I spent the afternoon getting the palace ready for my parents' return. Fish had been right, the weather brightened up in the late afternoon, and although I could hardly call it a sunny day, at least the rain abated. After getting ready, Emma and I jumped into the royal carriage. The one I'd take to my parents' hideout had been inconspicuous, but this one bore the royal insignia in gold along the side. Four guards on horseback accompanied the carriage. This time, I wanted to be seen.

"Nervous?" Emma asked me as we traveled through the town to the marina.

I gave her a wide grin. "Not with you here. You've been at my side the whole time. I couldn't have done this without you." I took a deep breath at the same time as taking her hand. "Thank you."

"The pleasure is all mine." She grinned back.

The last few weeks had been the hardest of my life, and yet, look at what had come out of it. A new best friend, a boyfriend, and most importantly, I'd grown up. I was setting out to host my first-ever party. Okay, I'd hosted the Valentine's Day Ball, but that had all been planned in advance by my mother. This party was all mine, and with some luck, my mother and father would be home in time to attend.

The cheer that went up as we turned the corner to the short road that would lead us down to the marina almost deafened me. My lips turned up at the edges at the warm welcome I was being afforded, and my fears went out the window. The people were happy to see me.

"This is going to be some party," Emma grinned, gazing out of the window at the thousands of people who had turned up. The crowd parted to let the carriage through, and when it came to a stop outside the restaurant, I stepped down with the aid of the palace guards. Their presence was not overwhelming, but it reassured me to see them dotted around in case of trouble. The El Mar had done a magnificent job, filling long tables with food inside the restaurant. The people all sat outside on chairs brought out for the occasion. The whole street had been shut down, so the party ran all the way to the sea where the merfolk had shown up by the hundreds. Fish was at the very front, waving wildly. I would have preferred him to come with me as my guest, but having him in the carriage and having to have him carried around would have been unwieldy. He was better off where he was. I waved back before heading up some stairs to a podium that had been erected for me.

When everyone's eyes fixed on me, I said, "Ladies and gentlemen, thank you so much for coming to this last-minute celebration. No one will deny that the last three weeks have been chaotic and filled with tension on all sides." I let my words sink in. "But we have managed to put aside our differences and found a way to work together, thereby making both the merpeople and the humans safe." Several people nodded, and many smiled. "My family and I appreciate your efforts in shutting down the hatred incited by the AML. The information provided by the group was based on lies. But by your actions, the potential damage to both our kingdoms if it had festered is now obliterated. I have complete faith that all of us will continue this peaceful work and make both our kingdoms greater. In unity there is peace and power."

I waited until their applause died down before I raised a glass of champagne and scanned the deck below to see everyone lift their own glasses. Fish, surrounded by his friends, touched his finger and blew it my way. I tipped my glass slightly toward him.

"To all the people of Atlantice and the kingdom underneath the sea, thank you. To our peace." I sipped the bubbly drink, enjoying the coolness as it slid its way down my throat. "Now, let's have some fun!"

The people applauded as the orchestra began to play.

A few people stood and began to dance, their feet splashing in the puddles caused by the morning's squall, not that any of them seemed to mind.

Emma waited for me downstairs and clapped gently. "That speech will make a bigger impact than this party."

"Really? Do you think they liked it?"

Emma bobbed her head. "Yes, look around you. Everyone is having fun and smiling. The merfolk are chatting to the land folk. There is no animosity, not anymore. "

"What are you talking about?" Hannah's voice came from behind me, making me jump. "This is a disgraceful party."

Emma's eyes widened, and she stepped back into the shadows.

I turned and fixed the biggest smile I could muster. "Hannah, I'm so glad you could make it. Have you had a chance to sample the cook's delicious pies? I know you love the shepherd and the chicken potpies. And the cook at El Mar has outdone herself with her seafood selection." I kept the smile on my face as I noticed some AML members behind her. I made a quick count of them in my head. Fifteen.

Where are the rest of the members?

A sinking feeling like something awful was about to happen hit my stomach. This was the moment Hannah had been waiting for. I caught the eyes of one of the guards nearby, which calmed my racing mind. I'd planned this. We had a lot of guards here, a lot of whom were in plain clothes. If Hannah and the AML did have something planned, we would be ready for them.

She narrowed her eyes. "Food? Is that all you can think about?"

I pointed to the buffet behind her. "This is a party, so food, music, dancing, and having a good time are all on the schedule. Why don't you mingle?"

"UGH! Are you insane? Our world is falling apart, and you're throwing a party! You disgust me."

She curled her mouth into a sneer, which was enough to tell me she had no intention of making up with the merfolk. She wasn't even going to try.

"I know you're upset. I can understand that. But look around you. Everyone is having fun. Look over there..." I pointed to where a group of landfolk were splashing the merfolk. Both sides were giggling. "This is what you're trying to stop, but no one wants to fight. No one ever did."

"The merfolk are foul creatures. Just because some people are too stupid to see that doesn't make it not so."

"They are not disgusting, Hannah, your attitude on the other hand..."

She asked in a quiet, menacing tone, "You believe their lies? Over me? Your best friend since forever?" She scoffed and threw her hands over her head. "Why? Why would you believe them over me?"

Let it go already.

In a calming tone, I responded, "You have been my best friend for as long as I can remember, but I've changed. I've grown up. Maybe it's time that you did the same?"

She inched forward and pointed her index finger in my face. Immediately, the guards surrounded us with their hands on the hilt of their swords.

Upon seeing them, she lowered her hand and backed up. "Hey, I'm not about to harm my best friend. We're just talking." The guards didn't budge but stood at ease with their hands close to their swords, ready to pounce.

"It's fine," I said, and they moved seamlessly back into the crowd.

"Setting your guards on me now? Some friend you've turned out to be."

"I didn't set anyone on you. They thought you were going to attack me."

She huffed. "Yeah, well, maybe I will. You've obviously

completely lost your mind fraternizing with that scum." She turned to point to the merfolk, but something stopped her.

Smack! The loud sound of a hand meeting a face prompted her to freeze. When I saw what had happened, my lower jaw dropped.

Emma shook her wrist. The pink outline of a handprint appeared on Hannah's face.

Hannah screamed, "How dare you!" The sounds of people enjoying the party stopped, and everyone looked our way.

"You are a maid, and you dare touch me?" She glared at me, pointing to Emma. "Are you going to let her get away with that?"

I held back the laughter that threatened to erupt and shrugged. "Maybe in the future, you should watch what you say."

Hannah's eyes glistened, but not one tear fell. "I'm out of here." She snapped her fingers, and her AML members marched over to her.

As soon as the group marched out through the doors, I slumped against a table with a loud sigh.

Emma stared at her red hand. She croaked as she whispered, "I'm so sorry. I shouldn't have slapped her."

I put my arm around her shoulder. "Don't worry about it."

"Are you sure? I hit her. I hit your friend."

"If you hadn't, I would have, and I don't think that would have looked very good in tomorrow's edition of the Daily Conch." I nodded my head toward Mr. Scribble, who pointed to his camera and gave me a thumbs up.

Emma hid her face behind her hands. "I'm going to be on the front page!" she hissed through her fingers.

"Yeah, well, don't worry about that either. I'll give Mr. Scribble something more interesting to print."

I left her and headed over to Fish. Making sure Mr. Scribble was watching, I bent down and gave him a kiss.

"Was that so your reporter friend would have something to print?" He asked with a gleam in his eye.

"Yes, it was," I replied, pulling my shoes off, "but this one isn't." I sat right on the edge of the wall letting my feet dangle in the water and brought him into a kiss. This one was anything but staged, and yet, I heard a chorus of oohs and aahs, and I was pretty sure I heard the clicking of a camera.

"I should probably stop kissing you now," I whispered, aware that hundreds of people were watching us.

"I don't know. It's kinda fun being a spectacle."

I playfully pushed his shoulder. "Thank you for coming."

"I wouldn't miss it for the world. Actually, I was hoping you would do something for me?"

I raised my eyebrows. "Anything."

"Seeing as I brought you all that tuna and those oysters, I was wondering if you'd let me sample some hot landfolk food. I've never had a hot meal in my life!"

"I'll grab you a pie," I said with a grin. "You'll love it."

"Do me a favor, though. Don't take it into the water. The pastry will get soggy."

Putting my shoes back on, I headed inside to the food. It was all laid out buffet style. Grabbing a plate for Fish and one for myself, I piled them both with food.

I was almost done when one of the guards apprehended me.

Immediately, my thoughts went to Hannah's threat.

"Is it the AML?" I asked.

"No, Your Highness, Captain McDougall is on his way."

"Why?"

Captain McDougall was with my parents. Or, at least, he should have been.

"He's bringing the king and queen."

My heart leapt with joy. "They are nearly here?"

"I believe so," the guard said. "They sent a messenger ahead. He told me ten minutes."

"Thank you!" I squealed, handing him my plate of food.

Rushing through the people, many of whom wanted to talk to me, I had to side step them all, to be able to give Fish his food.

"There are some people I think you should meet," Fish said as I handed his food over to him.

"I can't at the moment. My parents are coming. I need to make sure everything is ready."

I gave him a quick kiss and ran back to the podium.

"Ladies and Gentlemen. Once again, thank you for coming. I hope you are all enjoying the food. There's plenty left, so if you haven't already, go eat. I'd like to announce that His Majesty the King and Her Majesty the Queen are on their way. They didn't want to miss this special occasion."

The cheer that went up in the crowd almost deafened me. I grinned as I saw the merfolk clapping and waving. Inside I felt peace. Things were finally returning to normal.

The cheering was still happening as my parents' coach pulled up. The guards I'd asked to come swarmed to the carriage. I held my breath as my father stepped down. This was my mother's first royal occasion since turning back into a mermaid. McDougal carried her out to riotous applause. A quick scan of the crowd was enough for me to be assured that the AML had all gone. Whatever Hannah had planned, she didn't have the guts to follow through with it.

I ran to my father as my mother was carried to the sea. She was smiling, as she always did to the public, but I sensed a tenseness about her. I wasn't surprised. Fish had told me that she'd left the sea all those years ago in less than perfect circumstances. My father gripped my hand as McDougall lowered her to the wall. She didn't wait but pushed herself off into the sea.

My father and I walked through the crowd to the edge, my heart in my mouth the whole time, but it wasn't needed. My mother was swarmed by well-wishers and merfolk lining up to hug her.

"Did you plan all this yourself?" my father asked, extending his hand.

"I had a lot of help," I admitted. "It was all a bit last minute, but I figured that it was about time the Conch had something positive to print. "I'm so glad you are here to see it."

He brought me into a hug. "Me too. We shouldn't have stayed away for so long. I'm sorry."

"It's fine. Look at how happy Mother is."

"She fretted all the way home in the carriage. I told her things would be fine, but she didn't believe me."

"The tank in the ballroom is ready for her."

My father shook his head. "You know, I think she'd rather spend a few days out in the sea rather than being cooped up in a tank. At least, until we figure out a way to get her legs back."

Darkness filled me. There was no way she was going to get her legs back now. The spell was broken, and I didn't have the first clue how to bring it back again.

"Now point me to the food. I'm famished."

I put my arm in my father's and escorted him inside. This time, I managed to eat something. As we ate, people came up to us, congratulating me on the party, and talking to my father about merpeople relations.

My heart was filled with joy at how everything had turned out. My only regret was that I'd lost Hannah as a friend. We had been so close, but now she was so fanatical against the Merpeople, I didn't think it was a friendship I'd ever be able to rebuild. I was just thinking of all the fun times we'd had together as children when McDougall tapped my father on the shoulder and whispered something in his ear.

My father dropped his plate onto a nearby table and followed McDougall to the royal carriage at great speed. I ran after them, catching up as my father hopped into the carriage.

"What is it?" I asked, noting the fear in my father's eyes.

Captain McDougall was the one to answer. "The palace is under attack."

"What!?" I took in a huge breath. Hannah had threatened me as she left. I'd not taken it seriously at the time, or at least, not seriously enough to actually have her followed. I thought she was just mouthing off. It was perfect. The guard presence at the palace was low as most of them were at the party. I mentally kicked myself for messing up so much and leaving the palace vulnerable to attack. I hopped up into the carriage beside my father.

"What has the AML done?" I asked as McDougall closed the door behind us.

"It's not the AML," my father answered. "It's worse. Much worse."

"What could be worse than the AML?" I queried.

"It's the Sea Witch. She's taken over the palace."

GODDESS OF WATER

1

19TH FEBRUARY

The town clock struck midnight, but my tiredness had dissipated, and fear had taken its place.

It couldn't remain with all the adrenaline pumping through my body from the bombshell Captain McDougall had just dropped on me.

How did the sea witch manage to invade the palace? She was a creature of the sea. She didn't even have legs.

All these thoughts pounded through my mind as the carriage cut through the frosty night. My father and I had left the party behind in full swing without having time to inform anyone that we were leaving. My mother would wonder where we'd gone. Fish would too, and Emma. We should have told them, but it was too late now. I'd have to ask one of the guards to head back to the party and let my mother know what was going on as soon as I knew what was going on myself. I believed McDougall; he had no reason to lie. And yet, I couldn't picture the sea witch away from her natural habitat.

Of course, this all depended on how many guards I could actually ask. If the sea witch had taken over the palace, it stood to reason they were busy trying to oust her, though how she'd managed it was beyond me. One sea creature against how many guards? It didn't add up. By the time the carriage pulled up outside the palace gates, my curiosity was in overdrive, and fear gnawed at the pit of my stomach.

The captain's voice rose, "Please stay in the carriage while I assess the current situation, Sire."

He held up his hand to stop my father from getting out. My father was not accustomed to being told what to do, and I was interested to see how he'd react to such orders. I could see he was itching to follow McDougall out of the carriage. His palace was under attack, his home...my home.

"If the sea witch is in my home, I need to get out and fight!" he said gruffly, making to follow McDougall.

The captain turned and furrowed his brow. "Sire, the situation is dire. The guards have been fighting since Princess Blaise left last evening. It's imperative that we protect you from her men. The fighting can spill out here. I'd rather you wait until I've assessed the situation."

My father's eyes scanned the area over McDougall's head, narrowing as he took in the scene. I wanted to peek out of the carriage door, too, but with the way my father was looking, I knew it was best to wait it out. I'd see soon enough what mess I'd brought to the palace, for I was sure that this was my doing. The witch had never been spotted on land before now, and it was no coincidence that I'd escaped from her only a week or so before. She was here to get me. I was sure of it, and yet, I didn't feel scared. No, I was angry with myself for letting this happen. I should have been better.

"Get out of my way, man," My father ordered, pushing McDougall to the side. "My duty as king of this kingdom is to protect it. Yours is only to protect me. I understand that you are trying to do just that, but I need you working with me and not treating me like some kid who doesn't know what he's doing."

McDougall opened his mouth to answer, but before he could say a word, A cackled laugh sounded through the night, raising that hairs on my neck.

Grabbing my father's arm before he was fully out of the carriage,

I whispered, "Let's leave. We can make plans somewhere away from here."

I met the captain's gaze.

"There's a hut for the guard on the outer perimeter of the palace walls. We use it for training and our break times. It's not been taken over yet. We'll be safe there."

My father mulled it over and then nodded. "Let's go."

We jumped out of the carriage and sprinted toward the locked metal door of the guard's hut. It was less a hut and more of a full building separate from the palace. Captain McDougall pulled out some large brass keys and unlocked the door.

The smell of old socks and wet leather assaulted me as the door opened, but I refrained from pinching my nose. Barely.

The captain pointed at the chairs around a large rectangular table near the fireplace. It easily sat thirty men. "If you would like to sit, your majesty?"

My father looked like the last thing he wanted to do was sit when all hell was breaking loose in the palace on the other side of the walls, but he pulled a chair out from under the table and sat down.

"Tell me what's going on," He ordered as I sat in the chair next to him.

McDougall carried on standing.

"After the princess left last night, a woman... If you can call her that, invaded us from the sea."

"I am aware of the sea witch," my father commented. "We've already established that. Let's not be polite about this. The woman is a witch. Let's speak of her as such."

McDougall nodded and then carried on. "As most of the guards were at the party, the palace was left greatly under-protected. I lay the blame on myself. I should have left more guards here."

My father waved his hand. "Let's not start laying blame here. You did your job. How did one witch manage to overthrow the guards that were here? Even at low capacity, the guards should have been able to debilitate one woman, witch or not."

McDougall cleared his throat. "I haven't been clear. It wasn't just the sea witch. She came from the sea with an army of...I want to say men, but they weren't exactly men. They were green and scaly and had legs as well as long tails."

My father flung his hands in the air, and his voice hardened. "There is an army of sea creatures holding up the palace? Do you know how many we're dealing with?"

The captain raised his eyes. "I don't have a number at this point. I only know that the guards remaining here at the palace were overwhelmed. I've managed to pull everyone back, and there have been no major casualties, but since they got in, they've managed to barricade the doors so we can't."

My father slammed his palm against the wooden table. "If that's all the information you have, then let's go. There's no more to discuss as far as I'm concerned. I'm joining the fight. Do we have any weapons here?" His eyes scanned the room as the cackle sounded out again, making me shiver. There was something menacing about how loud she was and how filled with glee. The guards may have been out there fighting, but she sounded like she was enjoying it.

The captain said, "No, we'll have to enter the armory. We can arm you there, and then you can see for yourself where we are."

My father's green eyes darkened. "No, Captain McDougall. You will have someone escort Blaise to the cottage on the north of the island and pick the queen up along the way. While that's being organized, I'll go to the armory with the remaining men before we enter the palace. Get someone to head back to the party to round the guards up. They are no use back there."

A few weeks ago, I would have been glad to get away from something like this, but things had changed. I was no longer the little kid who was afraid of everything. The irony didn't escape me that I'd spent the last few years hating the merfolk, only to change my mind about them and then to decide to go to war against some other sea creature. But whereas I'd been wrong about the merfolk, there was no way I was wrong about any type of creature the sea witch had brought with her.

"Father, I'm not leaving you. I can fight side by side with you."

His harsh tone surprised me. "No!" He stood and strode to the door.

I raced after him, barely keeping up as he raced out of the guard's hut and through the palace gates to the armory.

We reached the armory, with its mahogany inner walls filled with battle axes, long and short swords, thin and thick swords, wooden lances, and bows and arrows. The smaller weapons, daggers and knives, lay in wooden cases with glass covers.

My mouth curled up at the side as I picked up a sword with a blade longer than my arm from its place on the wall. The gilt from the diamond and ruby hilt danced light on the walls as I tried to balance the exquisite sword on two fingers. Unfortunately, the blade dipped lower than the hilt. "This is an amazing sword. Too bad it's unbalanced."

Captain McDougall's deep voice vibrated off the walls. "It's not for fighting. The blade is sharp, but the hilt is too heavy. It was a gift to his majesty from one of the other royal families and is for ceremonial use only." He strolled over to the wall and picked a plain sword with about the same blade length but a slightly smaller hilt and without jewels. "This one might be better."

My father didn't even notice as he picked out his own weapons.

A couple of guards came in and bowed. "Captain, we are at an impasse. The sea witch is refusing to talk to us, and we cannot get in. What would you have us do?"

"Are there any staff left in there?" my father asked.

"No," I said as the guard echoed the same word. "I let them all have the night off. They'd worked so hard on getting the party ready that I let them all leave early." At least, that was one decision I'd made right in this whole fiasco.

"All the guards are accounted for, your majesty."

"Thank you."

McDougall stepped toward his guards. "One of you take a

carriage back to the town and round up any guards left at the party. You'll have to take extra carriages to pick them all up. We need them all back here now."

He glanced my way. I held up the sword he'd given me and mouthed the words, "Let me stay." I wanted to fight. I should be allowed to fight.

"Her majesty should be taken someplace safe." He turned to the second guard. "You go and let the guards here at the palace know that we are preparing to fight."

Both guards saluted and then left us. I noticed that he'd made no plans to get me out of here. Fortunately, my father had not either.

My father followed them out of the building back into the grounds.

The grip of the lighter sword fit my hand better, probably because of the shorter distance between the rain-guard and the pommel. Our crest stood out on the pommel, and I caressed it before I balanced the sword.

Perfection!

I gripped it tightly, and after grabbing a couple of knives along the way, ran out after my father into the night.

The whole palace was dark and silent. I'd never seen it so dark. There was always a light burning somewhere, but now, it looked desolate in its darkened state—an omen of things to come. At the palace gates, the guards congregated, and it was to them that my father walked with determination.

"Can anyone tell me where we are at?" he barked as McDougall caught up with us.

The guard that had, only moments before, come to speak to us in the armory shook his head. "We cannot get in. The palace is in full lockdown. She hasn't made any demands, and she is refusing to speak with us."

"So I understand. The rest of the guards should arrive shortly. I want everyone equipped for battle. When we have a full contingent of guards, we will attack."

An excited murmur ran through the men. I gripped the hilt of my sword tighter, readying myself to fight.

My father caught my attention as I whispered words of bravery to myself.

"What do you think you're doing with that sword? This isn't time to be playing games, Blaise. The guards need the swords."

"I need the sword if I'm going to fight, Father. I can't fight without one, that would be madness."

I waited for him to blast me with his words, but he never got the chance. The rumble of galloping horses took his attention away. One of the royal carriages pulled up next to us, and Sergeant Jimenez jumped out, quickly followed by some of the guards. He was here too quickly to have been told of the situation from the other guard. They must have passed at some point.

He said, "Your Majesty, Your highness, we have a problem. We were attacked at the party. The merfolk came from the sea and began to attack the people. I told you that the merfolk couldn't be trusted."

I sucked in a breath. "The merfolk attacked?" It made no sense. Why would the merfolk attack? Everything was fine when we left. Something didn't add up.

"These merfolk attacking. What did they look like?"

Jimenez eyed me curiously. It was evident in his expression that he didn't like to be questioned.

"They were exactly as you'd expect a merperson to look," he said, his voice dripping in disdain. "Human looking upper bodies and fishtails."

He lifted his nose as though he'd just smelled something rotten. I had a feeling that the only thing rotten around here was him.

"What color were they?" I pressed him.

"Is this really necessary?" Jimenez asked, looking toward my father.

"Just answer my daughter's question," he barked.

"They were green."

"All over?" I asked. Jimenez nodded and looked toward the ground.

My father barked at the sergeant. "That's not the merfolk you imbecile. They are the sea witch's army. The same creatures are currently ransacking the palace. Is my wife safe?"

Sergeant Jimenez took a deep breath and shuffled his feet. "Yes, she's with a merman with long hair. He could have been protecting her, I don't know."

My father tightened his fingers until his knuckles lost their color. "Why aren't you with her? Helping to defend her?"

"I'm sorry, Your Majesty, but she went underwater with the merman where we couldn't join her."

My father's eyes rounded like a marble, but he quickly recovered. "We fight now. Guards, you follow me. Jimenez, you stay here and wait for the other guards to join us. Tell them to get what they need from the armory and join us."

"But, Sire..."

"Then get back in the carriage and do what you can to help at the El Mar. I have no doubt the merfolk can handle themselves, but I need someone there to take charge. The rest of you, follow me."

Jimenez liked his position in the ranks and had spent his life working his way up. Being told to stay behind while the rest of the guards fought was the worst kind of punishment to someone like him, but then again, he'd left my mother to fend for herself, so it served him right.

My father's long legs pumped as he strode toward the back of the palace, the guards following behind with me at the back. He'd made it clear that I was not to fight alongside him, but his mind was too occupied with what was going on inside the palace to notice I was following behind.

I wondered what my father's plan was to get inside the palace, but it soon became apparent he wouldn't need one. The staff entrance door to the palace opened, and twenty huge ocean men, puke-green in color, barreled toward our guards. I shifted my feet into a fighting stance and raised my sword above my shoulder. Fear rippled through me as I realized what I'd done. I was no fighter, and yet, here I was, ready to be attacked by creatures of the deep. I didn't think my father was planning to be attacked so soon, either. His plan had been to wait for back up before trying to get inside, but it was too late for that now. The danger was coming toward us in droves.

The guards surrounded my father and me, making me feel slightly less queasy about my decision to stay, but my father stepped out of their protection, lifted his sword, and in one swoop hit the first man to reach us straight in the arm. The sea witch's man or beast, or whatever the foul creature was, instantly collapsed on the ground, clutching what was left of his arm and squealing in a high pitched voice that belied the size of him. The sight of it made my stomach curdle, but my father stepped over him and plunged his sword into the second man's chest.

The man's chest exploded in a riot of blue blood as he crumpled forward, then literally disappeared in a puff of blue smoke. Seconds later, the first one also turned into blue smoke, dissipating in the night air.

Seeing my father fight was a sight to behold. If only I knew how to fight like him. If only I knew how to fight at all. The willingness was there, but the training was sorely lacking.

My father squeezed his fist and motioned for the sea witch's men to step closer. "Come prepared to die, you swine."

Five of the creatures rushed forward, but one of them circled around, avoiding my father.

So far, the guards we did have hadn't moved one iota. My father was doing all the work, but the way he fearlessly felled the creatures mesmerized me, and I had a feeling I wasn't the only one. Safe in the cocoon of guards, it was fascinating to watch. As more of the vile creatures filed out, it became apparent that my father could not fight alone, no matter how amazing he was, the guards went in to help, leaving me without protection. I only had myself and my own wits.

The creature that had side-stepped my father now moved

toward me, his beady evil eyes glowered, and his hoarse voice barked, "You're mine, little girl!"

Hot blood traveled through my body, and I almost threw up on the grass. I'd asked for this. I'd wanted it. It was I and I alone that had taken the sword from the armory. To show weakness now would be dangerous to everyone. I took a deep breath and looked the repugnant creature in the eyes. "Are you ready to die, you disgusting piece of whale excrement?"

The beady eyed-monster, his body wider than my throne chair, raised his sword. Taking the offensive stand, I swung my sword. Hard. His eyes widened, and he stepped back. I swung again, but he was ready, and our swords met in the middle. Once, twice, three times. The fourth time our swords connected a little more violently than I was prepared for. I couldn't maintain my grip on the sword and released it.

Clank, clank.

The metal struck the stone pathway. I bent to reach for my sword's pommel, but he stepped on the blade, his repulsive scaly green feet with what looked to be half-chewed-off toenails made me scrunch my nose up in distaste.

As I pulled on the sword, his mouth curled into a sneer, and then he bared his teeth at me and laughed.

My body froze at the sound.

"Such a weakling," he said, raising his sword to my head.

The rotten egg smell from his armpits almost knocked me over. So much so that I wondered briefly if his sword was even needed to do me in. I rolled on my side, pulled a knife from my belt, and sliced his knee cap, causing him to drop his sword and grab his knee in agony. As the other one had, he emitted a high pitch squeal . I almost had to cover my ears at the sound of it. I gripped my other knife and jabbed it into the middle of his chest, twisting it before I yanked it out of him.

Hatred reflected in his eyes as he staggered and fell backward. Finally, the screeching stopped.

I crouched, wiped my knife on his pants, and whispered in his ear, "Not much of a weakling now, am I?"

He grunted, and his eyes rolled back in his head. He vanished, and blue smoke appeared where he had fallen

Keeping an eye on my father, I inched back toward my sword. Another creature saw me and charged with his sword high in the air.

About a foot away, I bent my knees and stuck one leg out. He stumbled forward and fell on his own sword. Maybe I took after my father in the fighting department, after all.

Picking up my sword, I turned away and sprinted toward my father. I plunged my sword into a creature right as he was about to pierce my father's back. He plunged to the floor. I didn't bother to make sure he was dead.

There wasn't any time.

The guards around us fought two creatures at a time, while my father took on three or more. The noise of swords clashing, and the sound of groans filled the air. I slashed at all the creatures near my father, hoping that their strength would decrease, and my father's job would be easier.

It seemed as if the sea witch had brought half the ocean with her. Every time I thought we had defeated them, another twenty green men magically appeared.

I'd been lulled into a false sense of security. Watching my father and killing a few of the creatures with my own hand made me feel invincible, but as the creatures swamped us, I realized how wrong I'd been. I was in the middle of tackling one of the disgusting creatures when Emma ran past, a sword in her hand. I was so surprised that I forgot what I was doing, and the creature managed to push me to the ground. A swish of metal and a squelch later and the creature's head went flying clean from its shoulders. Emma kicked the body over before it could fall on me. She extended her hand and I took it.

"What are you doing here?"

She looked so strange, covered in ocean creature blood which was more blue than red, and still in her party dress. It was then, I remembered that I was still dressed up too. The pair of us must have looked a real sight.

"I overheard the guards talking at the party. I jumped in one of the carriages and grabbed a sword from the armory, and besides, this is my home." Emma held up her sword, and I couldn't help but grin at her. Who knew that my maid was so fearless?

To one side, I heard my father yell. Jerking my head, I saw he was being attacked from all sides. I was just about to run to his aid when Emma caught my wrist.

She picked up a stone and threw it at the back of the creature attacking my father from behind. It hit his head, felling him instantly.

"Nice throwing!"

"I can't wield a sword or a knife, but I'm an expert thrower." She said with a wink. She threw another stone at a creature about to swing at my father. The creature faltered, and my father was able to run his sword through him.

Rushing to catch a creature before he stabbed my father, I drove my sword into his huge back and pulled it out. He turned around with hatred in his eyes and held his dagger in both hands. He jabbed, and his blade grazed my thigh. I pushed through the pain and slashed across his stomach. Once he fell, I retreated into a corner and ripped a piece of cloth from my skirt to wrap it around my cut.

We fought hundreds of the creatures throughout the morning without rest. Unfortunately, the more we brought down, the more they multiplied.

It was overwhelming and, undoubtedly, magic. And I didn't wonder anymore how our guards were overcome in the first place. The whole palace was crawling with the vile things. Those that hadn't come out to fight with us were throwing things from the palace windows. Beautiful furniture and our personal possessions were being hurled at us from all directions, and most of the stuff was now lying broken on the ground. Whatever the witch wanted, she really wanted it badly. If only she would tell us, then we could decide what to do. Not that I expected what she wanted would be something we would give her. Looking around me at the detritus and the injured men, I saw that we could not win against her. The creatures were not so great with swords, and their unwieldy bodies prohibited them from moving with much speed, but as each one was killed, it turned to blue smoke, magically dissipating in the air. It meant that they were made of nothing but magic. The guards, being trained in combat, were mostly unharmed, and I'd seen no sign of any deaths on our side. But the injuries were piling up, and fatigue showed in all their faces. I, for one, was exhausted.

As if she'd read my mind, the sea witch's voice boomed out from somewhere. I raced around to the front of the palace along with many of the guards, to see her standing on the royal balcony. At least I assumed she was somehow standing. I couldn't see below her waist, and I remembered her tail not looking like it would support her weight out of the water, but if she could conjure up thousands of slimy creatures with swords, she could use magic to stand.

The sea witch cackled and screeched. "Where are the King and his daughter, The Little Mermaid? They will die in front of you."

"We need to retreat, now, Sire!" Captain McDougall grabbed my wrist and started wrestling me toward the gates. He pointed to a couple of guards nearby. "Head to the carriage with the king. We need to get them to a safe location."

I bit McDougall's hand, and he let me go. I wasn't going anywhere. Not while the sea witch was still in the palace.

A bolt of light narrowly missed me, followed by the cackle of the sea witch. A guard next to me got the full blast of the witch's magic. His face contorted into an expression of agony before it completely froze. His coloring greyed in front of my eyes. The sea witch had turned him to stone.

"Blaise, come here!" my father screamed as he stabbed another of the creatures. I ran toward him. I could ignore McDougall, but I couldn't ignore the fact the sea witch wanted to petrify me. When my father was happy I was at his side, he barked an order at

McDougall. "Find the queen, Captain. I have no doubts that the merfolk will keep her safe, but these creatures will be better fighters under the water than they are out of it. The sea witch wants Blaise, and I'm not prepared to let her have her. I'm taking her to safety at the cottage. I want you to get some of your guards to find the queen and bring her to us as soon as possible."

McDougall gave my father a salute and a quick nod of the head.

Emma followed us as we ran to the awaiting carriage surrounded by guards.

I recognized the guard by the carriage as one who had been at the El Mar.

"How bad is it in town?" I asked, fearful of the answer.

"Terrible. The sea witch's army is fighting at the seafront by the El Mar. The merfolk and land folk are managing to keep them back to some extent, but you've seen what it's like here. They keep on coming."

"And the queen?" I asked. I wanted to ask about Fish too, but I didn't know how.

"She was fighting admirably the last time I saw her. The merfolk were doing everything they could to protect her."

"How many have we lost?" My father asked as we reached the carriage.

The guard yanked the door open. "We don't have a count, but there are casualties. The queen is not among them."

My father jumped in, and I scrambled into the carriage without waiting for his help.

"Emma?" I called out when I saw that she'd not followed us in.

"Your highness, I cannot go. You have been so kind to me, but I'm a maid. I cannot leave when so many of the guards are staying behind to fight." She spoke with a slight tremble in her voice.

"Are you sure you'll be safe? Do you have anywhere to go?" I wanted her to come with us, but I couldn't force her. "There is room for you in here."

She glanced over her shoulder and shook her head vehemently.

"No, I swore to do my duty when I started working, and that means to the palace."

"No!" I glanced behind her to where the sea witch was sending bolt after bolt of magic, turning the screaming guards to stone. "You can't stay here."

One of the palace guards, a young man named Jaxon, rushed forward. "Emma!"

She looked at him, and I saw the hint of a sparkle in her eyes.

It was then that I understood the real reason she was staying behind. She had a crush on the guard. It had nothing to do with duty. She just didn't want to leave him for fear he would die.

"Yes, I'm sure," she said, turning back to me. If we weren't in such a grave situation, I'd have grinned at the way her cheeks were turning cherry red.

"Promise me you'll get away from here!" I said as the first guard closed the door.

"Emma, we need to leave now!" Jaxon came over and took Emma's hand. "They need to leave."

"Bye, Your Highness." She waved as we pulled away.

I smiled, knowing that she would be indeed safe with him.

My thoughts turned to my mom and Fish, wishing that there was something I could do to keep them safe.

Safe from the clutches of the evil sea witch.

The carriage jolted forward. I sat next to my father and leaned against the velvet cushions.

His leg bounced as he pulled back the curtain. He stuck his head through the carriage window and shouted at the driver. "Are we going to go faster?"

"Yes, Sire."

Our carriage flew onto the empty road. As we bolted through the cobbled streets, I noticed how quiet everywhere was. We'd been fighting all night, and the sun was now climbing in the sky. I had no idea what the time was. I was still wearing the same dress I'd gone to the party in, only now, it was ripped and covered in the blood of the sea creatures. As far as I could tell, none of the blood was mine, and apart from a few bruises I was uninjured. Looking out and seeing the empty streets made me wonder where everyone was.

Our town was desolate.

There was no doubt that the news of the sea witch invading the palace had gotten out. The usual hustle and bustle of the town's street was markedly absent. The people were too afraid to leave their homes.

2
20TH FEBRUARY

I stretched my arms and hit the wooden wall. The pain jerked me awake. The sun streamed in from a worn paisley colored curtain, and I rubbed my eyes. *What the heck?* Waking up in a room the size of my closet was disconcerting until I remembered.

The fighting.

The bloodshed.

The evil sea witch's cackle.

My insides trembled.

Her threat to kill us as she turned our people to stone made my blood run both cold and hot. It allowed fear and anger to comingle inside me.

I leapt out of the bed, craving a long bath. The one from the night before had eased my muscle aches but had done nothing to erase the horrors I had witnessed.

We'd returned to the cottage on the north end of the island. It meant we were safe, but it also meant we were too far away to know what was going on. I hated that we'd run away again, and I hated not knowing what had happened to Fish and my mother even more. I'd gone to bed early, not wanting to talk to anyone, but I'd not slept.

At some point in the night, I'd heard the sound of a carriage drawing up and my father's whispered words with one of the guards. As he'd not come down from his room early as I had, I assumed the news was good, but without waking him, I couldn't know for sure. Waking him after the night he'd had would be unkind, and as the guards were nowhere in sight, I had to hope for the best. I'd found a bag of clothes on the cottage kitchen table. They weren't mine, but they were my size. someone had been thoughtful enough to bring them here. I had my bath and pulled on a swimsuit, covering it with a sweater and pants and headed out to the cove.

A glint of sea glass caught my eye, and I picked it up. Turning the light turquoise glass in my hand, I thought about my mom and her transformation. My thoughts quickly turned to Fish, and all that he meant to me. I tucked the glass in my pocket. I couldn't bear it if I lost either one of them. I knew my father had his guards searching for my mom, but no one was searching for Fish. The guard that had brought us here last night had said himself that there had been casualties.

Where are they?

My impatience prompted me to shed my sweater and pants and run into the cool sea. I dove under the clear blue water searching for either one of them.

But nothing. Not a single sign.

She wasn't there. Fish wasn't there.

The ocean remained calm and almost motionless except for tiny waves that had me bobbing on the surface. I swam out as far as I dared. I couldn't go too far. My father would worry if he couldn't find me. I was just about to turn back to shore when I caught sight of something that made my heart soar.

Ripples on the water's surface about twenty feet from where I was treading water.

Ripples that could only be from a merperson tail.

Fish!

His warm arms encircled my waist, and a moment later, I found myself being pulled under the water in his embrace, I kissed him until I could no longer breathe, either above water or below it. I was so happy to see him that I could have stayed underwater with him all day, but my mother was not yet back, and I needed to know what I'd left behind in Antla. We swam to the surface. In the morning light, he'd never looked more beautiful with the sun giving him a halo around his long wet hair. My breath caught in my throat at how devastating he was. Just a look from him could both lift me and destroy me.

He was alive and looked to be unscathed, and that was all that mattered.

"How did you find us?" I asked. If my mother was with him, I would know, but I didn't see her. "And how are you? Were you hurt?"

"Perfectly fine and protecting your mom just as you requested." He kissed my forehead. "A guard came to us and told us where you and the king were being taken. We asked him to send word that we would head up here as soon as possible."

"Thank you so much." I gently pulled on his long wavy hair, completely wet. "Is my mother alright? Why isn't she with you?"

"She's fine. The mer village has been barricaded, and the only entrance and exit are too small to let the witch's creatures through. Your mom wanted to come to you last night, but the mer king didn't think it was a good idea. When I left this morning, there were none of those creatures left, so he was probably right. Either they were all killed in battle or they retreated, but it doesn't mean they won't come back."

"So, my mother is back in the mer village?" I asked, my stomach clenching with disappointment.

"No, she's just behind me. I swam on ahead so I could sneak a kiss before she saw us. I promised her I'd swim up here with her, but I need to leave soon."

My heart lurched at his words. "You're leaving? Why can't you stay here with me?"

"The king wants us close to the underwater kingdom because he doesn't trust the sea witch." He caressed my cheek. "We managed to sneak the queen out, but the sea witch doesn't know that. She thinks she's still in the mer village. Because of that, the whole mer village is in danger. I need to go back and help protect it."

"I don't want you to leave," I said, suddenly feeling the chill of the water. Without him, it would be cold. Too cold. It always was.

"Neither do I, but I must obey my king." He leaned in. "I'm really sorry, but I can come see you again. I'll try and get back to you tomorrow."

I pouted. "Okay."

His face split into a grin. "Don't worry, I'll find a way to come back." He kissed me before he pulled back and flapped his tail.

Behind him, my mother's turquoise tail flipped in the ocean, filling my heart with joy.

She breached the surface and swam over to us.

"Mom!" I used a breaststroke to reach her. "Are you okay? Did she hurt you?" I hugged her tightly, not daring to let go.

"Blaise, I'm fine because my people protected me. Your boyfriend protected me."

I felt my cheeks redden as she turned to him. "Thank you for delivering me safely back to my family."

"My pleasure, Your Majesty," he replied, bowing his head. With a flick of his tail, he was under the water and away, back to the mer village, taking my heart with him.

I took my mother's hand, and we swam back to the cove where my father was waiting for us. When he saw who I'd brought with me, his face positively beamed. He jumped into the water, drenching his trousers and waded out to greet us.

"My darling love, how are you?" She propelled herself right into his embrace, and their lips locked.

I cleared my throat a couple of times, but they didn't pull apart or look my way. "I need some water, do either of you want anything?"

Silence.

Complete silence.

I leisurely headed back to the small cottage feeling much better than I had when I'd left it only twenty minutes earlier.

Dripping cold water all over the stone floor of the kitchen, I put the kettle on and waited for it to boil. When it did, I poured out two containers of coffee. I figured my parents would appreciate a warm drink over plain water.

"Thank you, Blaise." my father said as he pulled himself into the boat that had been moored here since last time. I'd forgotten that he didn't get heat from my mother in the same way I did when I was in the water.

I handed him the containers of coffee and swam next to my mother, feeling her warmth.

"So much has happened in the last two days that I need to share everything I've gone through or else I'll explode," she said, clutching the side of the boat.

"How did you escape from the sea witch?" I asked. What I wanted to know was if the sea witch had been defeated, but if she had, Fish would have mentioned it.

Her tail stirred the water while she described what she had been through. While my father and I had been fighting in the palace grounds, she had been embroiled in a battle of her own below the ocean surface. It sounded like the merfolk's fight against the witch was as disastrous as ours, and they'd retreated rather than risk dying.

After she finished, my father and I took turns describing the battle we had undergone. Despite having fought alongside him, listening to his version boiled my blood. We'd left our guards behind. People were still fighting for us, and we were here bobbing merrily in a pretty little cove.

My mother began to sob next to me. Before all the trouble started, I'd never seen my mother cry, but it was becoming a regular habit. I swam closer and put my arm around her.

"There has been so much destruction. So many deaths and injuries."

"Do you know how many?" my father asked somberly. No one

had died up at the palace, but we already knew there had been deaths under the water.

"I don't know exactly," my mother said, wiping her eyes pointlessly with the back of her wet hand. "I was taken to the palace in the mer village. I left early before the official count was done."

My father sat up straight in the boat and spoke, "We need to decide how we're going to reclaim the palace. Now that you are both here and safe, I need to return."

"No!" my mother wailed. "It's too dangerous. Let the guards do their jobs."

"I have to go back, Antonella. I'm the king. I cannot let people die for me while I sit here twiddling my thumbs."

However much I hated to hear him say it, I agreed with him. Hiding out here was cowardly, and it was about time we stood up to the witch.

"If you must go, please do me one thing before you set off."

"Anything," he said, taking her hand.

"It has been so long since we had a meal together. I want to have just one meal with my family and be able to remember it."

She didn't add in case he didn't survive, but I knew that was what she meant. It wasn't an idle request. She needed it. I could see the fear in her eyes. I felt it in my own heart.

My father sighed and then nodded. "I'll have one of the guards bring us some food out."

"No," she shook her head. "I want to feel normal again. Carry me out of the water and let me sit at a restaurant like a normal person. I'll dry myself off and wear a long skirt to cover my tail."

I could see my father didn't want to waste time eating when he could be back at the palace fighting alongside his guard, but he acquiesced as he always did where my mother was concerned.

An hour later and we were all sitting in a small cafe overlooking the sea about three miles from the cottage. It wasn't a fine restaurant, but my mother didn't seem to mind. In fact, she seemed happy enough to order off the limited menu and just be herself. Herself before she got her tail. I'd had to lend her a skirt I'd found in the bag because no clothes had been brought for her. She no longer looked like the elegant queen I'd grown up with, but her pink cheeks and messy hair made her all the more beautiful to me. I could almost pretend we weren't at war. Almost.

We'd just finished our dessert when Hannah and some of the AML walked in. I almost choked on my cheesecake when I caught her eye.

My mother looked over to where I was staring.

"Just ignore them, Blaise. Let's not start any trouble."

"But how do they know where we are?" I whispered. If Hannah knew, did everyone else? We were miles away from Antla.

"The cabin belongs to her father, the admiral," My father said. "I suspect this is all just a coincidence."

Or she'd overheard her father talking and decided to pay us a little visit. Great! Just what I needed. Wasn't it bad enough that my home was currently inhabited by a magical sea creature, without her showing up with more needling about the merfolk?

While I didn't think she would start anything, I still hoped to avoid speaking to her.

All the hope in the world did not help me as Hannah pushed back her chair and filed into our area with her minions flanking her as if prepared for a battle.

"Well, well. If it isn't the royal disaster of a family," she said with a sneer

Her minions laughed, and I clenched my fists under the table.

Had things gotten so bad that she thought it was alright to disrespect my parents? She had always toed the line with them, even when she occasionally overstepped her bounds with me.

"Hannah Fallon," my mother began, keeping her voice much more even than I would have. "If you don't show us the respect we deserve as the royal family, as human beings, we'll have a talk with your father and your fiancée. You're no longer a child where your insolent behavior will be tolerated. Grow up and treat people decently."

Go, Mom!

Hannah's eyes widened as though she was not expecting the queen to speak to her in such a manner. Not that I could blame her. I'd not expected it either.

Hannah lowered her eyes. "I'm sorry, Queen Antonella. I was totally out of line." She cleared her throat. "Do you need a ride back to the palace? I didn't see another carriage or the guards. We have space."

My lips slightly lifted at my friend's olive branch so she could weave herself back into my mom's good graces.

My mom asked, "Are you coming from Antla?"

"No, we left the town after I spoke to Blaise the night of the party. We're picking up supplies and won't return to Antla until tomorrow afternoon."

The slight pinkness spreading from her cheeks to her ears and the way she responded sparked my interest. "Oh? Where have you been?"

She bit her lip before she said, "I was staying at a friend's house. We were on the way to my father's cottage. It's not far from here."

"I'm afraid that won't be possible," my father said. "We are staying at your father's cottage."

Hannah's brows furrowed, and I wondered if I'd been wrong. Maybe it was just a coincidence she was here after all. If she'd left the party when she said she had, she wouldn't know anything about the sea witch.

Her eyes narrowed. "Why are you staying there? It's no place for the royal family. There barely is enough room for four people. I assume you have guards with you?"

My father dropped his spoon into the cup, and sounding exasperated, lowered his voice. "It certainly isn't the palace, but after the sea witch invaded it, we had no other choice." He ran his hand through his hair. "We needed a safe place near the water, and your father generously let us stay at his cottage. I'll be heading back to Antla shortly."

"What? What do you mean invaded?" she asked, raising her voice at least an octave higher. "What sea witch?"

I jumped in, incredulous that the Conch had not distributed its newspaper, or that she hadn't seen it yet. "A sea witch overtook the guards at the palace the night before last. We fought her, but ultimately, she beat us. The guards are still fighting."

Hannah's face took on a picture of astonishment. I knew Hannah. she was a great actress and liar, but this was real. She really didn't know anything about it.

"But how?"

"The sea witch managed to surprise the few guards patrolling the palace on the night of the party. She had an army of sea creatures with her."

"What about the guards, the palace staff?" Her hand flew to her mouth as the enormity of it finally came to her. Her father and Fiancé had undoubtedly been fighting out in the ocean.

"Unfortunately, the sea witch still has possession of the palace. Some of the guards have been turned to stone, and there are casualties. As far as I'm aware, your father and your fiancée are still alive. I've not heard otherwise."

She shook her head like she didn't believe it. She'd come over here looking for a fight, and we'd ended up telling her that her loved ones were embroiled in a fight with a psychopathic, magical maniac. "Stone?" She asked weakly. "Like a rock, stone?"

My father nodded. "Yes. She is very powerful, but as I said, I believe your father is fine."

"Magic. She has strong magical powers," my mother added. "Always has."

"She must have serious magical powers to be able to do that." Hannah's eyes tapered until they were only slits. "Is that who changed you from a mermaid and gave you human legs?" she asked with her tough voice.

"Does it really matter how I obtained my legs?" my mother asked with her voice steady and met the eyes of all the members.

Now that Hannah knew her father and husband to be were alright, she adopted the same sneer she'd had when she first saw us. "You all brought this on yourselves with your house of cards." She pointed at my mom. "The fact that you were a mermaid must be the reason the sea witch has attacked the palace." She turned to me and glowered as if she wanted to kill me. "And you're no better. How could you not tell me that your mom was a mermaid while you paraded around the AML pretending to be one of us? Were you a spy? Learning all our secrets so you could undermine my authority? It doesn't matter." She shook her head. "The sea witch is now after you for your lies. It's payback for you and your family."

"Hannah," I cautioned her. "Stop it."

"Why? Your mother's transformation is why the sea witch is attacking. It has to be tied to your mother. You and your family deserve everything that is happening. Any bloodshed is because of your family." She snapped her fingers. "Let's go. I have had enough of this family with their lies. We need to return to Antla and be with people who aren't deceivers." She pointed at me. "Mark my words, this isn't over."

Hannah marched out and left us speechless.

My father laid some shells on the table to pay for the food and sighed. "Let's return to the cove. We may have just given the sea witch the keys to our location."

"What do you mean?" I asked, but then it dawned on me. He was worried Hannah would tell the witch where we were.

3

21ST FEBRUARY

In the end, my father decided it was too risky to stay at the cottage, so we'd all been driven back to the outskirts of Antla and stayed in a house there. I didn't even know whom this one belonged to, and I didn't want to. Who cared? The kingdom was a mess, my mother was a mermaid, and my once-upon-a-time best friend was now so untrustworthy that my father thought that there was a possibility that she'd give us up. At least, the view of the sea from the windows was nice, I thought, trying to cheer myself up. And I still had both my parents with me. My mother had traveled in the carriage with us.

After enjoying their company during breakfast at the cafe, the somber mood still lingered like a disease without a cure.

Even the soothing sound of the sea failed to lift my spirits.

My eyes strayed in the direction of the sea above the underwater kingdom, hoping for a glimpse of Fish, while my parents, with their own defeated facial expressions, discussed our future.

Defeat wasn't a normal state of mind for the royal family but understandable, considering everything we had endured during the last three weeks and the worry of not knowing what Hannah would do.

"I shouldn't have told her where we were staying," my father mumbled under his breath. "I should have gone back yesterday. Maybe if I surrender to the sea witch, she might leave everyone else alone."

"No, Father. No. You can't take the blame yourself, and you certainly can't sacrifice yourself for us. I won't allow you to do that." I vehemently shook my head."The three of us must stay together. Remember, from your sailing days, how a cord of three strands is so much stronger than those with two. You can't leave us to be vulnerable by ourselves."

He smiled. "You two are never vulnerable. Your individual strengths rival all the soldiers of the world. And together, you're a force to be reckoned with."

My mother grabbed his hand. "We need you."

My father only mumbled. I could see on his face how much hiding out was hurting him. He needed to be on the front line, and instead, he was stuck here with us.

I knew how he felt because I felt the same way. I was sick of being cooped up. I longed to dive back into the ocean. Looking out of the window, I wondered just how far away the mer village was. If we were on the outskirts of Antla, it couldn't be too far away. I wondered if I could get away with swimming there. Fish had told me that he'd seen none of the witch's sea creatures when he'd brought my mother to the cottage. Just thinking of him made my heart ache. He'd told me he'd come and see me, but we'd left the cottage so abruptly that I didn't even know if he'd made the trip.

"I'm going for a walk," I said, standing up from the breakfast table.

My father raised his eyes. "No. It's too dangerous."

"Let her go," my mother said, placing her hand on my father's arm. "We are out of town. No one knows we are here."

"Just don't be long," my father said gruffly, "and don't go too far, I don't want to have to come looking for you."

"Thank you, Daddy!" I said, kissing him quickly on the forehead. "Thanks, Mom."

I ran out before either of them could change their mind and found a path that would take me down the cliff to the water. There was no pretty little boat here and no beach, but the water was there. Saltwater, I craved. Without a swimming costume, I had to be content to swim in only my underwear. Without looking back, I dived into the ocean and began to swim.

Without Fish, the cold water nipped at my skin, and somehow, the ocean seemed darker than it had before. A strong sense of foreboding hit me, but I couldn't see any danger ahead. I forged ahead, keeping my wits about me. If I saw a hint of one of the witch's army, I'd turn around and swim back. Eventually, I began to feel calmer and began to let my mind wander to Hannah.

Deep down, my best friend was generally a good person, but she let her emotions rule her, and right now, she was mad. I guess her good side was really deeply hidden at the moment.

If only I could live in the mer village, I wouldn't have to worry about any of this. But although my mother would be able to join me, my father wouldn't. Besides, he wouldn't leave the people of Atlantice even if he wanted to. Sure, he'd hide out on the advice of his military staff occasionally, but he'd never leave for good. Especially not in our current situation.

The toughest part of any decision we made as a royal family was that we always needed to weigh how the outcome would affect the capital and the people of Atlantice. All these thoughts were swirling in my head as the sea darkened again. Although I felt I was close to the mer village, the sense of foreboding I felt came back, and this time, it made my body tremble. I was cold without Fish, and if I wasn't careful, I was going to get hypothermia. Reluctantly I gave up and turned back, swimming home much more quickly than I'd swam out. When I got back to the shore, I wasn't expecting half the guards to be watching me out of the window. Ok, half was a tad over-exaggerating, but there were enough, and I was in nothing but my wet underwear. Grabbing my clothes from where I'd left them on the rock. I quickly pulled them on and headed back to the house.

I expected my father to berate me for going into the water, but when I went in, it seemed he'd not even noticed. A number of guards were sitting around a long table in the kitchen, which was now filled with food.

"There you are, Blaise," my father said when he caught sight of me. "Come join us...is it raining outside?"

I shrugged my shoulders and quickly darted into the bedroom. Pulling all the clothes off, I found a towel and rubbed myself dry before getting dressed in dry clothes.

"What's this?" I asked as I squeezed in between two of the guards.

"The guards are here with news from the palace. It's not good news, I'm afraid. The sea witch is still in the palace, and there are more casualties. I've invited these men to eat with us. They've been telling me they haven't eaten much in days, so a warm meal is the least I can do."

My heart fell at the news. Of course, I knew that it was unlikely we'd gotten the witch out, but I'd still hoped. The news of more casualties made me feel sick to my stomach.

The guards chatted as they ate, but the whole table became quiet as a woman dressed in cargo pants and a plain shirt was escorted into the room with two other guards flanking her.

My eyes widened as I recognized her.

Emma!

She curtsied once she stopped near the table, and her face beamed. "Your Highness! I'm so glad you're here with Queen Antonella and King Ermias!"

Royal protocol forgotten, I jumped up from the table and hugged her. "Emma, you're safe. Tell me everything that's happened since we've left."

My mom cleared her throat and said in a reprimanding tone, "Blaise."

I turned with a sheepish look. "Yes, Mother?"

My mother raised an eyebrow at me before turning her attention to Emma. "Emma, why don't you join us?"

Emma faced me and lowered her voice, "It's okay. I needed that hug." The sunlight caught her glistening eyes. They reminded me of flecks of sunlight on sprinkled glitter.

But it definitely was not glitter but tears forming.

"What's wrong?" I tapped my fingers on my thigh, anticipating having to hear more bad news.

She looked toward my parents and whispered, "The sea witch is destroying Antla." She sniffed as if holding back her tears. "It's terrible. We don't know what to do." Her voice trembled.

The guard said, "You need to tell the king and queen everything."

"Jaxon told me you were here. He brought me in a carriage. I had to come see for myself. I needed to tell you what's been going on."

"Please continue, Emma. Blaise, scooch up so Emma can sit beside you."

"Once you left, all hell broke loose. The guards evacuated the town of Antla, or at least most of it. The children were sent to the outskirts of town as well as the pregnant women and the elderly. Anyone deemed vulnerable was asked to leave with the children. Most did, but many of the retired fishermen refused to leave. They barricaded their homes. Then things got quiet."

Nobody moved, and all eyes focused on her as she took a breath.

"We were lulled into thinking that the fighting was over. In the evening, most of the people headed to the town center to see what was happening. They believed that they were safe."

She pushed back a strand of hair with her hand that trembled. "They were wrong. The sea witch's army swarmed the town. The people needed to use whatever was near them to defend themselves. We fought all night and all this morning, but the creatures continued to come. It was like a herd of cattle that multiplied every ten minutes."

We didn't move. We barely breathed as we listened.

Emma's tears ran down her face.

I wanted to hug her, but I needed to hear what she was going to say next.

Instead, my mother grabbed Emma's hand and said, "Let it all out. Don't hold back."

Emma sniffled. "A few guards retrieved weapons from the armory, but it was useless. The creatures didn't seem real. They were huge, bigger than the ones we fought at the palace while you were still there. They were vicious and relentless. They didn't care who they killed. Men, women, children, dogs, cats. Anyone who'd refused or was unable to leave. Anyone that stood in their way was slashed." She closed her eyes. "Meanwhile, as everyone fought those creatures, the sea witch turned our people to stone. So between her army and people being turned into stone, we've lost about half of Antla." Emma put her head down, and the tears ran freely.

I gasped at her words, and opposite me, my mother let out a strangled sob.

Emma lifted her head. "The town is destroyed. The old buildings are hanging by rebar, and we fear that one strong wind will blow them over. It's terrible. We're hoping for reinforcements."

My father slammed his fist on the table, making us all jump. "I've stayed away too long. We must return and fight the sea witch and her men. We'll arm ourselves and prepare for the fiercest battle the island of Atlantice has ever seen. I won't back away from my duty any longer."

He stood up, and the guards around the table followed suit. Not one of them looked upset by the meal they would now have to leave behind.

My mother nodded her head. "There is no question we need to acquire whatever weapons are left from the armory."

I turned my head to stare at the horizon.

So much bloodshed, and for what? What did the sea witch want? What was her purpose?

"Blaise, I want you to leave Atlantice and head to the mainland. Away from the fighting. You can take Emma if she's willing to go with you."

"No, Father. I will not run away. You need every able person to fight."

"She's right, Ermias. We need her. Did you tell me yourself that she brought down dozens of men twice her size and also protected your back." My mom smiled. "Our daughter is one brave young lady."

"She is, but I'd rather have her safe." He touched my mom's cheek. "We can't lose her."

"Father, it's my duty to fight with you. I want to fight!" I stood and pulled on my boots. Emma ran over to me and handed me my coat from its hook. When I looked back up, the guards were all looking at my father in askance.

My father shook his head. "I don't know. This fight is rougher than the first battle. The way Emma describes it, this one is worse. Much worse. She's turning people into stone."

Like I needed the reminder. "I know Father, but you also have fewer men than before." I walked back toward him. "One day, I'll be running this kingdom. I need to be able to run it in any eventuality, and that includes war."

"I'm sorry, Blaise. I let you fight the other day because you really gave me no choice, but now I do have a choice. You and the queen will stay here while I go back and organize the troops. I need to bring in the whole of the Palace guard and the Atlantice navy. I can't do that if I'm worried about you."

"You wish me to stay behind too?" My mother asked.

"Yes, I do."

My mother looked at him in exactly the same way that I felt. Anger flitted across her face.

"Do I have to remind you that while you and Blaise were fighting at the palace, I was taking care of the creatures under the water? And let me tell you, they were a lot more dangerous down there."

"I imagine they were, but what I said still stands. The pair of you will remain here until I send for you. Come on guards, We need to go back. We need to finish this."

They all filed out, most of them with embarrassment on their faces after witnessing a full-on royal family argument. Only Emma, my mother, and I were left behind. It suddenly felt very quiet.

"I should probably head back too," Emma said, cutting through the silence.

"You're going back to fight?" I asked, not really surprised.

"I'm sorry, Blaise. I know how much you want to come. You've changed so much over the last few weeks. A month or so ago, I couldn't imagine you ever wanting to drop everything and fight against magical frog things, but look at you now."

I snorted at her description of the sea witch's army. They did look a little like overgrown frogs, with big bellies and spindly legs.

"You can fight as well as any of the guards. Better than some of them, and that's without the training they received. You would be an asset to any team your father puts together."

"So, you think I should sneak back with you?"

"Actually, despite everything I've just said, no, I don't. I know you will be amazing if you go back, but I think if your father knows you are back in Antla, he will lose his concentration. He will be so worried about you that he'll make mistakes. I don't think for one minute he doesn't think you are an amazing fighter, but he knows himself."

I let out a loud sigh. As much as I hated to admit it, she was right, and that was pretty much what he'd said. She'd just explained it better.

Emma gave me a hug and then left. The house felt very empty without anyone in it.

"Why don't you help me clean up?" my mother said. The plates from lunch were still set out on the table, and my mother couldn't walk to move them to the sink due to her lack of legs.

I worked in silence, clearing up the mess that the guards had left behind. It was almost an hour later when I could finally sit down. Two guards had been left behind to watch over us. I asked one of them to carry my mother to the living area.

"Who owns this house?" I asked, glancing around the sparsely decorated room. I'd not had much time to really take a look at the place, but now that I did, I could see that it was very minimalistic with white walls and only the bare minimum amount of furniture. The only picture on the wall was a painting of the sea. There were no family pictures or knick-knacks.

"It belongs to us...or should I say, to the palace. It's used as a holiday home for members of the staff we think deserve it. Sometimes we donate it to people who can't afford vacations. I never thought I'd see the day when I stayed here myself."

Now that she was out from under the table and I could see her leg, it made me realize just how weird, how out of place she looked on dry land. She'd always been the epitome of sophistication, but now, she looked unwieldy. She was still wearing the long skirt I'd lent her, not that any of the clothes either of us was wearing actually belonged to me. My clothes, my mother's clothes, were all back at the palace, no doubt being ruined by the frog army.

A thought of the sea witch trying to cram her large body into my mother's beautiful clothes made me shudder, so I tried to think of something else.

"Are you angry at Father for not letting us go and fight?"

"I was," my mother said, closing her eyes and massaging her temples, "but then in my heart, I knew it was the right thing to do. He loves us both so much, and we've been in so much danger these past few months. He just wants to keep us safe. Emma said it so well. If your father knew we were in danger, he wouldn't be able to do his job properly. Atlantice needs a strong leader right now. Your father has only known peace for his entire reign, but he's been desperate to prove himself. To show Atlantice that he can be a strong leader. Hiding out at the cottage nearly killed him. He needs this, Blaise."

"What if he gets hurt?" I asked in a small voice. It was all well and good, my father worrying about us, but what about us worrying about him?

"Then that is something we will deal with when the time comes. He has a strong army of men and women behind him. The palace guard, the navy. He's not doing this alone."

Maybe she was right. Maybe they were all right, but that didn't stop my feeling of unease and helplessness. I ended up going to bed early, through lack of anything else to do. Despite the chilly night, I opened the window to listen to the sound of the waves crashing on the rocks below. Yet another storm had blown in, which matched my mood perfectly. I'd thought we were over the weird storms, but apparently not. This whole year, so far, had been awful. First the storms, then the AML crap I'd had to deal with, not to mention my mother turning into a mermaid, and then the sea witch attacking.

Urgh. The sea witch. I wanted to forget about what she was doing, seeing as I couldn't do a thing about it, but my mind kept wandering back to it.

It was only hours later, in the middle of the night, when the window banged the frame, waking me up, that I realized I could do something about it. I could help save Antla without my father being any the wiser.

I jumped out of bed, my mind whirring. It would have been easier to run away without telling my mother, but I had a sneaking suspicion she would let me go. She would probably want to come with me.

I knocked on her bedroom door quietly, not wanting the guards to hear.

"Blaise?"

"I know how we can help Father," I whispered, padding into her room.

"What time is it?" she asked bleary-eyed as she lit her lamp.

"It's the middle of the night. That's not important. I know about the tunnels under the palace. We can get to her from there."

"We?" she asked, sitting up in bed. She was still wearing the same shirt she'd been wearing all day. No one had thought to bring clothes for her. Mind you, if we went with my plan, she'd have no need for clothes, beyond the bikini top she wore in the ocean.

"We. You , me, the merfolk."

Her eyes widened. "Of course! The whole mer village is in hiding, but they want to fight. I'll need to persuade my father, of course." She pulled the blankets back. "Help me, Blaise. I'll not be able to get down to the sea by myself, and we can't ask the guards. We'll have to sneak out the back."

"I can carry you!" I said, helping her out of bed. "You aren't mad at me?"

"Mad at you? No. not at all. It's a genius idea. I can't promise your father won't be mad at the pair of us, but once we win, he'll get over it."

I pulled her over my shoulder into a half fireman's lift. she was heavier than I expected, but I only needed to get her to the sea. It wasn't far. "You think we'll win?"

"Honestly?" she asked he face behind me. "I don't know, but I'm sure going to try. That witch has been the bane of my life for far too long. It's time we took her out."

It took every ounce of energy I had. Muscles I didn't even know I had, burned as I carefully made my way through the darkness down the cliff-side path. The water was savage. Huge waves sent droplets of saltwater all over us, long before we got to the bottom of the path. My old fear of the sea was beginning to come back with a vengeance, but this was too important to back out now. I visualized Fish's face and kept on until I could go no farther. "The waves will batter us against the rocks," I said, gently pulling my mother from my shoulder and lowering her to the path.

She glanced around at the churning sea. "I'm a strong swimmer. Very strong. I can see a point that we might be able to make it to. If I get enough force, I might be able to break through the current. Once we are under the water and away from the rocks, we'll be fine."

"There's an awful lot of might's in that sentence," I joked feebly.

"Just hold my hand and don't let go," she said, pulling her clothes off. She was still wearing her bikini underneath her shirt. I followed suit, and when I was in my underwear, she grabbed my hand and inched to the edge of the path. Sea spray hit my face, sending terror through my veins. I couldn't see any space between the rocks, and even if there was one, the waves were battering them so hard, we'd never get through them. She gripped my hand more tightly, and I closed my eyes. I had to trust her. She knew the ocean better than I did. And then I felt myself falling. I braced myself for hitting the rocks below, but we plunged into the icy water. Less than a second later, I was being spirited through the waves away from the rocks. In less than a minute, we were under the ocean far away from harm. Well, the cliff edge at least. We still had an army of magical frog men ahead of us.

"I'm taking you to meet my father first," my mother said in the strange underwater way I was getting used to. "It's about time you met your grandfather."

I was going to meet the mer king. No one had come out with it and said that my mother was a sea princess long before she was a land-dwelling queen, but there'd been enough clues. My grandfather was the king of the ocean. I was both a land princess and sea princess. Once again, I thanked my mother—my real mother—for leaving me with my parents. I had no idea who she was, and I'd probably never know, but she'd done the kindest thing for me. I just needed to find a way to survive the next few days so that if I ever did meet her, I could thank her face to face.

4
22ND FEBRUARY

*W*e passed through the dark patch of water I'd encountered the day before. Like night wasn't enough, and it needed something extra. As we passed through it, it felt colder too. Even with the magical mermaid energy my mother provided, the cold still seeped into my bones.

"What is this?" I asked.

"I don't know, but I do know it's spreading. It's not normal water, that's for sure. It has a current of evil running through it. I'm hoping we can swim through it."

A current of evil? Like we didn't have enough to deal with, now we had to deal with evil water too?

I grasped my mother's hand more tightly as we swam through. Above us, the sky began to turn orange as the sun made its way up the sky, but the light barely penetrated the surface.

"The mer village is just down there." My mother pointed down to a hole in the seabed. Or, at least, it looked like a hole. Everything was so dark it was hard to see. It turned out to be a tunnel like the one I'd traveled down before. This one took us to the back of the huge mer castle I'd seen the one time I was down here before.

It was so beautiful that I couldn't wait to see inside. A group of mer guards swam over when they saw us.

The largest one, a guy with long golden hair, held a trident to us. When he saw who it was, he lowered the trident immediately. "Your Highness," he said, dipping into a bow. "We thought you were more of the witch's army. Please forgive me."

"Just me and my daughter. Have there been any attacks since I left?"

"No. It's been quiet. I've heard that the land palace is still inhabited by the witch, but the king has ordered all the merfolk to stay in here until it's over. He doesn't want to get involved with the human war."

"It's not a human war," my mother argued, sounding exasperated. "The sea witch is from our world, and I rather think it's my fault that she's in the human world in the first place. I already told the king this. Let me pass."

She swam to the back door with me doing my best to keep up with her. Now that she'd let go of my hand, it was cold and I had to pump my legs as hard as I could just to keep up.

Inside the palace, we were ushered to a large room that was empty apart from the sand on the floor and various seashells. It wasn't long before my grandfather swam in. My mouth fell open at the sight of him; he was so much bigger than any merman I'd ever seen with muscular arms and chest and long flowing white hair. He, too, held a trident. I dropped into a bow as best as I could as I floated in the water.

"Daddy. This is Blaise, your granddaughter."

"Pleased to meet you, Your Majesty," I said, holding my hand out to him. It felt strange to be the one bowing. I was used to other people doing it to me.

"Let's not float on ceremony," he said, pulling me into a hug that almost crushed my bones.

"I can't believe I have a grandchild. My daughters had denied me," he said, throwing a glance at a group of red-haired mermaids that looked like my mother. "I'm glad at least one of my daughters saw fit to provide me with a grandchild and what a delightful one at that."

He held me at arm's length so he could look at me properly. He was so enthusiastic about meeting me that I couldn't help but grin at him.

"I'm adopted. I think you should know, sir."

"Adopted, shmadopted," he said, finally letting me go and waving his large meaty hand around. "You are my granddaughter, and I won't let anyone tell me differently. Please tell me you are here to visit for a while. I have eighteen years to catch up on."

"Actually, we are here to ask for your help," my mother cut in. "Ermias is fighting the witch. He can't do it alone."

"Not this again, Antonella," my grandfather sighed. "He isn't alone. He has guards, people who are fighting with him. I don't want to get involved in a human war."

She swam to him, her finger outstretched. "You know as well as I do that it is a war I started twenty years ago. I made a mistake. I asked the witch for something and gave her nothing in return. I cannot stand by and let my husband's kingdom fall because of some stupid mistake I made when I was too young to know any better."

"Hmm," my father grimaced. "I knew I should have had sons. Less trouble. What is it you expect me to do?"

"I want everyone in the mer village to fight. There are a number of tunnels below the land palace. We can invade from there."

"Invade? How do you think we are going to do that? We don't have legs, remember? Do you want us to float up through the palace on air, or do you expect us to pull ourselves up using our arms?"

"Ermias is dealing with the creatures outside the palace. We just need to thin the herd a bit to make it easier on him."

"I don't think we can," I said, realizing what my grandfather said was true. None of the merfolk could walk, and even if they could, how could they defeat an army that was everlasting? They were made of magic and nothing more. If one was killed, ten more popped up in its place. "The creatures aren't even real. We could be fighting them on the lower levels, but it wouldn't make a difference. The witch will continue conjuring them."

"No," my mother said forcefully. "She isn't invincible; there is a limit to her magic. The more of those creatures she makes, the more energy she uses. If we fight from the tunnels, she'll have to make creatures to fight us as well as creatures to fight your father and his guards. Double the energy. If she's doing that, she will be weakened quicker. Please, Father. I've not asked for anything from you in such a long time."

"Yes, well, that's because you ran away for a long time," he grumbled. "Ok, I'll let those that want to fight go with you. But I'm not pressuring anyone, and I'll need some of my guards kept here to guard the mer village in case any of those things decide to come back."

"If I'm at the palace, they won't come here, but thank you, Father."

The three of us swam out of the palace, followed by my aunts and a number of guards. I'd expected it to take hours rounding people up and asking them if they wanted to fight, but right outside the front of the palace, what looked to be most of the village were already there, most of them armed with tridents. Right at the very front was Fish.

"I heard a rumor that there was a beautiful girl with very nice legs in town," he said to me. "I thought I'd come and check it out."

"With a trident?" I asked, raising an eyebrow.

"Ok, I might have got the idea that you were planning on fighting alongside your father."

I shook my head. "Actually, my father doesn't know. He thinks I'm safely tucked up in bed in a house just outside of Antla."

"You are such a rebel," he teased, pulling me toward him and kissing my forehead. Come on, let's get this show on the seabed.

I couldn't count how many merpeople followed us, but it was a lot. I guess they were sick of the sea witch as much as I was. Even the girls who'd been rude to me on my first visit, were there, waving their tridents, ready to dive into action.

Almost as soon as the entrance to the palace tunnels came into sight, we were swarmed. Hundreds of the frog creatures swam out at us. The water around us had darkened again despite the storm above clearing. As they swarmed toward us, a shot of adrenaline pumped through me. I'd killed them before, I could do it again. Taking a trident from one of the merfolk that had two, I swam toward them with as much of a war cry as I could muster underwater.

The fork went right through one of their hearts, and it disappeared in a flash of magical blue energy. All around me, blue flashes lit up the dark sea as we took the creatures down.

They were no match for trident-wielding merfolk, but there were so many of them. Even though the merpeople were stronger, more skilled, and superior in every way, the creatures outnumbered us three to one, and the more I killed, the more seemed to come out of the tunnel to replace them. As I sliced the head from one of them, I told myself that it was worth it. Every creature the witch conjured, the more magical energy it took. At least, that's what my mother had said. I couldn't even see her in the melee. I hoped that we were weakening her enough to make it easier for my father and his troops because down here, we were swamped. The only saving grace was that the frog creatures didn't have weapons like they had on land. Instead, they swarmed the merfolk, grabbing onto them and throwing punches where they could.

I jabbed one with a trident, watching it turn to magical blue light dust, as another grabbed hold of my leg. As I kicked out with my other leg, sending it flying away from me, another grabbed my waist, and another put its arms around my head.

I gave a strangled yell as green scaly limbs consumed me, blocking out the little light I had.

I thrust my arms and legs around, trying to rid myself of the nasty beasts, but there were too many of them. With one clamped on my face, I found I couldn't breathe. However I was able to magically breathe underwater, the ability to do so was hampered by having frog creatures all over me.

I couldn't even shout out for help. All around me, the world turned black. Something sharp cut into my leg, and by the feel of it, it was one of the frog men's teeth. They were biting me now?

I should have felt fear. I was dying. Drowning covered in scaly magical monsters wasn't exactly how I planned to die. But it wasn't fear that was causing the ball of energy in my stomach. It was anger. They'd taken my home, they'd taken my mother's legs, or at least their creator had, and now, they were biting me.

With a primordial scream, I let out a roar and spread my arms and legs wide. The anger I'd been feeling spilled out of me from every pore. I could see it. Pink light lit up the whole ocean, turning their blue magical energy to purple and dissolving hundreds of them, including the five or six that had been holding onto me.

Looking around, I saw the faces of dozens of merfolk gazing at me with shock on their faces. Whatever monster I'd unleashed from within me, it hadn't seemed to have any effect on the merfolk. Unless you could count shocked expressions as an effect. I was as shocked as they were. Had I just produced magic? There were no frog men within fifty feet of me in any direction. I'd evaporated them all. But how? The people of Atlantice didn't do magic. The merfolk knew a bit, but not the kind where they had to wave wands around. They knew how to keep me warm by touch. They understood the sea currents better than anyone, but none of them could do anything like I'd just done. No one in Atlantice could do that. Magic was reserved for the people of Enchantia and the magical creatures in other kingdoms.

"What did you do?" Fish asked, swimming to me and taking my hand. I warmed to his touch immediately. "...Because it was awesome."

"I don't know."

The creatures further than fifty feet away from me, the ones that had survived my blast had gotten over their shock and were now swarming in again. I'd done it once, but I could feel the energy drained from me. I didn't think I'd be able to do it again.

"Let's get out of here," my mother said, grabbing my other hand

and pulling me away from the chaos. Fish kept hold, so the two of us were pulled along in my mother's wake.

"I'm not leaving the fight!" I said, trying to pull my hand from my mother's. My magical energy, or whatever it was, had depleted, but my physical energy was as strong as it ever had been. I might not be able to magic the frogs to death again, but I could throw a trident...at least I could have if I had one. In the confusion, I'd dropped mine somewhere.

"I'm not asking you to leave," my mother said without slowing down. "I'm taking you into the palace."

She pulled us all down a tunnel I'd never seen before. This wasn't the tunnel that took us to the basement nor the one where the dolphins delivered the mail, so where exactly was she taking us?

She pressed a button that started some kind of mechanism. Before I 'd had a chance to figure out what, the water pressure increased shooting us up a tube that carried us right into the palace. Water pressure pushed me along as I swam upwards. It was the strangest thing. It curved slightly, and then, I fell out into a huge tank. A huge tank I'd never seen before. Glancing through the glass, I saw that we were in a massive room. The tank took up most of it, but there was enough space for a bed and a small table.

"What is this place?" I asked as Fish splashed down into the tank behind me.

"It's a room in the palace. It's hidden behind a trick wall." My mother said, pulling herself over the glass and onto a kind of slide at the other side that helped her get to the floor without falling.

"But what is it?"

She turned a cherry red and averted my gaze. I hopped over the glass and slid down to her.

"When your father and I were still hiding from everyone..."

My eyes found the bed once more, and I held up my hand. "I don't think I want to know, after all," I said, amazed they'd managed to hide out in the palace without being caught. How my father had managed this without his parents knowing was beyond me. Still, that was a story for another day. We had bloodthirsty monsters to kill and a sea witch to capture. My mother pulled herself onto the bed.

"We need a plan. I've never seen anything like what you did back there. It was magic. Since when could you do magic?"

I shook my head, unsure of how to answer. "I don't know. A few weeks back, I found that I could breathe underwater. I've felt that getting stronger, but the light show I just did. That was as new to me as it was to you. I felt the energy, and I felt it explode out of me, but I didn't control it. I don't feel it now. I can't do it again."

She considered me for a minute as Fish tumbled to the floor behind me.

It was only then that I realized that I'd messed up. I'd brought two people right into the witch's lair without weapons. My mother had thought I could defeat the witch with magic, but I couldn't.

"I'm sorry. We should have brought tridents with us."

She took my hand and pulled me to her. "No. I didn't expect you would be able to. I didn't bring you here to fight. I brought you here because I'm going to give the sea witch what she wants. I can't walk so, I need you to be my legs."

My eyes widened as I took in her earnest face.

"You are giving up? What the sea witch wants is revenge."

"She wants my voice. I think that's a small price to pay to save the kingdom, don't you?"

"Your Highness," began Fish on the carpet behind me. "I don't want to sound disrespectful, but I think she's beyond that now. She doesn't just want your voice, she wants all of you. She wants to possess every part of you until there is nothing left."

My mother lowered her eyes. "I know. That's why I brought you here. I need you to fight the witch if she attempts to hurt Blaise. I'll happily sacrifice myself for the good of the kingdom, but I won't let her take Blaise."

"No," I cried, crumpling to her feet. My mother was talking about killing herself. Anguish filled me, and tears poured down my face as I wept over her tail.

"It's the only way," she said, stroking my hair as she used to do when I was a child.

"We can't do this," I said, looking up at her through tear-filled lashes. "I might be able to carry you, but I can't carry both of you. I'm not strong enough."

There. A fatal flaw in her plan. We'd have to go back out of the tube and find some other way to deal with the witch.

"Look over there," she said, pointing to a cart. It was the type a maid might bring lunch out on. We had one just like it in the parlor for when my mother had afternoon teas.

"You want me to fight the witch with a tea cart?"

"No, my darling. I want you to push me to the witch. If we squeeze together, your friend and I will just about be able to fit on."

I shook my head as the whole palace shook around us. It sounded like thunder was actually in the palace. Either my father was sending cannonballs through the palace walls, or the sea witch had upped her game. It didn't bode well either way.

"Bring the cart over, Blaise."

Fighting a sea witch was one thing, but fighting my mother when she was so determined was another. I lapsed into an almost dream-like state as I did as she asked.

As both Fish and my mother hauled themselves onto the cart, my mind kept exploring other outcomes to the inevitable. The witch had never explicitly said what she wanted from us, but I was pretty sure Fish was right. She wanted revenge. Wasn't that the third most likely reason to kill someone behind money and jealousy? Well, we had enough money for her to take with her if she so chose. The witch looked like something dragged from the bottom of the ocean. Take away her glimmer, and she had every reason to be jealous of my mother. Bam! All three reasons to kill her.

I opened the door, surprised to find myself on the third floor of the palace along a corridor we didn't use that much. No wonder I hadn't noticed the discrepancy in wall size. I thought this corridor was used for things like palace cleaning supplies and laundry. The staff lived on this floor in this particular wing. When the door closed behind us, I turned to see that the wood paneling slotted right back into place. I would never have noticed the tiny crack between the panels where the door was cut out.

So, maybe I'd not noticed the secret room, but the creatures sure noticed us. Within fifteen seconds of us coming through the door, the whole corridor was swarming with the frog beasts. My gut instinct was to fight, but what was the point if my mom planned suicide by witch anyway?

They must have known something was up because they didn't attack, and as I pushed the cart down the corridor, they parted, letting me walk a path right through them.

I asked one of them where the sea witch was. It didn't speak, but it raised its gnarled finger and pointed. As one symbiotic mass, they all pointed the same way, and I knew where she was. They were pointing to the main wing, luckily or unluckily, she was on this floor. She was in the room that the balcony jutted off from, the room where we held our press conferences and had official portraits painted.

She was ready for us as though she knew we were coming. Of course, she did; the frogmen were a part of her magic. What they knew, she knew.

My stomach heaved at the sight of her. Even more ugly on land that she had ever been underwater, her dull, grey hair and skin had lost their vibrant tone, but her eyes remained yellow. The mystery of how she had managed to walk out of the water was revealed. She floated. Her whole body sat on a cloud of purple magic, two feet from the ground.

"The Little Mermaid and her daughter, how precious," she shrieked. "You know, in all of my years, you two are the only ones to get away from me. And you..." she said, floating closer and running her grey finger down my mother's face, making my mother cringe, "are the first person to steal from me."

"I did steal from you, and I'm deeply sorry."

"Your repentance will not save you," she cackled.

My mother let her tail swing, and she pulled herself up straight.

"I understand that. I wronged you. I'm not here to bargain with you, nor am I here to fight. I made a mistake when I was young, and I'm here to offer myself to you. You know, the irony was that the king loved me. He loved me as a mermaid, he loved me as a human. He loved me for who I was. None of this had to happen. Take my voice, take what you want of me."

"What a touching story, but it isn't just you who betrayed me. Your daughter did too."

"No!" my mother shouted, raising her finger to the witch's face. "You leave her out of this. She didn't betray you. She escaped from you. It's hardly the same thing. You only captured her because you wanted to get to me. Well, now, you have me. You take me, you let them go."

The witch tapped her chin and walked slowly away,

"I've waited a long time for this moment. Eighteen years, to come back and finish what was started. It's a long time to wait." She turned. "But then my powers returned. They've been gaining strength for a while now. I don't know what took them away, and I don't know why they are back, but I do know something. Your daughter isn't who she says she is."

"She's my daughter. That's all you need to know."

The witch shook her head and walked over to me. "She's not human. Look at her eyes. No human has eyes like that."

"What are you talking about?" my mother demanded.

"I captured her, as you say, because I wanted to get you, but very quickly, I saw something in her. At first, I thought she was just some run of the mill half-mermaid, but then she escaped my bubble."

"I heard your magic words, that's all. It was no trick. I heard your words to get through the bubble, and when you were gone, I repeated them, and I swam through."

"It sounds so simple, doesn't it?" she trilled. "And yet, magic words, without magic, are just words. No human could have gotten through that bubble, no matter what words they said."

"I'm not magic," I blurted out, but even as I said it, I knew it was a lie.

"Tell that to my creations that you blasted. Over fifty of them in one go. You are more powerful than you think, and that intrigues me. I thought that after all this time, I wanted your mother, but as it turns out, I want you."

"Not a chance!" my mother screamed. She leapt forward from the cart, unsettling it. Fish fell backward as my mother caught the witch's arm. She sank her teeth into the flesh, causing the witch to scream out loudly. Because of her pain, or whatever, the frog creatures all disappeared in a puff of blue smoke.

"We need to get out of here," Fish yelled, trying to turn the cart back around the right way.

I looked at the witch. Her features were contorted with pain, but I knew it was a temporary thing. Getting Fish and my mother on the cart and then pushing it down the corridor would take time, time we didn't have.

I felt angry, and that anger churned in my gut. I now recognized it as something else. If I could do magic, maybe I could do more with it. I wasn't strong enough to fight the sea witch...yet , but I was sure I could pick up Fish and my mother. Using all the energy I had, I focused on the two of them, both lying on the floor. Picking them up with only the power of my mind took more energy than I thought it would. My plan was to float them down the corridor, but that wasn't going to happen. I had to be content with dumping them back on the cart.

"When this is all over, we really need to have a talk," my mother said as she gripped the side of the cart.

"Let's get out of here first, though, eh?"

I expected my mother to complain about me pushing them away from the witch. After all, she'd come here to sacrifice herself, but I guessed the sea witch deciding she wanted me had changed her mind. I bolted down the corridor quickly away from the witch. Behind me, I could hear her monsters had returned and were now hot on our heels. This time, they were out for blood. Back in the corridor at the secret door, I had to let my mother open it. She touched a panel, and the door sprang open. I pushed the cart through, diving through after it and slammed my feet against the door to close it. On the other side, I heard a bang and then a number of squeaks as the creature ran into the closed door.

"How did you get out of here?" I asked, looking at the tank. The tube still had water pouring out of it

"Not that way," my mother said, pulling herself across the floor with her arms. She pushed the table to one side to reveal a hole. When I peered down it, I saw another slide. This one had water gushing downwards.

The bangs from the door increased in both volume and frequency. The monsters were trying to get through.

I lifted my mother to the hole and watched as she disappeared into the void. Fish followed behind. As the door finally gave way, I leaped into the hole behind them.

Spiraling downwards, I ended up splashing into a pool in the darkness. Fish's hand caught my arm, and the three of us together swam through another tunnel to the light.

The scene before us was terrible. The merfolk were fighting the creatures in the sea, and a quick look toward the palace showed me that there were still thousands of them on land.

"I need to go and help my father," I said. I knew I was a hindrance under the water. My magic had saved me once, but it wouldn't work again. Just that little bit I'd used in the palace had wiped me out. I still needed the merfolk for warmth. It was just something I couldn't do alone.

My mother kissed my forehead. "I understand. You'll need some clothes..."

"I'll head to the guard's building. There are uniforms there."

"Be safe, my darling."

I gave her a smile. Fish took my hand and pulled me to the shore.

"I don't like this," he said as I stood on the sandy floor and began the walk up to the beach. When I'd gone as far as Fish could go with me, I stopped.

"I don't like it either, but I'll be back."

He pulled me to him and brought me into a kiss that destroyed my very soul. I knew it might be the last we ever shared.

I wouldn't let my tears fall. "What's your name?" I asked when we pulled apart.

Fish shook his head. "I'm not telling you. I'll tell you when this is over."

I stroked the side of his face. "I want to know. I can't keep calling you Fish."

"I'll tell you when this is over," he repeated. It was his way of telling me that we'd both survive.

I gave him one last peck on the cheek and entered the battle.

My muscles ached, my bones protested every time I asked them to move.

To slash.

To stab.

To kick.

I pushed my screaming body parts, hoping that they wouldn't fail me.

But it wasn't enough. We did not have enough men to fight. Emma's defeated face brought me to reality.

We were losing.

There was no backup cavalry. No assembly line of more guards.

We had given it our all, and we had lost.

I looked out to the ocean and saw my mom and Fish fighting the creatures in the water.

They looked exhausted beyond belief. It was impossible. The more people we brought in to fight, the more creatures the witch manufactured. I should have hit her over the head with a chair when I had the chance. But I hadn't. I'd been too busy wondering what she meant about me not being human. It was the same question I'd asked myself a thousand times since my adoption came to light. No one knew where I came from, so how could anyone know what I was? I'd been selfish, but I'd also been scared. Scared for me, for my mother, for Fish. I'd run away...again, and striking the creatures now, felling them with a sword picked up from the armory didn't assuage the guilt I felt.

I continued to fight, but my faith in our victory vanished with our numbers dwindling.

The situation appeared hopeless.

The sounds of screams and moans punctuated the air as our guards fell one by one.

The sea witch's voice rose above the noise. "I will have my revenge!"

As I looked up to the balcony to where she stood watching over the events playing out below her, an elbow smacked my head, and I dropped my sword. I bent to pick it up amidst a puddle of blood. Our blood. I gripped the pommel and turned around to face the giant frogman. He attacked and attacked until my arms felt as if they were burning embers. Somehow I managed to drive my sword into his chest but not before he slashed at my thigh. Reopening my thigh wound.

I fell to the ground and inched my way to a wall.

Everything moved in slow motion.

It seemed as if the sea witch's men had knocked every one of our men and women to the ground.

My father and the captain continued fighting, taking longer and longer to bring down their opponents.

We're doomed. We can't go on like this.

I was completely empty. I had nothing left to give. We couldn't win. I knew that now. We were literally fighting to the death, and there had been so many.

In the corner of my eye, I saw Admiral Fallon's navy ship moving forward, and a loud boom sounded. The witch turned around.

"Really? Is that all you have? I will pin your boat to the bottom of the sea."

The admiral raised his hand, and Hannah wearing her red navy jacket, threw a red cloth into the air. *What is she doing?*

It fell in slow motion, and the booming noise echoed as an iron cannonball shot out.

I watched as the cannonball soared through the air. Everything stopped as we all looked skyward. Silence rained over us as we all held our breath, waiting to see if the cannonball would hit its mark.

It arced through the sky and then began its descent. The last thing I heard before the balcony was completely obliterated was the deathly scream of the witch. Blue smoke erupted, mixing with the grey as the balcony collapsed. Almost immediately, the froglike monsters all turned into blue smoke and dissipated in the air. The smoke cleared. Someone coughed, breaking the silence.

I watched as one of the guards checked through the rubble.

"She's gone!" he shouted. A huge cheer went through the air, but a thrill of fear ran through my veins. She's gone wasn't the same as she's dead. Until I saw her mangled body with my own eyes, I wouldn't believe this was all over.

I looked out to the sea beyond the palace and spotted my mom and Fish inside a circle of merpeople. Relief flooded through me. They were alive. They were safe.

A couple of small boats launched into the water from the large ship. Hannah and her father were in the first boat.

Ripping my top, I tied it around my thigh as a makeshift bandage and hobbled over to the pier.

Hannah climbed out of the boat and ran up to me. "Blaise, are you okay? You have blood all over your clothes."

I looked down. A smear of dried blood covered my top to match the blood on my pants. Unlike the blood on the pants, this blood was not mine. I didn't even know whom it belonged to. I didn't answer her. What was there to say?

"Oh, Blaise, I've been so wrong," she cried. A lone tear fell. "You were right about the merpeople. I'm sorry I ever doubted you." She held up her hand, and another couple of tears dropped from her blue eyes.

I nodded. It was a bit late for her apology, but I was surprised.

"What caused this sudden change of heart?" I asked.

"My mom. The sea witch turned her into stone. Stone. In front of my eyes." Her tears flowed freely.

She sniffled and wiped her nose with her sleeve. A disgusting habit she had kept from our childhood. "She was down by the sea in front of our house. The merpeople tried to stop the sea witch from hurting her. Despite that they were hurt, they still continued to protect my mom, knowing that they might be killed. They were so brave. It wasn't enough, though. The sea witch's magic got through."

"I'm so sorry, Hannah," I said, and I meant it. No matter our differences over the past month, she didn't deserve that. None of us did. "Your mom was amazing." I brought her into a hug, and the anger melted away as she sobbed onto my shoulder.

I was aware that all around me, the people were picking up the pieces of what was left. In the distance, I saw Emma helping a wounded guard. The admiral was talking to my father, who looked unhurt. All around me, I could see death and destruction, but I also saw something else. The people coming together. Members of the AML mingling with the guards, helping each other.

As I watched something else happened. The people who had been turned to stone began to move. The color appeared in their skin again.

"Hannah!" I said. "Look." She turned and saw what I saw. The petrified people, no longer bound by the witch's magic, were coming back to life.

5

23RD FEBRUARY

The paper and rubber cement smell wafted by my nose as I ambled into Mr. Worthpaper's print shop for the hundredth time since early that morning. My heart wanted to break as I entered the room.

Hannah picked up a bunch of the AML flyers and invitations that had been scattered on the floor. The whole place was a mess, as so many other businesses were in Antla.

Ruined.

A tiny bit of me wanted to cry as I picked one of the invitations up and carefully placed it on the recycle pile.

I stood rubbing the red and blue painted balloons on the child's invitation. No longer would it reach the intended child. The little boy or girl would not be able to open up that card, filled with balloons, inviting the child to the party.

The wedding guest would miss inhaling the sweet rose-scented invitation

Such a waste.

Hannah handed me a thick pile, including the AML flyers that should, indeed, be shredded beyond recognition, breaking my somber thoughts.

I shook my head. "Please tell me this is the last pile we have to bring to the recycle bins." It was only five feet away from the print shop, but I had made ten trips in the last ten minutes. To add more pain to my situation, despite that my stomach had stopped loudly protesting an hour ago, it had decided to revolt every two minutes, stirring up the bile. But food could wait. The sea witch had destroyed half the town because of my mother and me. It was my duty to help to restore it. One good thing to have come from all the mess was the fact that the whole town had come together to rebuild. AML members joined in with everyone else to help salvage what we could.

It was a nice sight to see, except the feeling that the sea witch was somehow still alive gnawed at me. Her body hadn't been found despite extensive cleaning up at the palace. I looked over at Hannah. She was working harder than anyone else. Her mother had miraculously turned from a statue to normal, along with the others. We'd spent quite a bit of the morning sobbing into each other's arms as she apologized profusely over and over again for her part in the mess. Not that she really did have much of a part in it. She was never in league with the sea witch, and despite hinting that she might tell her our location, I suspected she never would have. We were back to being friends again. It wasn't the same as before. We'd lost our closeness, and we had a lot to rebuild, but we'd stared down that path.

She smirked. "It is."

Spotting a few more strewn AML flyers in the next room, I lowered my head down, tilted it to the side, and raised my narrowed eyes. I must have resembled a librarian about to reprimand a child for not whispering. "Are you sure?"

"I'm not lying. There's no more..." Hannah bit her lower lip as she noticed the pile I was referring to . Hate mail printed for the AML. "Ok, there may be some more," she conceded, picking them all up. "I think I'll take these out to be shredded."

I nodded, expecting her to walk past me, but she stopped right where I was.

"I wish I could go back in time and, instead of attacking you, join you and your father. My mom would not have been turned to stone. I've been so stupid."

"You don't know that," I said. I touched my friend's arm before I hugged her. "And you were never stupid. You were only blinded by lies that sparked and built up your hatred." Pulling back, I caught her gaze. "I was too. So many of us were."

"Thanks for being my friend. You know, I found out that the lies were all coming from pirates. Who would ever believe those sleaze-ball pirates?"

I smiled. I'd said that to her weeks ago. Still, what was done was done. "It's all in the past, and here you are helping to clean up those flyers that you must have spent a lot of shells on."

"Don't even ask me how many because it's a ridiculous amount. I requested a rush on the order so you can just imagine." She wiped her eyes and touched her heart. "How hate drives us to do crazy things."

"You and your father saved us all, and that's what matters."

"Thank you, Blaise. I had a serious talk with the remaining members of the AML, and we burned all the material in our office. Not one piece of propaganda is left, so I can now say that the AML officially does not exist. We've all promised to help rebuild Antla."

She finally went out, taking the leaflets with her as Mr. Worth-paper emerged from his office that had also been destroyed.

"All my orders are gone," he grumbled. "The printing press is still working fine, but the paperwork I need to complete the orders is in such a mess."

He looked so despondent that my heart went out to him. His was not the only business that was in tatters. Most of them were.

"People will understand. They'll come back. My father has pledged to help the businesses of Antla. He's pledging a lot of money. Enough for you to rebuild."

He nodded. "Thank you. I do appreciate everything you've done to help me."

The bell over the door jangled, and Hannah walked back in. Her hair was soaked through.

"It's raining cats and dogs out there. Yet another storm. The sky is dark as night. I swear I don't remember a winter ever being as bad as this one."

Her words scared me. I'd connected the bad weather to the sea witch in my mind. The storm blowing in only cemented my theory that she was still alive somehow. She was still out there, biding her time until she would strike again. I'd not told anyone my theory. Everyone was so happy that she was gone that I didn't want to even think of the notion that she might not be, but I knew I wouldn't rest until either the strange weather fully passed or I knew for certain that she was dead.

"I think we've done all we can here," I said to her. "Let's go and check in on Mrs. Farina at the bakery. Maybe we can grab something to eat if she has not given out all her bread. I heard that her kitchen is still in operation."

Hannah's stomach growled, and we both laughed. "Food might be good."

We moved from Mr. Worthpaper's shop to Mrs. Farina Martinez's bakery. The shop appeared almost the same as the day of the El Mar party, so it seemed she'd already tidied the mess. Mrs. Farina wasn't there, but plenty of goodies had been left out on a table for the people who were helping to rebuild the town. After grabbing a sandwich and cupcake, Hanna and I made our way to The Conch offices.

Mr. Scribble was delighted to see us.

"I was just on my way out. I'm going to take photos of the people cleaning up the town," he said with a grin. "I was hoping to fill the front page with photos of good deeds, alongside a tidbit of information I'd heard about the wolves in Elder. It'll make a nice human interest story after yesterday's edition."

"You mean a human and merfolk interest story," Hannah corrected him.

I had to turn my head so that she didn't see the smile on my face. How things had changed.

We organized the shop while Mr. Scribble and his sons took pictures of us before heading out into the town.

After we finished at The Conch, we decided to head over to El Mar. When I got there, the level of damage made me feel sick.

Tables were missing legs, the chandelier was missing its golden arms, sconces had been torn off the walls, ceramic plates, glass vases shattered beyond recognition, forks and knives stuck to the wall, and more destruction.

Glancing out of the window to the turbulent sea, I wondered what Fish was doing. The mer village had been left pretty much unscathed, but they had dead and injured to deal with. I'd have given anything to be able to jump into the sea and help down there, but I had to show my face up here. Me just being here was more important than anything I actually did while I was here.

Emma came out from the kitchen area and stopped when she saw Hannah. They'd not gotten along well since the first time they met.

Emma closed her brown eyes and bit her lip. "There's so much destruction," she sighed. "And now we have to figure out how to help fix this place. The damage to El Mar is just overwhelming."

Hannah walked toward her, and I held my breath. "A little daunting, but we have the former AML members chipping in. We're able, strong, and have the desire to restore Antla to its former beauty." Hannah smiled. "We're thinking of rebranding as the AWP to provide help whenever the community needs it. What do you think?"

"What does AWP stand for?" Emma scrunched her forehead. "Antla Women's Pact?"

Hannah shook her head. "I like the suggestion, but it stands for the Atlantice Working for Peace group. No propaganda, no required membership, just a bunch of people that are willing to volunteer in the community."

I hooked my arm through hers. "Hannah, that sounds like a great idea. I may just join your group."

Emma grinned. "That is one group I'd love to join. And be a full-time member."

"Well, great, because the more people we have, the more fun we can have. And we're kinda already working on one of our goals for the group." She met my eyes. "We want to completely restore Antla."

More people entered the room. With their help, we were able to sort the furniture into repairable and trash piles. Unfortunately, the unrepairable piles seemed twice as big as the repairable ones.

On the way from the only working restroom upstairs, I snuck out to the balcony and looked out over to the pier. I spotted Fish with his friends carrying the hull of a wooden boat. A few of the royal guards picked it up and strode toward the front of the building.

I watched him work, mesmerized by him. His muscles bulged every time he collected debris before he handed it over to the guards.

I smiled at the thought of us all coming together. Everyone from the merpeople to the guards to the town people to the monarchy contributed to the restoration of the town. How it should be.

The realization that everyone pitched in motivated me further, and I returned to my own group.

By the time the sun's orange rays were lowering over the water, most of the crowd had gathered in the town square to celebrate the progress we had made. My body was ready to escape to my bed.

The town had seen its fair share of cleaning, but there was a long way to go. I joined in the celebration, wishing the merpeople could be here to join in. In the back of my mind, I planned a proper celebration, one where everyone could be included. It was only right. I'd have to leave it for another day, though. I was tired. I yawned as I made the decision to return home. I'd not slept in my own bed for such a long time. My father had spent the day cleaning up the palace. I was in no doubt it would still be a mess, but it was where I belonged. It was my home.

"I'm heading back to the palace," I said to Emma. She'd been joined at the party by Jaxon, who had barely left her side for a second.

"Do you want to come back with me?"

A shiver ran down my back as I felt someone staring at me. I didn't hear Emma's answer as my arms erupted in goosebumps. Scanning the area, I didn't see anything out of the ordinary. Lots of people were there. I was the princess. It made sense that people were looking at me. People always looked at me.

"You okay?" Emma said, furrowing her brow.

"Yes, sure. Just felt cold all of a sudden."

She shrugged. "The sun is setting, and since you're no longer working so hard, your body is probably cooling off. Do you want me to find you a jacket?"

"I think I'll be fine."

She yawned. "I'm tired too. I'd love to walk back with you."

"Great. If you can wait here a minute, I'll find out if Hannah wants to head back as well. None of us should be walking back alone."

Not that Emma would be. Not with Jaxon. As a guard in the palace, he'd probably come with us.

As I ambled toward Hannah, I felt eyes boring through the back of my head. I jerked my head back and inhaled in shock as I caught sight of a woman with golden-rimmed irises staring back at me. Her hair and part of her face were hidden underneath a purple hoodie, but her eyes shocked me to the core. It was like staring into a mirror.

I stepped toward her when a teen boy bumped into me. He fell to the ground, and I extended my hand. "Are you okay?"

"Yes, princess. I'm so sorry." He stood and shook the dust from his pants. "My friend knocked me over, and I couldn't stop myself from bumping into you, and then my foot slipped on…"

I held up my hand. "No worries, it wasn't your fault. We're both good."

"Yes, princess. Thank you." He bowed and took after the friend already halfway down the block.

I turned completely around, but the purple-hoodie woman had left.

Disappeared into the crowd, leaving me wondering if I'd imagined her.

6
24TH FEBRUARY

The morning sun invaded my bedroom window, waking me from mixed dreams. I stayed in bed until I remembered that my parents had declared today a free day.

Freedom. A day of complete and utter freedom to do what I wanted and not what needed to be done. No more gathering up debris, or fixing furniture, or removing blood from the walls and floors. The bulk of the cleaning up had been done yesterday, and there was still much to do, but my father had declared a day of mourning of the dead. We'd restart the clean up later.

I thought about Fish. I'd not spoken to him since the battle, and I missed him. I got out of bed and, after grabbing a sandwich from the kitchen, sprinted down the beach to the shoreline, scanning the horizon for him.

Nothing.

I finished my sandwich as I reached the water.

Walking slowly, I ambled along the small pier and sat, letting my legs dip in the water. The storm had cleared from the day before, but the sky was still a miserable grey, reminding me of my theory that this was not yet over.

A minute later, he popped out of the water. His long, wavy brown hair dripping and causing droplets to trail down his chest.

I dove into the water to meet him. The ripples from his movements reached me before he did.

He engulfed me in his muscular arms. "I've missed you so much."

"I missed you too." I leaned in and rested my head on his chest, listening to his heart beat a slow, steady rhythm.

My heart skipped a beat as I pulled back and looked into his emerald-colored eyes. "The kingdom is officially in mourning. Thirty people died. I'm amazed it wasn't more. All those that had been petrified came back to life, so at one point, it had looked a lot worse. Please tell me that the merfolk didn't lose too many?"

Fish stroked my hair, and in an instant, everything seemed perfect, back to normal, but it wasn't. It would never be normal again. "We had a few minor injuries, but no one died in the final battle. You should have seen your mother. She's a pretty amazing fighter."

"I don't doubt it," I said, imagining her fighting off those creatures. I'd rebuilt my relationship with my mother, and I'd never been more glad about anything. If I could be half the queen she was, I'd be a fine queen indeed. "Do you have any plans for today?"

"I'm game for whatever you want to do." His cute dimples appeared when he grinned. "If you want, we can return to the village. I know your grandfather wants to get to know you better."

"I'd love to visit my grandfather, but I don't want to be around too many people. I'd like to just spend time with you."

He nodded. "Your wish is my command." He held out his hand. "We'll take our time and explore the reefs on the way to the cave." It sounded bliss, just the two of us being able to get away from everything. It was the escape I needed.

"Great idea." My fingers found his, and I gently squeezed them. "Thank you. You're so wonderful."

A wave pushed us toward the pier, and I raised my eyes at the darkening sky. "Should we leave before it starts to rain?"

He laughed. "Afraid of a little rain?"

It sounded so stupid when he said it like that. The pair of us was already soaked to the skin. But I had reasons to fear the storm, reasons I wasn't sure I wanted to share, not even with Fish.

"Ha, ha, you're so hilarious. I just don't want to be here if it starts to thunder."

The sea that had been terrifying to me, once more made me restless. Even with Fish by my side, I couldn't truly relax, wondering, as I was, if the sea witch might appear at any second.

We spent the morning and afternoon swimming from one cave to another, and the whole time, I spent looking over my shoulder. I was happy when Fish decided to stop at the cave we'd watched the sun rise in before. He pulled himself up onto the soft sand and I lay down next to him, letting my head rest on his chest. He played with my wet salty hair as he spoke to me. We talked about the battle, about the people, and about everything that had happened. I told him about Hannah and her father saving everyone. I almost told him that I thought the sea witch was still alive, that I could feel her presence, but it sounded foolish, so I didn't. Instead, I asked him a question I'd been wanting to ask for a while.

"Can I ask you a personal question?"

"Sure. I don't have any secrets."

"What happened to your parents? You told me they died."

It broke my heart to think about it. He was too young to lose both of them.

He sighed.

"They traveled a lot. The house in the mer village wasn't their only one. They had houses everywhere. Their main one was in a mer town by the Urbis Prison. A few years back, there was an attempted escape. Some of the inmates thought they could swim to the mainland at Badalah, but the seas are rough there, and they got into trouble. My parents knew they were prisoners. No one else would be foolish enough to swim in those waters unless they had tails, but my parents couldn't let them die. They took them to the mainland, but there was an altercation with the prison guards, and the prisoners and my parents got caught in the crossfire. Both died on the Badalah Beach."

My heart ached for him. I couldn't even imagine living through something so horrific. I'd almost lost my parents a couple of days ago, and the pain of that was unbearable even though both of them had left the battle unscathed.

"I'm sorry."

I looked up at him. He leaned forward, and his lips touched mine. They were warm despite the chill in the air.

"I left my home there and came here. I've not looked back. This is my home now."

I smiled up at him. "You are my home."

He gazed into my eyes. "You're so beautiful, do you know that?" The back of his hand gently stroked my cheek. "And you have such a wonderful heart."

With the waves crashing at our feet and thunder ripping through the sky, I could have stayed like that forever.

"I love you, Fish," I whispered, my heart beating almost eclipsed the sound of the thunder.

His fingers squeezed mine. "I love you too...You know my name isn't Fish, though, right?"

"Of course. I remember you telling me we shouldn't reveal our names because you wanted to keep the mystery."

He laughed. "Well, I know you are Blaise. I knew right from the start."

"So why the mystery about your name?"

"My name is Abelard."

"Abelard?" I scoffed, trying to keep the corners of my mouth from rising. "No wonder you didn't want to tell me."

"Yeah, that's pretty much ruined the mystery in our relationship."

"How about I call you Abe?" I said, pulling him in for a kiss.

He pulled away from my arms, and I instantly missed his warmth.

"Why are you pulling away? Is it the name thing because I'm sorry I laughed."

He shook his head. "I would have been shocked if you hadn't laughed. We will have company in less than a minute. I can hear a boat."

I strained my ears to hear, but all I could hear was the roaring of the ocean. Less than a minute later, a small boat pulled up. Fish..., Abe, had to swim over to bring them up to the sand. A couple of the palace guards stepped out.

This didn't bode well. How did they even know I was here?

I raised my eyes to greet the guard, who saluted me.

He cleared his throat. "Your Highness. We've been searching for you everywhere. We've checked half the coastline."

My heart started to pound, and thoughts of the sea witch flittered across my mind.

"What has happened now?"

He shook his head with his brown eyes not moving from mine. "Nothing to worry about. You have a visitor."

"You came looking for me because I have a visitor? Surely it could wait. You should have told them I'd be back later."

"We tried, Your Highness, but she was very persistent. When your mother saw her, she asked that we come to look for you. She's waiting in the palace."

"Who is she?" I asked my curiosity spiking. Hannah could be persistent, but the guards wouldn't be sent out to look for me if it was only she.

He shook his head. "She didn't say her name, but she told us that she was from Draconis."

I scrunched up my eyebrows. Almost all foreign visitors wanted to meet with my parents or at least my father. "Did she request that my parents also meet with her?"

"No, she specifically mentioned you and only you. Your mother seemed to know her."

"Thank you. Please let them know I'll be along shortly."

Abe and I helped them into the boat that swayed dangerously in the swell of the sea. Abe took my hand, and we followed the boat back to the shore, afraid that it might tip over at any second. When the guards were safely on shore, and the boat was pulled up high onto the sand, Abe kissed my cheek and said farewell.

"I'll come and see you tomorrow."

"I hope so. This visitor of yours sounds intriguing."

"I don't even know anyone from Draconis. It's probably all some silly mistake."

Before heading to my mother's parlor, I ran to my room to dry and dress and attempt to run a comb through my matted hair. A quick look in the mirror told me I was far from the well turned out princess I was expected to be, but the woman had shown up unannounced, so what did she expect?

My nerves were on edge as I headed to the parlor. When I opened the parlor door, my heart leapt. My mouth opened into an o shape as I took in the girl sitting across from my mother. Part of it was the tiny purple dragon sitting on her shoulder. I mean, that would be the thing that most people noticed first, but not me. She was the girl from the town center yesterday. The girl with eyes exactly like mine.

She was about my age, maybe older but not by much, and pretty with curly hair the color of a golden pecan. Not quite a light brown but not a true blonde.

"Hello, Blaise, I'm Princess Azia."

"Azia is King Alec and Queen Briar Rose of Draconis's daughter," my mother added. It explained why the guard said that my mother knew her. She had met with the king and queen of Draconis on a number of occasions, but I had a feeling she'd not met their daughter before. She would have mentioned it if she'd seen her eyes.

I smiled and responded, "Welcome to Atlantice."

I took a seat, not really knowing what to think. I must have been staring because of what she said next.

She smiled. "Extraordinary, isn't it? That our eyes are the same?"

"I've never met anyone with eyes like mine before."

"Neither had I before now,"Azia admitted. "I was quite taken aback when I saw you in town yesterday."

"So it was you. I saw you, but when I looked back, you'd gone."

"I must apologize for that. I had come to see you, but I wasn't expecting your eyes to have the gold rings around the irises. I was shocked. I took a room in a local inn to recoup. Your mother was telling me that you are adopted."

I glanced over at my mother, who nodded and then took a sip of her coffee. It surprised me that she'd let that bit of information slip, especially to a stranger.

"Yes, I just found out."

"I'm adopted too. When I saw you yesterday, I wondered if we were somehow related."

I shook my head. This was too much to take in. "I was brought here by two women as a newborn."

"An old woman and a young one at some point in late December eighteen years ago?"

I nodded, dumbfounded.

"I guess we are probably sisters. Twin sisters."

My mind could barely wrap itself around what she was saying. I had a twin? She didn't really look like me. We were both fair, but my hair was red and wavy, whereas hers was dark blond with a curl.

"Why, though?" I asked as my mother passed me a coffee.

"Why what?"

"Why split us up and put us with the royals of two different kingdoms?"

"That, I don't know. I came here looking for answers, and all I've found are more questions."

The little dragon stretched out its wings and did a little dance on her shoulder. Azia picked up a cupcake from a plate on the coffee table and tossed it into the air. The dragon snapped it in its jaws then hopped down to eat it.

"I thought dragons were dangerous?" I said, watching the dragon chomping on the cupcake. A second later and it was gone. The dragon curled up beside Azia and closed its eyes.

"Only if you want someone to steal all your food," she teased. The dragon opened a lazy eye, sent two smoke rings from its nostrils, and then went back to sleep.

"That's Nyre. She's my traveling companion."

"So, what brings you to Atlantice?" I sipped my coffee, knowing that her answer would be something important. She wasn't here on vacation. I knew that much.

"I mean, you said that you didn't know about my eyes until yesterday, so you couldn't be here to find me."

"Actually, I did come here to find you. Well, not you exactly. You might have seen in the papers what's been happening in Draconis."

"I'm afraid not. Things have been pretty dire here these last few months, and none of us have had time to read what's going on in other kingdoms."

"Things have been...weird. The weather, the dragons, my mother's illness."

I waited for her to expand, but she didn't.

"Your mother is sick?" I thought of my own mother and how she'd turned back into a mermaid. A quick glance over at her told me she was fine with having her tail on show. It peeked out of the bottom of her skirt.

"One moment, everything was amazing and peaceful as it has been for the last eighteen years and then boom." She snapped her fingers. "Things started to go haywire. My mom fell into a deep sleep that not even my father's kiss could wake her from. We've tried everything, but the spell is too powerful. I was planning on heading to Urbis, but when I read in The Conch about your—"

"No way!" I interrupted her. "It's similar to what happened here. My mom lost her human legs, which led to huge rioting and chaos between our people and the merfolk. We've had weird storms since the start of the year. It's as though something just.."

"Changed?"

"Yeah."

"I think it's something to do with a witch," we both said at the same time.

My mother cleared her throat. "Come now, Blaise. The witch is dead. The admiral made sure of that."

"The witch is dead?" Azia asked her brow furrowed. "That can't be true."

"We killed the sea witch off a few days ago. There's nothing to worry about," my mother added.

"The sea witch? I'm not talking about a sea witch; I'm talking about Derillen."

I shrugged my shoulders. "I don't think the sea witch had a name."

"But she was tall and slim, with a black headdress?"

"The sea witch was huge and wide."

Azia shook her head. "I don't get it. I'm so confused. I thought a witch did this, but it sounds like a completely different witch ruined your kingdom to the one that ruined mine."

"Two evil witches?" I said weakly.

"That's impossible, surely?" My mother said.

"It must be all tied together," Azia said, bumping the small dragon as she pulled her hand back and almost spilled coffee over the dragon's head. "I think the answer is in Urbis, and I want to go there."

My eyes automatically pulled to the side as her small dragon hopped to the floor and headed toward me.

"Nyre." She pointed to her shoulder, and the purple dragon jumped on her shoulder. Her iridescent scales provided a show of the most beautiful colors.

I didn't know whether to stare at the obeying dragon or her.

"Why Urbis?"

Her eyes reflected sadness before she said, "I have close friends that live there. And I think it's where I was...we were born, and it may hold the key to what is happening in Draconis and here. I won't go alone. We shall go to Urbis."

"Your dragon and you?"

Her dragon jumped up and down on her shoulder. Azia looked at it and said, "Please, relax, Nyre."

The dragon instantly laid its head against her neck.

"Well, she'll also come with us. But I meant I'd like you to come to Urbis with us." She pointed at me. "It'll be the three of us, and you know the saying."

The small dragon gently inched its way across to her other shoulder, not scratching her, not hurting her.

"Yeah, the blind leading the blind."

She laughed. "No, silly. A cord of three strands is much stronger than those of two. We can watch each other's back."

I waved hands. "No. I can't. I can't leave. Antla is still rebuilding. They need me."

I looked to my mother for support.

"It's your choice, Blaise. I'd never keep you from going to find your birth mother."

"I know you wouldn't, but it isn't just about that, is it?" I said, looking toward Azia.

She shook her head. "No. I want to make my mother well again. I think that her curse is connected to my past. Our past."

A curse. I'd never thought of it like that, but my mother was cursed too. Cursed by the witch that was supposed to be dead.

"When would you leave?"

"Tomorrow. I don't want to waste any time. My mother's health is fading."

I swallowed. Would my mother's health fade too?

"Why don't I sleep on it?" I said

It seemed inconceivable that the answer to my mother's problems lay outside of Atlantic. The sea witch was here...probably. The thought of leaving Abe behind caused my chest to restrict, but it was hardly as though I could take him. He couldn't walk on land. But then there was my mother. I owed it to her to go and find help. This wasn't going to be an easy decision. Not an easy decision at all.

7

25TH FEBRUARY

The rooster crowed around five, but I stayed in bed processing how Atlantice and Draconis had experienced similar magical anomalies. Nothing about the last few weeks made any sense to me, but it made less sense when I added another witch into the mix. I'd never heard the name Derillen before yesterday, but I was sure that it wasn't the sea witch. But how would I know for sure if I did not venture from the safety of my kingdom? How would I help save my mother if I didn't go with Azia?

But did I want to head to Urbis? Not really. It would mean leaving Abe and my parents. It would also mean leaving my friends, the cook's delicious meals, Mrs. Farinah's deserts, and all the comforts of home, to search for something I didn't even know existed. Azia had been so hell-bent on me going with her, but even she didn't really know what she was looking for. She spoke about dream gods and friends in Urbis, but none of it made any sense. She also was of the firm belief that our birth was somehow connected. I had to admit that the timing seemed a bit weird. We'd both shown up as babies in our respective kingdoms just after the great war had ended. It wasn't a war as such, just a long period of bickering and fighting and darkness that everyone seemed to partake of. I couldn't call it anything as organized as war. And here we were, eighteen years later, and both our kingdoms were falling apart again. Once again, a storm raged outside, rattling the windows and pelting rain. It was almost worth leaving the kingdom to get away from the cold and damp, although Azia had told me the usually dry and arid Draconis had seen an unusual amount of snow this year.

My mind wandered back to Abe. Our relationship was so new. Would it survive me being away?

My gut instinct told me it would, but I wished all the same that he could come with me.

Finally, my thoughts turned to my mother. She'd faced such hardships and was still the most generous person I knew. Azia's mother was dying. I wondered if mine was too? Maybe the tail was just the first part of it. In my heart, I knew that I needed to find the truth so that our mothers could return to the way they were for the last eighteen years. So that Queen Briar Rose could wake up, so my mom could live in her own home without the ignominy of being carried everywhere by the staff.

As the sun warmed my room, the idea of joining Azia became easier to accept.

I hurled out of bed, took a quick shower, and selected a simple dress with deep pockets.

The new maid, Alicia, knocked on the door with the distinct knock I had taught her the night before.

I would miss Emma, but when my parents promoted her to headmistress of the palace, she was thrilled. It meant more responsibility and pay. And she had already taken on the role when the former hadn't returned.

Emma deserved the position after helping to keep the palace running while both my parents were away and all the times I ventured off with Abe.

"Come in, Alicia."

The maid came in and curtsied, leaving a tray of food on the table next to my bed.

"Your Highness, Her Majesty asked me to bring you breakfast in bed. She said you might need it."

I furrowed my brow, trying to figure out who she was talking about. "My mother? She said I needed breakfast in bed?"

It didn't sound like her at all. She liked me to be up and ready before I even thought about breakfast.

"Has Her Highness the Princess Azia had breakfast in bed?" I asked. My mother had invited her and the cute little dragon to stay in one of the guest suites rather than go back to the inn.

"Yes, Your Highness. I delivered it before I delivered yours."

I gave her a wry smile. My mother was trying to make Azia feel at home, which explained the breakfast. Still, if I knew my mother, she wouldn't expect me to dilly-dally. After thanking Alicia, I ate the breakfast quickly before heading out.

I found my mother alone in the breakfast room. No breakfast in bed for her.

She smiled as I walked in.

"I was wondering when you'd surface. I figured you might have missed out on sleep with such a huge decision to make."

I sat at the table beside her and poured myself a coffee.

"What do you think I should do? I've never left Atlantice for more than a few days. I've never been to Urbis before."

"I can't make that decision for you, Blaise. You must decide for yourself."

"But if you were in my position?"

She handed me a pot of cream, which I poured into the coffee, watching the white dissolve into the black. It reminded me of the weird dark patches of seawater that had been cropping up lately.

"When I was your age, I was already living in this palace and engaged to your father. I'd been a bit of a rebel, as you already know. You, on the other hand, have lived a much more sheltered life. You've never rebelled. Maybe it's about time you did?"

"You want me to rebel?" I asked, choking on my coffee.

"You've shown such bravery these past few weeks. I've watched my little princess grow into a strong woman. If you'd have asked me at the beginning of the year if I'd want my daughter swanning off to Urbis with a stranger, I'd have said no, but now..."

"Now?"

"I would never ask you to go away just so you can help me get my legs back. I don't even know if that's possible. I've made my peace with spending half my life in the palace being carried around and the other half under the water with my father and sisters. I fought it for so long, but now I kind of like it, but I don't think that's the reason you're seriously considering this, is it?"

I shook my head.

"Honey. I totally understand that you'd want to meet your birth mother. It's natural to want to know where you came from."

"Actually, I wasn't even thinking of my birth mother. I want to go for another reason."

Curiosity painted her features.

"Why, then?"

I took a deep breath. "I don't think the witch is dead." There I'd told her.

"Don't be absurd. Of course, she's dead. We all saw Admiral Fallon and his crew kill her."

I thought back to the scene. Everything had been in chaos, but I could picture it well.

"Actually, we all saw the witch go up in blue smoke when the cannonball tore through the balcony. It will go down in the history of scales and legends. No body was ever recovered."

"But the petrified people came back to life. How could they do that if the witch was still living?"

I shrugged my shoulders. "I don't know. It's just a feeling I have. The weather is still bad, the sea is still dark. Something's not right. What if Azia is right, and it's all connected somehow?"

My mother shivered. "I hope you're wrong, Blaise."

"You don't think I am, though, do you?"

Her eyes lowered. "I hoped she was dead. I wanted to believe it. Everyone was so happy, but no. I don't think you are wrong. That feeling you have. I feel it too—like I'm connected to her somehow."

"Yes," I said, pointing at her. "I feel connected to her. I feel connected to Azia too. It's weird, like something I can't explain, but I feel as though this connection, whatever it is, needs to be played out."

"To the bitter end."

We sat in silence until my father entered the room. He sat in his usual chair and grabbed a croissant.

"I hear you'll be leaving us," he said, spreading jam on the croissant and looking right at me. A blob of strawberry jam missed the croissant and ended up on the white tablecloth below it. It reminded me of the bloodshed that had occurred, and all the work we still had to do to clean up the palace and the town.

"I've not fully decided yet," I sighed. My heart was torn in two. A big part of me felt that I needed to go, but another knew how much good I could do if I stayed.

"I'm yet to meet the lovely Azia, but I hear she has a pet dragon. What a wonderful thing to own."

"She's not a pet," Azia said, coming through the door and making my father's cheeks turn red. "She's my traveling companion." The dragon blew a smoke ring then flew over to us, landing on the back of one of the chairs.

"Well, she's a mighty fine companion," my father said, stroking the dragon's head. The dragon closed its eyes and let my father stroke it. He was braver than I was. I didn't want to go near the thing.

"I have to say, I feel much less worried about Blaise leaving if she has a dragon to protect her," my father added.

"I wouldn't count on Nyre protecting anything," Azia teased, sitting at the table. The dragon stuck its tongue out and moved to the back of my father's chair. My father chortled and passed it a croissant, which it swallowed back in one.

"I'm not even sure if I'm going yet. Azia, what is your timeline? When do we need to set off?"

"I can't wait. I'll be leaving tonight. I hope you'll be with me."

"Tonight?" I stared at her open-mouthed. I'd only just met her the day before.

"My mother is worsening daily. I need answers. I'm sorry, I can't give you more time. If you don't want to come, that's fine, but I'll be heading out tonight whatever your decision."

I shook my head. "I can't make such a big decision so quickly. I need more time. Maybe I can meet you in Urbis in a few days?"

"I won't be in Urbis in a few days. It will take me a good week, perhaps more, to walk."

"Walk?" My parents and I said at once.

"Why wouldn't you just catch the Urbis Express?" I asked.

"I'm sure we could loan you one of our carriages," my mother added.

"Thank you for your kind offer, but we must travel incognito. One princess traveling with a dragon is bad enough, but two is going to be hard to hide. Nyre hides in my hood when we are in towns, but we've tended to stick to the outskirts so as not to be spotted. That's why it's taken me so long to get here. I hitched rides when I could, but only when I thought the person wouldn't recognize me. I'm not going to lie to you, your majesties. It's not going to be an easy trip, but Urbis isn't too far away."

My mother and father gave each other a look, and I knew what they were thinking. Azia's words scared me too.

"Please come for a walk with me, Blaise?" Azia said. I glanced to the window. The storm had passed, but the sky was still grey and miserable. It was hardly fine weather for a walk. And yet, I found myself saying yes to her.

We walked along the beach slowly, neither of us speaking. Abe was nowhere to be seen, but I knew if I called for him, he'd come. It was as if he had an extra sense when it came to me.

"I hear there are merfolk in this water. I've never met one."

"I've never met a dragon before either," I said, looking at Nyre, who was flying over the sea. "I thought they were much bigger."

"They are, usually. Nyre isn't fully grown, but she's exceptionally small for her age."

"Oh," I said, not really knowing what to say. My knowledge of dragons was limited.

"I know you're on the fence about coming with me. I understand that. I'm the kind of person that always craved adventure, but I know not all people are like me."

"Indeed. before yesterday it hadn't occurred to me that I'd ever leave Atlantice. Not for a long time anyway. I've been to Floris a couple of times for the annual flower show, but that's about it. The thought of Urbis scares me."

Beside me, Azia let out a snort. "A little birdie told me that you were fighting weird creatures with a sword a few days ago. I think you are braver than you give yourself credit for. I wouldn't want to fight an army of sea creatures."

She lapsed into silence again. A couple of the merfolk played in the water nearby. When I pointed them out to Azia they noticed me and waved.

Azia hardly noticed. "I want you to come with me. I only just found out I was adopted a few weeks back, but even before that, I knew there was something missing. There is something about you that makes me feel like we are connected."

"I was just saying the same thing to mother this morning. I feel like she is connected somehow too, and the sea witch. I don't think the sea witch is dead, but I don't think she is Derillen either."

"When I found out I was adopted, I looked into my past. It was hard because there were no records. I did find out that when I was brought to the castle, there was another baby with me. That must have been you. I believe that everything is connected to that. Something happened before we were born that started something...I just don't know what, but I have a feeling that we are meant to end it."

As I gazed out to sea, I devoured the sight as I knew that I wasn't going to see it again for a while.

"I think the same thing. I never wanted to leave Atlantice, but I know I must. I'll be leaving behind my friends, my family, my..."

"Someone special?" she followed my gaze. "Is he a merman?"

I nodded. I didn't know how I was going to break it to him.

"I guess I should go home and pack."

Azia took my hand in hers, and immediately, I felt the connection grow stronger. Never having brothers or sisters before, I didn't know if I was supposed to feel this way, but I felt much more powerful with her touch. The magic that had lain dormant was coming alive. Azia whistled for Nyre, and the three of us headed back to the palace as the rain began to pour once again.

Alice helped me pack my bags. My mother wanted to help too, but it would have been difficult with her tail, so she sat on my bed and lectured me on proper attire as Alice passed me my clothes. I'd need no dresses or pretty blouses. I wouldn't even need my swimwear that I'd pretty much lived in these past weeks. Instead, my bag was packed with jeans and sweaters and anything that would not make me stand out.

After many tears and hugs from my mother and father, I'd come to accept my decision and was looking forward to it. Azia had told me it would take just over a week to get to Urbis, but she'd failed to mention how long we'd need to be in Urbis. I don't think she knew herself. Urbis was the governmental capital of all the kingdoms, and although it wasn't a kingdom itself, it housed many of the kingdoms' powerful men and women. It was the most cosmopolitan of the kingdoms, and even though each kingdom was ruled by royalty, the government officials in Urbis had the final say on laws and the most important matters. I could send my parents letters, and once I found somewhere to stay, they would be able to write back. Azia mentioned some friends there, but when I pushed her, she'd been vague about it.

Once everything was packed and there was nothing left to do, my mother mentioned that there was someone waiting for me at Mrs. Farina's Bakery.

She was mysterious as to who it was, but she told me with a grin, so it wasn't another mysterious visitor wanting to whisk me off to somewhere else.

I pulled my rain hood up as I trudged through the town. No one looked my way as I made my way through the streets. When my red hair was covered, no one batted an eyelid. Maybe I could do this undercover thing, after all.

I entered Mrs. Farina's Bakery but stood in the doorway, enjoying the aroma of the treats I would certainly miss. Scanning the crowd of people, I saw my two best friends seated in the back booth with almost the entire table covered with food that would have fed a dozen teenagers after a three-day hunger strike.

"What are you doing here?" I asked as I sat next to Emma at the table. "And what's all this?"

Mrs. Farina sauntered over with a tray full of caramel truffles. "You have to try these, Your Highness. I made them this morning, and they are still warm."

They all looked as if they would melt in my mouth, but the dark chocolate one called my name. Taking a small bite, I allowed it to melt before I swallowed it. "This is amazing."

"Your mother sent Emma to come get me a couple of hours ago," Hannah said.

I looked at Emma, who nodded to confirm it. "She told me that you had something big to tell us and that I should head to the bakery and ask Mrs. Farina to prepare a feast. What was it you wanted to tell us?"

"I bet that you are getting engaged!" Hannah said with apparent delight. "I wonder what an underwater wedding will look like? Would you still wear a dress?"

"Calm your horses, I'm not engaged. Abe and I have only just started dating."

"Who's Abe?" Emma asked her face a picture of confusion.

"Abe is Fish's real name. It's short for Abelard."

"So, if you aren't getting married, what are we celebrating?" Hannah pouted, her dreams of a double wedding drifting away from her, no doubt.

My fingers tapped my thigh, and I took a deep breath, struggling with the words I didn't want to say.

"I'm leaving." My fingers beat faster.

"Leaving?" Emma gasped. "Leaving why?"

"I'm leaving Atlantice because…"

All three of them stared at me. Mrs. Farina hadn't left her spot beside the table despite a line of people forming by the cash register.

"I met someone yesterday. I think she is related to me."

"You think?"

I squirmed in my seat. Hannah and Emma were my best friends, but Mrs. Farina was a chatterbox. I couldn't tell her who Azia was. It would spread around town like wildfire.

"Mrs. Farina, I think you have customers," I said, pointing to the line. She huffed like they were taking her away from a good bit of gossip. I waited until she was deep in conversation about the wolves in Elder before speaking.

"No one knows this, but I'm adopted. I only just found out. The girl I met yesterday is my twin sister,…or at least. we think she is."

Both of my friends' mouths dropped open.

"She doesn't look like me, so we're not identical, but we both have the golden ring around our irises."

When neither of them spoke, I told them the whole story in hushed tones, and afterward, I swore them both to secrecy.

Emma was the first to recover from the shock. "So where are you off to? How long will you be gone?"

"I'm not sure. Azia is setting everything up. I'm kinda just going along for the ride. She thinks our birth mother might be in Urbis."

Hannah hugged me. She hugged me as though she would never see me again.

"You know I should be back in a few weeks. I'm not going forever. You know I'd never leave Atlantice."

She twisted her mouth. "When you come back, I may be up to my eyeballs in wedding planning stuff. Geraldo says that his mom wants to help me when she returns from Floris, and you know how I hate her taste. I need you here. I can't get married without my chief bridesmaid."

My stomach churned. Her wedding was in April, and I didn't know if I'd be back in time. I couldn't tell her that, though. She was expecting me to be there. Looking at how chummy she and Emma were now, I knew that if I didn't return in time, she'd have a replacement bridesmaid. Emma and I were about the same size, so she'd fit into the dress.

"I'm really going to miss you."

The three of us ate the food and talked about our memories. Emma giggled at the stories of all the stupid things we used to do in the AML. Eventually, it was time to leave. Leaving my two best friends was hard, but it was nothing compared to the one person I was going to see next. Telling Abe that I was leaving was going to be painful.

It's only for a few weeks, I told myself, but as the lie flittered around my mind, I knew it would be longer. Just as I'd told Hannah I'd be back for her wedding, I wasn't sure that I would be.

I'd never called out to Abe from the walkways near town, but this was where we'd first met. I remembered the seagull causing me to slip into the water and gave a wry smile. I'd been so scared, and yet, it had ended up being the best thing that could ever happen to me.

I shouted for Abe, but he didn't appear, so when no one was looking, I stripped down to my underwear and dived into the water. Minutes later, I was swimming above the mer village. I shouted for him again, and this time, he appeared.

"So who was the mysterious girl?" he said as he swam up next to me and took my hand. His warmth ran through me, and I realized what I was giving up. I was always warm with him.

"Let's go to the cave, and I'll tell you everything."

The journey was swift, and my stomach churned the whole way. Telling Abe would be ten times harder than telling Emma and Hannah.

In the end, I blurted it out as soon as we pulled ourselves up onto the sand. "I'm leaving Atlantice."

He lost all color in his face. "What do you mean?"

"The girl we saw yesterday, Princess Azia of Draconis, is my twin sister." I shook my hands. "And what happened here also happened in Draconis. Her mother, the queen of Draconis, fell into a deep sleep, and they can't wake her up. Azia says it's a curse. I think the dark sea and the weather are connected to that."

His index finger and thumb rubbed his chin. "What does her mother's curse have to do with you, and why do you need to go anywhere?"

"I think the sea witch is still alive, and I think she has something to do with all this. Azia is taking me to find our birth mother in Urbis. She thinks everything has to do with our birth."

"I'll go with you." He caressed my cheeks.

I shook my head. "Urbis is surrounded by water, but we'll be traveling by land. Besides, this is something I have to do myself."

"Oh."

The dejection in that one word almost broke me.

A couple of tears rolled down my cheeks.

I laid my head against his chest, listening to his strong beating heart. "I'm going to miss you so much, Abe. I won't be gone long. A few weeks...maybe a bit longer."

"A bit longer?"

"I guess it depends on how long it takes us to find our mother. I have a feeling it might take a while, but I promise, as soon as this mess is all cleared up, I'll come straight home."

He kissed the top of my head. "And I will miss you. Are you sure you don't want me to come with you? To protect you and your twin?"

"I really wish you could, but it's better if you stay here and protect the waters just in case the sea witch returns."

"You're right. If she is still alive, she'll be back. I'll tell the mer king. We'll be ready for her."

"I've asked my father to make sure the naval fleet is ready, just in case. He wasn't sure, but..."

He didn't let me finish but kissed me until my toes curled up, and all my nerve endings shot warmth and tingles all over my body.

"I'm going to miss your kiss, especially," I said, grinning up at him.

"Then, I should give you something to remember me by."

"I won't forget you."

"Just to make sure." He leaned forward and kissed me again, and this time, I fell into it, knowing that this kiss would be the last in a long time.

A few hours later, we ended up at the pier in front of the palace.

Saying goodbye was breaking my heart, and I had to keep telling myself that it wasn't forever.

"Is that your sister?" he asked, pointing to a girl in a purple hoody sitting on the beach.

I looked over my shoulder, and Azia waved. "Yes, that's her."

"She's not as beautiful as you."

I touched my cheeks, feeling them flame. Azia was gorgeous.

"I love when your cheeks turn pink. Do you want to speak to her alone?"

"No, I want to introduce you."

Azia sat on the pier and touched her neck as if she touched a necklace, but Nyre was nowhere, at least that I could see. *Where do you hide a dragon?*

I waved my hand to motion her over. She stood and walked over to us, ending up at the very end of the low pier where she sat cross-legged.

"Hi, Azia. This is Abe. Abe, this is my sister, Azia."

It felt weird, referring to anyone as my sister, but I liked it. She already felt like part of my family.

"Nice meeting you, Princess Azia," Abe said, extending his hand to her, which she took.

"Likewise."

"You'll take care of her? This girl is special to me."

Azia pointed upward. I followed her gaze. In the sky, high enough that she looked like a purple dot was Nyre. "If I don't, my dragon will."

"You have a dragon?" Abe said incredulously. "Who's going to protect the pair of you from the dragon?"

Azia laughed. "She's perfectly safe, just a bit cheeky."

I wondered what she meant by a cheeky dragon.

A sharp pang touched my heart as I realized that this was good-bye. We'd be leaving in a few hours and I needed to prepare.

Azia walked away as I said my final goodbye with Abe. As I walked to Azia, we both watched him wave then disappear under the water with a swish of his tail.

"He's cute. I saw a photo of you in The Conch a couple of weeks back. The photo of you locking lips with him in The Conch was one thing, but seeing you two together is like whoa. I thought that only my parents had that kind of love."

"Do you have someone special back home?" I asked, feeling my cheeks go red again.

She nodded. "Yes. His name is Milo. He's one of the castle guards. I miss him so much, but finding out why this happened to my mom and Draconis is more important than being with him right now. But I do miss him, a whole bunch."

We began to walk slowly back to the palace.

"I was going to head into town to get us some supplies. Do you want to come with me?"

I nodded. I didn't want her doing all the work. Nyre stayed behind as we walked the short distance into the center of Antla. We stocked up on rations in the local supermarket. As we waited in line, a couple of sailors chatted in front of us.

The tall one said, "Why don't you want to go to Elder. You love that place."

"Not anymore. There are too many rumors that the werewolves are restless and that they want to take over. I'll quit before I step foot in Elder again."

Eventually, we had everything we needed. We stopped at Mrs. Farina's for a cake before our travels. I couldn't let Azia visit Antla without, at least, trying one of Mrs. Farina's cakes. Azia pulled her hoody up and held back as I handed some shells over for the cakes.

"Have you heard about Elder?" Mrs. Farina said. "It's shocking if what they say is true."

"No, I'm afraid I don't have time. I have to be going."

She passed the two cakes over. "It's a plague is what it is."

I handed Azia the cake as we left the shop.

"What was the lady saying about Elder?" Azia asked, before biting into her cake.

"Nothing. Mrs. Farina has a tendency to overreact and spread gossip. She makes great food, but I take everything she says with a pinch of salt."

"She was talking about Elder, wasn't she? About the wolves?"

"I really wouldn't put much stock into anything she says."

"But it isn't just her. Those sailors were talking about Elder too. What if it's not just Draconis and Atlantice? What if this thing is spreading? I think we should head there and see what's going on."

"We're not getting back in two weeks, are we?" I said, already knowing her answer.

She shook her head. "It doesn't look like it."

SPECIAL OFFER

We hope you enjoyed reading this book.

To thank you for reading, we'd like to offer you a discount on our other Kingdom of Fairytale books

Go to www.jaarmitage.com and add the code KOF10 for 10% your full order.

The discount is a one time offer, but will include as many books as you add to your first order.

A NOTE FROM THE AUTHOR

The Kingdom of Fairytales authors hope you enjoyed this new way of reading. We don't think that a series has ever been set with one chapter a day thought a whole year before and we hope we did it justice.

With this in mind, please leave a review, but when you do, remember that these books were always meant to be short breaks in your day and the blurb reflects that.

ABOUT J.A. ARMITAGE

J.A. Armitage lives in a total fantasy world (because reality is boring right?) When she's not writing all the crazy fun in her head, she can be found eating cake, designing pretty pictures and hanging upside down from the tallest climbing frame in the local playground while her children look on in embarrassment. She's travelled the world working as everything from a banana picker in Australia to a Pantomime clown, has climbed to the top of Mount Kilimanjaro and the bottom of the Grand Canyon and once gave birth to a surrogate baby for a friend of hers.

She spends way too much time gossiping on facebook and if you want to be part of her Reading Army, where you'll get lots of free-bies, exclusive sneak peeks and super secret sales, find her on Kingdom of Fairytales on Facebook

https://www.facebook.com/KingdomofFairytales

And for more books, check out:

www.jaarmitage.com

ALSO BY J.A. ARMITAGE

REVERSE FAIRYTALES CINDERELLA

Charm: A Cinderella Reverse Fairytale book 1

Lucky Charm: A Cinderella Reverse Fairytale book 2

Charmed

Charm: Books 1-3 boxset

REVERSE FAIRYTALES LITTLE MERMAID

Dark Water: A Little Mermaid Reverse Fairytale

Blue Water

Breakwater

Dark Water: Books 1-3 the full series

DRAGON TAMER

Slayer

Warrior

Protector

Savior

Dragon Tamer Boxset

Dragon Tamer colouring book

THE FAERIE RACE

The Sorcery Trial: A Fae Adventure Romance

The Elemental Trial: A Fae Adventure Romance

The Doomsday Trial: A Fae Adventure Romance

The Faerie Race: The Complete Fae Adventure Romance Series

REALM OF FIRE AND LIGHT

The Unicorn Key: A Dark Fae Adventure

The Unicorn Quest: A Dark Fae Adventure

The Unicorn Secret: A Dark Fae Adventure

KINGDOM OF FAIRYTALES

Queen of Dragons: A Sleeping Beauty retelling

Heiress of Embers: A Sleeping Beauty retelling

Throne of Fury: A Sleeping Beauty retelling

Goddess of Flames: A Sleeping Beauty retelling

Queen of mermaids: A Little Mermaid retelling

Heiress of the Sea: A Little Mermaid retelling

Throne of Change: A Little Mermaid retelling

Goddess of Water: A Little Mermaid retelling

King of Wolves: A Little Red Riding Hood retelling

Heir of the Curse: A Little Red Riding Hood retelling

Throne of Night: A Little Red Riding Hood retelling

God of Shifters: A Little Red Riding Hood retelling

King of Devotion: A Rapunzel retelling

Heir of Thorns: A Rapunzel retelling

Throne of Enchantment: A Rapunzel retelling

God of Loyalty: A Rapunzel retelling

Queen of Unicorns: A Rumpelstiltskin retelling

Heiress of Gold: A Rumpelstiltskin retelling

Throne of Sacrifice: A Rumpelstiltskin retelling

Goddess of Loss: A Rumpelstiltskin retelling

King of Beasts: A Beauty and the Beast retelling

Heir of Beauty: A Beauty and the Beast retelling

Throne of Betrayal: A Beauty and the Beast retelling

God of Illusion: A Beauty and the Beast retelling

Queen of the Sun: An Aladdin retelling

Heiress of Shadows: An Aladdin retelling

Throne of the Phoenix: An Aladdin Retelling

Goddess of Fire: An Aladdin retelling

Queen of Song: A Cinderella Retelling

Heiress of Melody: A Cinderella retelling

Throne of Symphony: A Cinderella retelling

Goddess of Harmony: A Cinderella Retelling

Queen of Clockwork: An Alice in Wonderland retelling

Heiress of Delusion: An Alice in Wonderland retelling

Throne of Cards: An Alice in Wonderland retelling

Goddess of Hearts: An Alice in Wonderland retelling

King of Traitors: A Wizard of Oz retelling

Heir of Fugitives: A Wizard of Oz retelling

Throne of Emeralds: A Wizard of Oz retelling

God of Storms: A Wizard of Oz retelling

Queen of Reflections: A Snow White retelling

Heiress of Mirrors: A Snow White retelling

Throne of Wands: A Snow White retelling

Goddess of Magic: A Snow White retelling

Queen of Skies: A Peter Pan retelling

Heiress of Stars: A Peter Pan retelling

Goddess of Air: A Peter Pan retelling

Throne of Feathers: A Peter Pan retelling

Kingdom of Power

Kingdom of Royalty

Kingdom of Fairytales

Kingdom of Ever After

Azia: Daughter of Sleeping Beauty

Blaise: Daughter of the Little Mermaid

Castiel: Son of Red Riding Hood

Deon: Son of Rapunzel

Eliana: Rapunzel's revenge

Fallon: Son of Beauty and the Beast

Gaia: Daughter of Aladdin

Halia: Daughter of Cinderella

Ivy: Daughter of Alice

Jakon:Son of Dorothy

Kelis: Daughter of Snow White

Lyric: Daughter of Peter Pan

Urbis: the final Fairytale

ABOUT AUDREY RICH

Audrey Rich is a New York City transplant living in South Florida, who writes sweet YA and NA Contemporary Romances and is an avid reader of novels where love conquers all.

She's married to her own happily-ever-after Hero, is an inactive CPA, and a stay-at-home mom who homeschooled her teenage daughter for two years, while also missing her son, who is away at college, even though it's only 25 minutes away.

Audrey enjoys volunteering with children of all ages at church, especially the enthusiastic teenagers, and teaching the Junior Achievement curriculums at local middle and high schools. She also loves to travel with her family and walking on the beach right near the homes of the mega-rich and billionaires.

Audrey is also the author of Thinking about Love, Where there's smoke there's Fire and Masquerading our Love along with many more.

Join her newsletter here

THE KINGDOM OF FAIRYTALES TEAM

These books would not be written without a great many people. Here is our team:

Many thanks to those who have made this possible.

Thank you to Rhi Parkes without whom, this series would never have come about.

Thanks to all the authors.

J.A. Armitage, Audrey Rich, B. Kristen Mcmichael, Emma Savant, Jennifer Ellision, Scarlett Kol, R. Castro, Margo Ryerkerk, Zara Quentin, Laura Greenwood and Anne Stryker

Also thank you to our amazing Beta team

Nadine Peterse-Vrijhof, Diane Major, Kalli Bunch and Stephanie Pittser.

Thanks to our Proof Reader

Tina Merritt

www.ingramcontent.com/pod-product-compliance
Lightning Source LLC
Chambersburg PA
CBHW020419030726
47495CB00006B/1580